# THE
# LAUGHING CORPSE

# THE
# LAUGHING
## CORPSE

LAURELL K. HAMILTON

B

BERKLEY BOOKS, NEW YORK

**B**

A Berkley Book
Published by The Berkley Publishing Group
A division of Penguin Group (USA) Inc.
375 Hudson Street
New York, New York 10014

PRINTING HISTORY
Ace mass market edition / September 1994
Jove mass market edition / October 2001
Berkley hardcover edition / December 2003

Library of Congress Cataloging-in-Publication Data

Hamilton, Laurell K.
    The laughing corpse / Laurell K. Hamilton.— Berkley hardcover ed.
        p.  cm.
    ISBN 0-425-19200-8
    1. Blake, Anita (Fictitious character)—Fiction. 2. Vampires—Fiction.  I. Title.

PS3558.A443357L38 2003
813'.54—dc22

                                                                2003061216

PRINTED IN THE UNITED STATES OF AMERICA

10  9  8  7  6  5  4  3  2

*To everyone who bought this book years ago,*
*because if you had not,*
*all those who recently found it*
*would never have had the chance*

## Acknowledgments

To J, who became my friend with this book, years before it would ever occur to us to date. Ginjer Buchanan, our editor, who believed in Anita and me from the start. Marcia Woolsey, who read the first Anita short story and pronounced it "good." (Marcia, please contact my publisher— I would love to talk to you!) Janni Lee Simner, Marella Sands, and Robert K. Sheaf, who made sure this book stood alone. Deborah Millitello, for holding my hand when I needed it. M. C. Sumner, for being a friend. Alternate Historians forever. Thanks to everyone who attended my readings at Windycon and Capricorn.

# 1

HAROLD GAYNOR'S HOUSE sat in the middle of intense green lawn and the graceful sweep of trees. The house gleamed in the hot August sunshine. Bert Vaughn, my boss, parked the car on the crushed gravel of the driveway. The gravel was so white, it looked like handpicked rock salt. Somewhere out of sight the soft whir of sprinklers pattered. The grass was absolutely perfect in the middle of one of the worst droughts Missouri has had in over twenty years. Oh, well. I wasn't here to talk with Mr. Gaynor about water management. I was here to talk about raising the dead.

Not resurrection. I'm not that good. I mean zombies. The shambling dead. Rotting corpses. Night of the living dead. That kind of zombie. Though certainly less dramatic than Hollywood would ever put up on the screen. I am an animator. It's a job, that's all, like selling.

Animating had only been a licensed business for about five years. Before that it had just been an embarrassing curse, a religious experience, or a tourist attraction. It still is in parts of New Orleans, but here in St. Louis it's a business. A profitable one, thanks in large part to my boss. He's a rascal, a scalawag, a rogue, but damn if he doesn't know how to make money. It's a good trait for a business manager.

Bert was six-four, a broad-shouldered, ex–college football player with the beginnings of a beer gut. The dark blue suit he wore was tailored so that the gut didn't show. For eight hundred dollars the suit should have hidden a herd of elephants. His white-blond hair was trimmed in a crew cut, back in style after all these years. A boater's tan made his pale hair and eyes dramatic with contrast.

Bert adjusted his blue and red striped tie, mopping a bead of sweat off his tanned forehead. "I heard on the news there's a movement there to use zombies in pesticide-contaminated fields. It would save lives."

"Zombies rot, Bert, there's no way to prevent that, and they don't stay smart enough long enough to be used as field labor."

"It was just a thought. The dead have no rights under law, Anita."

"Not yet."

It was wrong to raise the dead so they could slave for us. It was just wrong, but no one listens to me. The government finally had to get into the act. There was a nationwide committee being formed of animators and other experts. We were supposed to look into the working conditions of local zombies.

Working conditions. They didn't understand. You can't give a corpse nice working conditions. They don't appreciate it anyway. Zombies may walk, even talk, but they are very, very dead.

Bert smiled indulgently at me. I fought an urge to pop him one right in his smug face. "I know you and Charles are working on that committee," Bert said. "Going around to all the businesses and checking up on the zombies. It makes great press for Animators, Inc."

"I don't do it for good press," I said.

"I know. You believe in your little cause."

"You're a condescending bastard," I said, smiling sweetly up at him. He grinned at me. "I know."

I just shook my head; with Bert you can't really win an insult match. He doesn't give a damn what I think of him, as long as I work for him.

My navy blue suit jacket was supposed to be summer weight but it was a lie. Sweat trickled down my spine as soon as I stepped out of the car.

Bert turned to me, small eyes narrowing. His eyes lend themselves to suspicious squints. "You're still wearing your gun," he said.

"The jacket hides it, Bert. Mr. Gaynor will never know." Sweat started collecting under the straps of my shoulder holster. I could feel the silk blouse beginning to melt. I try not to wear silk and a shoulder rig at the same time. The silk starts to look indented, wrinkling where the straps cross. The gun was a Browning Hi-Power 9mm, and I liked having it near at hand.

"Come on, Anita. I don't think you'll need a gun in the middle of the afternoon, while visiting a client." Bert's voice held that patronizing tone that people use on children. Now, little girl, you know this is for your own good.

Bert didn't care about my well-being. He just didn't want to spook Gaynor. The man had already given us a check for five thousand dollars. And that was just to drive out and talk to him. The implication was that there was more money if we agreed to take his case. A lot of money. Bert was all excited about that part. I was skeptical. After all, Bert didn't have to raise the corpse. I did.

The trouble was, Bert was probably right. I wouldn't need the gun in broad daylight. Probably. "All right, open the trunk."

Bert opened the trunk of his nearly brand-new Volvo. I was already taking off the jacket. He stood in front of me, hiding me from the house. God forbid that they should see me hiding a gun in the trunk. What would they do, lock the doors and scream for help?

I folded the holster straps around the gun and laid it in the clean trunk. It smelled like new car, plastic and faintly unreal. Bert shut the trunk, and I stared at it as if I could still see the gun.

"Are you coming?" he asked.

"Yeah," I said. I didn't like leaving my gun behind, for any reason. Was that a bad sign? Bert motioned for me to come on.

I did, walking carefully over the gravel in my high-heeled black pumps. Women may get to wear lots of pretty colors, but men get the comfortable shoes.

Bert was staring at the door, smile already set on his face. It was his best professional smile, dripping with sincerity. His pale grey eyes sparkled with good cheer. It was a mask. He could put it on and off like a light switch. He'd wear the same smile if you confessed to killing your own mother. As long as you wanted to pay to have her raised from the dead.

The door opened, and I knew Bert had been wrong about me not needing a gun. The man was maybe five-eight, but the orange polo shirt he wore strained over his chest. The black sport jacket seemed too small, as if when he moved the seams would split, like an insect's skin that had been outgrown. Black acid-washed jeans showed off a small waist, so he looked like someone had pinched him in the middle while the clay was still wet. His hair was very blond. He looked at us silently. His eyes were empty, dead as a doll's. I caught a glimpse of shoulder holster under the sport jacket and resisted an urge to kick Bert in the shins.

Either my boss didn't notice the gun or he ignored it. "Hello, I'm Bert Vaughn and this is my associate, Anita Blake. I believe Mr. Gaynor is expecting us." Bert smiled at him charmingly.

The bodyguard—what else could he be—moved away from the door. Bert took that for an invitation and walked inside. I followed, not at all sure I wanted to. Harold Gaynor was a very rich man. Maybe he needed a bodyguard. Maybe people had threatened him. Or maybe he was one of those men who have enough money to keep hired muscle around whether they need it or not.

Or maybe something else was going on. Something that needed guns and muscle, and men with dead, emotionless eyes. Not a cheery thought.

The air-conditioning was on too high and the sweat gelled instantly. We followed the bodyguard down a long central hall that was paneled in dark, expensive-looking wood. The hall runner looked oriental and was probably handmade.

Heavy wooden doors were set in the right-hand wall. The bodyguard opened the doors and again stood to one side while we walked through. The room was a library, but I was betting no one ever read any of the books. The place was ceiling to floor in dark wood bookcases. There was even a second level of books and shelves reached by an elegant sweep of narrow staircase. All the books were hardcover, all the same size, colors muted and collected together like a collage. The furniture was, of course, red leather with brass buttons worked into it.

A man sat near the far wall. He smiled when we came in. He was a large man with a pleasant round face, double-chinned. He was sitting in an electric wheelchair, with a small plaid blanket over his lap, hiding his legs.

"Mr. Vaughn and Ms. Blake, how nice of you to drive out." His voice went with his face, pleasant, damn near amiable.

A slender black man sat in one of the leather chairs. He was over six feet tall, exactly how much over was hard to tell. He was slumped down, long legs stretched out in front of him with the ankles crossed. His legs were taller than I was. His brown eyes watched me as if he were trying to memorize me and would be graded later.

The blond bodyguard went to lean against the bookcases. He couldn't quite cross his arms, jacket too tight, muscles too big. You really shouldn't lean against a wall and try to look tough unless you can cross your arms. Ruins the effect.

Mr. Gaynor said, "You've met Tommy." He motioned towards the sitting bodyguard. "That's Bruno."

"Is that your real name or just a nickname?" I asked, looking straight into Bruno's eyes.

He shifted just a little in his chair. "Real name."

I smiled.

"Why?" he asked.

"I've just never met a bodyguard who was really named Bruno."

"Is that supposed to be funny?" he asked.

I shook my head. Bruno. He never had a chance. It was like naming a girl Venus. All Brunos had to be bodyguards. It was a rule. Maybe a cop? Naw, it was a bad guy's name. I smiled.

Bruno sat up in his chair, one smooth, muscular motion. He wasn't wearing a gun that I could see, but there was a presence to him. Dangerous, it said, watch out.

Guess I shouldn't have smiled.

Bert interrupted, "Anita, please. I do apologize, Mr. Gaynor . . . Mr. Bruno. Ms. Blake has a rather peculiar sense of humor."

"Don't apologize for me, Bert. I don't like it." I don't know what he was so sore about anyway. I hadn't said the really insulting stuff out loud.

"Now, now," Mr. Gaynor said. "No hard feelings. Right, Bruno?"

Bruno shook his head and frowned at me, not angry, sort of perplexed.

Bert flashed me an angry look, then turned smiling to the man in the wheelchair. "Now, Mr. Gaynor, I know you must be a busy man. So, exactly how old is the zombie you want raised?"

"A man who gets right down to business. I like that." Gaynor hesitated, staring at the door. A woman entered.

She was tall, leggy, blond, with cornflower-blue eyes. The dress, if it was a dress, was rose-colored and silky. It clung to her body the way it was supposed to, hiding what decency demanded, but leaving very little to the imagination. Long pale legs were stuffed into pink spike heels, no hose. She stalked across the carpet, and every man in the room watched her. And she knew it.

She threw back her head and laughed, but no sound came out. Her face brightened, her lips moved, eyes sparkled, but in absolute silence, like someone had turned the sound off. She leaned one hip against Harold Gaynor, one hand on his shoulder. He encircled her waist, and the movement raised the already short dress another inch.

Could she sit down in the dress without flashing the room? Naw.

"This is Cicely," he said. She smiled brilliantly at Bert, that little soundless laugh making her eyes sparkle. She looked at me and her eyes faltered, the smile slipped. For a second uncertainty filled her eyes. Gaynor patted her hip. The smile flamed back into place. She nodded graciously to both of us.

"I want you to raise a two-hundred-and-eighty-three-year-old corpse."

I just stared at him and wondered if he understood what he was asking.

"Well," Bert said, "that is nearly three hundred years old. Very old to raise as a zombie. Most animators couldn't do it at all."

"I am aware of that," Gaynor said. "That is why I asked for Ms. Blake. She can do it."

Bert glanced at me. I had never raised anything that old. "Anita?"

"I could do it," I said.

He smiled back at Gaynor, pleased.

"But I won't do it."

Bert turned slowly back to me, smile gone.

Gaynor was still smiling. The bodyguards were immobile. Cicely looked pleasantly at me, eyes blank of any meaning.

"A million dollars, Ms. Blake," Gaynor said in his soft pleasant voice.

I saw Bert swallow. His hands convulsed on the chair arms. Bert's idea of sex was money. He probably had the biggest hard-on of his life.

"Do you understand what you're asking, Mr. Gaynor?" I asked.

He nodded. "I will supply the white goat." His voice was still pleasant as he said it, still smiling. Only his eyes had gone dark; eager, anticipatory.

I stood up. "Come on, Bert, it's time to leave."

Bert grabbed my arm. "Anita, sit down, please."

I stared at his hand until he let go of me. His charming mask slipped, showing me the anger underneath, then he was all pleasant business again. "Anita. It is a generous payment."

"The white goat is a euphemism, Bert. It means a human sacrifice."

My boss glanced at Gaynor, then back to me. He knew me well enough to believe me, but he didn't want to. "I don't understand," he said.

"The older the zombie the bigger the death needed to raise it. After a few centuries the only death 'big enough' is a human sacrifice," I said.

Gaynor wasn't smiling anymore. He was watching me out of dark eyes. Cicely was still looking pleasant, almost smiling. Was there anyone home behind those so blue eyes? "Do you really want to talk about murder in front of Cicely?" I asked.

Gaynor beamed at me, always a bad sign. "She can't understand a word we say. Cicely's deaf."

I stared at him, and he nodded. She looked at me with pleasant eyes. We were talking of human sacrifice and she didn't even know it. If she could read lips, she was hiding it very well. I guess even the handicapped, um, physically challenged, can fall into bad company, but it seemed wrong.

"I hate a woman who talks constantly," Gaynor said.

I shook my head. "All the money in the world wouldn't be enough to get me to work for you."

"Couldn't you just kill lots of animals, instead of just one?" Bert asked. Bert is a very good business manager. He knows shit about raising the dead.

I stared down at him. "No."

Bert sat very still in his chair. The prospect of losing a million dollars must have been real physical pain for him, but he hid it. Mr. Corporate Negotiator. "There has to be a way to work this out," he said. His voice was calm. A professional smile curled his lips. He was still trying to do business. My boss did not understand what was happening.

"Do you know of another animator that could raise a zombie this old?" Gaynor asked.

Bert glanced up at me, then down at the floor, then at Gaynor. The professional smile had faded. He understood now that it was murder we were talking about. Would that make a difference?

I had always wondered where Bert drew the line. I was about to find out. The fact that I didn't know whether he would refuse the contract told you a lot about my boss. "No," Bert said softly, "no, I guess I can't help you either, Mr. Gaynor."

"If it's the money, Ms. Blake, I can raise the offer."

A tremor ran through Bert's shoulders. Poor Bert, but he hid it well. Brownie point for him.

"I'm not an assassin, Gaynor," I said.

"That ain't what I heard," Tommy of the blond hair said.

I glanced at him. His eyes were still as empty as a doll's. "I don't kill people for money."

"You kill vampires for money," he said.

"Legal execution, and I don't do it for the money," I said.

Tommy shook his head and moved away from the wall. "I hear you like staking vampires. And you aren't too careful about who you have to kill to get to 'em."

"My informants tell me you have killed humans before, Ms. Blake," Gaynor said.

"Only in self-defense, Gaynor. I don't do murder."

Bert was standing now. "I think it is time to leave."

Bruno stood in one fluid movement, big dark hands loose and half-cupped at his sides. I was betting on some kind of martial arts.

Tommy was standing away from the wall. His sport jacket was pushed back to expose his gun, like an old-time gunfighter. It was a .357 Magnum. It would make a very big hole.

I just stood there, staring at them. What else could I do? I might be able to do something with Bruno, but Tommy had a gun. I didn't. It sort of ended the argument.

They were treating me like I was a very dangerous person. At five-three I am not imposing. Raise the dead, kill a few vampires, and people start considering you one of the monsters. Sometimes it hurt. But now . . . it had possibilities. "Do you really think I came in here unarmed?" I asked. My voice sounded very matter-of-fact.

Bruno looked at Tommy. He sort of shrugged. "I didn't pat her down."

Bruno snorted.

"She ain't wearing a gun, though," Tommy said.

"Want to bet your life on it?" I said. I smiled when I said it, and slid my hand, very slowly, towards my back. Make them think I had a hip holster at the small of my back. Tommy shifted, flexing his hand near his gun. If he went for it, we were going to die. I was going to come back and haunt Bert.

Gaynor said, "No. No need for anyone to die here today, Ms. Blake."

"No," I said, "no need at all." I swallowed my pulse back into my throat and eased my hand away from my imaginary gun. Tommy eased away from his real one. Goody for us.

Gaynor smiled again, like a pleasant beardless Santa. "You of course understand that telling the police would be useless."

I nodded. "We have no proof. You didn't even tell us who you wanted raised from the dead, or why."

"It would be your word against mine," he said.

"And I'm sure you have friends in high places." I smiled when I said it.

His smile widened, dimpling his fat little cheeks. "Of course."

I turned my back on Tommy and his gun. Bert followed. We walked outside into the blistering summer heat. Bert looked a little shaken. I felt almost friendly towards him. It was nice to know that Bert had limits, something he wouldn't do, even for a million dollars.

"Would they really have shot us?" he asked. His voice sounded matter-of-fact, firmer than the slightly glassy look in his eyes. Tough Bert. He unlocked the trunk without being asked.

"With Harold Gaynor's name in our appointment book and in the computer?" I got my gun out and slipped on the holster rig. "Not knowing who we'd mentioned this trip to?" I shook my head. "Too risky."

"Then why did you pretend to have a gun?" He looked me straight in the eyes as he asked, and for the first time I saw uncertainty in his face. Ol' money bags needed a comforting word, but I was fresh out.

"Because, Bert, I could have been wrong."

# 2

THE BRIDAL SHOP was just off 70 West in St. Peters. It was called The Maiden Voyage. Cute. There was a pizza place on one side of it and a beauty salon on the other. It was called Full Dark Beauty Salon. The windows were blacked out, outlined in bloodred neon. You could get your hair and nails done by a vampire, if you wanted to.

Vampirism had only been legal for two years in the United States of America. We were still the only country in the world where it was legal. Don't ask me; I didn't vote for it. There was even a movement to give the vamps the vote. Taxation without representation and all that.

Two years ago if a vampire bothered someone I just went out and staked the son of a bitch. Now I had to get a court order of execution. Without it, I was up on murder charges, if I was caught. I longed for the good ol' days.

There was a blond mannequin in the wedding shop window wearing enough white lace to drown in. I am not a big fan of lace, or seed pearls, or sequins. Especially not sequins. I had gone out with Catherine twice to help her look for a wedding gown. It didn't take long to realize I was no help. I didn't like any of them.

Catherine was a very good friend or I wouldn't have been here at all. She told me if I ever got married I'd change my mind. Surely being in love doesn't cause you to lose your sense of good taste. If I ever buy a gown with sequins on it, someone just shoot me.

I also wouldn't have chosen the bridal dresses Catherine picked out, but it was my own fault that I hadn't been around when the vote was taken. I worked too much and I hated to shop. So, I ended up plunking down $120 plus tax on a pink taffeta evening gown. It looked like it had run away from a junior high prom.

I walked into the air-conditioned hush of the bridal shop, high heels sinking into a carpet so pale grey it was nearly white. Mrs. Cassidy, the manager, saw me come in. Her smile faltered for just a moment before she got it under control. She smiled at me, brave Mrs. Cassidy.

I smiled back, not looking forward to the next hour.

Mrs. Cassidy was somewhere between forty and fifty, trim figure, red hair so dark it was almost brown. The hair was tied in a French knot like Grace Kelly used to wear. She pushed her gold wire-framed glasses more securely on her nose and said, "Ms. Blake, here for the final fitting, I see."

"I hope it's the final fitting," I said.

"Well, we have been working on the . . . problem. I think we've come up with something." There was a small room in back of the desk. It was filled with racks of plastic-covered dresses. Mrs. Cassidy pulled mine out from between two identical pink dresses.

She led the way to the dressing rooms with the dress draped over her arms. Her spine was very straight. She was gearing for another battle. I didn't have to gear up, I was always ready for battle. But arguing with Mrs. Cassidy about alterations to a formal beat the heck out of arguing with Tommy and Bruno. It could have gone very badly, but it hadn't. Gaynor had called them off, for today, he had said.

What did that mean exactly? It was probably self-explanatory. I had left Bert at the office still shaken from his close encounter. He didn't deal with the messy end of the business. The violent end. No, I did that, or Manny, or Jamison, or Charles. We, the animators of Animators, Inc, we did the dirty work. Bert stayed in his nice safe office and sent clients and trouble our way. Until today.

Mrs. Cassidy hung the dress on a hook inside one of the dressing stalls and went away. Before I could go inside, another stall opened, and

Kasey, Catherine's flower girl, stepped out. She was eight, and she was glowering. Her mother followed behind her, still in her business suit. Elizabeth (call me Elsie) Markowitz was tall, slender, black-haired, olive-skinned, and a lawyer. She worked with Catherine and was also in the wedding.

Kasey looked like a smaller, softer version of her mother. The child spotted me first and said, "Hi, Anita. Isn't this dress dumb-looking?"

"Now, Kasey," Elsie said, "it's a beautiful dress. All those nice pink ruffles."

The dress looked like a petunia on steroids to me. I stripped off my jacket and started moving into my own dressing room before I had to give my opinion out loud.

"Is that a real gun?" Kasey asked.

I had forgotten I was still wearing it. "Yes," I said.

"Are you a policewoman?"

"No."

"Kasey Markowitz, you ask too many questions." Her mother herded her past me with a harried smile. "Sorry about that, Anita."

"I don't mind," I said. Sometime later I was standing on a little raised platform in front of a nearly perfect circle of mirrors. With the matching pink high heels the dress was the right length at least. It also had little puff sleeves and was an off-the-shoulder look. The dress showed almost every scar I had.

The newest scar was still pink and healing on my right forearm. But it was just a knife wound. They're neat, clean things compared to my other scars. My collarbone and left arm have both been broken. A vampire bit through them, tore at me like a dog with a piece of meat. There's also the cross-shaped burn mark on my left forearm. Some inventive human vampire slaves thought it was amusing. I didn't.

I looked like Frankenstein's bride goes to the prom. Okay, maybe it wasn't that bad, but Mrs. Cassidy thought it was. She thought the scars would distract people from the dress, the wedding party, the bride. But Catherine, the bride herself, didn't agree. She thought I deserved to be in the wedding, because we were such good friends. I was paying good money to be publicly humiliated. We must be good friends.

Mrs. Cassidy handed me a pair of long pink satin gloves. I pulled them on, wiggling my fingers deep into the tiny holes. I've never liked gloves. They make me feel like I'm touching the world through a curtain. But the bright pink things did hide my arms. Scars all gone. What a good girl. Right.

The woman fluffed out the satiny skirt, glancing into the mirror. "It will do, I think." She stood, tapping one long, painted fingernail against her lipsticked mouth. "I believe I have come up with something to hide that, uh . . . well . . ." She made vague hand motions towards me.

"My collarbone scar?" I said.

"Yes." She sounded relieved.

It occurred to me for the first time that Mrs. Cassidy had never once said the word "scar." As if it were dirty, or rude. I smiled at myself in the ring of mirrors. Laughter caught at the back of my throat.

Mrs. Cassidy held up something made of pink ribbon and fake orange blossoms. The laughter died. "What is that?" I asked.

"This," she said, stepping towards me, "is the solution to our problem."

"All right, but what is it?"

"Well, it is a collar, a decoration."

"It goes around my neck?"

"Yes."

I shook my head. "I don't think so."

"Ms. Blake, I have tried everything to hide that, that . . . mark. Hats, hairdos, simple ribbons, corsages . . ." She literally threw up her hands. "I am at my wit's end."

This I could believe. I took a deep breath. "I sympathize with you, Mrs. Cassidy, really I do. I've been a royal pain in the ass."

"I would never say such a thing."

"I know, so I said it for you. But that is the ugliest piece of fru-fru I've ever laid eyes on."

"If you, Ms. Blake, have any better suggestions, then I am all ears." She half crossed her arms over her chest. The offending piece of "decoration" trailed nearly to her waist.

"It's huge," I protested.

"It will hide your"—she set her mouth tight—"scar."

I felt like applauding. She'd said the dirty word. Did I have any better suggestions? No. I did not. I sighed. "Put it on me. The least I can do is look at it."

She smiled. "Please lift your hair."

I did as I was told. She fastened it around my neck. The lace itched, the ribbons tickled, and I didn't even want to look in the mirror. I raised my eyes, slowly, and just stared.

"Thank goodness you have long hair. I'll style it myself the day of the wedding so it helps the camouflage."

The thing around my neck looked like a cross between a dog collar and the world's biggest wrist corsage. My neck had sprouted pink ribbons like mushrooms after a rain. It was hideous, and no amount of hairstyling was going to change that. But it hid the scar completely, perfectly. Ta-da.

I just shook my head. What could I say? Mrs. Cassidy took my silence for assent. She should have known better. The phone rang and saved us both. "I'll be just a minute, Ms. Blake." She stalked off, high-heels silent on the thick carpet.

I just stared at myself in the mirrors. My hair and eyes match, black hair, eyes so dark brown they look black. They are my mother's Latin darkness. But my skin is pale, my father's Germanic blood. Put some makeup on me and I look not unlike a china doll. Put me in a puffy pink dress and I look delicate, dainty, petite. Dammit.

The rest of the women in the wedding party were all five-five or above. Maybe some of them would actually look good in the dress. I doubted it.

Insult to injury, we all had to wear hoop skirts underneath. I looked like a reject from *Gone With the Wind*.

"There, don't you look lovely." Mrs. Cassidy had returned. She was beaming at me.

"I look like I've been dipped in Pepto-Bismol," I said.

Her smile faded around the edges. She swallowed. "You don't like this last idea." Her voice was very stiff.

Elsie Markowitz came out of the dressing rooms. Kasey was trailing behind, scowling. I knew how she felt. "Oh, Anita," Elsie said, "you look adorable."

Great. Adorable, just what I wanted to hear. "Thanks."

"I especially like the ribbons at your throat. We'll all be wearing them, you know."

"Sorry about that," I said.

She frowned at me. "I think they just set off the dress."

It was my turn to frown. "You're serious, aren't you?"

Elsie looked puzzled. "Well, of course I am. Don't you like the dresses?"

I decided not to answer on the grounds that it might piss someone off. I guess, what can you expect from a woman who has a perfectly good name like Elizabeth, but prefers to be named after a cow?

"Is this the absolutely last thing we can use for camouflage, Mrs. Cassidy?" I asked.

She nodded, once, very firmly.

I sighed, and she smiled. Victory was hers, and she knew it. I knew I was beaten the moment I saw the dress, but if I'm going to lose, I'm going to make someone pay for it. "All right. It's done. This is it. I'll wear it."

Mrs. Cassidy beamed at me. Elsie smiled. Kasey smirked. I hiked the hoop skirt up to my knees and stepped off the platform. The hoop swung like a bell with me as the clapper.

The phone rang. Mrs. Cassidy went to answer it, a lift in her step, a song in her heart, and me out of her shop. Joy in the afternoon.

I was struggling to get the wide skirt through the narrow little door that led to the changing rooms when she called, "Ms. Blake, it's for you. A Detective Sergeant Storr."

"See, Mommy, I told you she was a policewoman," Kasey said.

I didn't explain because Elsie had asked me not to, weeks ago. She thought Kasey was too young to know about animators and zombies and vampire slayings. Not that any child of eight could not know what a vampire was. They were pretty much the media event of the decade.

I tried to put the phone to my left ear, but the damned flowers got in the way. Pressing the receiver in the bend of my neck and shoulder, I reached back to undo the collar. "Hi, Dolph, what's up?"

"Murder scene." His voice was pleasant, like he should sing tenor.

"What kind of murder scene?"

"Messy."

I finally pulled the collar free and dropped the phone.

"Anita, you there?"

"Yeah, having some wardrobe trouble."

"What?"

"It's not important. Why do you want me to come down to the scene?"

"Whatever did this wasn't human."

"Vampire?"

"You're the undead expert. That's why I want you to come take a look."

"Okay, give me the address, and I'll be right there." There was a notepad of pale pink paper with little hearts on it. The pen had a plastic cupid on the end of it. "St. Charles, I'm not more than fifteen minutes from you."

"Good." He hung up.

"Good-bye to you, too, Dolph." I said it to empty air just to feel superior. I went back into the little room to change.

I had been offered a million dollars today, just to kill someone and raise a zombie. Then off to the bridal shop for a final fitting. Now a murder scene. Messy, Dolph had said. It was turning out to be a very busy afternoon.

*3*

MESSY, DOLPH HAD called it. A master of understatement. Blood was everywhere, splattered over the white walls like someone had taken a can of paint and thrown it. There was an off-white couch with brown and gold patterned flowers on it. Most of the couch was hidden under a sheet. The sheet was crimson. A bright square of afternoon sunlight came through the clean, sparkling windows. The sunlight made the blood cherry-red, shiny.

Fresh blood is really brighter than you see it on television and the movies. In large quantities. Real blood is screaming fire-engine red, in large quantities, but darker red shows up on the screen better. So much for realism.

Only fresh blood is red, true red. This blood was old and should have faded, but some trick of the summer sunshine kept it shiny and new.

I swallowed very hard and took a deep breath.

"You look a little green, Blake," a voice said almost at my elbow.

I jumped, and Zerbrowski laughed. "Did I scare ya?"

"No," I lied.

Detective Zerbrowski was about five-seven, curly black hair going grey, dark-rimmed glasses framed brown eyes. His brown suit was rumpled; his yellow and maroon tie had a smudge on it, probably from lunch. He was grinning at me. He was always grinning at me.

"I gotcha, Blake, admit it. Is our fierce vampire slayer gonna upchuck on the victims?"

"Putting on a little weight there, aren't you, Zerbrowski?"

"Ooh, I'm hurt," he said. He clutched hands to his chest, swaying a little. "Don't tell me you don't want my body, the way I want yours."

"Lay off, Zerbrowski. Where's Dolph?"

"In the master bedroom." Zerbrowski gazed up at the vaulted ceiling with its skylight. "Wish Katie and I could afford something like this."

"Yeah," I said. "It's nice." I glanced at the sheet-covered couch. The sheet clung to whatever was underneath, like a napkin thrown over spilled juice. There was something wrong with the way it looked. Then it hit me, there weren't enough bumps to make a whole human body. Whatever was under there was missing some parts.

The room sort of swam. I looked away, swallowing convulsively. It had been months since I had actually gotten sick at a murder scene. At least the air-conditioning was on. That was good. Heat always makes the smell worse.

"Hey, Blake, do you really need to step outside?" Zerbrowski took my arm as if to lead me towards the door.

"Thanks, but I'm fine." I looked him straight in his baby-browns and lied. He knew I was lying. I wasn't all right, but I'd make it.

He released my arm, stepped back, and gave me a mock salute. "I love a tough broad."

I smiled before I could stop it. "Go away, Zerbrowski."

"End of the hall, last door on the left. You'll find Dolph there." He walked away into the crowd of men. There are always more people than you need at a murder scene, not the gawkers outside but uniforms, plainclothes, technicians, the guy with the video camera. A murder scene was like a bee swarm, full of frenzied movement and damn crowded.

I threaded my way through the crowd. My plastic-coated ID badge was clipped to the collar of my navy-blue jacket. It was so the police would know I was on their side and hadn't just snuck in. It also made carrying a gun into a crowd of policemen safer.

I squeezed past a crowd that was gathered like a traffic jam beside a door in the middle of the hall. Voices came, disjointed, "Jesus, look at the blood . . . Have they found the body yet? . . . You mean what's left of it? . . . No."

I pushed between two uniforms. One said, "Hey!" I found a cleared space just in front of the last door on the left-hand side. I don't know how Dolph had done it but he was alone in the room. Maybe they were just finished in here.

He knelt in the middle of the pale brown carpet. His thick hands, encased in surgical gloves, were on his thighs. His black hair was cut so short it left his ears sort of stranded on either side of a large blunt face. He saw me and stood. He was six-eight, built big like a wrestler. The canopied bed behind him suddenly looked small.

Dolph was head of the police's newest task force, the spook squad. Official title was the Regional Preternatural Investigation Team, R-P-I-T, pronounced "rip it." It handled all supernatural crime. It was a place to dump the troublemakers. I never wondered what Zerbrowski had done to get on the spook squad. His sense of humor was too strange and absolutely merciless. But Dolph. He was the perfect policeman. I had always sort of figured he had offended someone high up, offended them by being too good at his job. Now that I could believe.

There was another sheet-covered bundle on the carpet beside him.

"Anita." He always talks like that, one word at a time.

"Dolph," I said.

He knelt between the canopy bed and the blood-soaked sheet. "You ready?"

"I know you're the silent type, Dolph, but could you tell me what I'm supposed to be looking for?"

"I want to know what you see, not what I tell you you're supposed to see."

For Dolph it was a speech. "Okay," I said, "let's do it."

He pulled back the sheet. It peeled away from the bloody thing underneath. I stood and I stared and all I could see was a lump of bloody meat. It could have been from anything: a cow, horse, deer. But human? Surely not.

My eyes saw it, but my brain refused what it was being shown. I squatted beside it, tucking my skirt under my thighs. The carpeting squeezed underfoot like rain had gotten to it, but it wasn't rain.

"Do you have a pair of gloves I can borrow? I left my crime scene gear at the office."

"Right jacket pocket." He lifted his hands in the air. There were blood marks on the gloves. "Help yourself. The wife hates me to get blood on the dry cleaning."

I smiled. Amazing. A sense of humor is mandatory at times. I had to reach across the remains. I pulled out two surgical gloves; one size fits all. The gloves always felt like they had powder in them. They didn't feel like gloves at all, more like condoms for your hands.

"Can I touch it without damaging evidence?"

"Yes."

I poked the side of it with two fingers. It was like poking a side of fresh beef. A nice, solid feel to it. My fingers traced the bumps of bone, ribs under the flesh. Ribs. Suddenly I knew what I was looking at. Part of the rib cage of a human being. There was the shoulder, white bone sticking out where the arm had been torn away. That was all. All there was. I stood too quickly and stumbled. The carpet squeeshed underfoot.

The room was suddenly very hot. I turned away from the body and found myself staring at the bureau. Its mirror was splattered so heavily with blood, it looked like someone had covered it in layers of red fingernail polish. Cherry Blossom Red, Carnival Crimson, Candy Apple.

I closed my eyes and counted very slowly to ten. When I opened them the room seemed cooler. I noticed for the first time that a ceiling fan was slowly turning. I was fine. Heap big vampire slayer. Ri-ight.

Dolph didn't comment as I knelt by the body again. He didn't even look at me. Good man. I tried to be objective and see whatever there was to see. But it was hard. I liked the remains better when I couldn't figure out what part of the body they were. Now all I could see was the bloody remains. All I could think of was this used to be a human body. "Used to be" was the operative phrase.

"No signs of a weapon that I can see, but the coroner will be able to tell you that." I reached out to touch it again, then stopped. "Can you help me raise it up so I can see inside the chest cavity? What's left of the chest cavity."

Dolph dropped the sheet and helped me lift the remains. It was lighter than it looked. Raised on its side there was nothing underneath.

All the vital organs that the ribs protect were gone. It looked for all the world like a side of beef ribs, except for the bones where the arm should have connected. Part of the collarbone was still attached.

"Okay," I said. My voice sounded breathy. I stood, holding my blood-spattered hands out to my sides. "Cover it, please."

He did, and stood. "Impressions?"

"Violence, extreme violence. More than human strength. The body's been ripped apart by hand."

"Why by hand?"

"No knife marks." I laughed, but it choked me. "Hell, I'd think some-one had used a saw on the body like butchering a cow, but the bones . . ." I shook my head. "Nothing mechanical was used to do this."

"Anything else?"

"Yeah, where is the rest of the fucking body?"

"Down the hall, second door on the left."

"The rest of the body?" The room was getting hot again.

"Just go look. Tell me what you see."

"Dammit, Dolph, I know you don't like to influence your experts, but I don't like walking in there blind."

He just stared at me.

"At least answer one question."

"Maybe, what?"

"Is it worse than this?"

He seemed to think about that for a moment. "No, and yes."

"Damn you."

"You'll understand after you've seen it."

I didn't want to understand. Bert had been thrilled that the police wanted to put me on retainer. He had told me I would gain valuable experience working with the police. All I had gained so far was a wider variety of nightmares.

Dolph walked ahead of me to the next chamber of horrors. I didn't really want to find the rest of the body. I wanted to go home. He hesitated in front of the closed door until I stood beside him. There was a cardboard cutout of a rabbit on the door like for Easter. A nee-dlework sign hung just below the bunny. Baby's Room.

"Dolph," my voice sounded very quiet. The noise from the living room was muted.

"Yes."

"Nothing, nothing." I took a deep breath and let it out. I could do this. I could do this. Oh, God, I didn't want to do this. I whispered a prayer under my breath as the door swung inward. There are moments in life when the only way to get through is with a little grace from on high. I was betting this was going to be one of them.

Sunlight streamed through a small window. The curtains were white with little duckies and bunnies stitched around the edges. Animal cutouts danced around the pale blue walls. There was no crib, only one of those beds with handrails halfway down. A big boy bed, wasn't that what they were called?

There wasn't as much blood in here. Thank you, dear God. Who says prayers never get answered? But in a square of bright August sunshine sat a stuffed teddy bear. The teddy bear was candy-coated with blood. One glassy eye stared round and surprised out of the spiky fake fur.

I knelt beside it. The carpet didn't squeeze, no blood soaked in. Why was the damn bear sitting here covered in congealing blood? There was no other blood in the entire room that I could see.

Did someone just set it here? I looked up and found myself staring at a small white chest of drawers with bunnies painted on it. When you have a motif, I guess you stick with it. On the white paint was one small, perfect handprint. I crawled towards it and held up my hand near it comparing size. My hands aren't big, small even for a woman's, but this handprint was tiny. Two, three, maybe four. Blue walls, probably a boy.

"How old was the child?"

"Picture in the living room has Benjamin Reynolds, age three, written on the back."

"Benjamin," I whispered it, and stared at the bloody handprint. "There's no body in this room. No one was killed here."

"No."

"Why did you want me to see it?" I looked up at him, still kneeling.

"Your opinion isn't worth anything if you don't see everything."

"That damn bear is going to haunt me."

"Me, too," he said.

I stood, resisting the urge to smooth my skirt down in back. It was amazing how many times I touched my clothing without thinking and smeared blood on myself. But not today.

"Is it the boy's body under the sheet in the living room?" As I said it, I prayed that it wasn't.

"No," he said.

Thank God. "Mother's body?"

"Yes."

"Where is the boy's body?"

"We can't find it." He hesitated, then asked, "Could the thing have eaten the child's body completely?"

"You mean so there wouldn't be anything left to find?"

"Yes," he said. His face looked just the tiniest bit pale. Mine probably did, too.

"Possible, but even the undead have a limit to what they can eat." I took a deep breath. "Did you find any signs of—regurgitation."

"Regurgitation." He smiled. "Nice word. No, the creature didn't eat and then vomit. At least we haven't found it."

"Then the boy's probably still around somewhere."

"Could he be alive?" Dolph asked.

I looked up at him. I wanted to say yes, but I knew the answer was probably no. I compromised. "I don't know."

Dolph nodded.

"The living room next?" I asked.

"No." He walked out of the room without another word. I followed. What else could I do? But I didn't hurry. If he wanted to play tough, silent policeman, he could damn well wait for me to catch up.

I followed his broad back around the corner through the living room into the kitchen. A sliding glass door led out onto a deck. Glass was everywhere. Shiny slivers of it sparkled in the light from yet another skylight. The kitchen was spotless, like a magazine ad, done in blue tile and rich light-colored wood. "Nice kitchen," I said.

I could see men moving around the yard. The party had moved outside. The privacy fence hid them from the curious neighbors, as it had hidden the killer last night. There was just one detective standing beside the shiny sink. He was scribbling something in a notebook.

Dolph motioned me to have a closer look. "Okay," I said. "Something crashed through the sliding glass door. It must have made a hell of a lot of noise. This much glass breaking even with the air-conditioning on . . . You'd hear it."

"You think so?" he asked.

"Did any of the neighbors hear anything?" I asked.

"No one will admit to it," he said.

I nodded. "Glass breaks, someone comes to check it out, probably the man. Some sexist stereotypes die hard."

"What do you mean?" Dolph asked.

"The brave hunter protecting his family," I said.

"Okay, say it was the man, what next?"

"Man comes in, sees whatever crashed through the window, yells for his wife. Probably tells her to get out. Take the kid and run."

"Why not call the police?" he asked.

"I didn't see a phone in the master bedroom." I nodded towards the phone on the kitchen wall. "This is probably the only phone. You have to get past the bogeyman to reach the phone."

"Go on."

I glanced behind me into the living room. The sheet-covered couch was just visible. "The thing, whatever it was, took out the man. Quick, disabled him, knocked him out, but didn't kill him."

"Why not kill?"

"Don't test me, Dolph. There isn't enough blood in the kitchen. He was eaten in the bedroom. Whatever did it wouldn't have dragged a dead man off to the bedroom. It chased the man into the bedroom and killed him there."

"Not bad, want to take a shot at the living room next?"

Not really, but I didn't say it out loud. There was more left of the woman. Her upper body was almost intact. Paper bags enveloped her hands. We had samples of something under her fingernails. I hoped it helped. Her wide brown eyes stared up at the ceiling. The pajama top clung wetly to where her waist used to be. I swallowed hard and used my index finger and thumb to raise the pajama top.

Her spine glistened in the hard sunshine, wet and white and dangling, like a cord that had been ripped out of its socket.

Okay. "Something tore her apart, just like the . . . man in the bedroom."

"How do you know it's a man?"

"Unless they had company, it has to be the man. They didn't have a visitor, did they?"

Dolph shook his head. "Not as far as we know."

"Then it has to be the man. Because she still has all her ribs, and both arms." I tried to swallow the anger in my voice. It wasn't Dolph's fault. "I'm not one of your cops. I wish you'd stop asking me questions that you already have the answers to."

He nodded. "Fair enough. Sometimes I forget you're not one of the boys."

"Thank you for that."

"You know what I mean."

"I do, and I even know you mean it as a compliment, but can we finish discussing this outside, please?"

"Sure." He slipped off his bloody gloves and put them in a garbage sack that was sitting open in the kitchen. I did the same.

The heat fastened round me like melting plastic, but it felt good, clean somehow. I breathed in great lungfuls of hot, sweating air. Ah, summer.

"I was right though, it wasn't human?" he asked.

There were two uniformed police officers keeping the crowd off the lawn and in the street. Children, parents, kids on bikes. It looked like a freaking circus.

"No, it wasn't human. There was no blood on the glass that it came through."

"I noticed. What's the significance?"

"Most dead don't bleed, except for vampires."

"Most?"

"Freshly dead zombies can bleed, but vampires bleed almost like a person."

"You don't think it was a vampire then?"

"If it was, then it ate human flesh. Vampires can't digest solid food."

"Ghoul?"

"Too far from a cemetery, and there'd be more destruction of the house. Ghouls would tear up furniture like wild animals."

"Zombie?"

I shook my head. "I honestly don't know. There are such things as flesh-eating zombies. They're rare, but it happens."

"You told me that there have been three reported cases. Each time the zombies stay human longer and don't rot."

I smiled. "Good memory. That's right. Flesh-eating zombies don't rot, as long as you feed them. Or at least don't rot as quickly."

"Are they violent?"

"Not so far," I said.

"Are zombies violent?" Dolph asked.

"Only if told to be."

"What does that mean?" he asked.

"You can order a zombie to kill people if you're powerful enough."

"A zombie as a murder weapon?"

I nodded. "Something like that, yes."

"Who could do something like that?"

"I'm not sure that's what happened here," I said.

"I know. But who could do it?"

"Well, hell, I could, but I wouldn't. And nobody I know that could do it would do it."

"Let us decide that," he said. He had gotten his little notebook out.

"You really want me to give you names of friends so you can ask them if they happened to have raised a zombie and sent it to kill these people?"

"Please."

I sighed. "I don't believe this. All right, me, Manny Rodriguez, Peter Burke, and . . ." I stopped words already forming a third name.

"What is it?"

"Nothing. I just remembered that I've got Burke's funeral to go to this week. He's dead so I don't think he's a suspect."

Dolph was looking at me hard, suspicion plain on his face. "You sure this is all the names you want to give me?"

"If I think of anyone else, I'll let you know," I said. I was at my wide-eyed most sincere. See, nothing up my sleeve.

"You do that, Anita."

"Sure thing."

He smiled and shook his head. "Who are you protecting?"

"Me," I said. He looked puzzled. "Let's just say I don't want to get someone mad at me."

"Who?"

I looked up into the clear August sky. "You think we'll get rain?"

"Dammit, Anita, I need your help."

"I've given you my help," I said.

"The name."

"Not yet. I'll check it out, and if it looks suspicious, I promise to share it with you."

"Well, isn't that just generous of you?" A flush was creeping up his neck. I had never seen Dolph angry before. I feared I was about to.

"The first death was a homeless man. We thought he'd passed out from liquor and ghouls got him. We found him right next to a cemetery. Open and shut, right?" His voice was rising just a bit with each word.

"Next we find this couple, teenagers caught necking in the boy's car. Dead, still not too far from the cemetery. We called in an exterminator and a priest. Case closed." He lowered his voice, but it was like he had swallowed the yelling. His voice was strained and almost touchable with its anger.

"Now this. It's the same beastie, whatever the hell it is. But we are miles from the nearest frigging cemetery. It isn't a ghoul, and maybe if I had called you in with the first or even the second case, this wouldn't have happened. But I figure I'm getting good at this supernatural crap. I've had some experience now, but it isn't enough. It isn't nearly enough." His big hands were crushing his notebook.

"That's the longest speech I've ever heard you make," I said.

He half laughed. "I need the name, Anita."

"Dominga Salvador. She's the voodoo priest for the entire Midwest. But if you send police down there she won't talk to you. None of them will."

"But they'll talk to you?"

"Yes," I said.

"Okay, but I better hear something from you by tomorrow."

"I don't know if I can set up a meeting that soon."

"Either you do it, or I do it," he said.

"Okay, okay, I'll do it, somehow."

"Thanks, Anita. At least now we have someplace to start."

"It might not be a zombie at all, Dolph. I'm just guessing."

"What else could it be?"

"Well, if there had been blood on the glass, I'd say maybe a lycanthrope."

"Oh, great, just what I need—a rampaging shapeshifter."

"But there was no blood on the glass."

"So probably some kind of undead," he said.

"Exactly."

"You talk to this Dominga Salvador and give me a report ASAP."

"Aye, aye, Sergeant."

He made a face at me and walked back inside the house. Better him
than me. All I had to do was go home, change clothes, and prepare to
raise the dead. At full dark tonight I had three clients lined up or would
that be lying down?

Ellen Grisholm's therapist thought it would be therapeutic for Ellen
to confront her child-molesting father. The trouble was the father had
been dead for several months. So I was going to raise Mr. Grisholm
from the dead and let his daughter tell him what a son of a bitch he
was. The therapist said it would be cleansing. I guess if you have a
doctorate, you're allowed to say things like that.

The other two raisings were more usual; a contested will, and a pros-
ecution's star witness that had had the bad taste to have a heart attack
before testifying in court. They still weren't sure if the testimony of a
zombie was admissible in court, but they were desperate enough to try,
and to pay for the privilege.

I stood there in the greenish-brown grass. Glad to see the family
hadn't been addicted to sprinklers. A waste of water. Maybe they had
even recycled their pop cans, newspapers. Maybe they had been decent
earth-loving citizens. Maybe not.

One of the uniforms lifted the yellow Do-Not-Cross tape and let me out. I ignored all the staring people and got in my car. It was a late-model Nova. I could have afforded something better but why bother? It ran.

The steering wheel was too hot to touch. I turned on the air-conditioning and let the car cool down. What I had told Dolph about Dominga Salvador had been true. She wouldn't talk to the police, but that hadn't been the reason I tried to keep her name out of it.

If the police came knocking on Señora Dominga's door, she'd want to know who sent them. And she'd find out. The Señora was the most powerful vaudun priest I knew of. Raising a murderous zombie was just one of many things she could do, if she wanted to.

Frankly, there were things worse than zombies that could come crawling through your window some dark night. I knew as little about that side of the business as I could get away with. The Señora had invented most of it.

No, I did not want Dominga Salvador angry with me. So it looked like I was going to have to talk with her tomorrow. It was sort of like getting an appointment to see the godfather of voodoo. Or in this case the godmother. The trouble was this godmother was unhappy with me. Dominga had sent me invitations to her home. To her ceremonies. I had politely declined. I think my being a Christian disappointed her. So I had managed to avoid a face to face, until now.

I was going to ask the most powerful vaudun priest in the United States, maybe in all of North America, if she just happened to raise a zombie. And if that zombie just happened to be going around killing people, on her orders? Was I crazy? Maybe. It looked like tomorrow was going to be another busy day.

# 4

THE ALARM SCREAMED. I rolled over swatting at the buttons on top of the digital clock. Surely to God, I'd hit the snooze button soon. I finally had to prop myself up on one elbow and actually open my eyes. I turned off the alarm and stared at the glowing numbers. 6:00 A.M. Shit. I'd only gotten home at three.

Why had I set the alarm for six? I couldn't remember. I am not at my best after only three hours of sleep. I lay back down in the still warm nest of sheets. My eyes were fluttering shut when I remembered. Dominga Salvador.

She had agreed to meet me at 7:00 A.M. today. Talk about a breakfast meeting. I struggled out of the sheet, and just sat on the side of the bed for a minute. The apartment was absolutely still. The only sound was the hush-hush of the air-conditioning. Quiet as a funeral.

I got up then, thoughts of blood-coated teddy bears dancing in my head.

Fifteen minutes later I was dressed. I always showered after coming in from work no matter how late it was. I couldn't stand the thought of going to bed between nice clean sheets smeared with dried chicken blood. Sometimes it's goat blood, but more often chicken.

I had compromised on the outfit, caught between showing respect and not melting in the heat. It would have been easy if I hadn't planned

to carry a gun with me. Call me paranoid, but I don't leave home without it.

The acid washed jeans, jogging socks, and Nikes were easy. An Uncle
Mike's inter-pants holster complete with a Firestar 9mm completed the
outfit. The Firestar was my backup piece to the Browning Hi-Power.
The Browning was far too bulky to put down an inter-pants holster, but
the Firestar fit nicely.

Now all I needed was a shirt that would hide the gun, but leave it
accessible to grab and shoot. This was harder than it sounded. I finally
settled on a short, almost middrift top that just barely fell over my
waistband. I turned in front of the mirror.

The gun was invisible as long as I didn't forget and raise my arms
too high. The top, unfortunately, was a pale, pale pink. What had pos-
sessed me to buy this top, I really didn't remember. Maybe it had been
a gift? I hoped so. The thought that I had actually spent money on
anything pink was more than I could bear.

I hadn't opened the drapes at all yet. The entire apartment was in
twilight. I had special-ordered very heavy drapes. I rarely saw sunlight,
and I didn't miss it much. I turned on the light over my fish tank. The
angelfish rose towards the top, mouths moving in slow-motion begging.

Fish are my idea of pets. You don't walk them, pick up after them,
or have to housebreak them. Clean the tank occasionally, feed them,
and they don't give a damn how many hours of overtime you work.

The smell of strong brewed coffee wafted through the apartment
from my Mr. Coffee. I sat at my little two-seater kitchen table sipping
hot, black Colombian vintage. Beans fresh from my freezer, ground on
the spot. There was no other way to drink coffee. Though in a pinch
I'll take it just about any way I can get it.

The doorbell chimed. I jumped, spilling coffee onto the table. Nervous? Me? I left my Firestar on the kitchen table instead of taking it to
the door with me. See, I'm not paranoid. Just very, very careful.

I checked the peephole and opened the door. Manny Rodriguez stood
in the doorway. He's about two inches taller than I am. His coal-black
hair is streaked with grey and white. Thick waves of it frame his thin
face and black mustache. He's fifty-two, and with one exception, I would

still rather have him backing me in a dangerous situation than anyone else I know.

We shook hands, we always do that. His grip was firm and dry. He grinned at me, flashing very white teeth in his brown face. "I smell coffee."

I grinned back. "You know it's all I have for breakfast." He walked in, and I locked the door behind him, habit.

"Rosita thinks you don't take care of yourself." He dropped into a near-perfect imitation of his wife's scolding voice, a much thicker Mexican accent than his own. "She doesn't eat right, so thin. Poor Anita, no husband, not even a boyfriend." He grinned.

"Rosita sounds like my stepmother. Judith is sick with worry that I'll be an old maid."

"You're what, twenty-four?"

"Mm-uh."

He just shook his head. "Sometimes I do not understand women."

It was my turn to grin. "What am I, chopped liver?"

"Anita, you know I didn't mean . . ."

"I know, I'm one of the boys. I understand."

"You are better than any of the boys at work."

"Sit down. Let me pour coffee in your mouth before your foot fits in again."

"You are being difficult. You know what I meant." He stared at me out of his solid brown eyes, face very serious.

I smiled. "Yeah, I know what you meant."

I picked one of the dozen or so mugs from my kitchen cabinet. My favorite mugs dangled from a mug-tree on the countertop.

Manny sat down, sipping coffee, glancing at his cup. It was red with black letters that said, "I'm a coldhearted bitch but I'm good at it." He laughed coffee up his nose.

I sipped my own coffee from a mug decorated with fluffy baby penguins. I'd never admit it, but it is my favorite mug.

"Why don't you bring your penguin mug to work?" he asked.

Bert's latest brainstorm was that we all use personalized coffee cups at work. He thought it would add a homey note to the office. I had brought in a grey on grey cup that said, "It's a dirty job and I get to do it." Bert had made me take it home.

"I enjoy yanking Bert's chain."

"So you're going to keep bringing in unacceptable cups."

I smiled. "Mm-uh."

He just shook his head.

"I really appreciate you coming to see Dominga with me."

He shrugged. "I couldn't let you go see the devil woman alone, could I?"

I frowned at the nickname, or was it an insult? "That's what your wife calls Dominga, not what I call her."

He glanced down at the gun still lying on the tabletop. "But you'll take a gun with you, just in case."

I looked at him over the top of my cup. "Just in case."

"If it comes to shooting our way out, Anita, it will be too late. She has bodyguards all over the place."

"I don't plan to shoot anybody. We are just going to ask a few questions. That's all."

He smirked. "*Por favor*, Señora Salvador, did you raise a killer zombie recently?"

"Knock it off, Manny. I know it's awkward."

"Awkward?" He shook his head. "Awkward, she says. If you piss off Dominga Salvador, it's a hell of a lot more than just awkward."

"You don't have to come."

"You called me for backup." He smiled that brilliant teeth-flashing smile that lit up his entire face. "You didn't call Charles or Jamison. You called me, and, Anita, that is the best compliment you could give an old man."

"You're not an old man." And I meant it.

"That is not what my wife keeps telling me. Rosita has forbidden me to go vampire hunting with you, but she can't curtail my zombie-related activities, not yet anyway."

The surprise must have shone on my face, because he said, "I know she talked to you two years back, when I was in the hospital."

"You almost died," I said.

"And you had how many broken bones?"

"Rosita made a reasonable request, Manny. You have four children to think of."

"And I'm too old to be slaying vampires." His voice held irony, and almost bitterness.

"You'll never be too old," I said.

"A nice thought." He drained his coffee mug. "We better go. Don't want to keep the Señora waiting."

"God forbid," I said.

"Amen," he said.

I stared at him as he rinsed his mug out in the sink. "Do you know something you're not telling me?"

"No," he said.

I rinsed my own cup, still staring at him. I could feel a suspicious frown between my eyes. "Manny?"

"Honest Mexican, I don't know nuthin'."

"Then what's wrong?"

"You know I was vaudun before Rosita converted me to pure Christianity."

"Yeah, so?"

"Dominga Salvador was not just my priestess. She was my lover."

I stared at him for a few heartbeats. "You're kidding?"

His face was very serious as he said, "I wouldn't joke about something like that."

I shrugged. People's choices of lovers never failed to amaze me. "That's why you could get me a meeting with her on such short notice."

He nodded.

"Why didn't you tell me before?"

"Because you might have tried to sneak over there without me."

"Would that have been so bad?"

He just stared at me, brown eyes very serious. "Maybe."

I got my gun from the table and fitted it to the inter-pants holster. Eight bullets. The Browning could hold fourteen. But let's get real; if I needed more than eight bullets, I was dead. And so was Manny.

"Shit," I whispered.

"What?"

"I feel like I'm going to visit the bogeyman."

Manny made a back and forth motion with his head. "Not a bad analogy."

Great, just freaking, bloody great. Why was I doing this? The image of Benjamin Reynolds's blood-coated teddy bear flashed into my mind. All right, I knew why I was doing it. If there was even a remote chance that the boy could still be alive, I'd go into hell itself—if I stood a chance of coming back out. I didn't mention this out loud. I did not want to know if hell was a good analogy, too.

## 5

THE NEIGHBORHOOD WAS older houses; fifties, forties. The lawns were dying to brown for lack of water. No sprinklers here. Flowers struggled to survive in beds close to the houses. Mostly petunias, geraniums, a few rosebushes. The streets were clean, neat, and one block over you could get yourself shot for wearing the wrong color of jacket.

Gang activity stopped at Señora Salvador's neighborhood. Even teenagers with automatic pistols fear things you can't stop with bullets no matter how good a shot you are. Silver-plated bullets will harm a vampire, but not kill it. It will kill a lycanthrope, but not a zombie. You can hack the damn things to pieces, and the disconnected body parts will crawl after you. I've seen it. It ain't pretty. The gangs leave the Señora's turf alone. No violence. It is a place of permanent truce.

There are stories of one Hispanic gang that thought it had protection against gris-gris. Some people say that the gang's ex-leader is still down in Dominga's basement, obeying an occasional order. He was great show-and-tell to any juvenile delinquents who got out of hand.

Personally, I had never seen her raise a zombie. But then I'd never seen her call the snakes either. I'd just as soon keep it that way.

Señora Salvador's two-story house is on about a half acre of land. A nice roomy yard. Bright red geraniums flamed against the whitewashed walls. Red and white, blood and bone. I was sure the symbolism was not lost on casual passersby. It certainly wasn't lost on me.

Manny parked his car in the driveway behind a cream-colored Impala. The two-car garage was painted white to match the house. There was a little girl of about five riding a tricycle furiously up and down the sidewalk. A slightly older pair of boys were sitting on the steps that led up to the porch. They stopped playing and looked at us.

A man stood on the porch behind them. He was wearing a shoulder holster over a sleeveless blue T-shirt. Sort of blatant. All he needed was a flashing neon sign that said "Bad Ass."

There were chalk markings on the sidewalk. Pastel crosses and un-readable diagrams. It looked like a children's game, but it wasn't. Some devoted fans of the Señora had chalked designs of worship in front of her house. Stubs of candles had melted to lumps around the designs. The girl on the tricycle peddled back and forth over the designs. Normal, right?

I followed Manny over the sun-scorched lawn. The little girl on the tricycle was watching us now, small brown face unreadable.

Manny removed his sunglasses and smiled up at the man. "*Buenos días*, Antonio. It has been a long time."

"*Sí,*" Antonio said. His voice was low and sullen. His deeply tanned arms were crossed loosely over his chest. It put his right hand right next to his gun butt.

I used Manny's body to shield me from sight and casually put my hands close to my own gun. The Boy Scout motto, "Always be prepared." Or was that the Marines?

"You've become a strong, handsome man," Manny said.

"My grandmother says I must let you in," Antonio said.

"She is a wise woman," Manny said.

Antonio shrugged. "She is the Señora." He peered around Manny at me. "Who is this?"

"Señorita Anita Blake." Manny stepped back so I could move forward. I did, right hand loose on my waist like I had an attitude, but it was the closest I could stay to my gun.

Antonio looked down at me. His dark eyes were angry, but that was all. He didn't have near the gaze of Harold Gaynor's bodyguards. I smiled. "Nice to meet you."

He squinted at me suspiciously for a moment, then nodded. I continued to smile at him, and a slow smile spread over his face. He thought I was flirting with him. I let him think it.

He said something in Spanish. All I could do was smile and shake my head. He spoke softly, and there was a look in his dark eyes, a curve to his mouth. I didn't have to speak the language to know I was being propositioned. Or insulted.

Manny's neck was stiff, his face flushed. He said something from between clenched teeth.

It was Antonio's turn to flush. His hand started to go for his gun. I stepped up two steps, touching his wrist as if I didn't know what was going on. The tension in his arm was like a wire, straining.

I beamed up at him as I held his wrist. His eyes flicked from Manny to me, then the tension eased, but I didn't let go of his wrist until his arm fell to his side. He raised my hand to his lips, kissing it. His mouth lingered on the back of my hand, but his eyes stayed on Manny. Angry, rage-filled.

Antonio carried a gun, but he was an amateur. Amateurs with guns eventually get themselves killed. I wondered if Dominga Salvador knew that? She may have been a whiz at voodoo but I bet she didn't know much about guns, and what it took to use one on a regular basis. Whatever it took, Antonio didn't have it. He'd kill you all right. No sweat. But for the wrong reasons. Amateur's reasons. Of course, you'll be just as dead.

He guided me up on the porch beside him, still holding my hand. It was my left hand. He could hold that all day. "I must check you for weapons, Manuel."

"I understand," Manny said. He stepped up on the porch and Antonio stepped back, keeping room between them in case Manny jumped him. That left me with a clear shot of Antonio's back. Careless; under different circumstances, deadly.

He made Manny lean against the porch railing like a police frisk. Antonio knew what he was doing, but it was an angry search, lots of quick jerky hand movements, as if just touching Manny's body enraged him. A lot of hate in old Tony.

It never occurred to him to pat me down for weapons. Tsk-tsk.

A second man came to the screen door. He was in his late forties, maybe. He was wearing a white undershirt with a plaid shirt unbuttoned over it. The sleeves were folded back as far as they'd go. Sweat stood out on his forehead. I was betting there was a gun at the small of his back. His black hair had a pure white streak just over the forehead. "What is taking so long, Antonio?" His voice was thick and held an accent.

"I searched him for weapons."

The older man nodded. "She is ready to see you both."

Antonio stood to one side, taking up his post on the porch once more. He made a kissing noise as I walked past. I felt Manny stiffen, but we made it into the living room without anyone getting shot. We were on a roll.

The living room was spacious, with a dining-room set taking up the left-hand side. There was a wall piano in the living room. I wondered who played. Antonio? Naw.

We followed the man through a short hallway into a roomy kitchen. Golden oblongs of sunshine lay heavy on a black and white tiled floor. The floor and kitchen were old, but the appliances were new. One of those deluxe refrigerators with an ice maker and water dispenser took up a hunk of the back wall. All the appliances were done in a pale yellow: Harvest Gold, Autumn Bronze.

Sitting at the kitchen table was a woman in her early sixties. Her thin brown face was seamed with a lot of smile lines. Pure white hair was done in a bun at the nape of her neck. She sat very straight in her chair, thin-boned hands folded on the tabletop. She looked terribly harmless. A nice old granny. If a quarter of what I'd heard about her was true, it was the greatest camouflage I'd ever seen.

She smiled and held out her hands. Manny stepped forward and took the offering, brushing his lips on her knuckles. "It is good to see you, Manuel." Her voice was rich, a contralto with the velvet brush of an accent.

"And you, Dominga." He released her hands and sat across from her.

Her quick black eyes flicked to me, still standing in the doorway. "So, Anita Blake, you have come to me at last."

It was a strange thing to say. I glanced at Manny. He gave a shrug with his eyes. He didn't know what she meant either. Great. "I didn't know you were eagerly awaiting me, Señora."

"I have heard stories of you, *chica*. Wondrous stories." There was a hint in those black eyes, that smiling face, that was not harmless.

"Manny?" I asked.

"It wasn't me."

"No, Manuel does not talk to me anymore. His little wife forbids it." That last sentence was angry, bitter.

Oh, God. The most powerful voodoo priestess in the Midwest was acting like a scorned lover. Shit.

She turned those angry black eyes to me. "All who deal in vaudun come to Señora Salvador eventually."

"I do not deal in vaudun."

She laughed at that. All the lines in her face flowed into the laughter. "You raise the dead, the zombie, and you do not deal in vaudun. Oh, *chica*, that is funny." Her voice sparkled with genuine amusement. So glad I could make her day.

"Dominga, I told you why we wished this meeting. I made it very clear . . ." Manny said.

She waved him to silence. "Oh, you were very careful on the phone, Manuel." She leaned towards me. "He made it very clear that you were not here to participate in any of my pagan rituals." The bitterness in her voice was sharp enough to choke on.

"Come here, *chica*," she said. She held out one hand to me, not both. Was I supposed to kiss it as Manny had done. I didn't think I'd come to see the pope.

I realized then that I didn't want to touch her. She had done nothing wrong. Yet, the muscles in my shoulders were screaming with tension. I was afraid, and I didn't know why.

I stepped forward and took her hand, uncertain what to do with it. Her skin was warm and dry. She sort of lowered me to the chair closest to her, still holding my hand. She said something in her soft, deep voice.

I shook my head. "I'm sorry I don't understand Spanish."

She touched my hair with her free hand. "Black hair like the wing of a crow. It does not come from any pale skin."

"My mother was Mexican."

"Yet you do not speak her tongue."

She was still holding my hand, and I wanted it back. "She died when I was young. I was raised by my father's people."

"I see."

I pulled my hand free and instantly felt better. She had done nothing to me. Nothing. Why was I so damn jumpy? The man with the streaked hair had taken up a post behind the Señora. I could see him clearly. His hands were in plain sight. I could see the back door and the entrance to the kitchen. No one was sneaking up behind me. But the hair at the base of my skull was standing at attention.

I glanced at Manny, but he was staring at Dominga. His hands were gripped together on the tabletop so tightly that his knuckles were mottled.

I felt like someone at a foreign film festival without subtitles. I could sort of guess what was going on, but I wasn't sure I was right. The creeping skin on my neck told me some hocus-pocus was going on. Manny's reaction said that just maybe the hocus-pocus was meant for him.

Manny's shoulders slumped. His hands relaxed their awful tension. It was a visible release of some kind. Dominga smiled, a brilliant flash of teeth. "You could have been so powerful, *mi corazón*."

"I did not want the power, Dominga," he said.

I stared from one to the other, not exactly sure what had just happened. I wasn't sure I wanted to know. I was willing to believe that ignorance was bliss. It so often is.

She turned her quick black eyes to me. "And you, *chica*, do you want power?" The creeping sensation at the base of my skull spread over my body. It felt like insects marching on my skin. Shit.

"No." A nice simple answer. Maybe I should try those more often.

"Perhaps not, but you will."

I didn't like the way she said that. It was ridiculous to be sitting in a sunny kitchen at 7:28 in the morning, and be scared. But there it was. My gut was twitching with it.

She stared at me. Her eyes were just eyes. There was none of that seductive power of a vampire. They were just eyes, and yet . . . The hair on my neck tried to crawl down my spine. Goose bumps broke out on my body, a rush of prickling warmth. I licked my lips and stared at Dominga Salvador.

It was a slap of magic. She was testing me. I'd had it done before. People are so fascinated with what I do. Convinced that I know magic. I don't. I have an affinity with the dead. It's not the same.

I stared into her nearly black eyes and felt myself sway forward. It was like falling without movement. The world sort of swung for a moment, then steadied. Warmth burst out of my body, like a twisting rope of heat. It went outward to the old woman. It hit her solid, and I felt it like a jolt of electricity.

I stood up, gasping for air. "Shit!"

"Anita, are you all right?" Manny was standing now, too. He touched my arm gently.

"I'm not sure. What the hell did she do to me?"

"It is what you have done to me, *chica*," Dominga said. She looked a little pale around the edges. Sweat beaded on her forehead.

The man stood away from the wall, his hands loose and ready. "No," Dominga said, "Enzo, I am all right." Her voice was breathy as if she had been running.

I stayed standing. I wanted to go home now, please.

"We did not come here for games, Dominga," Manny said. His voice had deepened with anger and, I think, fear. I agreed with that last emotion.

"It is not a game, Manuel. Have you forgotten everything I taught you. Everything you were?"

"I have forgotten nothing, but I did not bring her here to be harmed."

"Whether she is harmed or not is up to her, *mi corazón*."

I didn't much like that last part. "You're not going to help us. You're just going to play cat and mouse. Well, this mouse is leaving." I turned to leave, keeping a watchful eye on Enzo. He wasn't an amateur.

"Don't you wish to find the little boy that Manny said was taken? Three years old, very young to be in the hands of the bokor."

It stopped me. She knew it would. Damn her. "What is a bokor?"

She smiled. "You really don't know, do you?"

I shook my head.

The smile widened, all surprised pleasure. "Place your right hand palm up on the table, *por favor*."

"If you know something about the boy, just tell me. Please."

"Endure my little tests, and I will help you."

"What sort of tests?" I hoped I sounded as suspicious as I felt.

Dominga laughed, an abrupt and cheery sound. It went with all the smile lines in her face. Her eyes were practically sparkling with mirth. Why did I feel like she was laughing at me?

"Come, *chica*, I will not hurt you," she said.

"Manny?"

"If she does anything that may harm you, I will say so."

Dominga gazed up at me, a sort of puzzled wonder on her face. "I have heard that you can raise three zombies in a night, night after night. Yet, you truly are a novice."

"Ignorance is bliss," I said.

"Sit, *chica*. This will not hurt, I promise."

This will not hurt. It promised more painful things later. I sat. "Any delay could cost the boy his life." Try to appeal to her good side.

She leaned towards me. "Do you really think the child is still alive?" Guess she didn't have a good side.

I leaned back from her. I couldn't help it, and I couldn't lie to her. "No."

"Then we have time, don't we?"

"Time for what?"

"Your hand, *chica*, *por favor*, then I will answer your questions."

I took a deep breath and placed my right hand on the table, palm up. She was being mysterious. I hated people who were mysterious.

She brought a small black bag from under the table, as if it had been sitting in her lap the whole time. Like she'd planned this.

Manny was staring at the bag like something noisome was about to crawl out. Close. Dominga Salvador pulled something noisome out of it.

It was a charm, a gris-gris made of black feathers, bits of bone, a mummified bird's foot. I thought at first it was a chicken until I saw the thick black talons. There was a hawk or eagle out there somewhere with a peg leg.

I had visions of her digging the talons into my flesh, and was all tensed to pull away. But she simply placed the gris-gris on my open palm. Feathers, bits of bone, the dried hawk foot. It wasn't slimy. It didn't hurt. In fact, I felt a little silly.

Then I felt it, warmth. The thing was warm, sitting there in my hand. It hadn't been warm a second ago. "What are you doing to it?"

Dominga didn't answer. I glanced up at her, but her eyes were staring at my hand, intent. Like a cat about to pounce.

I glanced back down. The talons flexed, then spread, then flexed. It was moving in my hand. "Shiiit!" I wanted to stand up. To fling the vile thing to the floor. But I didn't. I sat there with every hair on my body tingling, my pulse thudding in my throat, and let the thing move in my hand. "All right," my voice sounded breathy, "I've passed your little test. Now get this thing the hell out of my hand."

Dominga lifted the claw gently from my hand. She was careful not to touch my skin. I didn't know why, but it was a noticeable effort.

"Dammit, dammit!" I whispered under my breath. I rubbed my hand against my stomach, touching the gun hidden there. It was comforting to know that if worse came to worst, I could just shoot her. Before she scared me to death. "Can we get down to business now?" My voice sounded almost steady. Bully for me.

Dominga was cradling the claw in her hands. "You made the claw move. You were frightened, but not surprised. Why?"

What could I say? Nothing I wanted her to know. "I have an affinity with the dead. It responds to me like some people can read thoughts."

She smiled. "Do you really believe that your ability to raise the dead is like mind reading? Parlor tricks?"

Dominga had obviously never met a really good telepath. If she had, she wouldn't have been scornful. In their own way, they were just as scary as she was.

"I raise the dead, Señora. It is just a job."

"You do not believe that any more than I do."

"I try real hard," I said.

"You've been tested before by someone." She made it a statement.

"My grandmother on my mother's side tested me, but not with that." I pointed to the still flexing foot. It looked like one of those fake hands that you can buy at Spencer's. Now that I wasn't holding it, I could pretend it just had tiny little batteries in it somewhere. Right.

"She was vaudun?"

I nodded.

"Why did you not study with her?"

"I have an inborn gift for raising the dead. That doesn't dictate my religious preferences."

"You are Christian." She made the word sound like something bad.

"That's it." I stood. "I wish I could say it's been a pleasure, but it hasn't."

"Ask your questions, *chica*."

"What?" The change of subject was too fast for me.

"Ask whatever you came here to ask," she said.

I glanced at Manny. "If she says she will answer, she will answer." He didn't look completely happy about it.

I sat down, again. The next insult and I'm outta here. But if she could really help . . . oh, hell, she was dangling that thin little thread of hope. And after what I'd seen at the Reynolds house, I was grabbing for it.

I had planned to be as polite as possible on the wording of the question, now I didn't give a shit. "Have you raised a zombie in the last few weeks?"

"Some," she said.

Okay. I hesitated over the next question. The feel of that thing moving in my hand flashed back on me. I rubbed my hand against my pants leg as if I could rub the sensation away. What was the worst she could do to me if I offended her? Don't ask. "Have you sent any zombies out on errands . . . of revenge?" There; that was polite, amazing.

"None."

"Are you sure?" I asked.

She smiled. "I'd remember if I loosed murderers from the grave."

"Killer zombies don't have to be murderers," I said.

"Oh?" Her pale eyebrows raised. "Are you so very familiar with raising 'killer' zombies?"

I fought the urge to squirm like a schoolchild caught at a lie. "Only one."

"Tell me."

"No." My voice was very firm. "No, that is a private matter." A private nightmare that I was not going to share with the voodoo lady.

I decided to change the subject just a little. "I've raised murderers before. They weren't more violent than regular undead."

"How many dead have you called from the grave?" she asked.

I shrugged. "I don't know."

"Give me an"—she seemed to be groping for a word—"estimation."

"I can't. It must have been hundreds."

"A thousand?" she asked.

"Maybe, I haven't kept count," I said.

"Has your boss at Animators, Incorporated, kept count?"

"I would assume that all my clients are on file, yes," I said.

She smiled. "I would be interested in knowing the exact number."

What could it hurt? "I'll find out if I can."

"Such an obedient girl." She stood. "I did not raise this 'killer' zombie of yours. If that is what is eating citizens." She smiled, almost laughed, as if it were funny. "But I know people that would never speak to you. People that could do this horrible deed. I will question them, and they will answer me. I will have truth from them, and I will pass this truth on to you, Anita."

She said my name like it was meant to be said, Ahneetah. Made it sound exotic.

"Thank you very much, Señora Salvador."

"But there is one favor I will ask in return for this information," she said.

Something unpleasant was about to be said, I'd have bet on it. "What would that favor be, Señora?"

"I want you to pass one more test for me."

I stared at her, waiting for her to go on, but she didn't. "What sort of test?" I asked.

"Come downstairs, and I will show you." Her voice was mild as honey.

"No, Dominga," Manny said. He was standing now. "Anita, nothing the Señora could tell you would be worth what she wants."

"I can talk to people and things that will not talk to you, either of you. Good Christians that you are."

"Come on, Anita, we don't need her help." He had started for the door. I didn't follow him. Manny hadn't seen the slaughtered family. He hadn't dreamed about blood-coated teddy bears last night. I had. I couldn't leave if she could help me. Whether Benjamin Reynolds was dead or not wasn't the point. The thing, whatever it was, would kill again. And I was betting it had something to do with voodoo. It wasn't my area. I needed help, and I needed it fast.

"Anita, come on." He touched my arm, pulling me a little towards the door.

"Tell me about the test."

Dominga smiled triumphantly. She knew she had me. She knew I wasn't leaving until I had her promised help. Damn.

"Let us retire to the basement. I will explain the test there."

Manny's grip on my arm tightened. "Anita, you don't know what you're doing."

He was right, but . . . "Just stay with me, Manny, back me up. Don't let me do anything that will really hurt. Okay?"

"Anita, anything she wants you to do down there will hurt. Maybe not physically, but it will hurt."

"I have to do this, Manny." I patted his hand and smiled. "It'll be all right."

"No," he said, "it won't be."

I didn't know what to say to that, except that he was probably right. But it didn't matter. I was going to do it. Whatever she asked, within reason, if it would stop the killings. If it would fix it so that I never had to see another half-eaten body.

Dominga smiled. "Let us go downstairs."

"May I speak with Anita alone, Señora, *por favor*," Manny said. His hand was still on my arm. I could feel the tension in his hand.

"You will have the rest of this beautiful day to talk to her, Manuel. But I have only this short time. If she does this test for me now, I promise to aid her in any way I can to catch this killer."

It was a powerful offer. A lot of people would talk to her just out of pure terror. The police can't inspire that. All they can do is arrest you. It wasn't enough of a deterrent. Having the undead crawl through your window . . . that was a deterrent.

Four, maybe five people were already dead. It was a bad way to die. "I've already said I'd do it. Let's go."

She walked around the table and took Manny's arm. He jumped like she'd struck him. She pulled him away from me. "No harm will come to her, Manuel. I swear."

"I do not trust you, Dominga."

She laughed. "But it is her choice, Manuel. I have not forced her."

"You have blackmailed her, Dominga. Blackmailed her with the safety of others."

She looked back over her shoulder. "Have I blackmailed you, *chica?*"

"Yes," I said.

"Oh, she is your student, *corazón*. She has your honesty. And your bravery."

"She is brave, but she has not seen what lies below."

I wanted to ask what exactly was in the basement, but I didn't. I really didn't want to know. I've had people warn me about supernatural shit before. Don't go in that room; the monster will get you. There usually is a monster, and it usually tries to get me. But up till now I've been faster or luckier than the monsters. Here's to my luck holding.

I wished that I could heed Manny's warning. Going home sounded very good about now, but duty reared its ugly head. Duty and a whisper of nightmares. I didn't want to see another butchered family.

Dominga led Manny from the room. I followed with Enzo bringing up the rear. What a day for a parade.

# 6

THE BASEMENT STAIRS were steep, wooden slats. You could feel the vibrations in the stairs as we tromped down them. It was not comforting. The bright sunlight from the door spilled into absolute darkness. The sunlight faltered, seemed to fade as if it had no power in this cavelike place. I stopped on the grey edge of daylight, staring down into the night-dark of the room. I couldn't even make out Dominga and Manny. They had to be just in front of me, didn't they?

Enzo the bodyguard waited at my back like some patient mountain. He made no move to hurry me. Was it my decision then? Could I just pack up my toys and go home?

"Manny," I called.

A voice came distantly. Too far away. Maybe it was an acoustic trick of the room. Maybe not. "I'm here, Anita."

I strained to see where the voice was coming from, but there was nothing to see. I took two steps farther down into the inky dark and stopped like I'd hit a wall. There was the damp rock smell of most basements, but under that something stale, sour, sweet. That almost indescribable smell of corpses. It was faint here at the head of the stairs. I was betting it would get worse the farther down I went.

My grandmother had been a priestess of vaudun. Her Humfo had not smelled like corpses. The line between good and evil wasn't as clear cut in voodoo as in Wicca or Christianity and satanism, but it was there. Dominga Salvador was on the wrong side of the line. I had known that when I came. It still bothered me.

Grandmother Flores had told me that I was a necromancer. It was more than being a voodoo priestess, and less. I had a sympathy with the dead, all dead. It was hard to be vaudun and a necromancer and not be evil. Too tempting, Grandma said. She had encouraged my being Christian. Encouraged my father to cut me off from her side of the family. Encouraged it for love of me and fear for my soul.

And here I was going down the steps into the jaws of temptation. What would Grandma Flores say to that? Probably, go home. Which was good advice. The tight feeling in my stomach was saying the same thing.

The lights came on. I blinked on the stairs. The one dim bulb at the foot of the staircase seemed as bright as a star. Dominga and Manny stood just under the bulb, looking up at me.

Light. Why did I feel instantly better? Silly, but true. Enzo let the door swing shut behind us. The shadows were thick, but down a narrow bricked hallway more bare light bulbs dangled.

I was almost at the bottom of the stairs. That sweet, sour smell was stronger. I tried breathing through my mouth, but that only made it clog the back of my throat. The smell of rotting flesh clings to the tongue.

Dominga led the way between the narrow walls. There were regular patches in the walls. Places where it looked like cement had been put over—doors. Paint had been smoothed over the cement, but there had been doors, rooms, at regular intervals. Why wall them up? Why cover the doors in cement? What was behind them?

I rubbed fingertips across the rough cement. The surface was bumpy and cool. The paint wasn't very old. It would have flaked in this dampness. It hadn't. What was behind this blocked up door?

The skin just between my shoulder blades started to itch. I fought an urge to glance back at Enzo. I was betting he was behaving himself. I was betting that being shot was the least of my worries.

The air was cool and damp. A very basement of a basement. There were three doors, two to the right, one to the left that were just doors.

One door had a shiny new padlock on it. As we walked past it, I heard the door sigh as if something large had leaned against it.

I stopped. "What's in there?"

Enzo had stopped when I stopped. Dominga and Manny had rounded a corner, and we were alone. I touched the door. The wood creaked, rattling against its hinges. Like some giant cat had rubbed against the door. A smell rolled out from under the door. I gagged and backed away. The stench clung to my mouth and throat. I swallowed convulsively and tasted it all the way down.

The thing behind the door made a mewling sound. I couldn't tell if it was human or animal. It was bigger than a person, whatever it was. And it was dead. Very, very dead.

I covered my nose and mouth with my left hand. The right was free just in case. In case that thing should come crashing out. Bullets against the walking dead. I knew better, but the gun was still a comfort. In a pinch I could shoot Enzo. But somehow I knew that if the thing rattling the door got out, Enzo would be in as much danger as I was.

"We must go on, now," he said.

I couldn't tell anything from his face. We might have been walking down the street to the corner store. He seemed impervious, and I hated him for it. If I'm terrified, by God, everyone else should be, too.

I eyed the supposedly unlocked door to my left. I had to know. I yanked it open. The room was maybe eight by four, like a cell. The cement floor and whitewashed walls were clean, empty. It looked like a cell waiting for its next occupant. Enzo slammed the door shut. I didn't fight him. It wasn't worth it. If I was going to go one on one with someone who outweighed me by over a hundred pounds, I was going to be picky about where I drew the line. An empty room wasn't worth it.

Enzo leaned against the door. Sweat glimmered across his face in the harsh light. "Do not try any other doors, señorita. It could be very bad."

I nodded. "Sure, no problem." An empty room and he was sweating. Nice to know something frightened him. But why this room and not the one with the mewling stench behind it? I didn't have a clue.

"We must catch up with the Señora." He made a gracious motion like a maître d' showing me to a chair. I went where he pointed. Where else was I going to go?

The hallway fed into a large rectangular chamber. It was painted the same startling white as the cell had been. The whitewashed floor was covered in brilliant red and black designs. Verve it was called. Symbols drawn in the voodoo sanctuary to summon the lao, the gods of vaudun.

The symbols acted as walls bordering a path. They led to the altar. If you stepped off the path you messed up all those carefully formed symbols. I didn't know if that would be good or bad. Rule number three hundred sixty-nine when dealing with unfamiliar magic: when in doubt, leave it alone.

I left it alone.

The end of the room gleamed with candles. The warm, rich light flickered and filled the white walls with heat and light. Dominga stood in the midst of that light, that whiteness, and gleamed with evil. There was no other word for it. She wasn't just bad, she was evil. It gleamed around her like darkness made liquid and touchable. The smiling old woman was gone. She was a creature of power.

Manny stood off to one side. He was staring at her. He glanced at me. His eyes were showing a lot of white. The altar was directly behind Dominga's straight back. Dead animals spilled off the top of it to form a pool on the floor. Chickens, dogs, a small pig, two goats. Lumps of fur and dried blood that I couldn't identify. The altar looked like a fountain where dead things flowed out of the center, sluggish and thick.

The sacrifices were fresh. No smell of decay. The glazed eyes of a goat stared at me. I hated killing goats. They always seemed so much more intelligent than chickens. Or maybe I just thought they were cuter.

A tall woman stood to the right of the altar. Her skin gleamed nearly black in the candlelight as if she had been carved of some heavy, gleaming wood. Her hair was short and neat, falling to her shoulders. Wide cheekbones, full lips, expert makeup. She wore a long silky dress, the bright scarlet of fresh blood. It matched her lipstick.

To the right of the altar stood a zombie. It had once been a woman. Long, pale brown hair fell nearly to her waist. Someone had brushed it until it gleamed. It was the only thing about the corpse that looked alive. The skin had turned a greyish color. The flesh had narrowed down around the bones like shrink wrap. Muscles moved under the thin, rotting skin, stringy and shrunken. The nose was almost gone, giving it a half-finished look. A crimson gown hung loose and flapping on the skeletal remains.

There was even an attempt at makeup. Lipstick had been abandoned when the lips shriveled up but a dusting of mauve eye shadow outlined the bulging eyes. I swallowed very hard and turned to stare at the first woman.

She was a zombie. One of the best preserved and most lifelike I had ever seen, but no matter how luscious she looked, she was dead. The woman, the zombie, stared back at me. There was something in her perfect brown eyes that no zombie has for long. The memory of who and what they were fades within a few days, sometimes hours. But this zombie was afraid. The fear was like a shiny, bright pain in her eyes. Zombies didn't have eyes like that.

I turned back to the more decayed zombie and found her staring at me, too. The bulging eyes were staring at me. With most of the flesh holding the eyes in the socket gone, her facial expressions weren't as good, but she managed. It managed to be afraid. Shit.

Dominga nodded, and Enzo motioned me farther into the circle. I didn't want to go.

"What the hell is going on here, Dominga?"

She smiled, almost a laugh. "I am not accustomed to such rudeness."

"Get used to it," I said. Enzo sort of breathed down my back. I did my best to ignore him. My right hand was sort of casually near my gun, without looking like I was reaching for my gun. It wasn't easy. Reaching for a gun usually looks like reaching for a gun. No one seemed to notice though. Goody for our side.

"What have you done to the two zombies?"

"Inspect them yourself, *chica*. If you are as powerful as the stories say, you will answer your own question."

"And if I can't figure it out?" I asked.

She smiled, but her eyes were as flat and black as a shark's. "Then you are not as powerful as the stories."

"Is this the test?"

"Perhaps."

I sighed. The voodoo lady wanted to see how tough I really was. Why? Maybe there wasn't a reason. Maybe she was just a sadistic power-hungry bitch. Yeah, I could believe that. Then again, maybe there was a purpose to the theatrics. If so, I still didn't know what it was.

I glanced at Manny. He gave a barely perceivable shrug. He didn't know what was going on either. Great.

I didn't like playing Dominga's games, especially when I didn't know the rules. The zombies were still staring at me. There was something in their eyes. It was fear, and something worse—hope. Shit. Zombies didn't have hope. They didn't have anything. They were dead. These weren't dead. I had to know. Here's hoping that curiosity didn't kill the animator.

I stepped around Dominga carefully, watching her out of the corner of my eye. Enzo stayed behind blocking the path between the verve. He looked big and solid standing there, but I could get past him, if I wanted it bad enough. Bad enough to kill him. I hoped I wouldn't want it that bad.

The decayed zombie stared down at me. She was tall, almost six feet. Skeletal feet peeked out from underneath the red gown. A tall, slender woman, probably beautiful, once. Bulging eyes rolled in the nearly bare sockets. A wet, sucking sound accompanied the movements.

I'd thrown up the first time I heard that sound. The sound of eyeballs rolling in rotting sockets. But that was four years ago, when I was new at this. Decaying flesh didn't make me flinch anymore or throw up. As a general rule.

The eyes were pale brown with a lot of green in them. The smell of some expensive perfume floated around her. Powdery and fine, like talcum powder in your nose, sweet, flowery. Underneath was the stink of rotting flesh. It wrinkled my nose, caught at the back of my throat. The next time I smelled this delicate, expensive perfume, I would think of rotting flesh. Oh, well, it smelled too expensive to buy, anyway.

She was staring at me. She, not it, she. There was the force of personality in her eyes. I call most zombies "it" because it fits. They may come from the grave very alive-looking, but it doesn't last. They rot. Personality and intelligence goes first, then the body. It's always that order. God is not cruel enough to force anyone to be aware while their body decays around them. Something had gone very wrong with this one.

I stepped around Dominga Salvador. For no reason that I could name, I stayed out of reach. She had no weapon, I was almost sure of that. The danger she represented had nothing to do with knives or guns. I simply didn't want her to touch me, not even by accident.

The zombie on the left was perfect. Not a sign of decay. The look in her eyes was alert, alive. God help us. She could have gone anywhere and passed for human. How had I known she wasn't alive? I wasn't even sure. None of the usual signs were there, but I knew dead when I felt it. Yet . . . I stared up at the second woman. Her lovely, dark face stared back. Fear screamed out of her eyes.

Whatever power let me raise the dead told me this was a zombie, but my eyes couldn't tell. It was amazing. If Dominga could raise zombies like this, she had me beat hands down.

I have to wait three days before I raise a corpse. It gives the soul time to leave the area. Souls usually hover around for a while. Three days is average. I can't call shit from the grave if the soul's still present. It has been theorized that if an animator could keep the soul intact while raising the body, we'd get resurrection. You know, resurrection, the real thing, like in Jesus and Lazarus. I didn't believe that. Or maybe I just know my limitations.

I stared up at this zombie and knew what was different. The soul was still there. The soul was still inside both bodies. How? How in Jesus' name did she do it?

"The souls. The souls are still in the bodies." My voice held the distaste I felt. Why bother to hide it?

"Very good, *chica*."

I went to stand to her left, keeping Enzo in sight. "How did you do it?"

"The soul was captured at the moment it took flight from the body."

I shook my head. "That doesn't explain anything."

"Don't you know how to capture souls in a bottle?"

Souls in a bottle? Was she kidding? No, she wasn't. "No, I don't." I tried not to sound superior as I said it.

"I could teach you so much, Anita, so very much."

"No, thanks," I said. "You captured their souls, then you raised the body, and put the soul back in." I was guessing, but it sounded right.

"Very, very good. That is it exactly." She was staring at me so hard that it was uncomfortable. Her empty, black eyes were memorizing me.

"But why is the second zombie rotting? The theory is with the soul intact, the zombie won't decay?"

"It is no longer a theory. I have proved it," she said.

I stared at the rotted corpse, and it stared back. "Then why is that one rotting, and this one isn't?" Just two necromancers talking shop. Tell me, do you raise your zombies only during the dark of the moon?

"The soul may be put into the body, then removed again, as often as I wish."

I stared at Dominga Salvador now. I stared and tried not to let my jaw drop, not to let the dawning horror slip across my face. She would enjoy shocking me. I didn't want her taking pleasure from me, for any reason.

"Let me test my understanding here," I said in my best executive trainee voice. "You put the soul into the body and it didn't rot. Then you took the soul out of the body, making it an ordinary zombie, and it did rot."

"Exactly," she said.

"Then you put the soul back in the rotted corpse, and the zombie was aware and alive again. Did the rotting stop when the soul went back in?"

"Yes."

Shit. "So you could keep the zombie over there rotted just that much forever?"

"Yes."

Double shit. "And this one?" I pointed this time, like I was doing a lecture.

"Many people would pay dearly for her."

"Wait a minute, you mean sell her as a sex slave?"

"Perhaps."

"But . . ." The idea was too horrible. She was a zombie, which meant she didn't need to eat or sleep or anything. You could keep her in a closet and take her out like a toy. A perfectly obedient slave.

"Are they as obedient as normal zombies, or does the soul give them free will?"

"They seem to be very obedient."

"Maybe they're just scared of you," I said.

She smiled. "Perhaps."

"You can't just keep the soul imprisoned forever."

"I can't," she said.

"The soul needs to go on."

"To your Christian heaven or hell?"

"Yes," I said.

"These were wicked women, *chica*. Their own families gave them to me. Paid me to punish them."

"You took money for this?"

"It is illegal to tamper with dead bodies without permission of the family," she said.

I don't know if she had planned to horrify me. Maybe not. But with that one sentence she let me know that what she was doing was perfectly legal. The dead had no rights. This was the reason we needed some laws to protect zombies. Shit.

"No one deserves to spend eternity locked in a corpse," I said.

"We could do this to criminals on death row, *chica*. They could be made to serve society after death."

I shook my head. "No, it's wrong."

"I have created a nonrotting zombie, *chica*. Animators, I believe you call yourselves, have been searching for the secret for years. I have it, and people will pay for it."

"It's wrong. I may not know much about voodoo, but even among your own people, it's wrong. How can you keep the souls prisoner and not allow them to go on and join with the lao?"

She shrugged and sighed. She suddenly looked tired. "I was hoping, *chica*, that you would help me. With two of us working, we could create more zombies much faster. We could be wealthy beyond our dreams."

"You've asked the wrong girl."

"I see that now. I had hoped that since you were not vaudun, you would not see it as wrong."

"Christian, Buddhist, Moslem, you name it, Dominga, no one's going to think it's all right."

"Perhaps, perhaps not. It does not hurt to ask."

I glanced at the rotted zombie. "At least put your first experiment out of its misery."

Dominga glanced at the zombie. "She makes a powerful demonstration, does she not?"

"You've created a nonrotting zombie, great. Don't be sadistic."

"You think I am being cruel?"

"Yeah," I said.

"Manuel, am I being cruel?"

Manny stared at me while he answered. His eyes were trying to tell me something. I couldn't tell what. "Yes, Señora, you are being cruel."

She glanced over at him then, surprise in the movement of her body, her face. "Do you really think I am cruel, Manuel? Your beloved *amante*?"

He nodded slowly. "Yes."

"You were not so quick to judge a few years back, Manuel. You slew the white goat for me, more than once."

I turned towards Manny. It was like that moment in a movie where the main character has a revelation about someone. There should be music and camera angles when you learn one of your best friends participated in human sacrifice. More than once she had said. More than once.

"Manny?" My voice was a hoarse whisper. This, for me, was worse than the zombies. The hell with strangers. This was Manny, and it couldn't be true.

"Manny?" I said it again. He wouldn't look at me. Bad sign.

"You didn't know, *chica*? Didn't your Manny tell you of his past?"

"Shut up," I said.

"He was my most treasured helper. He would have done anything for me."

"Shut up!" I screamed it at her. She stopped, her face thinning with anger. Enzo took two steps into the altar area. "Don't." I wasn't even sure who I was saying it to. "I need to hear from him, not from you."

The anger was still in her face. Enzo loomed like an avalanche about to be unleashed. Dominga gave one sharp nod. "Ask him then, *chica*."

"Manny, is she telling the truth? Did you perform human sacrifices?" My voice sounded so normal. It shouldn't have. My stomach was so tight, it hurt. I wasn't afraid anymore, or at least not of Dominga. The truth; I was afraid of the truth.

He looked up. His hair fell across his face framing his eyes. A lot of pain in those eyes. Almost flinching.

"It's the truth, isn't it?" My skin felt cold. "Answer me, dammit." My voice still sounded ordinary, calm.

"Yes," he said.

"Yes, you committed human sacrifice?"

He glared at me now, anger helping him meet my eyes. "Yes, yes!"

It was my turn to look away. "God, Manny, how could you?" My voice was soft now, not ordinary. If I didn't know better, I'd say it sounded like I was on the verge of tears.

"It was nearly twenty years ago, Anita. I was vaudun and a necromancer. I believed. I loved the Señora. Thought I did."

I stared up at him. The look on his face made my throat tight. "Manny, dammit."

He didn't say anything. He just stood there looking miserable. And I couldn't reconcile the two images. Manny Rodriguez and someone who would slaughter the hornless goat in a ritual. He had taught me right from wrong in this business. He had refused to do so many things. Things not half as bad as this. It made no sense.

I shook my head. "I can't deal with this right now." I heard myself say it out loud, and hadn't really meant to. "Fine, you've dropped your little bombshell, Señora Salvador. You said you'd help us, if I passed your test. Did I pass?" When in doubt, concentrate on one disaster at a time.

"I wanted to offer you a chance to help me with my new business venture."

"We both know I'm not going to do that," I said.

"It is a pity, Anita. With training you could rival my powers."

Be just like her when I grew up. No thanks. "Thanks anyway, but I'm happy where I am."

Her eyes flicked to Manny, back to me. "Happy?"

"Manny and I will deal with it, Señora. Now will you help me?"

"If I help you without you helping me in some way, you will owe me a favor."

I didn't want to owe her a favor. "I would rather just trade information."

"What could you possibly know that would be worth all the effort I will expend hunting for your killer zombie?"

I thought about that for a moment. "I know that legislation is being written right now, about zombies. Zombies are going to have rights, and laws protecting them soon." I hoped it was soon. No need to tell her how early in the process the legislation was.

"So, I must sell a few nonrotting zombies soon, before it becomes illegal."

"I wouldn't think illegal would bother you much. Human sacrifice is illegal, too."

She gave a tiny smile. "I do not do such things anymore, Anita. I have given up my wicked ways."

I didn't believe that, and she knew I didn't believe it. Her smile widened. "When Manuel left, I stopped such evil practices. Without his urgings, I became a respectable bokar."

She was lying, but I couldn't prove it. And she knew that, too. "I gave you valuable information. Now will you help me?"

She nodded graciously. "I will search among my followers to see if any knows of your killer zombie." I had the sense that she was quietly laughing at me.

"Manny, will she help us?"

"If the Señora says she will do a thing, it will be done. She is good that way."

"I will find your killer if it has anything to do with vaudun," she said.

"Great." I didn't say thank you, because it seemed wrong. I wanted to call her a bitch and shoot her between the eyes, but then I would have had to shoot Enzo, too. And how would I explain that to the police? She was breaking no laws. Dammit.

"I don't suppose appealing to your better nature would make you forget this mad scheme to use your new improved zombies for slaves?"

She smiled. "*Chica, chica*, I will be rich beyond your wildest dreams. You can refuse to join me, but you cannot stop me."

"Don't bet on it," I said.

"What will you do, go to the police? I am breaking no laws. The only way to stop me is to kill me." She looked directly at me while she said it.

"Don't tempt me."

Manny moved up beside me. "Don't, Anita, don't challenge her."

I was sort of mad at him, too, so what the hell. "I will stop you, Señora Salvador. Whatever it takes."

"You call death magic against me, Anita, and it is you who will die."

I didn't know death magic from frijoles. I shrugged. "I was thinking something more down to earth, like a bullet."

Enzo surged into the altar area, moving to stand between his boss-lady and me. Dominga stopped him. "No, Enzo, she is angry this morn-ing, and shocked." Her eyes were still laughing at me. "She knows nothing of the deeper magics. She cannot harm me, and she is too morally superior to commit cold-blooded murder."

The worst part about it was that she was right. I couldn't just put a bullet between her eyes, not unless she threatened me. I glanced at the waiting zombies, patient as the dead, but underneath that endless pa-tience was fear, and hope, and . . . God, the line between life and death was getting thinner all the time.

"At least lay to rest your first experiment. You've proved you can put the soul in and out multiple times. Don't make her watch."

"But, Anita, I already have a buyer for her."

"Oh, Jesus, you don't mean . . . Oh, God, a necrophiliac."

"Those that love the dead better than you or I ever will, will pay extraordinary amounts for such as her."

Maybe I could just shoot her. "You are a cold-hearted, amoral bitch."

"And you, *chica*, need to learn respect for your elders."

"Respect has to be earned," I said.

"I think, Anita Blake, that you need to remember why people fear the dark. I will see that very soon you have a visitor to your window.

Some dark night when you are fast asleep in your warm, safe bed. Something evil will creep into your room. I will earn your respect, if that is the way you want it."

I should have been afraid, but I wasn't. I was angry and wanted to go home. "You can force people to be afraid of you, Señora, but you can't force them to respect you."

"We shall see, Anita. Call me after you have gotten my gift. It will be soon."

"Will you still help locate the killer zombie?"

"I said I would, and I will."

"Good," I said. "May we go now?"

She waved Enzo back beside her. "By all means run out into the daylight where you can be brave."

I walked to the pathway. Manny stayed right with me. We were careful not to look at each other. We were too busy watching the Señora and her pets. I stopped just inside the path. Manny touched my arm lightly, as if he knew what I was about to say. I ignored him.

"I may not be willing to kill you in cold blood, but hurt me first, and I'll put a bullet in you some bright, sunshiny day."

"Threats will not save you, *chica*," she said.

I smiled sweetly. "You either, bitch."

Her face went all thin and angry. I smiled wider.

"She does not mean it, Señora," Manny said. "She will not kill you."

"Is this true, *chica*?" Her voice was a rich growl of sound, pleasant and frightening at the same time.

I gave Manny a quick dirty look. It was a good threat. I didn't like weakening it with common sense, or truth. "I said, I'd shoot you. I didn't say I'd kill you. Now did I?"

"No, you did not."

Manny grabbed my arm and started pulling me backwards towards the stairs. He was pulling on my left arm, leaving my right free for my gun. Just in case.

Dominga never moved. Her black, angry eyes stared at me until we rounded the corner. Manny pulled me into the hallway with its cement covered doors. I pulled free of him. We stared at each other for a heartbeat.

"What's behind the doors?"

"I don't know."

Doubt must have shown on my face because he said, "God as my witness, Anita, I don't know. It wasn't like this twenty years ago."

I just stared at him as if looking would change things. I wish Dominga Salvador had kept Manny's secret to herself. I had not wanted to know.

"Anita, we have to get out of here, now." The light bulb over our head went out, like someone had snuffed it. We both looked up. There was nothing to see. My arms broke out in goose bumps. The bulb just ahead of us dimmed, then blinked off.

Manny was right. We needed to leave now. I broke into a half jog towards the stairs. Manny stayed with me. The door with its shiny padlock rattled and thumped as if the thing were trying to get out. Another light bulb flashed off. The darkness was snapping at our heels. We were at a full run by the time we hit the stairs. There were two bulbs left.

We were halfway up the stairs when the last light vanished. The world went black. I froze on the stairs unwilling to move without being able to see. Manny's arm brushed mine, but I couldn't see him. The darkness was complete. I could have touched my eyeballs and not seen my finger. We grabbed hands and held on. His hand wasn't much bigger than mine. It was warm and familiar, and damn comforting.

The cracking of wood was loud as a shotgun blast in the dark. The stench of rotting meat filled the stairwell. "Shit!" The word echoed and bounced in the blackness. I wished I hadn't said it. Something large pulled itself into the corridor. It couldn't be as big as it sounded. The wet, slithering sounds moved towards the stairs. Or sounded like they did.

I stumbled up two steps. Manny didn't need any urging. We stumbled through the darkness, and the sounds below hurried. The light under the door was so bright, it almost hurt. Manny flung open the door. The sunlight blazed against my eyes. We were both momentarily blinded.

Something screamed behind us, caught in the edge of daylight. The scream was almost human. I started to turn, to look. Manny slammed the door. He shook his head. "You don't want to see. I don't want to see."

He was right. So why did I have this urge to yank the door open, to stare down into the dark until I saw something pale and shapeless? A screaming nightmare of a sight. I stared at the closed door, and I let it go.

"Do you think it will come out after us?" I asked.

"Into the daylight?" Manny asked.

"Yeah," I said.

"I don't think so. Let's leave without finding out."

I agreed. The August sunlight streamed into the living room. Warm and real. The scream, the darkness, the zombies, all of it seemed wrong for the sunlight. Things that go bump in the morning. It didn't sound quite right.

I opened the screen door calmly, slowly. Panicked, me? But I was listening so hard I could hear blood rush in my ears. Listening for slithery sounds of pursuit. Nothing.

Antonio was still on guard outside. Should we warn him about the possibility of a Lovecraftian horror nipping at our heels?

"Did you fuck the zombie downstairs?" Antonio asked.

So much for warning old Tony.

Manny ignored him.

"Go fuck yourself," I said.

He said, "Heh!"

I kept walking down the porch steps. Manny stayed with me. Antonio didn't draw his gun and shoot us. The day was looking up.

The little girl on the tricycle had stopped by Manny's car. She stared up at me as I got in the passenger side door. I stared back into huge brown eyes. Her face was darkly tanned. She couldn't have been more than five.

Manny got in the driver's side door. He put the car in gear, and we pulled away. The little girl and I stared at each other. Just before we turned the corner she started pedaling up and down the sidewalk again.

# 7

THE AIR CONDITIONER blasted cold air into the car. Manny drove through the residential streets. Most of the driveways were empty. People off to work. Small children playing in the yards. A few moms out on the front steps. I didn't see any daddies at home with the kids. Things change, but not that much. The silence stretched out between us. It was not a comfortable silence.

Manny glanced at me furtively out of the corner of his eye.

I slumped in the passenger seat, the seat belt digging across my gun. "So," I said, "you used to perform human sacrifice."

I think he flinched. "Do you want me to lie?"

"No, I want to not know. I want to live in blessed ignorance."

"It doesn't work that way, Anita," he said.

"I guess it doesn't," I said. I adjusted the lap strap so it didn't press over my gun. Ah, comfort. If only everything else were that easy to fix. "What are we going to do about it?"

"About you knowing?" he asked. He glanced at me as he asked. I nodded.

"You aren't going to rant and rave? Tell me what an evil bastard I am?"

"Doesn't seem much point in it," I said.

He looked at me a little longer this time. "Thanks."

"I didn't say it was alright, Manny. I'm just not going to yell at you. Not yet, anyway."

He passed a large white car full of dark-skinned teenagers. Their car stereo was up so loud, my teeth rattled. The driver had one of those high-boned, flat faces, straight off an Aztec carving. Our eyes met as we moved by them. He made kissing motions with his mouth. The others laughed uproariously. I resisted the urge to flip them off. Mustn't encourage the little tykes.

They turned right. We went straight. Relief.

Manny stopped two cars back from a light. Just beyond the light was the turnoff 40 West. We'd take 270 up to Olive and then a short jaunt to my apartment. We had forty-five minutes to an hour of travel time. Not a problem normally. Today I wanted away from Manny. I wanted some time to digest. To decide how to feel.

"Talk to me, Anita, please."

"Honest to God, Manny, I don't know what to say." Truth, try to stick to the truth between friends. Yeah.

"I've known you for four years, Manny. You are a good man. You love your wife, your kids. You've saved my life. I've saved yours. I thought I knew you."

"I haven't changed."

"Yes," I looked at him as I said it, "you have. Manny Rodriguez would never under any circumstance take part in human sacrifice."

"It's been twenty years."

"There's no statute of limitations on murder."

"You going to the cops?" His voice was very quiet.

The light changed. We waited our turn and merged into the morning traffic. It was as heavy as it ever got in St. Louis. It's not the gridlock of L.A., but stop and jerk is still pretty darn annoying. Especially this morning.

"I don't have any proof. Just Dominga Salvador's word. I wouldn't exactly call her a reliable witness."

"If you had proof?"

"Don't push me on this, Manny." I stared out the window. There was a silver Miada with the top down. The driver was white-haired, male, and wore a jaunty little cap, plus racing gloves. Middle-age crisis.

"Does Rosita know?" I asked.

"She suspects, but she doesn't know for sure."

"Doesn't want to know," I said.

"Probably not." He turned and stared at me then.

A red Ford truck was nearly in front of us. I yelled, "Manny!"

He slammed on the brakes, and only the seat belt kept me from kissing the dashboard.

"Jesus, Manny, watch your driving!"

He concentrated on traffic for a few seconds, then without looking at me this time, "Are you going to tell Rosita?"

I thought about that for about a second. I shook my head, realized he couldn't see it, and said, "I don't think so. Ignorance is bliss on this one, Manny. I don't think your wife could deal with it."

"She'd leave me and take the kids."

I believed she would. Rosita was a very religious person. She took all the commandments very seriously.

"She already thinks I'm risking my eternal soul by raising the dead," Manny said.

"She didn't have a problem until the pope threatened to excommunicate all animators unless they stopped raising the dead."

"The Church is very important to Rosita."

"Me, too, but I'm a happy little Episcopalian now. Switch churches."

"It's not that easy," he said.

It wasn't. I knew that. But, hey, you do what you can, or what you have to. "Can you explain why you would do human sacrifice? I mean, something that will make sense to me?"

"No," he said. He pulled into the far lane. It seemed to be going a little faster. It slowed down as soon as we pulled in. Murphy's law of traffic.

"You won't even try to explain?"

"It's indefensible, Anita. I live with what I did. I can't do anything else."

He had a point. "This has to change the way I think about you, Manny."

"In what way?"

"I don't know yet." Honesty. If we were very careful, we could still be honest with each other. "Is there anything else you think I should know? Anything that Dominga might spill later on?"

He shook his head. "Nothing worse."

"Okay," I said.

"Okay," he said. "That's it, no interrogation?"

"Not now, maybe not ever." I was tired all at once. It was 9:23 in the morning, and I needed a nap. Emotionally drained. "I don't know how to feel about this, Manny. I don't know how it changes our friendship, or our working relationship, or even if it does. I think it does. Oh, hell, I don't know."

"Fair enough," he said. "Let's move on to something we aren't confused about."

"And what would that be?" I asked.

"The Señora will send something bad to your window, just like she said she would."

"I figured that."

"Why did you threaten her?"

"I didn't like her."

"Oh, great, just great," he said. "Why didn't I think of that?"

"I am going to stop her, Manny. I figured she should know."

"Never give the bad guys a head start, Anita. I taught you that."

"You also taught me that human sacrifice is murder."

"That hurt," he said.

"Yes," I said, "it did."

"You need to be prepared, Anita. She will send something after you. Just to scare you, I think, not to really harm."

"Because you made me 'fess up to not killing her," I said.

"No, because she doesn't really believe you'll kill her. She's intrigued with your powers. I think she'd rather convert you than kill you."

"Have me as part of her zombie-making factory."

"Yes."

"Not in this lifetime."

"The Señora is not used to people saying no, Anita."

"Her problem, not mine."

He glanced at me, then back to the traffic. "She'll make it your problem."

"I'll deal with it."

"You can't be that confident."

"I'm not, but what do you want me to do, break down and cry. I'll deal with it when, and if, something noisome drags itself through my window."

"You can't deal with the Señora, Anita. She is powerful, more powerful than you can ever imagine."

"She scared me, Manny. I am suitably impressed. If she sends something I can't handle, I'll run. Okay?"

"Not okay. You don't know, you just don't know."

"I heard the thing in the hallway. I smelled it. I'm scared, but she's just human, Manny. All the mumbo jumbo won't keep her safe from a bullet."

"A bullet may take her out, but not down."

"What does that mean?"

"If she were shot, say in the head or heart, and seemed dead, I'd treat her like a vampire. Head and heart taken out. Body burned." He glanced at me sort of sideways.

I didn't say anything. We were talking about killing Dominga Salvador. She was capturing souls and putting them into corpses. It was an abomination. She would probably attack me first. Some supernatural goodie come creeping into my home. She was evil and would attack me first. Would it be murder to ambush her? Yeah. Would I do it anyway? I let the thought take shape in my head. Rolled it over like a piece of candy, tasting the idea. Yeah, I could do it.

I should have felt bad that I could plan a murder, for any reason, and not flinch. I didn't feel bad. It was sort of comforting to know if she pushed me, I could push back. Who was I to cast stones at Manny for twenty-year-old crimes? Yeah, who indeed.

# 8

IT WAS EARLY afternoon. Manny had dropped me off without a word. He hadn't asked to come up, and I hadn't offered. I still didn't know what to think about him, Dominga Salvador, and nonrotting zombies, complete with souls. I decided not to think. What I needed was good physical activity. As luck would have it, I had judo class this afternoon.

I have a black belt, which sounds a lot more impressive than it really is. In the dojo with referees and rules, I do okay. Out in the real world where most bad guys outweigh me by a hundred pounds, I trust a gun.

I was actually reaching for the doorknob when the bell chimed. I put the overstuffed gym bag by the door and used the little peephole. I always had to stand on tiptoe to see out of it.

The distorted image was blond, fair-eyed, and barely familiar. It was Tommy, Harold Gaynor's muscle-bound bodyguard. This day was just getting better and better.

I don't usually take a gun to judo class. It's in the afternoon. In the summer that means daylight. The really dangerous stuff doesn't come out until after dark. I untucked the red polo shirt I was wearing and clipped my inter-pants holster back in place. The pocket-size 9mm dug in just a little. If I had known I was going to need it, I would have worn looser jeans.

The doorbell rang again. I hadn't called out to let him know I was in here. He didn't seem discouraged. He rang the doorbell a third time, leaning on it.

I took a deep breath and opened the door. I looked up into Tommy's pale blue eyes. They were still empty, dead. A perfect blankness. Were you born with a stare like that, or did you have to practice?

"What do you want?" I asked.

His lips twitched. "Aren't you going to invite me in?"

"I don't think so."

He shrugged massive shoulders. I could see the straps of his shoulder holster imprinted on his suit jacket. He needed a better tailor.

A door opened to my left. A woman came out with a toddler in her arms. She locked the door before turning and seeing us. "Oh, hi." She smiled brightly.

"Hello," I said.

Tommy nodded.

The woman turned and walked towards the stairs. She was murmuring something nonsensical and high-pitched to the toddler.

Tommy looked back at me. "You really want to do this in the hallway?"

"What are we doing?"

"Business. Money."

I looked at his face, and it told me nothing. The only comfort I had was that if Tommy meant to do me harm he probably wouldn't have come to my apartment to do it. Probably.

I stepped back, holding the door very wide. I stayed out of arm's reach as he walked into my apartment. He looked around. "Nice, clean."

"Cleaning service," I said. "Talk to me about business, Tommy. I've got an appointment."

He glanced at the gym bag by the door. "Work or pleasure?" he asked.

"None of your business," I said.

Again that bare twist of lips. I realized it was his version of a smile. "Down in the car I got a case full of money. A million five, half now, half after you raise the zombie."

I shook my head. "I gave Gaynor my answer."

"But that was in front of your boss. This is just you and me. No one'll know if you take it. No one."

"I didn't say no because there were witnesses. I said no because I don't do human sacrifice." I could feel myself smiling. This was ridiculous. I thought about Manny then. Alright, maybe it wasn't ridiculous. But I wasn't doing it.

"Everyone has their price, Anita. Name it. We can meet it."

He had never once mentioned Gaynor's name. Only I had. He was being so bloody careful, too careful. "I don't have a price, Tommy-boy. Go back to Mr. Harold Gaynor and tell him that."

His face clouded up then. A wrinkling between his eyes. "I don't know that name."

"Oh, give me a break. I'm not wearing a wire."

"Name your price. We can meet it," he said.

"There is no price."

"Two million, tax-free," he said.

"What zombie could be worth two million dollars, Tommy?" I stared at his softly frowning face. "What could Gaynor hope to gain that would allow him to make a profit on that kind of expenditure?"

Tommy just stared at me. "You don't need to know that."

"I thought you'd say that. Go away, Tommy. I'm not for sale." I stepped back towards the door, planning to escort him out. He moved forward suddenly, faster than he looked. Muscled arms wide to grab me.

I pulled the Firestar and pointed it at his chest. He froze. Dead eyes, blinking at me. His large hands balled into fists. A nearly purple flush crept up his neck into his face. Rage.

"Don't do it," I said, my voice sounded soft.

"Bitch," he wheezed it at me.

"Now, now, Tommy, don't get nasty. Ease down, and we can all live to see another glorious day."

His pale eyes flicked from the gun to my face, then back to the gun. "You wouldn't be so tough without that piece."

If he wanted me to offer to arm wrestle him, he was in for a disappointment. "Back off, Tommy, or I'll drop you here and now. All the muscle in the world won't help you."

I watched something move behind his dead eyes, then his whole body relaxed. He took a deep breath through his nose. "Okay, you got the drop on me today. But if you keep disappointing my boss, I'm gonna find you without that gun." His lips twitched. "And we'll see how tough you really are."

A little voice in my head said, "Shoot him now." I knew as surely as I knew anything that dear Tommy would be at my back someday. I didn't want him there, but . . . I couldn't just kill him because I thought he might come after me someday. It wasn't a good enough reason. And how would I ever have explained it to the police?

"Get out, Tommy." I opened the door without taking either my gaze or the gun off the man. "Get out and tell Gaynor that if he keeps annoying me, I'll start sending his bodyguards home in boxes."

Tommy's nostrils flared just a bit at that, veins straining in his neck. He walked very stiffly past me and out into the hall. I held the gun at my side and watched him, listening to his footsteps retreat down the stairs. When I was as sure as I could be that he was gone, I put my gun back in its holster, grabbed my gym bag, and headed for judo class. Mustn't let these little interruptions spoil my exercise program. Tomorrow I would miss my workout for sure. I had a funeral to attend. Besides, if Tommy really did challenge me to arm wrestling, I was going to need all the help I could get.

# 9

I HATE FUNERALS. At least this one wasn't for anyone I had particularly liked. Cold, but true. Peter Burke had been an unscrupulous SOB when alive. I didn't see why death should automatically grant him sainthood. Death, especially violent death, will turn the meanest bastard in the world into a nice guy. Why is that?

I stood there in the bright August sunlight in my little black dress and dark sunglasses, watching the mourners. They had set up a canopy over the coffin, flowers, and chairs for the family. Why was I here, you might ask, if I had not been a friend? Because Peter Burke had been an animator. Not a very good one, but we are a small, exclusive club. If one of us dies, we all come. It's a rule. There are no exceptions. Maybe your own death, but then again being that we raise the dead, maybe not.

There are things you can do to a corpse so it won't rise again as a vampire, but a zombie is a different beast. Short of cremation, an animator can bring you back. Fire was about the only thing a zombie respected or feared.

We could have raised Peter and asked him who put a gun to his head. But they had put a 357 Magnum with an expanding point just behind his ear. There wasn't enough left of his head to fill a plastic bag. You could raise him as a zombie, but he couldn't talk. Even the dead need mouths.

Manny stood beside me, uncomfortable in his dark suit. Rosita, his wife, stood spine absolutely straight. Thick brown hands gripping her black patent leather purse. She is what my stepmother used to call large-boned. Her black hair was cut just below the ears and loosely permed. The hair needed to be longer. It emphasized how perfectly round her face was.

Charles Montgomery stood just behind me like a tall dark mountain. Charles looks like he played football somewhere. He has the ability to frown and make people run for cover. He just looks like a hard ass. Truth is, Charles faints at the sight of anything but animal blood. It's lucky for him he looks like such a big black dude. He has almost no tolerance for pain. He cries at Walt Disney movies, like when Bambi's mother dies. It's endearing as hell.

His wife, Caroline, was working. She hadn't been able to switch shifts with anyone. I wondered how hard she had tried. Caroline is okay but she sort of looks down on what we do. Mumbo jumbo she calls it. She's a registered nurse. I guess after dealing with doctors all day, she has to look down on someone.

Up near the front of the crowd was Jamison Clarke. He was tall, thin, and the only red-haired, green-eyed black man I've ever met. He nodded at me across the grave. I nodded back.

We were all here; the animators of Animators, Incorporated. Bert and Mary, our daytime secretary, were holding down the fort. I hoped Bert didn't book us in anything we couldn't handle. Or would refuse to handle. He did that if you didn't watch him.

The sun slapped my back like a hot metal hand. The men kept pulling at their ties and high collars. The smell of chrysanthemums was thick like wax at the back of my throat. No one ever gives you football mums unless you die. Carnations, roses, snapdragons, they all have happier lives, but mums, and glads—they're the funeral flowers. At least the tall spires of gladiolus had no scent.

A woman sat in the front line of chairs under the canopy. She was leaning over her knees like a broken doll. Her sobs were loud enough to drown out the words of the priest. Only his quiet, soothing rhythm reached me as I stood near the back.

Two small children were gripping the hands of an older man. Grampa? The children were pale, hollow-eyed. Fear vied with tears on their faces. They watched their mother break down completely, useless to them. Her grief was more important than theirs. Her loss greater. Bullshit.

My own mother had died when I was eight. You never really filled in the hole. It was like a piece of you gone missing. An ache that never quite goes away. You deal with it. You go on, but it's there.

A man sat beside her, rubbing her back in endless circles. His hair was nearly black, cut short and neat. Broad-shouldered. From the back he looked eerily like Peter Burke. Ghosts in sunlight.

The cemetery was dotted with trees. The shade rustled and flickered pale grey in the sunlight. On the other side of the gravel driveway that twined through the cemetery were two men. They stood quietly, waiting. Grave diggers. Waiting to finish the job.

I looked back at the coffin under its blanket of pink carnations. There was a bulky mound just behind it, covered in bright green fake grass. Underneath was the fresh dug earth waiting to go back in the hole.

Mustn't let the loved ones think about red-clay soil pouring down on the gleaming coffin. Clods of dirt hitting the wood, covering your husband, father. Trapping them forever inside a lead-lined box. A good coffin will keep the water and worms out, but it doesn't stop decay.

I knew what would be happening to Peter Burke's body. Cover it in satin, wrap a tie round its neck, rouge the cheeks, close the eyes; it's still a corpse.

The funeral ended while I wasn't looking. The people rose gratefully in one mass movement. The dark-haired man helped the grieving widow to stand. She nearly fell. Another man rushed forward and supported her other side. She sagged between them, feet dragging on the ground.

She looked back over her shoulder, head almost lolling on her neck. She screamed, loud and ragged, then flung herself on the coffin. The woman collapsed against the flowers, digging at the wood. Fingers scrambling for the locks on the coffin. The ones that held the lid down.

Everyone just froze for a moment, staring. I saw the two children through the crowd still standing, wide-eyed. Shit. "Stop her," I said it too loud. People turned to stare. I didn't care.

I pushed my way through the vanishing crowd and the aisles of chairs. The dark-haired man was holding the widow's hands while she screamed and struggled. She had collapsed to the ground, and her black dress had worked up high on her thighs. She was wearing a white slip. Her mascara had run like black blood down her face.

I stood in front of the man and the two children. He was staring at the woman like he would never move again. "Sir," I said. He didn't react. "Sir?"

He blinked, staring down at me like I had just appeared in front of him. "Sir, do you really think the children need to see all this?"

"She's my daughter," he said. His voice was deep and thick. Drugged or just grief?

"I sympathize, sir, but the children should go to the car now."

The widow had begun to wail, loud and wordless, raw pain. The girl was beginning to shake. "You're her father, but you're their grandfather. Act like it. Get them out of here."

Anger flickered in his eyes then. "How dare you?"

He wasn't going to listen to me. I was just an intrusion on their grief. The oldest, a boy of about five, was staring up at me. His brown eyes were huge, his thin face so pale it looked ghostly.

"I think it is you who should go," the grandfather said.

"You're right. You are so right," I said. I walked around them out into the grass and the summer heat. I couldn't help the children. I couldn't help them, just as no one had been there to help me. I had survived. So would they, maybe.

Manny and Rosita were waiting for me. Rosita hugged me. "You must come to Sunday dinner after church."

I smiled. "I don't think I can make it, but thanks for asking."

"My cousin Albert will be there," she said. "He is an engineer. He will be a good provider."

"I don't need a good provider, Rosita."

She sighed. "You make too much money for a woman. It makes you not need a man."

I shrugged. If I ever did marry, which I'd begun to doubt, it wouldn't be for money. Love. Shit, was I waiting for love? Naw, not me.

"We have to pick up Tomas at kindergarten," Manny said. He was smiling at me apologetically around Rosita's shoulder. She was nearly a foot taller than he. She towered over me, too.

"Sure, tell the little guy hi for me."

"You should come to dinner," Rosita said, "Albert is a very handsome man."

"Thanks for thinking of me, Rosita, but I'll skip it."

"Come on, wife," Manny said. "Our son is waiting for us."

She let him pull her towards the car, but her brown face was set in disapproval. It offended some deep part of Rosita that I was twenty-four and had no prospects of marriage. Her and my stepmother.

Charles was nowhere to be seen. Hurrying back to the office to see clients. I thought Jamison had, too, but he stood in the grass, waiting for me.

He was dressed impeccably, crossed-lapels, narrow red tie with small dark dots on it. His tie clip was onyx and silver. He smiled at me, always a bad sign.

His greenish eyes looked hollow, like someone had erased part of the skin. If you cry enough, the skin goes from puffy red to hollow white. "I'm glad so many of us showed up," he said.

"I know he was a friend of yours, Jamison. I'm sorry."

He nodded and looked down at his hands. He was holding a pair of sunglasses loosely. He looked up at me, eyes staring straight into mine. All serious.

"The police won't tell the family anything," he said. "Peter gets blown away, and they don't have a clue who did it."

I wanted to tell him the police were doing their best, because they were. But there are a hell of a lot of murders in St. Louis over a year. We were giving Washington, D.C. a run for their money as murder capital of the United States. "They're doing their best, Jamison."

"Then why won't they tell us anything?" His hands convulsed. The sound of breaking plastic was a crumbling sharp sound. He didn't seem to notice.

"I don't know," I said.

"Anita, you're in good with the police. Could you ask?" His eyes were naked, full of such real pain. Most of the time I could ignore, or even dislike, Jamison. He was a tease, a flirt, a bleeding-heart liberal who thought that vampires were just people with fangs. But today . . . today he was real.

"What do you want me to ask?"

"Are they making any progress? Do they have any suspects? That sort of thing."

They were vague questions, but important ones. "I'll see what I can find out."

He gave a watery smile. "Thanks, Anita, really, thanks." He held out his hand. I took it. We shook. He noticed his broken sunglasses. "Damn, ninety-five dollars down the tubes."

Ninety-five dollars for sunglasses? He had to be kidding. A group of mourners were taking the family away at last. The mother was smothered in well-meaning male relatives. They were literally carrying her away from the grave. The children and Grampa brought up the rear. No one listens to good advice.

A man stepped away from the crowd and walked towards us. He was the one who reminded me of Peter Burke from the back. He was around six feet, dark-complected, a black mustache, and thin almost goateelike beard framing a handsome face. It was handsome, a dark movie-star face, but there was something about the way he moved. Maybe it was the white streak in his black hair just over the forehead. Whatever, you knew that he would always play the villain.

"Is she going to help us?" he asked, no preamble, no hello.

"Yes," Jamison said. "Anita Blake, this is John Burke, Peter's brother."

John Burke, *the* John Burke, I wanted to ask. New Orleans's greatest animator and vampire slayer? A kindred spirit. We shook hands. His grip was strong, almost painfully so, as if he wanted to see if I would flinch. I didn't. He let go. Maybe he just didn't know his own strength? But I doubted it.

"I am truly sorry about your brother," I said. I meant it. I was glad I meant it.

He nodded. "Thank you for talking to the police about him."

"I'm surprised you couldn't get the New Orleans police to give you some juice with our local police," I said.

He had the grace to look uncomfortable. "The New Orleans police and I have had a disagreement."

"Really?" I said, eyes wide. I had heard the rumors, but I wanted to hear the truth. Truth is always stranger than fiction.

"John was accused of participating in some ritual murders," Jamison said. "Just because he's a practicing vaudun priest."

"Oh," I said. Those were the rumors. "How long have you been in town, John?"

"Almost a week."

"Really?"

"Peter had been missing for two days before they found the . . . body." He licked his lips. His dark brown eyes flicked to the scene behind me. Were the grave diggers moving in? I glanced back, but the grave looked just the same to me.

"Anything you could find out would be most appreciated," he said.

"I'll do what I can."

"I have to get back to the house." He shrugged, as if to loosen the shoulder muscles. "My sister-in-law isn't taking it well."

I let it go. I deserved brownie points for that. One thing I didn't let go. "Can you look after your niece and nephew?"

He looked at me, a puzzled frown between his black eyebrows.

"I mean, keep them out of the really dramatic stuff if you can."

He nodded. "It was rough for me to watch her throw herself on the coffin. God, what must the kids be thinking?" Tears glittered in his eyes like silver. He kept them open very wide so the tears wouldn't spill out.

I didn't know what to say. I did not want to see him cry. "I'll talk to the police, find out what I can. I'll tell Jamison when I have anything."

John Burke nodded, carefully. His eyes were like a glass where only the surface tension kept the water from spilling over.

I nodded to Jamison and left. I turned on the air-conditioning in my car and let it run full blast. The two men were still standing in the hot sunshine in the middle of summer brown grass when I put the car in gear and drove away.

I would talk to the police and find out what I could. I also had another name for Dolph. John Burke, biggest animator in New Orleans, voodoo priest. Sounded like a suspect to me.

# 10

THE PHONE WAS ringing as I shoved the key into my apartment door. I yelled at it, "I'm coming, I'm coming!" Why do people do that? Yell at the phone as if the other person can hear you and will wait?

I shoved the door open and scooped up the phone on the fourth ring. "Hello."

"Anita?"

"Dolph," I said. My stomach tightened. "What's up?"

"We think we found the boy." His voice was quiet, neutral.

"Think," I said. "What do you mean, think?"

"You know what I mean, Anita," he said. He sounded tired.

"Like his parents?" It wasn't a question.

"Yeah."

"God, Dolph, is there much left?"

"Come and see. We're at the Burrell Cemetery. Do you know it?"

"Sure, I've done work there."

"Be here as soon as you can. I want to go home and hug my wife."

"Sure, Dolph, I understand." I was talking to myself. The phone had gone dead. I stared at the receiver for a moment. My skin felt cold. I did not want to go and view the remains of Benjamin Reynolds. I did not want to know. I pulled a lot of air in through my nose and let it out slowly.

I stared down at the dark hose, high heels, dress. It wasn't my usual crime scene attire, but it would take too long to change. I was usually the last expert called in. Once I was through, they could cover the body. And everyone could go home. I grabbed a pair of black Nikes for walking over grass and through blood. Once you got bloodstains on dress shoes, they never come clean.

I had the Browning Hi-Power, complete with holster sort of draped atop my little black clutch purse. The gun had been in my car during the funeral. I couldn't figure out a way to carry a gun of any kind while wearing a dress. I know you see thigh holsters on television, but does the word "chafing" mean anything to you?

I hesitated on getting my backup gun and shoving it in my purse, but didn't. My purse, like all purses, seems to have a traveling black hole in it. I'd never get the gun out in time if I really needed it.

I did have a silver knife in a thigh sheath under the short black skirt. I felt like Kit Carson in drag, but after Tommy's little visit, I didn't want to be unarmed. I had no illusions what would happen if Tommy did catch me with no gun. Knives weren't as good, but they beat the hell out of kicking my little feet and screaming.

I had never yet had to try to fast draw a knife from a thigh sheath. It was probably going to look vaguely obscene, but if it kept me alive . . . hey, I can take a little embarrassment.

BURRELL Cemetery is at the crest of a hill. Some of the gravestones go back centuries. The soft, weathered limestone is almost unreadable, like hard candy that's been sucked clean. The grass is waist tall, luxuriant with only the headstones standing like tired sentinels.

There is a house on the edge of the cemetery where the caretaker lives, but he doesn't have to take care of much. The graveyard is full and has been for years. The last person buried here could remember the 1904 World's Fair.

There is no road into the graveyard anymore. There is a ghost of one, like a wagon track where the grass doesn't grow quite so high. The caretaker's house was surrounded by police cars and the coroner's van. My Nova seemed underdressed. Maybe I should get some buggy whip antennae, or plaster Zombies "R" Us on the side of the car. Bert would probably get mad.

I got a pair of coveralls from the trunk and slipped into them. They covered me from neck to ankle. Like most coveralls the crotch hit at knee level, I never understood why, but it meant my skirt didn't bunch up. I bought them originally for vampire stakings, but blood is blood. Besides, the weeds would play hell with my panty hose. I got a pair of surgical gloves from the little Kleenex-like box in the trunk. Nikes instead of dress shoes, and I was ready to view the remains.

Remains. Nice word.

Dolph stood like some ancient sentinel, towering over everyone else in the field. I worked my way towards him, trying not to trip over broken bits of headstone. A wind hot enough to scald rustled the grass. I was sweating inside the overalls.

Detective Clive Perry came to meet me, as if I needed an escort. Detective Perry was one of the most polite people I had ever met. He had an old-world courtliness to him. A gentleman in the best sense of the word. I always wanted to ask what he had done to end up on the spook squad.

His slender black face was beaded with sweat. He still wore his suit jacket even though it had to be over a hundred degrees. "Ms. Blake."

"Detective Perry," I said. I glanced up at the crest of the hill. Dolph and a handful of men were standing around like they didn't know what to do. No one was looking at the ground.

"How bad is it, Detective Perry?" I asked.

He shook his head. "Depends on what you compare it to."

"Did you see the tapes and pictures of the Reynolds house?"

"I did."

"Is it worse than that?" It was my new "worst thing I ever saw" measurement. Before this it had been a vampire gang that had tried to move in from Los Angeles. The respectable vampire community had chopped them up with axes. The parts were still crawling around the room when we found them. Maybe this wasn't worse. Maybe time had just dimmed the memory.

"It isn't bloodier," he said, then he hesitated, "but it was a child. A little boy."

I nodded. He didn't need to explain. It was always worse when it was a child. I never knew exactly why. Maybe it was some primal instinct to protect the young. Some deep hormonal thing. Whatever, kids were always worse. I stared down at a white tombstone. It looked like dull, melted ice. I didn't want to go up the hill. I didn't want to see.

I went up the hill. Detective Perry followed. Brave detective. Brave me.

A sheet rested on the grass like a tent. Dolph stood closest to it. "Dolph," I said.

"Anita."

No one offered to pull back the sheet. "Is this it?"

"Yeah."

Dolph seemed to shake himself, or maybe it was a shiver. He reached down and grabbed the edge of the sheet. "Ready?" he asked.

No, I wasn't ready. Don't make me look. Please don't make me look. My mouth was dry. I could taste my pulse in my throat. I nodded.

The sheet flew back, caught by a gust of wind like a white kite. The grass was trampled down. Struggles? Had Benjamin Reynolds been alive when he was pulled down into the long grass? No, surely not. God, I hoped not.

The footed pajamas had tiny cartoon figures on them. The pajamas had been pulled back like the skin of a banana. One small arm was flung up over his head like he was sleeping. Long-lashed eyelids helped the illusion. His skin was pale and flawless, small cupid-bow mouth half open. He should have looked worse, much worse.

There was a dirty brown stain on his pajamas, the cloth covering his lower body. I did not want to see what had killed him. But that was why I was here. I hesitated, fingers hovering over the torn cloth. I took a deep breath, and that was a mistake. Hunkered over the body in the windy August heat the smell was fresh. New death smells like an out-house, especially if the stomach or bowels have been ripped open. I knew what I'd find when I lifted the bloody cloth. The smell told me.

I knelt with a sleeve over my mouth and nose for a few minutes, breathing shallow and through my mouth, but it didn't really help. Once you caught a whiff of it, your nose remembered. The smell crawled down my throat and wouldn't let go.

Quick or slow? Did I jerk the cloth back or pull it? Quick. I jerked on the cloth, but it stuck, dried blood catching. The cloth peeled back with a wet, sucking sound.

It looked like someone had taken a giant ice cream scoop and gutted him. Stomach, intestines, upper bowels, gone. The sunshine swam around me, and I had to put a hand on the ground to keep from falling.

I glanced up at the face. His hair was pale brown like his mother's. Damp curls traced his cheeks. My gaze was pulled back to the gaping ruin that was his abdomen. There was some dark, heavy fluid leaking out of the end of his small intestine.

I stumbled away from the crime scene, using the tombstones to help me stand. I would have run if I hadn't known I would fall. The sky was spinning to meet the ground. I collapsed in the smothering grass and vomited.

I threw up until I was empty and the world stopped spinning. I wiped my mouth on my sleeve and stood up using a crooked headstone for support.

No one said a word as I walked back to them. The sheet was covering the body. The body. Had to think of it that way. Couldn't dwell on the fact that it had been a small child. Couldn't. I'd go mad.

"Well?" Dolph asked.

"He hasn't been dead long. Dammit to hell, Dolph, it was late morning, maybe just before dawn. He was alive, alive when that thing took him!" I stared up at him and felt the hot beginnings of tears. I would not cry. I had already disgraced myself enough for one day. I took a deep careful breath and let it out. I would not cry.

"I gave you twenty-four hours to talk to this Dominga Salvador. Did you find out anything?"

"She says she knows nothing of it. I believe her."

"Why?"

"Because if she wanted to kill people she wouldn't have to do anything this dramatic."

"What do you mean?" he asked.

"She could wish them to death," I said.

He widened his eyes. "You believe that?"

I shrugged. "Maybe. Yes. Hell, I don't know. She scares me."

He raised one thick eyebrow. "I'll remember that."

"I have another name to add to your list though," I said.

"Who?"

"John Burke. He's up from New Orleans for his brother's funeral."

He wrote the name in his little notebook. "If he's just visiting, would he have time?"

"I can't think of a motive, but he could do it if he wanted to. Check him out with the New Orleans police. I think he's under suspicion down there for murder."

"What's he doing traveling out of state?"

"I don't think they have any proof," I said. "Dominga Salvador said she'd help me. She's promised to ask around and tell me anything she turns up."

"I've been asking around since you gave me her name. She doesn't help anyone outside her own people. How did you get her to cooperate?"

I shrugged. "My winning personality."

He shook his head.

"It wasn't illegal, Dolph. Beyond that I don't want to talk about it."

He let it go. Smart man. "Tell me as soon as you hear anything, Anita. We've got to stop this thing before it kills again."

"Agreed." I turned and looked out over the rolling grass. "Is this the cemetery near where you found the first three victims?"

"Yes."

"Maybe part of the answer's here then," I said.

"What do you mean?"

"Most vampires have to return to their coffins before dawn. Ghouls stay in underground tunnels, like giant moles. If it was either of those I'd say the creature was out here somewhere waiting for nightfall."

"But," he said.

"But if it's a zombie it isn't harmed by sunlight and it doesn't need to rest in a coffin. It could be anywhere, but I think it originally came from this cemetery. If they used voodoo there will be signs of the ritual."

"Like what?"

"A chalk verve, drawn symbols around the grave, dried blood, maybe a fire." I stared off at the rustling grass. "Though I wouldn't want to start an open fire in this place."

"If it wasn't voodoo?" he asked.

"Then it was an animator. Again you look for dried blood, maybe a dead animal. There won't be as many signs and it's easier to clean up."

"Are you sure it's some kind of a zombie?" he asked.

"I don't know what else it could be. I think we should act like that's what it is. It gives us someplace to look, and something to look for."

"If it's not a zombie we don't have a clue," he said.

"Exactly."

He smiled, but it wasn't pleasant. "I hope you're right, Anita."

"Me, too," I said.

"If it did come from here, can you find what grave it came from?"

"Maybe."

"Maybe?" he said.

"Maybe. Raising the dead isn't a science, Dolph. Sometimes I can feel the dead under the ground. Restlessness. How old without looking at the tombstone. Sometimes I can't." I shrugged.

"We'll give you any help you need."

"I have to wait until full dark. My . . . powers are better after dark."

"That's hours away. Can you do anything now?"

I thought about that for a moment. "No. I'm sorry but no."

"Okay, you'll come back tonight then?"

"Yeah," I said.

"What time? I'll send some men out."

"I don't know what time. And I don't know how long it will take. I could be wandering out here for hours and find nothing."

"Or?"

"Or I could find the beastie itself."

"You'll need backup for that, just in case."

I nodded. "Agreed, but guns, even silver bullets, won't hurt it."

"What will?"

"Flamethrowers, napalm like the exterminators use on ghoul tunnels," I said.

"Those aren't standard issue."

"Have an exterminator team standing by," I said.

"Good idea." He made a note.

"I need a favor," I said.

He looked up. "What?"

"Peter Burke was murdered, shot to death. His brother asked me to find out what progress the police are making."

"You know we can't give out information like that."

"I know, but if you can get the facts I can feed just enough to John Burke to keep in touch with him."

"You seem to be getting along well with all our suspects," he said.

"Yeah."

"I'll find out what I can from homicide. Do you know what jurisdiction he was found in?"

I shook my head. "I could find out. It would give me an excuse to talk to Burke again."

"You say he's suspected of murder in New Orleans."

"Mm-huh," I said.

"And he may have done this." He motioned at the sheet.

"Yep."

"You watch your back, Anita."

"I always do," I said.

"You call me as early tonight as you can. I don't want all my people sitting around twiddling their thumbs on overtime."

"As soon as I can. I've got to cancel three clients just to make it." Bert was not going to be pleased. The day was looking up.

"Why didn't it eat more of the boy?" Dolph asked.

"I don't know," I said.

He nodded. "Okay, I'll see you tonight then."

"Say hello to Lucille for me. How's she coming with her master's degree?"

"Almost done. She'll have it before our youngest gets his engineering degree."

"Great."

The sheet flapped in the hot wind. A trickle of sweat trailed down my forehead. I was out of small talk. "See you later," I said, and started down the hill. I stopped and turned back. "Dolph?"

"Yes?" he said.

"I've never heard of a zombie exactly like this one. Maybe it does rise from its grave more like a vampire. If you kept that exterminator team and backup hanging around until after dark, you might catch it rising from the grave and be able to bag it."

"Is that likely?"

"No, but it's possible," I said.

"I don't know how I'll explain the overtime, but I'll do it."

"I'll be here as soon as I can."

"What else could be more important than this?" he asked.

I smiled. "Nothing you'd like to hear about."

"Try me," he said.

I shook my head.

He nodded. "Tonight, early as you can."

"Early as I can," I said.

Detective Perry escorted me back. Maybe politeness, maybe he just wanted to get away from the corpus delicti. I didn't blame him. "How's your wife, Detective?"

"We're expecting our first baby in a month."

I smiled up at him. "I didn't know. Congratulations."

"Thank you." His face clouded over, a frown puckering between his dark eyes. "Do you think we can find this creature before it kills again?"

"I hope so," I said.

"What are our chances?"

Did he want reassurance or the truth. Truth. "I haven't the faintest idea."

"I was hoping you wouldn't say that," he said.

"So was I, Detective. So was I."

# 11

WHAT WAS MORE important than bagging the critter that had eviscerated an entire family? Nothing, absolutely nothing. But it was a while until full dark, and I had other problems. Would Tommy go back to Gaynor and tell him what I said? Yes. Would Gaynor let it go? Probably not. I needed information. I needed to know how far he would go. A reporter, I needed a reporter. Irving Griswold to the rescue.

Irving had one of those pastel cubicles that passes for an office. No roof, no door, but you got walls. Irving is five-three. I'd like him for that reason if nothing else. You don't meet many men exactly my height. Frizzy brown hair framed his bald spot like petals on a flower. He wore a white dress shirt, sleeves rolled up to the elbow, tie at half-mast. His face was round, pink-cheeked. He looked like a bald cherub. He did not look like a werewolf, but he was one. Even lycanthropy can't cure baldness.

No one on the St. Louis *Post-Dispatch* knew Irving was a shapeshifter. It is a disease, and it's illegal to discriminate against lycanthropes, just like people with AIDS, but people do it anyway. Maybe the paper's management would have been broad-minded, liberal, but I was with Irving. Caution was better.

Irving sat in his desk chair. I leaned in the doorway of his cubicle. "How's tricks?" Irving said.

"Do you really think you're funny, or is this just an annoying habit?" I asked.

He grinned. "I'm hilarious. Ask my girlfriend."

"I'll bet," I said.

"What's up, Blake? And please tell me whatever it is is on the record, not off."

"How would you like to do an article on the new zombie legislation that's being cooked up?"

"Maybe," he said. His eyes narrowed, suspicion gleamed forth. "What do you want in return?"

"This part is off the record, Irving, for now."

"It figures." He frowned at me. "Go on."

"I need all the information you have on Harold Gaynor."

"Name doesn't ring any bells," he said. "Should it?" His eyes had gone from cheerful to steady. His concentration was nearly perfect when he smelled a story.

"Not necessarily," I said. Cautious. "Can you get the information for me?"

"In exchange for the zombie story?"

"I'll take you to all the businesses that use zombies. You can bring a photographer and snap pictures of corpses."

His eyes lit up. "A series of articles with lots of semigruesome pictures. You center stage in a suit. Beauty and the Beast. My editor would probably go for it."

"I thought he might, but I don't know about the center stage stuff."

"Hey, your boss will love it. Publicity means more business."

"And sells more papers," I said.

"Sure," Irving said. He looked at me for maybe a minute. The room was almost silent. Most had gone home. Irving's little pool of light was one of just a few. He'd been waiting on me. So much for the press never sleeps. The quiet breath of the air conditioner filled the early evening stillness.

"I'll see if Harold Gaynor's in the computer," Irving said at last.

I smiled at him. "Remembered the name after me mentioning it just once, pretty good."

"I am, after all, a trained reporter," he said. He swiveled his chair back to his computer keyboard with exaggerated movements. He pulled imaginary gloves on and adjusted the long tails of a tux.

"Oh, get on with it." I smiled a little wider.

"Do not rush the maestro." He typed a few words and the screen came to life. "He's on file," Irving said. "A big file. It'd take forever to print it all up." He swiveled the chair back to look at me. It was a bad sign.

"I'll tell you what," he said. "I'll get the file together, complete with pictures if we have any. I'll deliver it to your sweet hands."

"What's the catch?"

He put his fingers to his chest. "*Moi*, no catch. The goodness of my heart."

"All right, bring it by my apartment."

"Why don't we meet at Dead Dave's, instead?" he said.

"Dead Dave's is down in the vampire district. What are you doing hanging around out there?"

His sweet cherubic face was watching me very steadily. "Rumor has it that there's a new Master Vampire of the City. I want the story."

I just shook my head. "So you're hanging around Dead Dave's to get information?"

"Exactly."

"The vamps won't talk to you. You look human."

"Thanks for the compliment," he said. "The vamps do talk to you, Anita. Do you know who the new Master is? Can I meet him, or her? Can I do an interview?"

"Jesus, Irving, don't you have enough troubles without messing with the king vampire?"

"It's a him then," he said.

"It's a figure of speech," I said.

"You know something. I know you do."

"What I know is that you don't want to come to the attention of a master vampire. They're mean, Irving."

"The vampires are trying to mainstream themselves. They want positive attention. An interview about what he wants to do with the vampire community. His vision of the future. It would be very up-and-coming. No corpse jokes. No sensationalism. Straight journalism."

"Yeah, right. On page one a tasteful little headline: THE MASTER VAMPIRE OF ST. LOUIS SPEAKS OUT."

"Yeah, it'll be great."

"You've been sniffing newsprint again, Irving."

"I'll give you everything we have on Gaynor. Pictures."

"How do you know you have pictures?" I said.

He stared up at me, his round, pleasant face cheerfully blank.

"You recognized the name, you little son of . . ."

"Tsk, tsk, Anita. Help me get an interview with the Master of the City. I'll give you anything you want."

"I'll give you a series of articles about zombies. Full-color pictures of rotting corpses, Irving. It'll sell papers."

"No interview with the Master?" he said.

"If you're lucky, no," I said.

"Shoot."

"Can I have the file on Gaynor?"

He nodded. "I'll get it together." He looked up at me. "I still want you to meet me at Dead Dave's. Maybe a vamp will talk to me with you around."

"Irving, being seen with a legal executioner of vampires is not going to endear you to the vamps."

"They still call you the Executioner?"

"Among other things."

"Okay, the Gaynor file for going along on your next vampire execution?"

"No," I said.

"Ah, Anita . . ."

"No."

He spread his hands wide. "Okay, just an idea. It'd be a great article."

"I don't need the publicity, Irving, not that kind anyway."

He nodded. "Yeah, yeah. I'll meet you at Dead Dave's in about two hours."

"Make it an hour. I'd like to be out of the District before full dark."

"Is anybody gunning for you down there? I mean I don't want to endanger you, Blake." He grinned. "You've given me too many lead stories. I wouldn't want to lose you."

"Thanks for the concern. No, no one's after me. Far as I know."

"You don't sound real certain."

I stared at him. I thought about telling him that the new Master of the City had sent me a dozen white roses and an invitation to go dancing. I had turned him down. There had been a message on my machine and an invitation to a black tie affair. I ignored it all. So far the Master was behaving like the courtly gentleman he had been a few centuries back. It couldn't last. Jean-Claude was not a person who took defeat easily.

I didn't tell Irving. He didn't need to know. "I'll see you at Dead Dave's in an hour. I'm gonna run home and change."

"Now that you mention it, I've never seen you in a dress before."

"I had a funeral today."

"Business or personal?"

"Personal," I said.

"Then I'm sorry."

I shrugged. "I've got to go if I'm going to have time to change and then meet you. Thanks, Irving."

"It's not a favor, Blake. I'll make you pay for those zombie articles."

I sighed. I had images of him making me embrace the poor corpse. But the new legislation needed attention. The more people who understood the horror of it, the better chance it had to pass. In truth, Irving was still doing me a favor. No need to let him know that, though.

I walked away into the dimness of the darkened office. I waved over my shoulder without looking back. I wanted to get out of this dress and into something I could hide a gun on. If I was going into Blood Square, I might need it.

## 12

DEAD DAVE'S IS in the part of St. Louis that has two names. Polite: the Riverfront. Rude: the Blood Quarter. It is our town's hottest vampire commercial district. Big tourist attraction. Vampires have really put St. Louis on the vacation maps. You'd think that the Ozark Mountains, some of the best fishing in the country, the symphony, Broadway level musicals, or maybe the Botanical Gardens would be enough, but no. I guess it's hard to compete with the undead. I know I find it difficult.

Dead Dave's is all dark glass and beer signs in the windows. The afternoon sunlight was fading into twilight. Vamps wouldn't be out until full dark. I had a little under two hours. Get in, look over the file, get out. Easy. Ri-ight.

I had changed into black shorts, royal-blue polo shirt, black Nikes with a matching blue swish, black and white jogging socks, and a black leather belt. The belt was there so the shoulder holster had something to hang on. My Browning Hi-Power was secure under my left arm. I had thrown on a short-sleeved dress shirt to hide the gun. The dress shirt was in a modest black and royal-blue print. The outfit looked great. Sweat trickled down my spine. Too hot for the shirt, but the Browning gave me thirteen bullets. Fourteen if you're animal enough to shove the magazine full and carry one in the chamber.

I didn't think things were that bad, yet. I did have an extra magazine shoved into the pocket of my shorts. I know it picks up pocket lint, but where else was I going to carry it? One of these days I promise to get a deluxe holster with spaces for extra magazines. But all the models I'd seen had to be cut down to my size and made me feel like the Frito Bandito.

I almost never carry an extra clip when I've got the Browning. Let's face it, if you need more than thirteen bullets, it's over. The really sad part was the extra ammo wasn't for Tommy, or Gaynor. It was for Jean-Claude. The Master Vampire of the City. Not that silver-plated bullets would kill him. But they would hurt him, make him heal almost human slow.

I wanted out of the District before dark. I did not want to run into Jean-Claude. He wouldn't attack me. In fact, his intentions were good, if not exactly honorable. He had offered me immortality without the messy part of becoming a vampire. There was some implication that I got him along with eternity. He was tall, pale, and handsome. Sexier than a silk teddy.

He wanted me to be his human servant. I wasn't anyone's servant. Not even for eternal life, eternal youth, and a little compromise of the soul. The price was too steep. Jean-Claude didn't believe that. The Browning was in case I had to make him believe it.

I stepped into the bar and was momentarily blind, waiting for my eyes to adjust to the dimness. Like one of those old westerns where the good guy hesitates at the front of the bar and views the crowd. I suspected he wasn't looking for the bad guy at all. He had just come out of the sun and couldn't see shit. No one ever shoots you while you're waiting for your eyes to adjust. I wonder why?

It was after five on a Thursday. Most of the bar stools and all the tables were taken. The place was cheek to jowl with business suits, male and female. A spattering of work boots and tans that ended at the elbow, but mostly upwardly mobile types. Dead Dave's had become trendy despite efforts to keep it at bay.

It looked like happy hour was in high gear. Shit. All the yuppies were here to catch a nice safe glimpse of a vampire. They would be slightly sloshed when it happened. Increase the thrill I guess.

Irving was sitting at the rounded corner of the bar. He saw me and waved. I waved back and started pushing my way towards him.

I squeezed between two gentlemen in suits. It took some maneuvering, and a very uncool-looking hop to mount the bar stool.

Irving grinned broadly at me. There was a nearly solid hum of conversation in the air. Words translated into pure noise like the ocean. Irving had to lean into me to be heard over the murmuring sound.

"I hope you appreciate how many dragons I had to slay to save that seat for you," he said. The faint smell of whiskey breathed along my cheek as he spoke.

"Dragons are easy, try vampires sometimes," I said.

His eyes widened. Before his mouth could form the question, I said, "I'm kidding, Irving." Sheesh, some people just don't have a sense of humor. "Besides, dragons were never native to North America," I said.

"I knew that."

"Sure," I said.

He sipped whiskey from a faceted glass. The amber liquid shimmered in the subdued light.

Luther, daytime manager and bartender, was down at the far end of the bar dealing with a group of very happy people. If they had been any happier they'd have been passed out on the floor.

Luther is large, not tall, fat. But it is solid fat, almost a kind of muscle. His skin is so black, it has purple highlights. The cigarette between his lips flared orange as he took a breath. He could talk around a cig better than anyone I'd ever met.

Irving picked up a scuffed leather briefcase from off the floor near his feet. He fished out a file over three inches thick. A large rubber band wrapped it together.

"Jesus, Irving. Can I take it home with me?"

He shook his head. "A sister reporter is doing a feature on local upstanding businessmen who are not what they seem. I had to promise her dibs on my firstborn to borrow it for the night."

I looked at the stack of papers. I sighed. The man on my right nearly rammed an elbow in my face. He turned. "Sorry, little lady, sorry. No harm done." Little came out liddle, and sorry slushed around the edges.

"No harm," I said.

He smiled and turned back to his friend. Another business type who laughed uproariously at something. Get drunk enough and everything is funny.

"I can't possibly read the file here," I said.

He grinned. "I'll follow you anywhere."

Luther stood in front of me. He pulled a cigarette from the pack he always carried with him. He put the tip of his still burning stub against the fresh cigarette. The end flared red like a live coal. Smoke trickled up his nose and out his mouth. Like a dragon.

He crushed the old cig in the clear glass ashtray he carried with him from place to place like a teddy bear. He chain smokes, is grossly overweight, and his grey hair puts him over fifty. He's never sick. He should be the national poster child for the Tobacco Institute.

"A refill?" he asked Irving.

"Yeah, thanks."

Luther took the glass, refilled it from a bottle under the bar, and set it back down on a fresh napkin.

"What can I get for ya, Anita?" he asked.

"The usual, Luther."

He poured me a glass of orange juice. We pretend it is a screwdriver. I'm a teetotaler, but why would I come to a bar if I didn't drink?

He wiped the bar with a spotless white towel. "Gotta message for you from the Master."

"The Master Vampire of the City?" Irving asked. His voice had that excited lilt to it. He smelled news.

"What?" There was no excited lilt to my voice.

"He wants to see you, bad."

I glanced at Irving, then back at Luther. I tried to telepathically send the message, not in front of the reporter. It didn't work.

"The Master's put the word out. Anybody who sees you gives you the message."

Irving was looking back and forth between us like an eager puppy. "What does the Master of the City want with you, Anita?"

"Consider it given," I said.

Luther shook his head. "You ain't going to talk to him, are you?"

"No," I said.

"Why not?" Irving asked.

"None of your business."

"Off the record," he said.

"No."

Luther stared at me. "Listen to me, girl, you talk to the Master. Right now all the vamps and freaks are just supposed to tell you the Master wants a powwow. The next order will be to detain you and take ya to him."

Detain, it was a nice word for kidnap. "I don't have anything to say to the Master."

"Don't let this get outta hand, Anita," Luther said. "Just talk to him, no harm."

That's what he thought. "Maybe I will." Luther was right. It was talk to him now or later. Later would probably be a lot less friendly.

"Why does the Master want to talk to you?" Irving asked. He was like some curious, bright-eyed bird that had spied a worm.

I ignored the question, and thought up a new one. "Did your sister reporter give you any highlights from this file? I don't really have time to read *War and Peace* before morning."

"Tell me what you know about the Master, and I'll give you the highlights."

"Thanks a lot, Luther."

"I didn't mean to sic him on you," he said. His cig bobbed up and down as he spoke. I never understood how he did that. Lip dexterity. Years of practice.

"Would everybody stop treating me like the bubonic fucking plague," Irving said. "I'm just trying to do my job."

I sipped my orange juice and looked at him. "Irving, you're messing with things you don't understand. I cannot give you info on the Master. I can't."

"Won't," he said.

I shrugged. "Won't, but the reason I won't is because I can't."

"That's a circular argument," he said.

"Sue me." I finished the juice. I didn't want it anyway. "Listen, Irving, we had a deal. The file info for the zombie articles. If you're going to break your word, deal's off. But tell me it's off. I don't have time to sit here and play twenty damn questions."

"I won't go back on the deal. My word is my bond," he said in as stagy a voice as he could manage in the murmurous noise of the bar.

"Then give me the highlights and let me get the hell out of the District before the Master hunts me up."

His face was suddenly solemn. "You're in trouble, aren't you?"

"Maybe. Help me out, Irving. Please."

"Help her out," Luther said.

Maybe it was the please. Maybe it was Luther's looming presence. Whatever, Irving nodded. "According to my sister reporter, he's crippled in a wheelchair."

I nodded. Nondirective, that's me.

"He likes his women crippled."

"What do you mean?" I remembered Cicely of the empty eyes.

"Blind, wheelchair, amputee, whatever, old Harry'll go for it."

"Deaf," I said.

"Up his alley."

"Why?" I asked. Clever questions are us.

Irving shrugged. "Maybe it makes him feel better since he's trapped in a chair himself. My fellow reporter didn't know why he was a deviant, just that he was."

"What else did she tell you?"

"He's never even been charged with a crime, but the rumors are real ugly. Suspected mob connections, but no proof. Just rumors."

"Tell me," I said.

"An old girlfriend tried to sue him for palimony. She disappeared."

"Disappeared as in probably dead," I said.

"Bingo."

I believed it. So he'd used Tommy and Bruno to kill before. Meant it would be easier to give the order a second time. Or maybe Gaynor's given the order lots of times, and just never gotten caught.

"What does he do for the mob that earns him his two bodyguards?"

"Oh, so you've met his security specialist."

I nodded.

"My fellow reporter would love to talk to you."

"You didn't tell her about me, did you?"

"Do I look like a stoolie?" He grinned at me.

I let that go. "What's he do for the mob?"

"Helps them clean money, or that's what we suspect."

"No evidence?" I said.

"None." He didn't look happy about it.

Luther shook his head, tapping his cig into the ashtray. Some ash spilled onto the bar. He wiped it with his spotless towel. "He sounds like bad news, Anita. Free advice, leave him the hell alone."

Good advice. Unfortunately. "I don't think he'll leave me alone."

"I won't ask, I don't want to know." Someone else was frantically signaling for a refill. Luther drifted over to them. I could watch the entire bar in the full-length mirror that took up the wall behind the bar. I could even see the door without turning around. It was convenient and comforting.

"I will ask," Irving said, "I do want to know."

I just shook my head.

"I know something you don't know," he said.

"And I want to know it?"

He nodded vigorously enough to make his frizzy hair bob.

I sighed. "Tell me."

"You first."

I had about enough. "I have shared all I am going to tonight, Irving. I've got the file. I'll look through it. You're just saving me a little time. Right now, a little time could be very important to me."

"Oh, shucks, you take all the fun out of being a hard-core reporter." He looked like he was going to pout.

"Just tell me, Irving, or I'm going to do something violent."

He half laughed. I don't think he believed me. He should have. "Alright, alright." He brought out a picture from behind his back with a flourish like a magician.

It was a black and white photo of a woman. She was in her twenties, long brown hair down in a modern style, just enough mousse to make it look spiky. She was pretty. I didn't recognize her. The photo was obviously not posed. It was too casual and there was a look to the face of someone who didn't know she was being photographed.

"Who is she?"

"She was his girlfriend until about five months ago," Irving said.

"So she's . . . handicapped?" I stared down at the pretty, candid face. You couldn't tell by the picture.

"Wheelchair Wanda."

I stared at him. I could feel my eyes going wide. "You can't be serious."

He grinned. "Wheelchair Wanda cruises the streets in her chair. She's very popular with a certain crowd."

A prostitute in a wheelchair. Naw, it was too weird. I shook my head. "Okay, where do I find her?"

"I and my sister reporter want in on this."

"That's why you kept her picture out of the file."

He didn't even have the grace to look embarrassed. "Wanda won't talk to you alone, Anita."

"Has she talked to your reporter friend?"

He frowned, the light of conquest dimming in his eyes. I knew what that meant. "She won't talk to reporters will she, Irving?"

"She's afraid of Gaynor."

"She should be," I said.

"Why would she talk to you and not us?"

"My winning personality," I said.

"Come on, Blake."

"Where does she hang out, Irving?"

"Oh, hell." He finished his dwindling drink in one angry swallow. "She stays near a club called The Grey Cat."

The Grey Cat, like that old joke, all cats are grey in the dark. Cute. "Where's the club?"

Luther answered. I hadn't seen him come back. "On the main drag in the Tenderloin, corner of Twentieth and Grand. But I wouldn't go down there alone, Anita."

"I can take care of myself."

"Yeah, but you don't look like you can. You don't want to have to shoot some dumb shmuck just because he copped a feel, or worse. Take someone who looks mean, save yourself the aggravation."

Irving shrugged. "I wouldn't go down there alone."

I hated to admit it, but they were right. I may be heap big vampire slayer but it doesn't show much on the outside. "Okay, I'll get Charles. He looks tough enough to take on the Green Bay Packers, but his heart is oh so gentle."

Luther laughed, puffing smoke. "Don't let ol' Charlie see too much. He might faint."

Faint once in public and people never let you forget.

"I'll keep Charles safe." I put more money down on the bar than was needed. Luther hadn't really given me much information this time, but usually he did. Good information. I never paid full price for it. I got a discount because I was connected with the police. Dead Dave had been a cop before they kicked him off the force for being undead. Short-sighted of them. He was still pissed about that, but he liked to help. So he fed me information, and I fed the police selected bits of it.

Dead Dave came out of the door behind the bar. I glanced at the dark glass windows. It looked the same, but if Dave was up, it was full dark. Shit. It was a walk back to my car surrounded by vampires. At least I had my gun. Comforting that.

Dave is tall, wide, short brown hair that had been balding when he died. He lost no more hair but it didn't grow back either. He smiled at me wide enough to flash fangs. An excited wiggle ran through the crowd, as if the same nerve had been touched in all of them. The whispers spread like rings in a pool. Vampire. The show was on.

Dave and I shook hands. His hand was warm, firm, and dry. Have you fed tonight, Dave? He looked like he had, all rosy and cheerful. What did you feed on, Dave? And was it willing? Probably. Dave was a good guy for a dead man.

"Luther keeps telling me you stopped by but it's always in daylight. Nice to see you're slumming after dark."

"Truthfully, I planned to be out of the District before full dark."

He frowned. "You packing?"

I gave him a discreet glimpse of my gun.

Irving's eyes widened. "You're carrying a gun." It only sounded like he shouted it.

The noise level had died down to a waiting murmur. Quiet enough for people to overhear. But then, that's why they had come, to listen to the vampire. To tell their troubles to the dead. I lowered my voice and said, "Announce it to the world, Irving."

He shrugged. "Sorry."

"How do you know newsboy over here?" Dave asked.

"He helps me sometimes with research."

"Research, well la-de-da." He smiled without showing any fang. A trick you learn after a few years. "Luther give you the message?"

"Yeah."

"You going to be smart or dumb?"

Dave is sorta blunt, but I like him anyway. "Dumb probably," I said.

"Just because you got a special relationship with the new Master, don't let it fool you. He's still a master vampire. They are freaking bad news. Don't fuck with him."

"I'm trying to avoid it."

Dave smiled broad enough to show fang. "Shit, you mean . . . Naw, he wants you for more than good tail."

It was nice to know he thought I'd be good tail. I guess. "Yeah," I said.

Irving was practically bouncing in his seat. "What the hell is going on, Anita?"

Very good question. "My business, not yours."

"Anita . . ."

"Stop pestering me, Irving. I mean it."

"Pestering? I haven't heard that word since my grandmother."

I looked him straight in the eyes and said, carefully, "Leave me the fuck alone. That better?"

He put his hands out in an I-give-up gesture. "Heh, just trying to do my job."

"Well, do it somewhere else."

I slid off the bar stool.

"The word's out to find you, Anita," Dave said. "Some of the other vampires might get overzealous."

"You mean try to take me?"

He nodded.

"I'm armed, cross and all. I'll be okay."

"You want me to walk you to your car?" Dave asked.

I stared into his brown eyes and smiled. "Thanks, Dave, I'll remember the offer, but I'm a big girl." Truth was a lot of the vampires didn't like Dave feeding information to the enemy. I was the Executioner. If a vampire stepped over the line, they sent for me. There was no such thing as a life sentence for a vamp. Death or nothing. No prison can hold a vampire.

California tried, but one master vampire got loose. He killed twenty-five people in a one-night bloodbath. He didn't feed, he just killed. Guess he was pissed about being locked up. They'd put crosses over the doors and on the guards. Crosses don't work unless you believe in them. And they certainly don't work once a master vampire has convinced you to take them off.

I was the vampire's equivalent of an electric chair. They didn't like me much. Surprise, surprise.

"I'll be with her," Irving said. He put money down on the bar and stood up. I had the bulky file under my arm. I guess he wasn't going to let it out of his sight. Great.

"She'll probably have to protect you, too," Dave said.

Irving started to say something, then thought better of it. He could say, but I'm a lycanthrope, except he didn't want people to know. He worked very, very hard at appearing human.

"You sure you'll be okay?" he asked. One more chance for a vampire guard to my car.

He was offering to protect me from the Master. Dave hadn't been dead ten years. He wasn't good enough. "Nice to know you care, Dave."

"Go on, get outta here," he said.

"Watch yourself, girl," Luther said.

I smiled brightly at both of them, then turned and walked out of the near silent bar. The crowd couldn't have overheard much, if any, of the conversation, but I could feel them staring at my back. I resisted an urge to whirl around and go "boo." I bet somebody would have screamed.

It's the cross-shaped scar on my arm. Only vampires have them, right? A cross shoved into unclean flesh. Mine had been a branding iron specially made. A now dead master vampire had ordered it. Thought it would be funny. Hardy-har.

Or maybe it was just Dave. Maybe they hadn't noticed the scar. Maybe I was overly sensitive. Make friendly with a nice law-abiding vampire, and people get suspicious. Have a few funny scars and people wonder if you're human. But that's okay. Suspicion is healthy. It'll keep you alive.

# 13

THE SWELTERING DARKNESS closed around me like a hot, sticky fist. A streetlight formed a puddle of brilliance on the sidewalk, as if the light had melted. All the streetlights are reproductions of turn-of-the-century gas lamps. They rise black and graceful, but not quite authentic. Like a Halloween costume. It looks good but is too comfortable to be real.

The night sky was like a dark presence over the tall brick buildings, but the streetlights held the darkness back. Like a black tent held up by sticks of light. You had the sense of darkness without the reality.

I started walking for the parking garage just off First Street. Parking on the Riverfront is damn near impossible. The tourists have only made the problem worse.

The hard soles of Irving's dress shoes made a loud, echoing noise on the stone of the street. Real cobblestones. Streets meant for horses, not cars. It made parking a bitch, but it was . . . charming.

My Nike Airs made almost no sound on the street. Irving was like a clattery puppy beside me. Most lycanthropes I've met have been stealthy. Irving may have been a werewolf but he was more dog. A big, fun-loving dog.

Couples and small groups passed us, laughing, talking, voices too shrill. They had come to see vampires. Real-live vampires, or was that real-dead vampires? Tourists, all of them. Amateurs. Voyeurs. I had seen more undead than any of them. I'd lay money on that. The fascination escaped me.

It was full dark now. Dolph and the gang would be awaiting me at Burrell Cemetery. I needed to get over there. What about the file on Gaynor? And what was I going to do with Irving? Sometimes my life is too full.

A figure detached itself from the darkened buildings. I couldn't tell if he had been waiting or had simply appeared. Magic. I froze, like a rabbit caught in headlights, staring.

"What's wrong, Blake?" Irving asked.

I handed him the file and he took it, looking puzzled. I wanted my hands free in case I had to go for my gun. It probably wouldn't come to that. Probably.

Jean-Claude, Master Vampire of the City, walked towards us. He moved like a dancer, or a cat, a smooth, gliding walk. Energy and grace contained, waiting to explode into violence.

He wasn't that tall, maybe five-eleven. His shirt was so white, it gleamed. The shirt was loose, long, full sleeves made tight at the wrist by three-buttoned cuffs. The front of the shirt had only a string to close the throat. He'd left it untied, and the white cloth framed the pale smoothness of his chest. The shirt was tucked into tight black jeans, and only that kept it from billowing around him like a cape.

His hair was perfectly black, curling softly around his face. The eyes, if you dared to look into them, were a blue so dark it was almost black. Glittering, dark jewels.

He stopped about six feet in front of us. Close enough to see the dark cross-shaped scar on his chest. It was the only thing that marred the perfection of his body. Or what I'd seen of his body.

He'd told me once that he killed the one who scarred him. Bully for him, so had I.

"Hello, Jean-Claude," I said.

"Greetings, *ma petite*," he said. His voice was like fur, rich, soft, vaguely obscene, as if just talking to him was something dirty. Maybe it was.

"Don't call me *ma petite*," I said.

He smiled slightly, not a hint of fang. "As you like." He looked at

Irving. Irving looked away, careful not to meet Jean-Claude's eyes. You never looked directly into a vampire's eyes. Never. So why was I doing it with impunity. Why indeed?

"Who is your friend?" The last word was very soft and somehow threatening.

"This is Irving Griswold. He's a reporter for the *Post-Dispatch*. He's helping me with a little research."

"Ah," he said. He walked around Irving as if he were something for sale, and Jean-Claude wanted to see all of him.

Irving gave nervous little glances so that he could keep the vampire in view. He glanced at me, widening his eyes. "What's going on?"

"What indeed, Irving?" Jean-Claude said.

"Leave him alone, Jean-Claude."

"Why have you not come to see me, my little animator?"

Little animator wasn't much of an improvement over *ma petite*, but I'd take it. "I've been busy."

The look that crossed his face was almost anger. I didn't really want him mad at me. "I was going to come see you," I said.

"When?"

"Tomorrow night."

"Tonight." It was not a suggestion.

"I can't."

"Yes, *ma petite*, you can." His voice was like a warm wind in my head.

"You are so damn demanding," I said.

He laughed then. Pleasant and resonating like expensive perfume that lingers in the room after the wearer has gone. His laughter was like that, lingering in the ears like distant music. He had the best voice of any master vampire I'd ever met. Everyone has their talents.

"You are so exasperating," he said, the edge of laughter still in his voice. "What am I to do with you?"

"Leave me alone," I said. I was utterly serious. It was one of my biggest wishes.

His face sobered completely, like someone had flipped a switch. On, happy, off, unreadable. "Too many of my followers know you are my human servant, *ma petite*. Bringing you under control is part of consolidating my power." He sounded almost regretful. A lot of help that did me.

"What do you mean, bringing me under control?" My stomach was tight with the beginnings of fear. If Jean-Claude didn't scare me to death, he was going to give me an ulcer.

"You are my human servant. You must start acting like one."

"I am not your servant."

"Yes, *ma petite*, you are."

"Dammit, Jean-Claude, leave me alone."

He was suddenly standing next to me. I hadn't seen him move. He had clouded my mind without me even blinking. I could taste my pulse at the back of my throat. I tried to step back, but one pale slender hand grabbed my right arm, just above the elbow. I shouldn't have stepped back. I should have gone for my gun. I hoped I would live through the mistake.

My voice came out flat, normal. At least I'd die brave. "I thought having two of your vampire marks meant you couldn't control my mind."

"I cannot bewitch you with my eyes, and it is harder to cloud your mind, but it can be done." His fingers encircled my arm. Not hurting. I didn't try to pull away. I knew better. He could crush my arm without breaking a sweat, or tear it from its socket, or bench press a Toyota. If I couldn't arm wrestle Tommy, I sure as hell couldn't match Jean-Claude.

"He's the new Master of the City, isn't he?" It was Irving. I think we had forgotten about him. It would have been better for Irving if we had.

Jean-Claude's grip tightened slightly on my right arm. He turned to look at Irving. "You are the reporter that has been asking to interview me."

"Yes, I am." Irving sounded just the tiniest bit nervous, not much, just the hint of tightness in his voice. He looked brave and resolute. Good for Irving.

"Perhaps after I have spoken with this lovely young woman, I will grant you your interview."

"Really?" Astonishment was plain in his voice. He grinned widely at me. "That would be great. I'll do it any way you want. It . . ."

"Silence." The word hissed and floated. Irving fell quiet as if it were a spell.

"Irving, are you alright?" Funny me asking. I was the one cheek to jowl with a vampire, but I asked anyway.

"Yeah," Irving said. That one word was squeezed small with fear. "I've just never felt anything like him."

I glanced up at Jean-Claude. "He is sort of one of a kind."

Jean-Claude turned his attention back to me. Oh, goody. "Still making jokes, *ma petite*."

I stared up into his beautiful eyes, but they were just eyes. He had given me the power to resist them. "It's a way to pass the time. What do you want, Jean-Claude?"

"So brave, even now."

"You aren't going to do me on the street, in front of witnesses. You may be the new Master, but you're also a businessman. You're mainstream vampire. It limits what you can do."

"Only in public," he said, so soft that only I heard him.

"Fine, but we both agree you aren't going to do violence here and now." I stared up at him. "So cut the theatrics and tell me what the bloody hell you want."

He smiled then, a bare movement of lips, but he released my arm and stepped back. "Just as you will not shoot me down in the street without provocation."

I thought I had provocation, but nothing I could explain to the police. "I don't want to be up on murder charges, that's true."

His smile widened, still not fangs. He did that better than any living vampire I knew. Was living vampire an oxymoron? I wasn't sure anymore.

"So, we will not harm each other in public," he said.

"Probably not," I said. "What do you want? I'm late for an appointment."

"Are you raising zombies or slaying vampires tonight?"

"Neither," I said.

He looked at me, waiting for me to say more. I didn't. He shrugged and it was graceful. "You are my human servant, Anita."

He'd used my real name, I knew I was in trouble now. "Am not," I said.

He gave a long sigh. "You bear two of my marks."

"Not by choice," I said.

"You would have died if I had not shared my strength with you."

"Don't give me crap about how you saved my life. You forced two marks on me. You didn't ask or explain. The first mark may have saved my life, great. The second mark saved yours. I didn't have a choice either time."

"Two more marks and you will have immortality. You will not age because I do not age. You will remain human, alive, able to wear your crucifix. Able to enter a church. It does not compromise your soul. Why do you fight me?"

"How do you know what compromises my soul? You don't have one anymore. You traded your immortal soul for earthly eternity. But I know that vampires can die, Jean-Claude. What happens when you die? Where do you go? Do you just go poof? No, you go to hell where you belong."

"And you think by being my human servant you will go with me?"

"I don't know, and I don't want to find out."

"By fighting me, you make me appear weak. I cannot afford that, *ma petite*. One way or another, we must resolve this."

"Just leave me alone."

"I cannot. You are my human servant, and you must begin to act like one."

"Don't press me on this, Jean-Claude."

"Or what, will you kill me? Could you kill me?"

I stared at his beautiful face and said, "Yes."

"I feel your desire for me, *ma petite*, as I desire you."

I shrugged. What could I say? "It's just a little lust, Jean-Claude, nothing special." That was a lie. I knew it even as I said it.

"No, *ma petite*, I mean more to you than that."

We were attracting a crowd, at a safe distance. "Do you really want to discuss this in the street?"

He took a deep breath and let it out in a sigh. "Very true. You make me forget myself, *ma petite*."

Great. "I really am late, Jean-Claude. The police are waiting for me."

"We must finish this discussion, *ma petite*," he said.

I nodded. He was right. I'd been trying to ignore it, and him. Master vampires are not easy to ignore. "Tomorrow night."

"Where?" he asked.

Polite of him not to order me to his lair. I thought about where best to do it. I wanted Charles to go down to the Tenderloin with me. Charles was going to be checking the zombie working conditions at a new comedy club. Good a place as any. "Do you know The Laughing Corpse?"

He smiled, a glimpse of fang touching his lips. A woman in the small crowd gasped. "Yes."

"Meet me there at, say, eleven o'clock."

"My pleasure." The words caressed my skin like a promise. Shit.

"I will await you in my office, tomorrow night."

"Wait a minute. What do you mean, your office?" I had a bad feeling about this.

His smile widened into a grin, fangs glistening in the streetlights. "Why, I own The Laughing Corpse. I thought you knew."

"The hell you did."

"I will await you."

I'd picked the place. I'd stand by it. Dammit. "Come on, Irving."

"No, let the reporter stay. He has not had his interview."

"Leave him alone, Jean-Claude, please."

"I will give him what he desires, nothing more."

I didn't like the way he said desires. "What are you up to?"

"Me, *ma petite*, up to something?" He smiled.

"Anita, I want to stay," Irving said.

I turned to him. "You don't know what you're saying."

"I'm a reporter. I'm doing my job."

"Swear to me, swear to me you won't harm him."

"You have my word," Jean-Claude said.

"That you will not harm him in any way."

"That I will not harm him in any way." His face was expressionless, as if all the smiles had been illusions. His face had that immobility of the long dead. Lovely to look at, but empty of life as a painting.

I looked into his blank eyes and shivered. Shit. "Are you sure you want to stay here?"

Irving nodded. "I want the interview."

I shook my head. "You're a fool."

"I'm a good reporter," he said.

"You're still a fool."

"I can take care of myself, Anita."

We looked at each other for a space of heartbeats. "Fine, have fun. May I have the file?"

He looked down at his arms as if he had forgotten he was holding it. "Drop it by tomorrow morning or Madeline is going to have a fit."

"Sure. No problem." I tucked the bulky file under my left arm as loosely as I could manage it. It hampered my being able to draw my gun, but life's imperfect.

I had information on Gaynor. I had the name of a recent ex-girlfriend. A woman scorned. Maybe she'd talk to me. Maybe she'd help me find clues. Maybe she'd tell me to go to hell. Wouldn't be the first time.

Jean-Claude was watching me with his still eyes. I took a deep breath through my nose and let it out through my mouth. Enough for one night. "See you both tomorrow." I turned and walked away. There was a group of tourists with cameras. One was sort of tentatively raised in my direction.

"If you snap my picture, I will take the camera away from you and break it." I smiled while I said it.

The man lowered his camera uncertainly. "Geez, just a little picture."

"You've seen enough," I said. "Move on, the show's over." The tourists drifted away like smoke when the wind blows through it. I walked down the street towards the parking garage. I glanced back and found the tourists had drifted back to surround Jean-Claude and Irving. The tourists were right. The show wasn't over yet.

Irving was a big boy. He wanted the interview. Who was I to play nursemaid on a grown werewolf? Would Jean-Claude find out Irving's secret? If he did, would it make a difference? Not my problem. My problem was Harold Gaynor, Dominga Salvador, and a monster that was eating the good citizens of St. Louis, Missouri. Let Irving take care of his own problems. I had enough of my own.

## 14

THE NIGHT SKY was a curving bowl of liquid black. Stars like pinprick diamonds gave a cold, hard light. The moon was a glowing patchwork of greys and goldish-silver. The city makes you forget how dark the night, how bright the moon, how very many stars.

Burrell Cemetery didn't have any streetlights. There was nothing but the distant yellow gleam of a house's windows. I stood at the top of the hill in my coveralls and Nikes, sweating.

The boy's body was gone. It was in the morgue waiting for the coroner's attentions. I was finished with it. Never had to look at it again. Except in my dreams.

Dolph stood beside me. He didn't say a word, just looked out over the grass and broken tombstones, waiting. Waiting for me to do my magic. To pull the rabbit out of the hat. The best that could happen was the rabbit to be in and to destroy it. Next best thing was finding the hole it had come from. That could tell us something. And something was better than what we had right now.

The exterminators followed a few paces behind. The man was short, beefy, grey hair cut in a butch. He looked like a retired football coach, but he handled the flamethrower strapped to his back like it was something alive. Thick hands caressing it.

The woman was young, no more than twenty. Thin blond hair tied back in a ponytail. She was a little taller than me, small. Wisps of hair trailed across her face. Her eyes were wide and searched the tall grass, side to side. Like a gunner on point.

I hoped she didn't have an itchy trigger finger. I didn't want to be eaten by a killer zombie, but I didn't want to be plastered with napalm either. Burned alive or eaten alive? Is there anything else on the menu?

The grass rustled and whispered like dry autumn leaves. If we did use the flamethrowers in here, it'd be a grass fire. We'd be lucky to outrun it. But fire was the only thing that could stop a zombie. If it was a zombie and not something else altogether.

I shook my head and started walking. Doubts would get us nowhere. Act like you know what you're doing; it was a rule I lived by.

I am sure that Señora Salvador would have had a specific rite or sacrifice to find a zombie's grave. Her way of doing all this had more rules than my way. Of course her way enabled her to trap souls in rotting corpses. I had never hated anyone enough to do that to them. Kill them, yes, but entrap their soul and make it sit and wait and feel its body rotting. No, that was worse than wicked. It was evil. She needed to be stopped, and only death would do that. I sighed. Another problem for another night.

It bothered me to hear Dolph's footsteps echoing mine. I glanced back at the two exterminators. They killed everything from termites to ghouls, but ghouls are cowards, scavengers mostly. Whatever we were after wasn't a scavenger.

I could feel the three of them at my back. Their footsteps seemed louder than mine. I tried to clear my mind and start the search, but all I could hear was their footsteps. All I could sense was the woman's fear. They were messing up my concentration.

I stopped. "Dolph, I need more room."

"What does that mean?"

"Hang back a little. You're ruining my concentration."

"We might be too far away to help."

"If the zombie rises out of the ground and leeches on me..." I shrugged. "What are you going to do, shoot it with napalm and crispy-critter me, too?"

"You said fire was the only weapon," he said.

"It is, but if the zombie actually grapples with anyone, tell the exterminators not to fry the victim."

"If the zombie grabs one of us, we can't use the napalm?" he said.

"Bingo."

"You could have said this sooner."

"I just thought of it."

"Great," he said.

I shrugged. "I'll take point. My oversight. Just hang back and let me do my job." I stepped in close to him to whisper, "And watch the woman. She looks scared enough to start shooting shadows."

"They're exterminators, Anita, not police or vampire slayers."

"For tonight, our lives could depend on them, so keep an eye on her, okay?"

He nodded and glanced back at the two exterminators. The man smiled and nodded. The girl just stared. I could almost smell her fear.

She was entitled to it. Why did it bother me so much? Because she and I were the only women here, and we had to be better than the men. Braver, quicker, whatever. It was a rule for playing with the big boys.

I walked out into the grass alone. I waited until the only thing I could hear was the grass; soft, dry, whispering. Like it was trying to tell me something in a scratchy, frantic voice. Frantic, fearful. The grass sounded afraid. That was stupid. Grass didn't feel shit. But I did, and there was sweat on every inch of my body. Was it here? Was the thing that had reduced a man to so much raw meat, here in the grass, hiding, waiting?

No. Zombies weren't smart enough for that, but of course, it had been smart enough to hide from the police. That was smart for a corpse. Too smart. Maybe it wasn't a zombie at all. I had finally found something that scared me more than vampires. Death didn't bother me much. Strong Christian and all that. Method of death did. Being eaten alive. One of my top three ways not to go out.

Who would ever have thought I'd be afraid of a zombie, any kind of zombie? Nicely ironic that. I'd laugh later when my mouth wasn't so damn dry.

There was that quiet waiting that all cemeteries have. As if the dead held their collective breath, waiting, but for what? The resurrection?

Maybe. But I've dealt with the dead too long to believe in just one answer. The dead are like the living. They do different things.

Most people die and go to heaven or hell, and that's that. But a few, for whatever reason, don't work that way. Ghosts, restless spirits, violence, evil, or simple confusion; all of these can trap a spirit on earth. I'm not saying that it traps the soul. I don't believe that, but some memory of the soul, the essence, lingers.

Was I expecting some specter to rise from the grass and rush screaming towards me? No. I had never seen a ghost yet that could cause actual physical harm. If it causes physical damage, it isn't a ghost; demon maybe, or the spirit of some sorcerer, black magic, but ghosts don't hurt.

That was almost a comforting thought.

The ground sloped out from under my feet. I stumbled and caught myself on one of the leaning headstones. Sunken earth, a grave without a marker. A tingling shock ran up my leg, a whisper of ghostly electricity. I jerked back and sat down hard on the ground.

"Anita, you all right?" Dolph yelled.

I glanced back at him and found the grass completely hid me from view. "I'm fine," I yelled. I got to my feet careful to avoid stepping on the old grave. Whatever person lay under the earth, he, or she, was not a happy camper. It was a hot spot, not a ghost, or even a haunt, but something. It had probably been a full-blown ghost once, but time had worn it away. Ghosts wear out like old clothes and go on to wherever old ghosts go.

The sunken grave would fade away, probably in my lifetime. If I could avoid killer zombies for a few years. And vampires. And gun-toting humans. Oh, hell, the hot spot would probably outlast me.

I looked back to find Dolph and the exterminators maybe twenty yards back. Twenty yards, wasn't that awfully far? I had told them to hang back, but I hadn't meant for them to leave me hanging in the wind. I was just never satisfied.

If I called them to come closer, you think they'd get mad? Probably. I started walking again, trying not to step on any more graves. But it was hard with most of the stones hidden in the long grass. So many unmarked graves, so much neglect.

I could wander aimlessly all bloody night. Had I really thought that I could just accidentally walk over the right grave? Yes. Hope springs eternal, especially when the alternative isn't very human.

Vampires were once ordinary human beings; zombies, too. Most lycanthropes start out human, though there are a few rare inherited curses. All the monsters start out normal except me. Raising the dead wasn't a career choice. I didn't sit down in the guidance counselor's office one day and say, "I'd like to raise the dead for a living." No, it wasn't that neat or clean.

I have always had an affinity for the dead. Always. Not the newly dead. No, I don't mess with souls, but once the soul departs, I know it. I can feel it. Laugh all you want. It's the truth.

I had a dog when I was little. Just like most kids. And like most kids' dogs, she died. I was thirteen. We buried Jenny in the backyard. I woke up a week after Jenny died and found her curled up beside me. Thick black fur coated with grave dirt. Dead brown eyes following my every move, just like when she was alive.

I thought for one wild moment she was alive. It had been a mistake, but I know dead when I see it. Feel it. Call it from the grave. I wonder what Dominga Salvador would think about that story. Calling an animal zombie. How shocking. Raising the dead by accident. How frightening. How sick.

My stepmother, Judith, never quite recovered from the shock. She rarely tells people what I do for a living. Dad? Well, Dad ignores it, too. I tried ignoring it, but couldn't. I won't go into details, but does the term "road kill" have any significance for you? It did for Judith. I looked like a nightmare version of the Pied Piper.

My father finally took me to meet my maternal grandmother. She's not as scary as Dominga Salvador, but she's . . . interesting. Grandma Flores agreed with Dad. I should not be trained in voodoo, only in enough control to stop the . . . problems. "Just teach her to control it," Dad said.

She did. I did. Dad took me back home. It was never mentioned again. At least not in front of me. I always wondered what dear stepmother said behind closed doors. For that matter Dad wasn't pleased either. Hell, I wasn't pleased.

Bert recruited me straight out of college. I never knew how he heard about me. I refused him at first, but he waved money at me. Maybe I was rebelling against parental expectations? Or maybe I had finally realized that there is damn little employment opportunity for a B.S. in biology with an emphasis on the supernatural. I minored in creatures of legend. That was real helpful on my résumé.

It was like having a degree in ancient Greek or the Romantic Poets, interesting, enjoyable, but then what the hell can you do with it? I had planned to go on to grad school and teach college. But Bert came along and showed me a way to turn my natural talent into a job. At least I can say I use my degree every day.

I never puzzled about how I came to do what I do. There was no mystery. It was in the blood.

I stood in the graveyard and took a deep breath. A bead of sweat trickled down my face. I wiped it with the back of my hand. I was sweating like a pig, and I still felt cold. Fear, but not of the bogeyman, of what I was about to do.

If it were a muscle, I would move it. If it were a thought, I would think it. If it were a magic word, I could say it. It is nothing like that. It is like my skin becomes cool even under cloth. I can feel all my nerve endings naked to the wind. And even in this hot, sweating August night, my skin felt cool. It is almost like a tiny, cool wind emanates from my skin. But it isn't wind, no one else can feel it. It doesn't blow through a room like a Hollywood horror movie. It isn't flashy. It's quiet. Private. Mine.

The cool fingers of "wind" searched outward. Within a ten-to-fifteen-foot circle I would be able to search the graves. As I moved, the circle would move with me, searching.

How does it feel to search through the hard-packed earth for dead bodies? Like nothing human. The closest I can come to describing it is like phantom fingers rifling through the dirt, searching for the dead. But, of course, that isn't quite what it feels like either. Close but no cigar.

The coffin nearest me had been water-ruined years ago. Bits of warped wood, shreds of bone, nothing whole. Bone and old wood, dirt, clean and dead. The hot spot flared almost like a burning sensation. I couldn't read its coffin. The hot spot could keep its secrets. It wasn't worth forcing the issue. It was a life force of sorts, trapped to a dead grave until it faded. That is bound to make you grumpy.

I walked slowly forward. The circle moved with me. I touched bones, intact coffins, bits of cloth in newer graves. This was an old cemetery. There were no decaying corpses. Death had progressed to the nice neat stage.

Something grabbed my ankle. I jumped and walked forward without looking down. Never look down. It's a rule. I got a brief glimpse just behind my eyes of something pale and mistlike with wide screaming eyes.

A ghost, a real-live ghost. I had walked over its grave and it had let me know it didn't like it. A ghost had grabbed me round the ankles. Big deal. If you ignored them, the spectral hands would fade. If you noticed them, you gave them substance, and you could be in deep shit.

Important safety tip with most of the spiritual world: if you ignore it, it has less power. This does not work with demons or other demibeings. Other exceptions to the rule are vampires, zombies, ghouls, lycanthropes, witches . . . Oh, hell, ignoring only works for ghosts. But it does work.

Phantom hands tugged at my pants leg. I could feel skeletal fingers pulling upwards, as if it would use me to pull itself from the grave. Shit! I was eating my pulse between my teeth. Just keep walking. Ignore it. It will go away. Dammit to hell

The fingers slipped away, reluctantly. Some types of ghost seem to bear a grudge against the living. A sort of jealousy. They cannot harm you, but they scare the bejesus out of you and laugh while they're doing it.

I found an empty grave. Bits of wood decaying into the earth, but no trace of bone. No body. Empty. The earth above it was thick with grass and weeds. The earth was hard-packed and dry from the drought. The grass and weeds had been disturbed. Bare roots were showing, almost as if someone had tried to pull the grass up. Or something had come up underneath the grass and left a trail.

I knelt on all fours above the dying grass. My hands stayed on top of the hard, reddish dirt, but I could feel the inside of the grave like rolling your tongue around your teeth. You can't see it, but you can feel it.

The corpse was gone. The coffin was undisturbed. A zombie had come from here. Was it the zombie we were looking for? No guarantees. But it was the only zombie raising I could sense.

I stared out away from the grave. It was hard using just my eyes to search the grass. I could almost see what lay under the dirt. But the grave showed behind my eyes in my head somewhere where there were no optic nerves. The graveyard that I could see with my eyes ended at a fence maybe five yards away. Had I walked it all? Was this the only grave that was empty?

I stood and looked out over the graves. Dolph and the two exterminators were still with me about thirty yards back. Thirty yards? Some backup.

I had walked it all. There was the grabby ghost. The hot spot was there. The newest grave over there. It was mine now. I knew this cemetery. And everything that was restless. Everything that wasn't quite dead was dancing above its grave. White misty phantoms. Sparkling angry lights. Agitated. There was more than one way to wake the dead.

But they would quiet down and sleep, if that was the word. No permanent damage. I glanced back down at the empty grave. No permanent damage.

I waved Dolph and the others over. I got a Ziploc bag out of the coverall pocket and scooped some grave dirt into it.

The moonlight suddenly seemed dimmer. Dolph was standing over me. He did sort of loom.

"Well?" he asked.

"A zombie came out of this grave," I said.

"Is it the killer zombie?"

"I don't know for sure."

"You don't know?"

"Not yet."

"When will you know?"

"I'll take it to Evans and let him do his touchie-feelie routine on it."

"Evans, the clairvoyant," Dolph said.

"Yep."

"He's a flake."

"True, but he's good."

"The department doesn't use him anymore."

"Bully for the department," I said. "He's still on retainer at Animators, Inc."

Dolph shook his head. "I don't trust Evans."

"I don't trust anybody," I said. "So what's the problem?"

Dolph smiled. "Point taken."

I had rolled some of the grass and weeds, roots carefully intact, inside a second bag. I crawled to the head of the grave and spread the weeds. There was no marker. Dammit! The pale limestone had been chipped away at the base. Shattered. Carried away. Shit.

"Why would they destroy the headstone?" Dolph asked.

"The name and date could have given us some clue to why the zombie was raised and to what went wrong."

"Wrong, how?"

"You might raise a zombie to kill one or two people but not wholesale slaughter. Nobody would do that."

"Unless they're crazy," he said.

I stared up at him. "That's not funny."

"No, it isn't."

A madman that could raise the dead. A murderous zombie corpse controlled by a psychotic. Great. And if he, or she, could do it once . . .

"Dolph, if we have a crazy man running around, there could be more than one zombie."

"And if it is crazy, then there won't be a pattern," he said.

"Shit."

"Exactly."

No pattern meant no motive. No motive meant we might not be able to figure this out. "No, I don't believe that."

"Why not?" he asked.

"Because if I do believe it, it leaves us no place to go." I took out a pocketknife that I brought for the occasion and started to chip at the remains of the tombstone.

"Defacing a gravemarker is against the law," Dolph said.

"Isn't it though." I scrapped a few smaller pieces into a third bag, and finally got a sizable chunk of marble, big as my thumb.

I stuffed all the bags into the pockets of my coveralls, along with the pocketknife.

"You really think Evans will be able to read anything from those bits and pieces?"

"I don't know." I stood and looked down at the grave. The two exterminators were standing just a short distance away. Giving us privacy. How very polite. "You know, Dolph, they may have destroyed the tombstone, but the grave is still here."

"But the corpse is gone," he said.

"True, but the coffin might be able to tell us something. Anything might help."

He nodded. "Alright, I'll get an exhumation order."

"Can't we just dig it up now, tonight?"

"No," he said. "I have to play by the rules." He stared at me very hard. "And I don't want to come back out here and find the grave dug up. The evidence won't mean shit if you tamper with it."

"Evidence? You really think this case will go to court?"

"Yes."

"Dolph, we just need to destroy the zombie."

"I want the bastards that raised it, Anita. I want them up on murder charges."

I nodded. I agreed with him, but I thought it unlikely. Dolph was a policeman, he had to worry about the law. I worried about simpler things, like survival.

"I'll let you know if Evans has anything useful to say," I said.

"You do that."

"Wherever the beastie is, Dolph, it isn't here."

"It's out there, isn't it?"

"Yeah," I said.

"Killing someone else while we sit here and chase our tails."

I wanted to touch him. To let him know it was all right, but it wasn't all right. I knew how he felt. We were chasing our tails. Even if this was the grave of the killer zombie, it didn't get us any closer to finding the zombie. And we had to find it. Find it, trap it, and destroy it. The sixty-four-thousand-dollar question was, could we do all that before it needed to feed again? I didn't have an answer. That was a lie. I had an answer. I just didn't like it. Out there somewhere, the zombie was feeding again.

# 15

THE TRAILER PARK where Evans lives is in St. Charles just off Highway 94. Acres of mobile homes roll out in every direction. Of course, there's nothing mobile about them. When I was a kid, trailers could be hooked to the back of a car and moved. Simple. It was one of their appeals. Some of these mobile homes had three and four bedrooms, multiple baths. The only thing moving these puppies was a semitruck, or a tornado.

Evans's trailer is an older model. I think, if he had to, he could chain it to the back of a pickup and move. Easier than hiring a moving van, I guess. But I doubt Evans will ever move. Hell, he hasn't left the trailer in nearly a year.

The windows were golden with light. There was a little makeshift porch complete with an awning, guarding the door. I knew he would be up. Evans was always up. Insomnia sounded so harmless. Evans had made it a disease.

I was back in my black shorts outfit. The three bags of goodies were stuffed in a fanny pack. If I went in there waving them around, Evans would freak. I needed to work up to it, be subtle. Just thought I'd drop by to see my old buddy. No ulterior motives here. Right.

I opened the screen door and knocked. Silence. No movement. Nothing. I raised my hand to knock again, then hesitated. Had Evans finally gotten to sleep? His first decent night's sleep since I'd known him. Drat. I was still standing there with my hand half-raised when I felt him staring at me.

I looked up at the little window in the door. A slice of pale face was staring out from between the curtains. Evans's blue eye blinked at me.

I waved.

His face disappeared. The door unlocked, then opened. There was no sight of Evans, just the open door. I walked in. Evans was standing behind the door, hiding.

He closed the door by leaning against it. His breathing was fast and shallow as if he'd been running. Stringy yellow hair trailed over a dark blue bathrobe. His face was covered in bristly reddish beard.

"How are you doing, Evans?"

He leaned against the door, eyes too wide. His breathing was still too fast. Was he on something?

"Evans, you all right?" When in doubt, reverse your word order.

He nodded. "What do you want?" His voice was breathy.

I didn't think he was going to believe I had just stopped by. Call it an instinct. "I need your help."

He shook his head. "No."

"You don't even know what I want."

He shook his head. "Doesn't matter."

"May I sit down?" I asked. If directness wouldn't work, maybe politeness would.

He nodded. "Sure."

I glanced around the small living-room area. I was sure there was a couch under the newspapers, paper plates, half-full cups, old clothes. There was a box of petrified pizza on the coffee table. The room smelled stale.

Would he freak if I moved stuff? Could I sit on the pile that I thought was the couch without everything collapsing? I decided to try. I'd sit in the freaking moldy pizza box if Evans would agree to help me.

I perched on a pile of papers. There was definitely something large and solid under the newspapers. Maybe the couch. "May I have a cup of coffee?"

He shook his head. "No clean cups."

This I could believe. He was still pressed against the door as if afraid to come any closer. His hands were plunged into the pockets of his bathrobe.

"Can we just talk?" I asked.

He shook his head. I shook my head with him. He frowned at that. Maybe somebody was home.

"What do you want?" he asked.

"I told you, your help."

"I don't do that anymore."

"What?" I asked.

"You know," he said.

"No, Evans, I don't know. Tell me."

"I don't touch things anymore."

I blinked. It was an odd way to phrase it. I stared around at the piles of dirty dishes, the clothes. It did look untouched. "Evans, let me see your hands."

He shook his head. I didn't imitate him this time. "Evans, show me your hands."

"No," it was loud, clear.

I stood up and started walking towards him. It didn't take long. He backed away into the corner by the door and the doorway into the bedroom. "Show me your hands."

Tears welled in his eyes. He blinked, and the tears slid down his cheeks. "Leave me alone," he said.

My chest was tight. What had he done? God, what had he done? "Evans, either you show me your hands voluntarily, or I make you do it." I fought an urge to touch his arm, but that was not allowed.

He was crying harder now, small hiccupy sobs. He pulled his left hand out of the robe pocket. It was pale, bony, whole. I took a deep breath. Thank you, dear God.

"What did you think I'd done?" he asked.

I shook my head. "Don't ask."

He was looking at me now, really looking at me. I did have his attention. "I'm not that crazy," he said.

I started to say, "I never thought you were," but obviously I had. I had thought he had cut his hands off so he wouldn't have to touch anymore. God, that was crazy. Seriously crazy. And I was here to ask him to help me with a murder. Which of us was crazier? Don't answer that.

He shook his head. "What are you doing here, Anita?" The tears weren't even dry on his face, but his voice was calm, ordinary.

"I need your help with a murder."

"I don't do that anymore. I told you."

"You told me once that you couldn't not have visions. Your clairvoyance isn't something you can just turn off."

"That's why I stay in here. If I don't go out, I don't see anybody. I don't have visions anymore."

"I don't believe you," I said.

He took a clean white handkerchief out of his pocket and wrapped it around the doorknob. "Get out."

"I saw a three-year-old boy today. He'd been eaten alive."

He leaned his forehead into the door. "Don't do this to me, please."

"I know other psychics, Evans, but no one with your success rate. I need the best. I need you."

He rubbed his forehead against the door. "Please don't."

I should have gone then, left, done what he said, but I didn't. I stood behind him and waited. Come on, old buddy, old pal, risk your sanity for me. I was the ruthless zombie raiser. I didn't feel guilt. Results were all that mattered. Ri–ight.

But in a way, results *were* all that mattered. "Other people are going to die unless we can stop it," I said.

"I don't care," he said.

"I don't believe you."

He stuffed the handkerchief back into his pocket and whirled around. "The little boy, you're not lying about that, are you?"

"I wouldn't lie to you."

He nodded. "Yeah, yeah." He licked his lips. "Give me what ya got."

I got the bags out of my purse and opened the one with the gravestone fragments in it. Had to start somewhere.

He didn't ask what it was, that would be cheating. I wouldn't even have mentioned the boy except I needed the leverage. Guilt is a wonderful tool.

His hand shook as I dropped the largest rock fragment into his palm. I was very careful that my fingers did not brush his hand. I didn't want Evans inside my secrets. It might scare him off.

His hand clenched around the stone. A shock ran up his spine. He jerked, eyes closed. And he was gone.

"Graveyard, grave." His head jerked to the side like he was listening to something. "Tall grass. Hot. Blood, he's wiping blood on the tombstone." He looked around the room with his closed eyes. Would he have seen the room if his eyes had been open?

"Where does the blood come from?" he asked that. Was I supposed to answer? "No, no!" He stumbled backwards, back smacking into the door. "Woman screaming, screaming, no, no!"

His eyes flew open wide. He threw the rock fragment across the room. "They killed her, they killed her!" He pressed his fists into his eyes. "Oh, God, they slit her throat."

"Who is they?"

He shook his head, fists still shoved against his face. "I don't know."

"Evans, what did you see?"

"Blood." He stared at me between his arms, shielding his face. "Blood everywhere. They slit her throat. They smeared the blood on the tombstone."

I had two more items for him. Dare I ask? Asking didn't hurt. Did it? "I have two more items for you to touch."

"No fucking way," he said. He backed away from me towards the short hall that led to the bedroom. "Get out, get out, get the fuck out of my house. Now!"

"Evans, what else did you see?"

"Get out!"

"Describe one thing about the woman. Help me, Evans!"

He leaned in the doorway and slid to sit on the floor. "A bracelet. She wore a bracelet on her left wrist. Little dangling charms, hearts, bow and arrow, music." He shook his head and buried his head against his eyes. "Go away now."

I started to say thank you, but that didn't cut it. I picked my way over the floor searching for the rock fragment. I found it in a coffee cup. There was something green and growing in the bottom of it. I picked up the stone and wiped it on a pair of jeans on the floor. I put it back in the bag and shoved all of it inside the purse.

I stared around at the filth and didn't want to leave him here. Maybe I was just feeling guilty for having abused him. Maybe. "Evans, thanks."

He didn't look up.

"If I had a cleaning person drop by, would you let her in to clean?"

"I don't want anybody in here."

"Animators, Inc., could pick up the tab. We owe you for this one."

He looked up then. Anger, pure anger was all that was in his face. "Evans, get some help. You're tearing yourself apart."

"Get-the-fuck-out-of-my-house." Each word was hot enough to scald. I had never seen Evans angry. Scared, yes, but not like this. What could I say? It was his house.

I got out. I stood on the shaky porch until I heard the door lock behind me. I had what I wanted, information. So why did I feel so bad? Because I had bullied a seriously disturbed man. Okay, that was it. Guilt, guilt, guilt.

An image flashed into my head, the blood-soaked sheet on the brown patterned couch. Mrs. Reynolds's spine dangling wet and glistening in the sunlight.

I walked to my car and got in. If abusing Evans could save one family, then it was worth it. If it would keep me from having to see another three-year-old boy with his intestines ripped out, I'd beat Evans with a padded club. Or let him beat me.

Come to think of it, wasn't that what we'd just done?

# *16*

I WAS SMALL in the dream. A child. The car was crushed in front where it had been broadsided by another car. It looked like it was made of shiny paper that had been crushed by hand. The door was open. I crawled inside on the familiar upholstery, so pale it was almost white. There was a dark liquid stain on the seat. It wasn't all that large. I touched it, tentatively.

My fingers came away smeared with crimson. It was the first blood I'd ever seen. I stared up at the windshield. It was broken in a spiderweb of cracks, bowed outward where my mother's face had smashed into it. She had been thrown out the door to die in a field beside the road. That's why there wasn't a lot of blood on the seat.

I stared at the fresh blood on my fingers. In real life the blood had been dry, just a stain. When I dreamed about it, it was always fresh.

There was a smell this time. The smell of rotten flesh. That wasn't right. I stared up in the dream and realized it was a dream. And the smell wasn't part of it. It was real.

I woke instantly, staring into the dark. My heart thudding in my throat. My hand went for the Browning in its second home, a sheath attached to the headboard of my bed. It was firm and solid, and comforting. I stayed on the bed, back pressed against the headboard, gun held in a teacup grip.

Through a tiny crack in the drapes moonlight spilled. The meager light outlined a man's shape. The shape didn't react to the gun or my movement. It shuffled forward, dragging its feet through the carpet. It had stumbled into my collection of toy penguins that spilled like a fuzzy tide under my bedroom window. It had knocked some of them over, and it didn't seem able to pick its feet up and walk over them. The figure was wading through the fluffy penguins, dragging its feet as if wading in water.

I kept the gun pointed one-handed at the thing and reached without looking to turn on my bedside lamp. The light seemed harsh after the darkness. I blinked rapidly willing my pupils to contract, to adjust. When they did, and I could see, it was a zombie.

He had been a big man in life. Shoulders broad as a barn door filled with muscle. His huge hands were very strong-looking. One eye had dehydrated and was shriveled like a prune. The remaining eye stared at me. There was nothing in that stare, no anticipation, no excitement, no cruelty, nothing but a blankness. A blankness that Dominga Salvador had filled with purpose. Kill she had said. I would have bet on it.

It was her zombie. I couldn't turn it. I couldn't order it to do anything until it fulfilled Dominga's orders. Once it killed me, it would be docile as a dead puppy. Once it killed me.

I didn't think I'd wait for that.

The Browning was loaded with Glazer Safety Rounds, silver-coated. Glazer Safety Rounds will kill a man if you hit him anywhere near the center of the body. The hole will be too big for salvage. A hole in its chest wouldn't bother the zombie. It would keep coming, heart or no heart. If you hit a person in the arm or leg with Safety Rounds, it will take off that arm or leg. Instant amputee. If you hit it right.

The zombie seemed in no hurry. He shuffled through the fallen stuffed toys with that single-minded determination of the dead. Zombies are not inhumanly strong. But they can use every ounce of strength; they don't save anything. Almost any human being could do a super-human feat, once. Pop muscles, tear cartilage, snap your spine, but you can lift the car. Only inhibitors in the brain prevent us all from destroying ourselves. Zombies don't have inhibitors. The corpse could literally tear me apart while it tore itself apart. But if Dominga had really wanted to kill me, she would have sent a less-decayed zombie. This one was so far gone I might have been able to dodge around it, and make the door. Maybe. But then again . . .

I cupped the butt of the gun in my left, the right where it was supposed to be, my finger on the trigger. I pulled the trigger and the explosion was incredibly loud in the small room. The zombie jerked, stumbled. Its right arm flew off in a welter of flesh and bone. No blood, it had been dead too long for that.

The zombie kept coming.

I sighted on the other arm. Hold your breath, squee-eeze. I was aiming for the elbow. I hit it. The two arms lay on the carpet and began to worm their way towards the bed. I could chop the thing to pieces, and all the pieces would keep trying to kill me.

The right leg at the knee. The leg didn't come loose completely, but the zombie toppled to one side, listing. It fell on its side, then rolled onto its stomach and began pushing with its remaining leg. Some dark liquid was leaking out of the shattered leg. The smell was worse.

I swallowed, and it was thick. God. I got off the bed on the far side away from the thing. I walked around the bed coming in behind the thing. It knew instantly that I had moved. It tried to turn and come at me, pushing with that last leg. The crawling arms turned faster, fingers scrambling on the carpet. I stood over it and blasted the other leg from less than two feet away. Bits and pieces of it splattered onto my penguins. Damn.

The arms were almost at my bare feet. I fired two quick shots and the hand shattered, exploding on the white carpet. The handless arms flopped and struggled. They were still trying to reach me.

There was a brush of cloth, a sense of movement just behind me, in the darkened living room. I was standing with my back to the open door. I turned and knew it was too late.

Arms grabbed me, clutching me to a very solid chest. Fingers dug into my right arm, pinning the gun against my body. I turned my head away, using my hair to shield my face and neck. Teeth sank into my shoulder. I screamed.

My face was pressed against the thing's shoulder. The fingers were digging in. It was going to crush my arm. The gun barrel was pressed against its shoulder. Teeth tore at the flesh of my shoulder, but it wasn't fangs. It only had human teeth to work with. It hurt like hell, but it would be alright, if I could get away.

I turned my face forward away from the shoulder and pulled the trigger. The entire body jerked backwards. The left arm crumbled. I rolled out of its grip. The arm dangled from my forearm, fingers hanging on.

I was standing in the doorway of my bedroom staring at the thing that had almost got me. It had been a white male, about six-one, built like a football player. It was fresh from the farm. Blood spattered where the shoulder had torn away. The fingers on my arm tightened. It couldn't crush my arm, but I couldn't make it let go either. I didn't have the time.

The zombie charged, one arm wide to grab me. I seemed to have all the time in the world to lift the gun, two-handed. The arm struggled and fought me as if it were still connected to the zombie's brain. I got off two quick shots. The zombie stumbled, its left leg collapsing, but it was too late. It was too close. As it fell, it took me with it.

We landed on the floor with me on the bottom. I managed to keep the Browning up, so that my arms were free and so was the gun. His weight pinned my body, nothing I could do about it. Blood glistened on his lips. I fired point-blank, closing my eyes as I pulled the trigger. Not just because I didn't want to see, but to save my eyes from bone shards.

When I looked, the head was gone except for a thin line of naked jawbone and a fragment of skull. The remaining hand scrambled for my throat. The hand still attached to my arm was helping its body. I couldn't get the gun around to shoot the arm. The angle was wrong.

A sound of something heavy sliding behind me. I risked a glance, craning my neck backwards to see the first zombie coming towards me. Its mouth, all that it had left to hurt me with, was open wide.

I screamed and turned back to the one on top of me. The attached hand fluttered at my neck. I pulled it away and gave it its own arm to hold. It grabbed it. With the brain gone, it wasn't as smart. I felt the fingers on my arm loosen. A shudder ran through the dangling arm. Blood burst out of it like a ripe melon. The fingers spasmed, releasing my arm. The zombie crushed its own arm until it spattered and bones snapped.

The scrambling sounds behind me were closer. "God!"

"Police! Come out with your hands up!" The voice was male and loud from the hallway.

The hell with being cool and self-sufficient. "Help me!"

"Miss, what's happening in there?"

The scrambling sounds were right next to me. I craned my neck and found myself almost nose to nose with the first zombie. I shoved the Browning in its open mouth. Its teeth scrapped on the barrel, and I pulled the trigger.

A policeman was suddenly in the doorway framed against the darkness. From my angle he was huge. Curly brown hair, going gray, mustache, gun in hand. "Jesus," he said.

The second zombie dropped its crushed arm and reached for me again. The policeman took a firm grip of the zombie's belt and pulled him upward with one hand. "Get her out of here," he said.

His partner moved in, but I didn't give him time. I scrambled out from under the half-raised body, scuttling on all fours into the living room. You didn't have to ask me twice. The partner lifted me to my feet by one arm. It was my right and the Browning came up with it.

Normally, a cop will make you drop your gun before anything else. There is usually no way to tell who the bad guy is. If you have a gun, you are a bad guy unless proven otherwise. Innocent until proven guilty does not work in the field.

He scooped the gun from my hand. I let him. I knew the drill.

A gunshot exploded behind us. I jumped, and the cop did, too. He was about my age, but right then I felt about a million years old. We turned and found the first cop shooting into the zombie. The thing had struggled free of his hand. It was on its feet, staggered by the bullets but not stopped.

"Get over here, Brady," the first cop said. The younger cop drew his gun and moved forward. He hesitated, glancing at me.

"Help him," I said.

He nodded and started firing into the zombie. The sound of gunfire was like thunder. It filled the room until my ears were ringing and the reek of gunpowder was almost overpowering. Bullet holes blossomed in the walls. The zombie kept staggering forward. They were just annoying it.

The problem for police is that they can't load up with Glazer Safety Rounds. Most cops don't run into the supernatural as much as I do. Most of the time they're chasing human crooks. The powers that be frown on taking off the leg of John Q. Public just 'cause he fired at you. You're not really supposed to kill people just because they're trying to kill you. Right?

So they had normal rounds, maybe a little silver coating to make the medicine go down, but nothing that could stop a zombie. They were being backed up. One reloaded while the other fired. The thing staggered forward. Its remaining arm sweeping in front of it, searching. For me. Shit.

"My gun's loaded with Glazer Safety Rounds," I said. "Use it."

The first cop said, "Brady, I told you to get her out of here."

"You needed help," Brady said.

"Get the civilian the fuck out of here."

Civilian, me?

Brady didn't question again. He just backed towards me, gun out but not firing. "Come on, miss, we gotta get out of here."

"Give me my gun."

He glanced at me, shook his head.

"I'm with the Regional Preternatural Investigation Team." Which was true. I was hoping he would assume I was a cop, which wasn't true.

He was young. He assumed. He handed me back the Browning. "Thanks."

I moved up with the older cop. "I'm with the Spook Squad."

He glanced at me, gun still trained on the advancing corpse. "Then do something."

Someone had turned on the living-room light. Now that no one was shooting it, the zombie was moving out. It walked like a man striding down the street, except it had no head and only one arm. There was a spring in its step. Maybe it sensed I was close.

The body was in better condition than the first zombie's had been. I could cripple it but not incapacitate it. I'd settle for crippled. I fired a third round into the left leg that I had wounded earlier. I had more time to aim, and my aim was true.

The leg collapsed under it. It pulled itself forward with the one arm, leg pushing against the rug. He was on his last leg. I started to smile, then to laugh, but it choked in my throat. I walked around the far side of the couch. I didn't want any accidents after what I'd seen it do to its own body. I didn't want any crushed limbs.

I came in behind it, and it scrambled quicker than it should have to try to face me. It took two shots for the other leg. I couldn't remember how many bullets I'd used. Did I have one more left, or two, or none?

I felt like Dirty Harry, except that this punk didn't give a damn how many bullets I had left. The dead don't scare easy.

It was still pulling itself and its damaged legs along. That one hand. I fired nearly point-blank, and the hand exploded like a crimson flower on the white carpet. It kept coming, using the wrist stump to push along.

I pulled the trigger, and it clicked empty. Shit. "I'm out," I said. I stepped back away from it. It followed me.

The older cop moved in and grabbed it by both ankles. He pulled it backwards. One leg slid slowly out of the pants and twisted free in his hand. "Fuck!" He dropped the leg. It wiggled like a broken-backed snake.

I stared down at the still determined corpse. It was struggling towards me. It wasn't making much progress. The policeman was holding it one-legged sort of in the air. But the zombie kept trying. It would keep trying until it was incinerated or Dominga Salvador changed her orders.

More uniformed cops came in the door. They fell on the butchered zombie like vultures on a wildebeest. It bucked and struggled. Fought to get away, to finish its mission. To kill me. There were enough cops to subdue it. They would hold it until the lab boys arrived. The lab boys would do what they could on-site. Then the zombie would be incinerated by an exterminator team. They had tried taking zombies down to the morgue and holding them for tests, but little pieces kept escaping and hiding out in the strangest places.

The medical examiner had decreed that all zombies were to be truly dead before shipping. The ambulance crew and lab techs agreed with her. I sympathized but knew that most evidence disappears in a fire. Choices, choices.

I stood to one side of my living room. They had forgotten me in the melee. Fine, I didn't feel like wrestling any more zombies tonight. I realized for the first time that I was wearing nothing but an oversize T-shirt and panties. The T-shirt clung wetly to my body, thick with blood. I started towards the bedroom. I think I meant to get a pair of pants. The sight on the floor stopped me.

The first zombie was like a legless insect. It couldn't move, but it was trying. The bloody stump of a body was still trying to carry out its orders. To kill me.

Dominga Salvador had meant to kill me. Two zombies, one almost new. She had meant to kill me. That one thought chased round my head like a piece of song. We had threatened each other, but why this level of violence? Why kill me? I couldn't stop her legally. She knew that. So why make such a damned serious attempt to kill me?

Maybe because she had something to hide? Dominga had given her word that she hadn't raised the killer zombie, but maybe her word didn't mean anything. It was the only answer. She had something to do with the killer zombie. Had she raised it? Or did she know who had? No. She'd raised the beast or why kill me the night after I talked to her? It was too big a coincidence. Dominga Salvador had raised a zombie, and it had gotten away from her. That was it. Evil as she was, she wasn't psychotic. She wouldn't just raise a killer zombie and let it loose. The great voodoo queen had screwed up royally. That, more than anything else, more than the deaths, or the possible murder charge, would piss her off. She couldn't afford her reputation to be trashed like that.

I stared past the bloody, stinking remnants in the bedroom. My stuffed penguins were covered in blood and worse. Could my long suffering dry cleaner get them clean? He did pretty good with my suits.

Glazer Safety Rounds didn't go through walls. It was another reason I liked them. My neighbors didn't get shot up. The police bullets had pierced the bedroom walls. Neat round holes were everywhere.

No one had ever attacked me at home before, not like this. It should have been against the rules. You should be safe in your own bed. I know, I know. Bad guys don't have rules. It's one of the reasons they're bad guys.

I knew who had raised the zombie. All I had to do was prove it. There was blood everywhere. Blood and worse things. I was actually getting used to the smell. God. But it stank. The whole apartment stank. Almost everything in my apartment is white; walls, carpet, couch, chair. It made the stains show up nicely, like fresh wounds. The bullet holes and cracked plaster board set off the blood nicely.

The apartment was trashed. I would prove Dominga had done this, then, if I was lucky, I'd get to return the favor.

"Sweets to the sweet," I whispered to no one in particular. Tears started to burn at the back of my throat. I didn't want to cry, but a scream was sort of tickling around in my throat, too. Crying or screaming. Crying seemed better.

The paramedics came. One was a short black woman about my own age. "Come on, honey, we got to take a look at you." Her voice was gentle, her hands sort of leading me away from the carnage. I didn't even mind her calling me honey.

I wanted very much to crawl up into someone's lap about now and be comforted. I needed that badly. I wasn't going to get it.

"Honey, we need to see how bad you're bleeding before we take you down to the ambulance."

I shook my head. My voice sounded far away, detached. "It's not my blood."

"What?"

I looked at her, fighting to focus and not drift. Shock was setting in. I'm usually better than this, but hey, we all have our nights.

"It's not my blood. I've got a bite on the shoulder, that's it."

She looked like she didn't believe me. I didn't blame her. Most people see you covered in blood, they just assume part of it has to be yours. They do not take into account that they are dealing with a tough-as-nails vampire slayer and corpse raiser.

The tears were back, stinging just behind my eyes. There was blood all over my penguins. I didn't give a damn about the walls and carpet.

They could be replaced, but I'd collected those damned stuffed toys over years. I let the paramedic lead me away. Tears trickling down my cheeks. I wasn't crying, my eyes were running. My eyes were running because there were pieces of zombie all over my toys. Jesus.

## 17

I'D SEEN ENOUGH crime scenes to know what to expect. It was like a play I'd seen too many times. I could tell you all the entrances, the exits, most of the lines. But this was different. This was my place.

It was silly to be offended that Dominga Salvador had attacked me in my own home. It was stupid, but there it was. She had broken a rule. One I hadn't even known I had. Thou shalt not attack the good guy in his, or her, own home. Shit.

I was going to nail her hide to a tree for it. Yeah, me and what army? Maybe, me and the police.

The living-room curtains billowed in the hot breeze. The glass had been shattered in the firefight. I was glad I had just signed a two-year lease. At least they couldn't kick me out.

Dolph sat across from me in my little kitchen area. The breakfast table with its two straight-backed chairs seemed tiny with him sitting at it. He sort of filled my kitchen. Or maybe I was just feeling small tonight. Or was it morning?

I glanced at my watch. There was a dark, slick smear obscuring the face. Couldn't read it. Would have to chip the damn thing clean. I tucked my arm back inside the blanket the paramedic had given me. My skin was colder than it should have been. Even thoughts of vengeance couldn't warm me. Later, later I would be warm. Later I would be pissed. Right now I was glad to be alive.

"Okay, Anita, what happened?"

I glanced at the living room. It was nearly empty. The zombies had been carried away. Incinerated on the street no less. Entertainment for the entire neighborhood. Family fun.

"Could I change clothes before I give a statement, please?"

He looked at me for maybe a second, then nodded.

"Great." I got up gripping the blanket around me, edges folded carefully. Didn't want to accidentally trip on the ends. I'd embarrassed myself enough for one night.

"Save the T-shirt for evidence," Dolph called.

I said, "Sure thing," without turning around.

They had thrown sheets over the worst of the stains so they didn't track blood all over the apartment building. Nice. The bedroom stank of rotted corpse, stale blood, old death. God. I'd never be able to sleep in here tonight. Even I had my limits.

What I wanted was a shower, but I didn't think Dolph would wait that long. I settled for jeans, socks, and a clean T-shirt. I carried all of it into the bathroom. With the door closed, the smell was very faint. It looked like my bathroom. No disasters here.

I dropped the blanket on the floor with the T-shirt. There was a bulky bandage over my shoulder where the zombie had bitten me. I was lucky it hadn't taken a hunk of flesh. The paramedic warned me to get a tetanus booster. Zombies don't make more zombies by biting, but the dead have nasty mouths. Infection is more of a danger but a tetanus booster is a precaution.

Blood had dried in flaking patches on my legs and arms. I didn't bother washing my hands. I'd shower later. Get everything clean at once.

The T-shirt hung almost to my knees. A huge caricature of Arthur Conan Doyle was on the front. He was peering through a huge magnifying glass, one eye comically large. I gazed into the mirror over the sink, looking at the shirt. It was soft and warm and comforting. Comforting was good right now.

The old T-shirt was ruined. No saving it. But maybe I could save some of the penguins. I ran cold water into the bathtub. If it was a shirt, I'd soak it in cold water. Maybe it worked with toys.

I got a pair of jogging shoes out from under the bed. I didn't really want to walk over the drying stains in only socks. Shoes were made for such occasions. Alright, so the creator of Nike Airs never foresaw walking over drying zombie blood. It's hard to prepare for everything.

Two of the penguins were turning brown as the blood dried. I carried them gingerly into the bathroom and laid them in the water. I pushed them under until they soaked up enough water to stay partially submerged, then I turned the water off. My hands were cleaner. The water wasn't. Blood trailed out of the two soft toys like water squeezed out of a sponge. If these two came clean, I could save them all.

I dried my hands on the blanket. No sense getting blood on anything else.

Sigmund, the penguin I occasionally slept with, was barely spattered. Just a few specks across his fuzzy white belly. Small blessings. I almost tucked him under my arm to hold while I gave a statement. Dolph probably wouldn't tell. I put Sigmund a little farther from the worst stains, as if that would help. Seeing the stupid toy tucked safely in a corner did make me feel better. Great.

Zerbrowski was peering at the aquarium. He glanced my way. "These are the biggest freaking angelfish I've ever seen. You could fry some of 'em up in a pan."

"Leave the fish alone, Zerbrowski," I said.

He grinned. "Sure, just a thought."

Back in the kitchen Dolph sat with his hands folded on the tabletop. His face unreadable. If he was upset that I'd almost cashed it in tonight, he didn't show it. But then Dolph didn't show much of anything, ever. The most emotion I'd ever seen him display was about this case. The killer zombie. Butchered civilians.

"You want some coffee?" I asked.

"Sure."

"Me, too," Zerbrowski said.

"Only if you say please."

He leaned against the wall just outside the kitchen. "Please."

I got a bag of coffee out of the freezer.

"You keep the coffee in the freezer?" Zerbrowski said.

"Hasn't anyone ever fixed real coffee for you?" I asked.

"My idea of gourmet coffee is Taster's Choice."

I shook my head. "Barbarian."

"If you two are finished with clever repartee," Dolph said, "could we start the statement now?" His voice was softer than his words.

I smiled at him and at Zerbrowski. Damned if it wasn't nice to see both of them. I must have been hurt worse than I knew to be happy to see Zerbrowski.

"I was asleep minding my own business when I woke up to find a zombie standing over me." I measured beans and poured them into the little black coffee grinder that I'd bought because it matched the coffee maker.

"What woke you?" Dolph asked.

I pressed the button on the grinder and the rich smell of fresh ground coffee filled the kitchen. Ah, heaven.

"I smelled corpses," I said.

"Explain."

"I was dreaming, and I smelled rotting corpses. It didn't match the dream. It woke me."

"Then what?" He had his ever present notebook out. Pen poised.

I concentrated on each small step to making the coffee and told Dolph everything, including my suspicions about Señora Salvador. The coffee was beginning to perk and fill the apartment with that wonderful smell that coffee always has by the time I finished.

"So you think Dominga Salvador is our zombie raiser?" Dolph said.

"Yes."

He stared at me across the small table. His eyes were very serious. "Can you prove it?"

"No."

He took a deep breath, closing his eyes for a moment. "Great, just great."

"The coffee smells done," Zerbrowski said. He was sitting on the floor, back propped against the kitchen doorway.

I got up and poured the coffee. "If you want sugar or cream, help yourself." I put the cream, real cream, out on the kitchen counter along with the sugar bowl. Zerbrowski took a lot of sugar and a dab of cream. Dolph went for black. It was the way I took it most of the time. Tonight I added cream and sweetened it. Real cream in real coffee. Yum, yum.

"If we could get you inside Dominga's house, could you find proof?" Dolph asked.

"Proof of something, sure, but of raising the killer zombie . . ." I shook my head. "If she did raise it and it got away, then she won't want to be tied to it. She'll have destroyed all the proof, just to save face."

"I want her for this," Dolph said.

"Me, too."

"She might also try and kill you again," Zerbrowski said from the doorway. He was blowing on his coffee to cool it.

"No joke," I said.

"You think she'll try again?" Dolph asked.

"Probably. How the hell did two zombies get inside my apartment?"

"Someone picked the lock," Dolph said. "Could the zombie . . ."

"No, a zombie would rip a door off its hinges, but it wouldn't take the time to pick a lock. Even if it had the fine motor skill to do it."

"So someone with skill opened the door and let them in," Dolph said.

"Appears so," I said.

"Any ideas on that?"

"I would bet one of her bodyguards. Her grandson Antonio or maybe Enzo. A big guy in his forties who seems to be her personal protection. I don't know if either of them have the skill, but they'd do it. Enzo, but not Antonio."

"Why cross him off?"

"If Tony had let the zombies in, he'd have stayed and watched."

"You sure?"

I shrugged. "He's that kind of guy. Enzo would do business and leave. He'd follow orders. The grandson wouldn't."

Dolph nodded. "There's a lot of heat from upstairs to solve this case. I think I can get us a search warrant in forty-eight hours."

"Two days is a long time, Dolph."

"Two days without one piece of proof, Anita. Except for your word. I'm going out on a limb for this one."

"She's in it, Dolph, somehow. I don't know why, and I don't know what could have caused her to lose control of the zombie, but she's in it."

"I'll get the warrant," he said.

"One of the brothers in blue said you told him you were a cop," Zerbrowski said.

"I told him I was with your squad. I never said I was a cop."

Zerbrowski grinned. "Mmm-huh."

"Will you be safe here tonight?" Dolph asked.

"I think so. The Señora doesn't want to get on the bad side of the law. They treat renegade witches sort of like renegade vampires. It's an automatic death sentence."

"Because people are too scared of them," Dolph said.

"Because some witches can slip through the fucking bars."

"How about voodoo queens?" Zerbrowski said.

I shook my head. "I don't want to know."

"We better go, leave you to get some sleep," Dolph said. He left his empty coffee cup on the table. Zerbrowski hadn't finished his, but he put it on the counter and followed Dolph out.

I walked them to the door.

"I'll let you know when we get the warrant," Dolph said.

"Could you arrange for me to see Peter Burke's personal effects?"

"Why?"

"There are only two ways to lose control of a zombie this badly. One, you are strong enough to raise it, but not to control it. Dominga can control anything she can raise. Second, someone of near equal power interferes, sort of a challenge." I stared up at Dolph. "John Burke might just be strong enough to have done it. Maybe if I'm helpful enough to take John down to go over his brother's effects—you know, does any of this look out of place, that type of thing—maybe this Burke will let something slip."

"You've already got Dominga Salvador pissed at you, Anita. Isn't that enough for one week?"

"For one lifetime," I said. "But it's something we can do while we wait for the warrant."

Dolph nodded. "Yeah. I'll arrange it. Call Mr. Burke tomorrow morning and set up a time. Then call me."

"Will do."

Dolph hesitated in the doorway for a moment. "Watch your back."

"Always," I said.

Zerbrowski leaned into me and said, "Nice penguins." He followed Dolph down the hallway. I knew the next time I saw the rest of the spook squad they'd all know I collected toy penguins. My secret was out. Zerbrowski would spread it far and wide. At least, he was consistent.

It was nice to know something was.

# 18

STUFFED ANIMALS ARE not meant to be submerged in water. The two in the bathtub were ruined. Maybe spot remover? The smell was thick and seemed permanent. I put an emergency message on my cleaning service's answering machine. I didn't give a lot of details. Didn't want to frighten them off.

I packed an overnight bag. Two changes of clothes and one penguin with his tummy freshly scrubbed, Harold Gaynor's file, and I was set. I also packed both guns: the Firestar in its inner pants holster; the Browning under my arm. A windbreaker hid the Browning from view. I had extra ammo in the jacket pockets. Between both guns I had twenty-two bullets. Twenty-two bullets. Why didn't I feel safe?

Unlike most walking dead, zombies can bear the touch of sunlight. They don't like it, but they can exist with it. Dominga could order a zombie to kill me in daylight just as easily as moonlight. She wouldn't be able to raise the dead during daylight, but if she planned it right, she could raise the dead the night before and send it out to get me the next day. A voodoo priestess with executive planning skills. It would be just my luck.

I didn't really believe that Dominga had backup zombies waiting to jump me. But somehow I was feeling paranoid this morning. Paranoia is just another word for longevity.

I stepped out into the quiet hallway, glancing both ways as if it were a street. Nothing. No walking corpses hiding in the shadows. No one but us fraidy-cats. The only sound was the hush of the air-conditioning. The hallway had that feel to it. I came home often enough at dawn to know the quality of silence. I thought about that for a minute. I knew it was almost dawn. Not by clock or window, but on some level deeper than that. Some instinct that an ancestor had found while hiding in a dark cave, praying for light.

Most people fear the dark in a vague way. They fear what might be out there. I raise the dead. I've slain over a dozen vampires. I know what's out there in the dark. And I am terrified of it. People are supposed to fear the unknown, but ignorance is bliss when knowledge is so damn frightening.

I knew what would have happened to me if I had failed last night. If I had been slower or a worse shot. Two years ago there had been three murders. Nothing connected them except the method of death. They had been torn apart by zombies. They had not been eaten. Normal zombies don't eat anything. They may bite a time or two, but that's the worst of it. There had been the man whose throat was crushed, but that had been accidental. The zombie just bit down on the nearest body part. It happened to be a killing blow. Blind luck.

A zombie will normally just wrestle you to pieces. Like a small boy tearing pieces off of a fly.

Raising a zombie for the purposes of being a murder weapon is an automatic death sentence. The court system has gotten rather quick on the draw the last few years. A death sentence meant what it said these days. Especially if your crime was supernatural in some way. You didn't burn witches anymore. You electrocuted them.

If we could get proof, the state would kill Dominga Salvador for me. John Burke, too, if we could prove he had knowingly caused the zombie to go ape-shit. The trouble with supernatural crimes is proving them in court. Most juries aren't up on the latest spells and incantations. Heck, neither am I. But I've tried explaining zombies and vampires in court before. I've learned to keep it simple and to add any gory details the defense will allow me. A jury appreciates a little vicarious adventure.

Most testimony is terribly boring or heartbreaking. I try to be interesting. It's a change of pace.

The parking area was dark. Stars still glimmered overhead. But they were fading like candles in a steady wind. I could taste dawn on the air. Roll it around on my tongue. Maybe it's all the vampire hunting I do, but I was more attuned to the passage of light and dark than I had been four years ago. I hadn't been able to taste the dawn.

Of course my nightmares were a lot less interesting four years ago. You gain something, you lose something else. It's the way life works.

It was after 5:00 A.M. when I got in my car and headed out for the nearest hotel. I wouldn't be able to stand my apartment until the cleaning crew got the smell out. If they could get the smell out. My landlord was not going to be pleased if they couldn't.

He was going to be even less pleased with the bullet holes and shattered window. Replace the window. Replaster the walls, maybe? I really didn't know what you did to repair bullet holes? Here I was hoping my lease couldn't be challenged in court.

The first hint of dawn was slipping over the eastern sky. A pure white light that spread like ice over the darkness. Most people think dawn is as colorful as sunset but the first color of dawn is white, a pure not-color, that is almost an absence of night.

There was a motel, but all its rooms were on one or two stories, some of them awfully isolated. I wanted a crowd. I settled on The Stouffer Concourse which wasn't terribly cheap but it would force zombies to ride up in elevators. People tended to notice the smell in an elevator. The Stouffer Concourse also had room service at this ungodly hour of dawn. I needed room service. Coffee, give me coffee.

The clerk gave me that wide-eyed-I'm-too-polite-to-say-it-out-loud look. The elevators were mirrored, and I had nothing to do for several floors but look at my reflection. Blood had dried in a stiff darkness in my hair. A stain went down the right side of my face just below the hairline and trailed down my neck. I hadn't noticed it in the mirror at home. Shock will make you forget things.

It wasn't the bloodstains that had made the clerk look askance. Unless you knew what to look for, you wouldn't know it was blood. No, the problem was that my skin was deathly pale, like clean paper. My eyes that are perfectly brown looked black. They were huge and dark and . . . strange. Startled, I looked startled. Surprised to be alive. Maybe. I was still fighting off the edge of shock. No matter how together I felt, my face told a different story. When the shock wore off, I'd be able to sleep. Until then, I'd read Gaynor's file.

The room had two double beds. More room than I needed, but what the heck. I got out clean clothes, put the Firestar in the drawer of the nightstand, and took the Browning into the bathroom with me. If I was careful and didn't turn the shower on full blast, I could fasten the shoulder holster to the towel rack in the back of the stall. It wouldn't even get wet. Though truthfully with most modern guns, wet doesn't hurt them. As long as you clean them afterwards. Most guns will shoot underwater.

I called room service wearing nothing but a towel. I'd almost forgotten. I ordered a pot of coffee, sugar, and cream. They asked if I wanted decaf. I said no thank you. Pushy. Like waiters asking if I wanted a diet Coke when I didn't ask for it. They never ask men, even portly men, if they want diet Cokes.

I could drink a pot of caffeine and sleep like a baby. It doesn't keep me awake or make me jumpy. It just tastes better.

Yes, they would leave the cart outside the door. No, they wouldn't knock. They would add the coffee to my bill. That was fine, I said. They had a credit card number. When they have plastic, people are always eager to add on to your bill. As long as the limit holds.

I propped the straight-backed chair under the doorknob to the hallway. If someone forced the door, I'd hear it. Maybe. I locked the bathroom door and had a gun in the shower with me. I was as secure as I was going to get.

There is something about being naked that makes me feel vulnerable. I would much rather face bad guys with my clothes on than off. I guess everyone's like that.

The bite on my shoulder with its thick bandage was a problem when I wanted to wash my hair. I had to get the blood out, bandage or no bandage.

I used their little bottles of shampoo and conditioner. They smelled like flowers are supposed to smell but never do. Blood had dried in patches on my body. I looked spotted. The water that washed down the drain was pinkish.

It took the entire bottle of shampoo before my hair was squeaky clean. The last rinse water soaked through the bandage on my right shoulder. The pain was sharp and persistent. I'd have to remember to get that tetanus booster.

I scrubbed my body with a washcloth and the munchkin bar of soap. When I had washed and soaked every inch of myself, and was as clean as I was going to get, I stood under the hot needling spray. I let the water pour over my back, down my body. The bandage had soaked through long ago.

What if we couldn't tie Dominga to the zombies? What if we couldn't find proof? She'd try again. Her pride was at stake now. She had set two zombies on me, and I had wasted them both. With a little help from the police. Dominga Salvador would see it as a personal challenge.

She had raised a zombie and it had escaped her control completely. She would rather have innocent people slaughtered than to admit her mistake. And she would rather kill me than have me prove it. Vindictive bitch.

Señora Salvador had to be stopped. If the warrant didn't help, then I'd have to be more practical. She'd made it clear that it was her or me. I preferred it to be her. And if necessary, I'd make sure of it.

I opened my eyes and turned off the water. I didn't want to think about it anymore. I was talking about murder. I saw it as self-defense, but I doubted a jury would. It'd be damn hard to prove. I wanted several things. Dominga out of the picture, dead or in jail. To stay alive. Not to be in jail on a murder charge. To catch the killer zombie before it killed again. Fat chance that. To figure out how John Burke fit into this mess.

Oh, and to keep Harold Gaynor from forcing me to perform human sacrifice. Yeah, I almost forgot that one.

It had been a busy week.

The coffee was outside the door on a little tray. I set it inside on the floor, locked the door, and put the chair against the doorknob again. Only then did I set the coffee tray on a small table by the curtained windows. The Browning was already sitting on the table, naked. The shoulder holster was on the bed.

I opened the drapes. Normally, I would have kept the drapes closed, but today I wanted to see the light. Morning had spread like a soft haze of light. The heat hadn't had time to creep up and strangle that first gentle touch of morning.

The coffee wasn't bad, but it wasn't great either. Of course, the worst coffee I've ever had was still wonderful. Well, maybe not the coffee at police headquarters. But even that was better than nothing. Coffee was my comfort drink. Better than alcohol, I guess.

I spread Gaynor's file on the table and started to read. By eight that morning, earlier than I usually get up, I had read every scribbled note, gazed at every blurry picture. I knew more about Mr. Harold Gaynor than I wanted to, none of it particularly helpful.

Gaynor was mob-connected, but it couldn't be proven. He was a self-made multimillionaire. Bully for him. He could afford the million five that Tommy had offered me. Nice to know a man can pay his bills.

His only family had been a mother who died ten years ago. His father was supposed to have died before he was born. There was no record of the father's death. In fact, the father didn't seem to exist.

An illegitimate birth, carefully disguised? Maybe. So Gaynor was a bastard in the original definition of the word. So what? I'd already known he was one in spirit.

I propped Wheelchair Wanda's picture against the coffeepot. She was smiling, almost like she'd known the picture was being taken. Maybe she was just photogenic. There were two pictures with her and Gaynor together. In one they were smiling, holding hands as Tommy pushed Gaynor's wheelchair and Bruno pushed Wanda. She was gazing at Gaynor with a look I had seen in other women. Adoration, love. I'd even experienced it myself for a brief time in college. You get over it.

The second picture was almost identical to the first. Bruno and Tommy pushing them. But they weren't holding hands. Gaynor was smiling. Wanda wasn't. She looked angry. Cicely of the blond hair and empty eyes was walking on the other side of Gaynor. They were holding hands. Ah-ha.

So Gaynor had kept both of them around for a while. Why had Wanda left? Jealousy? Had Cicely arranged it? Had Gaynor tired of her? The only way to know was to ask.

I stared at the picture with Cicely in it. I put it beside the laughing close-up of Wanda's face. An unhappy young woman, a scorned lover. If she hated Gaynor more than she feared him, Wanda would talk to me. She would be a fool to talk to the papers, but I didn't want to publish her secrets. I wanted Gaynor's secrets, so I could keep him from hurting me. Barring that, I wanted something to take to the police.

Mr. Gaynor would have other things to worry about if I could get him in jail. He might forget all about one reluctant animator. Unless, of course, he found out I'd had something to do with him being arrested. That would be bad. Gaynor struck me as vengeful. I had Dominga Salvador mad at me. I didn't need anyone else.

I closed the drapes and left a wake-up call for noon. Irving would just have to wait for his file. I had unintentionally given him the interview with the new Master of the City. Surely that cut me a little slack. If not, to hell with it. I was going to bed.

The last thing I did before going to bed was call Peter Burke's house. I figured that John would be staying there. It rang five times before the machine kicked on. "This is Anita Blake, I may have some information for John Burke on a matter we discussed Thursday." The message was a little vague, but I didn't want to leave a message saying, "Call me about your brother's murder." It would have seemed melodramatic and cruel.

I left the hotel's number as well as my own. Just in case. They probably had the ringers turned off. I would. The story had been front page because Peter was, had been, an animator. Animators don't get murdered much in the run-of-the-mill muggings. It's usually something more unusual.

I would drop off Gaynor's file on the way home. I wanted to drop it off at the receptionist desk. I didn't feel like talking to Irving about his big interview. I didn't want to hear that Jean-Claude was charming or had great plans for the city. He'd be very careful what he told a reporter. It would look good in print. But I knew the truth. Vampires are as much a monster as any zombie, maybe worse. Vamps usually volunteer for the process, zombies don't.

Just like Irving volunteered to go off with Jean-Claude. Of course, if Irving hadn't been with me the Master would have left him alone. Probably. So it was my fault, even if it had been his choice. I was achingly tired, but I knew I'd never be able to sleep until I heard Irving's voice. I could pretend I'd called to tell him I was dropping the file off late.

I wasn't sure if Irving would be on his way to work or not. I tried home first. He answered on the first ring.

"Hello."

Something tight in my stomach relaxed. "Hi, Irving, it's me."

"Ms. Blake, to what do I owe this early morning pleasure?" His voice sounded so ordinary.

"I had a bit of excitement at my apartment last night. I was hoping I could drop the file off later in the day."

"What sort of excitement?" His voice had that "tell me" lilt to it.

"The kind that's police business and not yours," I said.

"I thought you'd say that," he said. "You just getting to bed?"

"Yeah."

"I guess I can let a hardworking animator sleep in a little. My sister reporter may even understand."

"Thanks, Irving."

"You alright, Anita?"

No, I wanted to say, but I didn't. I ignored the question. "Did Jean-Claude behave himself?"

"He was great!" Irving's enthusiasm was genuine, all bubbly excitement. "He's a great interview." He was quiet for a moment. "Hey, you called to check up on me. To make sure I was okay."

"Did not," I said.

"Thanks, Anita, that means a lot. But really, he was very civilized."

"Great. I'll let you go then. Have a good day."

"Oh, I will, my editor is doing cartwheels about the exclusive interview with the Master of the City."

I had to laugh at the way he rolled the title off his tongue. "Good night, Irving."

"Get some sleep, Blake. I'll be calling you in a day or two about those zombie articles."

"Talk to you then," I said. We hung up.

Irving was fine. I should worry more about myself and less about everyone else.

I turned off the lights and cuddled under the sheets. My penguin was cradled in my arms. The Browning Hi-Power was under my pillow. It wasn't as easy to get to as the bed holster at home, but it was better than nothing.

I wasn't sure which was more comforting, the penguin or the gun. I guess both were equally comforting, for very different reasons.

I said my prayers like a good little girl. I asked very sincerely that I not dream.

## 19

THE CLEANING CREW had a cancellation and moved my emergency into the slot. By afternoon my apartment was clean and smelled like spring cleaning. Apartment maintenance had replaced the shattered window. The bullet holes had been smeared with white paint. The holes looked like little dimples in the wall. All in all, the place looked great.

John Burke had not returned my call. Maybe I'd been too clever. I'd try a more blunt message later. But right at this moment I had more pleasant things to worry about.

I was dressed for jogging. Dark blue shorts with white piping, white Nikes with pale blue swishes, cute little jogging socks, and tank top. The shorts were the kind with one of those inside pockets that shut with Velcro. Inside the pocket was a derringer. An American derringer to be exact; 6.5 ounces, .38 Special, 4.82 total length. At 6.5 ounces, it felt like a lumpy feather.

A Velcro pocket was not conducive to a fast draw. Two shots and spitting would be more accurate at a distance, but then Gaynor's men didn't want to kill me. Hurt me, but not kill me. They have to get in close to hurt me. Close enough to use the derringer. Of course, that was just two shots. After that, I was in trouble.

I had tried to figure out a way to carry one of my 9mms, but there was no way. I could not jog and tote around that much firepower. Choices, choices.

Veronica Sims was standing in my living room. Ronnie is five-nine, blond hair, grey eyes. She is a private investigator on retainer to Animators, Inc. We also work out together at least twice a week unless one of us is out of town, injured, or up to our necks in vampires. Those last two happen more often than I would like.

She was wearing French-cut purple shorts, and a T-shirt that said, "Outside of a dog, a book is man's best friend. Inside of a dog, it's too dark to read." There are reasons why Ronnie and I are friends.

"I missed you Thursday at the health club," she said. "Was the funeral awful?"

"Yeah."

She didn't ask me to elaborate. She knows funerals are not my best thing. Most people hate funerals because of the dead. I hate all the emotional shit.

She was stretching long legs parallel to her body, low on the floor. In a sort of stretching crouch. We always warm up in the apartment. Most leg stretches were never meant to be done while wearing short shorts.

I mirrored her movement. The muscles in my upper thighs moved and protested. The derringer was an uncomfortable but endurable lump.

"Just out of curiosity," Ronnie said, "why do you feel it necessary to take a gun with you?"

"I always carry a gun," I said.

She just looked at me, disgust plain in her eyes. "If you don't want to tell me, then don't, but don't bullshit me."

"Alright, alright," I said. "Strangely enough, no one's told me not to tell anyone."

"What, no threats about not going to the police?" she asked.

"Nope."

"My, how terribly friendly."

"Not friendly," I said, sitting flat on the floor, legs out at angles. Ronnie mirrored me. It looked like we were going to roll a ball across the floor. "Not friendly at all." I leaned my upper body over my left leg until my cheek touched my thigh.

"Tell me about it," she said.

I did. When I was done, we were limbered and ready to run.

"Shit, Anita. Zombies in your apartment and a mad millionaire after you to perform human sacrifices." Her grey eyes searched my face. "You're the only person I know who has weirder problems than I do."

"Thanks a lot," I said. I locked my door behind us and put my keys in the pocket along with the derringer. I know it would scratch hell out of it, but what was I supposed to do, run with the keys in my hand?

"Harold Gaynor. I could do some checking on him for you."

"Aren't you on a case?" We clattered down the stairs.

"I'm doing about three different insurance scams. Mostly surveillance and photography. If I have to eat one more fastfood dinner, I'm going to start singing jingles."

I smiled. "Shower and change at my place. We'll go out for a real dinner."

"Sounds great, but you don't want to keep Jean-Claude waiting."

"Cut it out, Ronnie," I said.

She shrugged. "You should stay as far away from that . . . creature as you can, Anita."

"I know it." It was my turn to shrug. "Agreeing to meet him seemed the lesser of evils."

"What were your choices?"

"Meeting him voluntarily or being kidnapped and taken to him."

"Great choices."

"Yeah."

I opened the double doors that led outside. The heat smacked me in the face. It was staggeringly hot, like stepping into an oven. And we were going to jog in this?

I looked up at Ronnie. She is six inches taller than I am, and most of that is leg. We can run together, but I have to set the pace and I have to push myself. It is a very good workout. "It has to be over a hundred today," I said.

"No pain, no gain," Ronnie said. She was carrying a sport water bottle in her left hand. We were as prepared as we were going to get.

"Four miles in hell," I said. "Let's do it." We set off at a slow pace, but it was steady. We usually finished the run in a half hour or less.

The air was solid with heat. It felt like we were running through semisolid walls of scalding air. The humidity in St. Louis is almost always around a hundred percent. Combine the humidity with hundred-plus temperatures and you get a small, damp slice of hell. St. Louis in the summertime, yippee.

I do not enjoy exercise. Slim hips and muscular calves are not incentive enough for this kind of abuse. Being able to outrun the bad guys is incentive. Sometimes it all comes down to who is faster, stronger, quicker. I am in the wrong business. Oh, I'm not complaining. But 106 pounds is not a lot of muscle to throw around.

Of course, when it comes to vampires, I could be two-hundred-plus of pure human muscles and it wouldn't do me a damn bit of good. Even the newly dead can bench press cars with one hand. So I'm outclassed. I've gotten used to it.

The first mile was behind us. It always hurts the worst. My body takes about two miles to be convinced it can't talk me out of this insanity.

We were moving through an older neighborhood. Lots of small fenced yards and houses dating to the fifties, or even the 1800s. There was the smooth brick wall of a warehouse that dated to pre-Civil War. It was our halfway point. Two miles. I was feeling loose and muscled, like I could run forever, if I didn't have to do it very fast. I was concentrating on moving my body through the heat, keeping the rhythm. It was Ronnie who spotted the man.

"I don't mean to be an alarmist," she said, "but why is that man just standing there?"

I squinted ahead of us. Maybe fifteen feet ahead of us the brick wall ended and there was a tall elm tree. A man was standing near the trunk of the tree. He wasn't trying to conceal himself. But he was wearing a jean jacket. It was much too hot for that, unless you had a gun under it.

"How long's he been there?"

"Just stepped out from around the tree," she said.

Paranoia reigns supreme. "Let's turn back. It's two miles either way."

Ronnie nodded.

We pivoted and started jogging back the other way. The man behind us did not cry out or say stop. Paranoia, it was a vicious disease.

A second man stepped out from the far corner of the brick wall. We jogged towards him a few more steps. I glanced back. Mr. Jean Jacket was casually walking towards us. The jacket was unbuttoned, and his hand was reaching under his arm. So much for paranoia.

"Run," I said.

The second man pulled a gun from his jacket pocket.

We stopped running. It seemed like a good idea at the time.

"Un-uh," the man said, "I don't feel like chasing anyone in this heat. All ya gotta be is alive, chickie, anything else is gravy." The gun was a .22 caliber automatic. Not much stopping power, but it was perfect for wounding. They'd thought this out. That was scary.

Ronnie was standing very stiff beside me. I fought the urge to grab her hand and squeeze it, but that wouldn't be very tough-as-nails vampire slayer, would it? "What do you want?"

"That's better," he said. A pale blue T-shirt gapped where his beer gut spilled over his belt. But his arms had a beefy look to them. He may have been overweight, but I bet it hurt when he hit you. I hoped I didn't have to test the theory.

I backed up so the brick wall was to my back. Ronnie moved with me. Mr. Jean Jacket was almost with us now. He had a Beretta 9mm loose in his right hand. It was not meant for wounding.

I glanced at Ronnie, then at Fatty who was nearly right beside her. I glanced at Mr. Jean Jacket, who was nearly beside me. I glanced back at Ronnie. Her eyes widened just a bit. She licked her lips once, then turned back to stare at Fatty. The guy with the Beretta was mine. Ronnie got the .22. Delegation at its best.

"What do you want?" I said again. I hate repeating myself.

"You to come take a little ride with us, that's all." Fatty smiled as he said it.

I smiled back, then turned to Jean Jacket, and his tame Beretta. "Don't you talk?"

"I talk," he said. He took two steps closer to me, but his gun was very steadily pointed at my chest. "I talk real good." He touched my hair, lightly, with his fingertips. The Beretta was damn near pressed against me. If he pulled the trigger now, it was all over. The dull black barrel of the gun was getting bigger. Illusion, but the longer you stare at a gun, the more important it gets to be. When you're on the wrong end of it.

"None of that, Seymour," Fatty said. "No pussy and we can't kill her, those are the rules."

"Shit, Pete."

Pete, alias Fatty, said, "You can have the blonde. No one said we couldn't have fun with her."

I did not look at Ronnie. I stared at Seymour. I had to be ready if I got that one second chance. Glancing at my friend to see how she was taking the news of her impending rape was not going to help. Really.

"Phallic power, Ronnie. It always goes to the gonads," I said.

Seymour frowned. "What the hell does that mean?"

"It means, Seymour, that I think you're stupid and what brains you have are in your balls." I smiled pleasantly while I said it.

He hit me with the flat of his hand, hard. I staggered but didn't go down. The gun was still steady, unwavering. Shit. He made a sound deep in his throat and hit me, closed fist. I went down. For a moment I lay on the gritty sidewalk, listening to the blood pound in my ears. The slap had stung. The closed fist hurt.

Someone kicked me in the ribs. "Leave her alone!" Ronnie screamed.

I lay on my stomach and pretended to be hurt. It wasn't hard. I groped for the Velcro pocket. Seymour was waving the Beretta in Ronnie's face. She was screaming at him. Pete had grabbed Ronnie's arms and was trying to hold her. Things were getting out of hand. Goody.

I stared up at Seymour's legs and struggled to my knees. I shoved the derringer into his groin. He froze and stared down at me.

"Don't move, or I'll serve up your balls on a plate," I said.

Ronnie drove her elbow back into Fatty's solar plexus. He bent over a little, hands going to his stomach. She twisted away and kneed him hard in the face. Blood spurted from his nose. He staggered back. She smashed him in the side of the face, getting all her shoulder and upper body into it. He fell down. She had the .22 in her hand.

I fought an urge to yell "Yea Ronnie," but it didn't sound tough enough. We'd do high-fives later. "Tell your friend not to move, Seymour, or I'll pull this trigger."

He swallowed loud enough for me to hear it. "Don't move, Pete, okay?"

Pete just stared at us.

"Ronnie, please get Seymour's gun from him. Thank you."

I was still kneeling in the gravel with the derringer pressed into the man's groin. He let Ronnie take his gun without a fight. Fancy that.

"I've got this one covered, Anita," Ronnie said. I didn't glance at her. She would do her job. I would do mine.

"Seymour, this is a .38 Special, two shots. It can hold a variety of ammunition, .22, .44, or .357 Magnum." This was a lie, the new light-weight version couldn't hold anything higher than .38s, but I was betting Seymour couldn't tell the difference. "Forty-four or .357 and you can kiss the family jewels good-bye. Twenty-two, maybe you'll just be very, very sore. To quote a role model of mine, 'Do you feel lucky today?' "

"What do you want, man, what do you want?" His voice was high and squeaky with fear.

"Who hired you to come after us?"

He shook his head. "No, man, he'll kill us."

"Three-fifty-seven Magnum makes a fucking big hole, Seymour."

"Don't tell her shit," Pete said.

"If he says anything else, Ronnie, shoot his kneecap off," I said.

"My pleasure," Ronnie said. I wondered if she would really do it. I wondered if I'd tell her to do it. Better not to find out.

"Talk to me, Seymour, now, or I pull the trigger." I shoved the gun a little deeper. That must have hurt all on its own. He sort of tried to tippy-toe.

"God, please don't."

"Who hired you?"

"Bruno."

"You asshole, Seymour," Pete said. "He'll kill us."

"Ronnie, please shoot him," I said.

"You said the kneecap, right?"

"Yeah."

"How about an elbow instead?" she asked.

"Your choice," I said.

"You're crazy," Seymour said.

"Yeah," I said, "you remember that. What exactly did Bruno tell you?"

"He said to take you to a building off Grand, on Washington. He said to bring you both, but we could hurt the blonde to get you to come along."

"Give me the address," I said.

Seymour did. I think he would have told me the secret ingredient in the magic sauce if I had asked.

"If you go down there, Bruno will know we told ya," Pete said.

"Ronnie," I said.

"Shoot me now, chickie, it don't matter. You go down there or send the police down there, we are dead."

I glanced at Pete. He seemed very sincere. They were bad guys but . . . "Okay, we won't bust in on him."

"We aren't going to the police," Ronnie asked.

"No, if we did that, we might as well kill them now. But we don't have to do that, do we, Seymour?"

"No, man, no."

"How much ol' Bruno pay you?"

"Four hundred apiece."

"It wasn't enough," I said.

"You're telling me."

"I'm going to get up now, Seymour, and leave your balls where they are. Don't come near me or Ronnie again, or I'll tell Bruno you sold him out."

"He'd kill us, man. He'd kill us slow."

"That's right, Seymour. We'll just all pretend this never happened, right?" He was nodding vigorously.

"That okay with you, Pete?" I asked.

"I ain't stupid. Bruno'd rip out our hearts and feed them to us. We won't talk." He sounded disgusted.

I got up and stepped carefully away from Seymour. Ronnie covered

Pete nice and steady with the Beretta. The .22 was tucked into the waistband of her jogging shorts. "Get out of here," I said.

Seymour's skin was pasty, and a sick sweat beaded his face. "Can I have my gun?" He wasn't very bright.

"Don't get cute," I said.

Pete stood. The blood under his nose had started to dry. "Come on, Seymour. We gotta go now."

They moved on down the street side by side. Seymour looked hunched in upon himself as if he were fighting an urge to clutch his equipment.

Ronnie let out a great whoosh of air and leaned back against the wall. The gun was still clutched in her right hand. "My God," she said.

"Yeah," I said.

She touched my face where Seymour had hit me. It hurt. I winced. "Are you all right?" Ronnie asked.

"Sure," I said. Actually, it felt like the side of my face was one great big ache, but it wouldn't make it hurt any less to say it out loud.

"Are we going down to the building where they were to drop us?"

"No."

"Why not?"

"I know who Bruno is and who gives him orders. I know why they tried to kidnap me. What could I possibly learn that would be worth two lives?"

Ronnie thought about that for a moment. "You're right, I guess. But you aren't going to report the attack to the police?"

"Why should I? I'm okay, you're okay. Seymour and Pete won't be back."

She shrugged. "You didn't really want me to shoot his kneecap off, did you? I mean we were playing good cop, bad cop, right?" She looked at me very steadily as she asked, her solid grey eyes earnest and true.

I looked away. "Let's walk back home. I don't feel much like jogging."

"Me either."

We set off walking down the street. Ronnie untucked her T-shirt and stuck the Beretta in the waistband. The .22 she sort of cupped in her hand. It wasn't very noticeable that way.

"We were pretending, right? Being tough, right?"

Truth. "I don't know."

"Anita!"

"I don't know, that's the truth."

"I couldn't have shot him to pieces just to keep him from talking."

"Good thing you didn't have to then," I said.

"Would you really have pulled the trigger on that man?"

There was a cardinal singing somewhere off in the distance. The song filled the stale heat and made it seem cooler.

"Answer me, Anita. Would you really have pulled the trigger?"

"Yes."

"Yes?" There was a lilt of surprise in her voice.

"Yes."

"Shit." We walked on in silence for a minute or two, then she asked, "What ammo is in the gun today?"

"Thirty-eights."

"It would have killed him."

"Probably," I said.

I saw her look at me sideways as we walked back. There was a look I'd seen before. A mixture of horror and admiration. I'd just never seen it on a friend's face before. That part hurt. But we went out to dinner that night at The Miller's Daughter in Old St. Charles. The atmosphere was pleasant. The food wonderful. As always.

We talked and laughed and had a very good time. Neither of us mentioned what had happened this afternoon. Pretend hard enough and maybe it will go away.

# 20

AT 10:30 THAT night I was down in the vampire district. Dark blue polo shirt, jeans, red windbreaker. The windbreaker hid the shoulder holster and the Browning Hi-Power. Sweat was pooling in the bends of my arms but it beat the hell out of not having it.

The afternoon fun and games had turned out all right, but that was partly luck. And Seymour losing his temper. And me being able to take a beating and keep on ticking. Ice had kept the swelling down, but the left side of my face was puffy and red, as if some sort of fruit was about to burst out of it. No bruise—yet.

The Laughing Corpse was one of the newest clubs in the District. Vampires are sexy. I'll admit that. But funny? I don't think so. Apparently, I was in the minority. A line stretched away from the club, curling round the block.

It hadn't occurred to me that I'd need a ticket or reservations or whatever just to get in. But, hey, I knew the boss. I walked along the line of people towards the ticket booth. The people were mostly young. The women in dresses, the men in dressy sports wear, with an occasional suit. They were chatting together in excited voices, a lot of casual hand and arm touching. Dates. I remember dates. It's just been a while. Maybe if I wasn't always ass deep in alligators, I'd date more. Maybe.

I cut ahead of a double-date foursome. "Hey," one man said.

"Sorry," I said.

The woman in the ticket booth frowned at me. "You can't just cut in line like that, ma'am."

Ma'am? "I don't want a ticket. I don't want to see the show. I am supposed to meet Jean-Claude here. That's it."

"Well, I don't know. How do I know you're not some reporter?"

Reporter? I took a deep breath. "Just call Jean-Claude and tell him Anita is here. Okay?"

She was still frowning at me.

"Look, just call Jean-Claude. If I'm a nosy reporter, he'll deal with me. If I'm who I say I am, he'll be happy that you called him. You can't lose."

"I don't know."

I fought an urge to scream at her. It probably wouldn't help. Probably. "Just call Jean-Claude, pretty please," I said.

Maybe it was the pretty please. She swiveled on her stool and opened the upper half of a door in the back of the booth. Small booth. I couldn't hear what she said, but she swiveled back around. "Okay, manager says you can go in."

"Great, thanks." I walked up the steps. The entire line of waiting people glared at me. I could feel their hot stares on my back. But I've been stared at by experts, so I was careful not to flinch. No one likes a line jumper.

The club was dim inside, as most clubs are. A guy just inside the door said, "Ticket, please?"

I stared up at him. He wore a white T-shirt that said, "The Laughing Corpse, it's a scream." A caricature of an open-mouthed vampire was drawn very large across his chest. He was large and muscled and had bouncer tattooed across his forehead. "Ticket, please," he repeated.

First the ticket lady, now the ticket man? "The manager said I could come through to see Jean-Claude," I said.

"Willie," the ticket man said, "you send her through?"

I turned around, and there was Willie McCoy. I smiled when I saw him. I was glad to see him. That surprised me. I'm not usually happy to see dead men.

Willie is short, thin, with black hair slicked back from his forehead.

I couldn't tell the exact color of his suit in the dimness, but it looked like a dull tomato-red. White button-up shirt, large shiny green tie. I had to look twice before I was sure, but yes, there was a glow-in-the-dark hula girl on his tie. It was the most tasteful outfit I'd ever seen Willie wear.

He grinned, flashing a lot of fang. "Anita, good to see ya."

I nodded. "You, too, Willie."

"Really?"

"Yeah."

He grinned even wider. His canines glistened in the dim light. He hadn't been dead a year yet.

"How long have you been manager here?" I asked.

" 'Bout two weeks."

"Congratulations."

He stepped closer to me. I stepped back. Instinctive. Nothing personal, but a vampire is a vampire. Don't get too close. Willie was new dead, but he was still capable of hypnotizing with his eyes. Okay, maybe no vampire as new as Willie could actually catch me with his eyes, but old habits die hard.

Willie's face fell. A flicker of something in his eyes—hurt? He dropped his voice but didn't try to step next to me. He was a faster study dead than he ever had been alive. "Thanks to me helping you last time, I'm in real good with the boss."

He sounded like an old gangster movie, but that was Willie. "I'm glad Jean-Claude's doing right by you."

"Oh, yeah," Willie said, "this is the best job I ever had. And the boss isn't . . ." He waggled his hands back and forth. "Ya know, mean."

I nodded. I did know. I could bitch and complain about Jean-Claude all I wanted, but compared to most Masters of the City, he was a pussycat. A big, dangerous, carnivorous pussycat, but still, it was an improvement.

"The boss's busy right this minute," Willie said. "He said if you was to come early, to give ya a table near the stage."

Great. Aloud I said, "How long will Jean-Claude be?"

Willie shrugged. "Don't know for sure."

I nodded. "Okay, I'll wait, for a little while."

Willie grinned, fangs flashing. "Ya want me to tell Jean-Claude to hurry it up?"

"Would you?"

He grimaced like he'd swallowed a bug. "Hell no."

"Don't sweat it. If I get tired of waiting, I'll tell him myself."

Willie looked at me sorta sideways. "You'd do it, wouldn't you?"

"Yeah."

He just shook his head and started leading me between the small round tables. Every table was thick with people. Laughing, gasping, drinking, holding hands. The sensation of being surrounded by thick, sweaty life was nearly overwhelming.

I glanced at Willie. Did he feel it? Did the warm press of humanity make his stomach knot with hunger? Did he go home at night and dream of ripping into the loud, roaring crowd? I almost asked him, but I liked Willie as much as I could like a vampire. I did not want to know if the answer was yes.

A table just one row back from the stage was empty. There was a big white cardboard foldy thing that said "Reserved." Willie tried to hold my chair for me, I waved him back. It wasn't women's liberation. I simply never understood what I was supposed to do while the guy shoved my chair in under me. Did I sit there and watch him strain to scoot the chair with me in it? Embarrassing. I usually hovered just above the chair and got it shoved into the backs of my knees. Hell with it.

"Would you like a drink while ya wait?" Willie asked.

"Could I have a Coke?"

"Nuthin' stronger?"

I shook my head.

Willie walked away through the tables and the people. On the stage was a slender man with short, dark hair. He was thin all over, his face almost cadaverous, but he was definitely human. His appearance was more comical than anything, like a long-limbed clown. Beside him, staring blank-faced out at the crowd, was a zombie.

Its pale eyes were still clear, human-looking, but he didn't blink. That familiar frozen stare gazed out at the audience. They were only half listening to the jokes. Most eyes were on the standing deadman. He was just decayed enough around the edges to look scary, but even one row away there was no hint of odor. Nice trick if you could manage it.

"Ernie here is the best roommate I ever had," the comedian said. "He doesn't eat much, doesn't talk my ear off, doesn't bring cute chicks home and lock me out while they have a good time." Nervous laughter from the audience. Eyes glued on ol' Ernie.

"Though there was that pork chop in the fridge that went bad. Ernie seemed to like that a lot."

The zombie turned slowly, almost painfully, to stare at the comedian. The man's eyes flickered to the zombie, then back to the audience, smile in place. The zombie kept staring at him. The man didn't seem to like it much. I didn't blame him. Even the dead don't like to be the butt of jokes.

The jokes weren't that funny anyway. It was a novelty act. The zombie was the act. Pretty inventive, and pretty sick.

Willie came back with my Coke. The manager waiting on my table, la-de-da. Of course, the reserved table was pretty good, too. Willie set the drink down on one of those useless paper lace dollies. "Enjoy," he said. He turned to leave, but I touched his arm. I wish I hadn't.

The arm was solid enough, real enough. But it was like touching wood. It was dead. I don't know what else to call it. There was no feeling of movement. Nothing.

I dropped his arm, slowly, and looked up at him. Meeting his eyes, thanks to Jean-Claude's marks. Those brown eyes held something like sorrow.

I could suddenly hear my heartbeat in my ears, and I had to swallow to calm my own pulse. Shit. I wanted Willie to go away now. I turned away from him and looked very hard at my drink. He left. Maybe it was just the sound of all the laughing, but I couldn't hear Willie walk away.

Willie McCoy was the only vampire I had ever known before he died. I remembered him alive. He had been a small-time hood. An errand boy for bigger fish. Maybe Willie thought being a vampire would make him a big fish. He'd been wrong there. He was just a little undead fish now. Jean-Claude or someone like him would run Willie's "life" for eternity. Poor Willie.

I rubbed the hand that had touched him on my leg. I wanted to forget the feel of his body under the new tomato-red suit, but I couldn't. Jean-Claude's body didn't feel that way. Of course, Jean-Claude could damn near pass for human. Some of the old ones could do that. Willie would learn. God help him.

"Zombies are better than dogs. They'll fetch your slippers and don't need to be walked. Ernie'll even sit at my feet and beg if I tell him to."

The audience laughed. I wasn't sure why. It wasn't that genuine ha-ha laughter. It was that outrageous shocked sound. The I-can't-believe-he-said-that laughter.

The zombie was moving toward the comedian in a sort of slow-motion jerk. Crumbling hands reached outward and my stomach squeezed tight. It was a flashback to last night. Zombies almost always attack by just reaching out. Just like in the movies.

The comedian didn't realize that Ernie had decided he'd had enough. If a zombie is simply raised without any particular orders, he usually reverts to what is normal for him. A good person is a good person until his brain decays, stripping him of personality. Most zombies won't kill without orders, but every once in a while you get lucky and raise one that has homicidal tendencies. The comedian was about to get lucky.

The zombie walked towards him like a bad Frankenstein monster. The comedian finally realized something was wrong. He stopped in mid-joke, turning eyes wide. "Ernie," he said. It was as far as he got. The decaying hands wrapped around his throat and started to squeeze.

For one pleasant second I almost let the zombie do him in. Exploiting the dead is one thing I feel strongly about, but . . . stupidity isn't punishable by death. If it was, there would be a hell of a population drop.

I stood up, glancing around the club to see if they had planned for this eventuality. Willie came running to the stage. He wrapped his arms around the zombie's waist and pulled, lifted the much taller body off its feet, but the hands kept squeezing.

The comedian slipped to his knees, making little argh sounds. His face was going from red to purple. The audience was laughing. They thought it was part of the show. It was a heck of a lot funnier than the act.

I stepped up to the stage and said softly to Willie, "Need some help?"

He stared at me, still clinging to the zombie's waist. With his extraordinary strength Willie could have ripped a finger at a time off the man's neck and probably saved him. But super-vampire strength doesn't help you if you don't think how to use it. Willie never thought. Of course, the zombie might crush the man's windpipe before even a vampire could peel its fingers away. Maybe. Best not to find out.

I thought the comedian was a putz. But I couldn't stand there and watch him die. Really, I couldn't.

"Stop," I said. Low and for the zombie's ears. He stopped squeezing, but his hands were still tight. The comedian was going limp. "Release him."

The zombie let go. The man fell in a near faint on the stage. Willie straightened up from his frantic tugging at the deadman. He smoothed his tomato-red suit back into place. His hair was still perfectly slick. Too much hair goop for a mere zombie wrestling to displace his hairdo.

"Thanks," he whispered. Then he stood to his full five feet four and said, "The Amazing Albert and his pet zombie, ladies and gentlemen." The audience had been a bit uncertain, but the applause began. When the Amazing Albert staggered to his feet, the applause exploded. He croaked into the microphone. "Ernie thinks it's time to go home now. You've been a great audience." The applause was loud and genuine.

The comedian left the stage. The zombie stayed and stared at me. Waiting, waiting for another order. I don't know why everyone can't speak and have zombies obey them. It doesn't even feel like magic to me. There is no tingle of the skin, no breath of power. I speak and the zombies listen. Me and E. F. Hutton.

"Follow Albert and obey his orders until I tell you otherwise." The zombie looked down at me for a second, then turned slowly and shuffled after the man. The zombie wouldn't kill him now. I wouldn't tell the comedian that, though. Let him think his life was in danger. Let him think he had to let me lay the zombie to rest. It was what I wanted. It was probably what the zombie wanted.

Ernie certainly didn't seem to like being the straight man in a comedy routine. Hecklers are one thing. Choking the comic to death is a little extreme.

Willie escorted me back to my table. I sat down and sipped my Coke.

He sat down across from me. He looked shaken. His small hands trembled as he sat across from me. He was a vampire, but he was still Willie McCoy. I wondered how many years it would take for the last remnants of his personality to disappear. Ten years, twenty, a century? How long before the monster ate the man?

If it took that long. It wouldn't be my problem. I wouldn't be there to see it. To tell the truth, I didn't want to see it.

"I never liked zombies," Willie said.

I stared at him. "Are you afraid of zombies?"

His eyes flickered to me, then down to the table. "No."

I grinned at him. "You're afraid of zombies. You're phobic."

He leaned across the table. "Don't tell. Please don't tell." There was real fear in his eyes.

"Who would I tell?"

"You know."

I shook my head. "I don't know what you're talking about, Willie."

"The MASTER." You could hear "master" was in all caps.

"Why would I tell Jean-Claude?"

He was whispering now. A new comedian had come up on stage, there was laughter and noise, and still he whispered. "You're his human servant, whether you like it or not. When we speak to you, he tells us we're speaking to him."

We were leaning almost face-to-face now. The gentle brush of his breath smelled like breath mints. Almost all vampires smell like breath mints. I don't know what they did before mints were invented. Had stinky breath, I guess.

"You know I'm not his human servant."

"But he wants you to be."

"Just because Jean-Claude wants something doesn't mean he gets it," I said.

"You don't know what he's like."

"I think I do . . ."

He touched my arm. I didn't jerk back this time. I was too intent on what he was saying. "He's been different since the old master died. He's a lot more powerful than even you know."

This much I had suspected. "So why shouldn't I tell him you're afraid of zombies?"

"He'll use it to punish me."

I stared at him, our eyes inches apart. "You mean he's torturing people to control them."

He nodded.

"Shit."

"You won't tell?"

"I won't tell. Promise," I said.

He looked so relieved, I patted his hand. The hand felt like a hand. His body didn't feel wood hard anymore. Why? I didn't know, and if I asked Willie, he probably wouldn't know either. One of the mysteries of . . . death.

"Thanks."

"I thought you said that Jean-Claude was the kindest master you've ever had."

"He is," Willie said.

Now that was a frightening truth. If being tormented by your darkest fear was the kindest, how much worse had Nikolaos been. Hell, I knew the answer to that one. She'd been psychotic. Jean-Claude wasn't cruel just for the sake of watching people squirm. There was reason to his cruelty. It was a step up.

"I gotta go. Thanks for helping with the zombie." He stood.

"You were brave, you know," I said.

He flashed a grin my way, fangs glinting in the dim light. The smile vanished from his face like someone had turned a switch. "I can't afford to be anything else."

Vampires are a lot like wolf packs. The weak are either dominated or destroyed. Banishment is not an option. Willie was moving up in the ranks. A sign of weakness could stop that rise or worse. I'd often wondered what vampires feared. One of them feared zombies. It would have been funny if I hadn't seen the fear in his eyes.

The comic on stage was a vampire. He was the new dead. Skin chalk-white, eyes like burned holes in paper. His gums were bloodless and receding from canines that would have been the envy of any German

shepherd. I had never seen a vampire look so monstrous. They all usually made an effort to appear human. This one wasn't.

I had missed the audience's reaction to his first appearance, but now
they were laughing. If I had thought the zombie jokes were bad, these
were worse. A woman at the next table laughed so hard, tears spilled
down her cheeks.

"I went to New York, tough city. A gang jumped me, but I put the
bite on them." People were holding their ribs as if in pain.

I didn't get it. It was genuinely not funny. I gazed around the crowd
and found every eye fixed on the stage. They peered up at him with the
helpless devotion of the bespelled.

He was using mind tricks. I'd seen vampires seduce, threaten, terrify,
all by concentrating. But I had never seen them cause laughter. He was
forcing them to laugh.

It wasn't the worst abuse of vampiric powers I'd ever seen. He wasn't
trying to hurt them. And this mass hypnosis was harmless, temporary.
But it was wrong. Mass mind control was one of the top scary things
that most people don't know vampires can do.

I knew, and I didn't like it. He was the fresh dead and even before
Jean-Claude's marks, the comic couldn't have touched me. Being an
animator gave you partial immunity to vampires. It was one of the reasons that animators are so often vampire slayers. We've got a leg up, so
to speak.

I had called Charles earlier, but I still didn't see him. He is not easy
to miss in a crowd, sort of like Godzilla going through Tokyo. Where
was he? And when would Jean-Claude be ready to see me? It was now
after eleven. Trust him to browbeat me into a meeting and then make
me wait. He was such an arrogant son of a bitch.

Charles came through the swinging doors that led to the kitchen area.
He strode through the tables, heading for the door. He was shaking his
head and murmuring to a small Asian man who was having to quick-
run to keep up.

I waved, and Charles changed direction towards me. I could hear the
smaller man arguing, "I run a very good, clean kitchen."

Charles murmured something that I couldn't hear. The bespelled
audience was oblivious. We could have shot off a twenty-one-gun salute,

and they wouldn't have flinched. Until the vampire comic was finished, they would hear nothing else.

"What are you, the damn health department?" the smaller man asked. He was dressed in a traditional chef's outfit. He had the big floppy hat wadded up in his hands. His dark uptilted eyes were sparkling with anger.

Charles is only six-one, but he seems bigger. His body is one wide piece from broad shoulders to feet. He seems to have no waist. He is like a moving mountain. Huge. His perfectly brown eyes are the same color as his skin. Wonderfully dark. His hand is big enough to cover my face.

The Asian chef looked like an angry puppy beside Charles. He grabbed Charles's arm. I don't know what he thought he was going to do, but Charles stopped moving. He stared down at the offending hand and said very carefully, voice almost painfully deep, "Do not touch me."

The chef dropped his arm like he'd been burned. He took a step back. Charles was only giving him part of the "look." The full treatment had been known to send would-be muggers screaming for help. Part of the look was enough for one irate chef.

His voice was calm, reasonable when he spoke again, "I run a clean kitchen."

Charles shook his head. "You can't have zombies near the food preparation. It's illegal. The health codes forbid corpses near food."

"My assistant is a vampire. He's dead."

Charles rolled his eyes at me. I sympathized. I'd had the same discussion with a chef or two. "Vampires are not considered legally dead anymore, Mr. Kim. Zombies are."

"I don't understand why."

"Zombies rot and carry disease just like any dead body. Just because they move around doesn't mean they aren't a depository for disease."

"I don't . . ."

"Either keep the zombies away from the kitchen or we will close you down. Do you understand that?"

"And you'd have to explain to the owner why his business was not making money," I said, smiling up at both of them.

The chef looked a bit pale. Fancy that. "I . . . I understand. It will be taken care of."

"Good," Charles said.

The chef darted one frightened look at me, then began to thread his way back to the kitchen. It was funny how Jean-Claude was beginning to scare so many people. He'd been one of the more civilized vampires before he became head bloodsucker. Power corrupts.

Charles sat down across from me. He seemed too big for the table. "I got your message. What's going on?"

"I need an escort to the Tenderloin."

It's hard to tell when Charles blushes, but he squirmed in his chair. "Why in the world do you want to go down there?"

"I need to find someone who works down there."

"Who?"

"A prostitute," I said.

He squirmed again. It was like watching an uncomfortable mountain. "Caroline is not going to like this."

"Don't tell her," I said.

"You know Caroline and I don't lie to each other, about anything."

I fought to keep my face neutral. If Charles had to explain his every move to his wife, that was his choice. He didn't have to let Caroline control him. He chose to do it. But it grated on me like having your teeth cleaned.

"Just tell her that you had extra animator business. She won't ask details." Caroline thought that our job was gross. Beheading chickens, raising zombies, how uncouth.

"Why do you need to find this prostitute?"

I ignored the question and answered another one. The less Charles knew about Harold Gaynor, the safer he'd be. "I just need someone to look menacing. I don't want to have to shoot some poor slob because he made a pass at me. Okay?"

Charles nodded. "I'll come. I'm flattered you asked."

I smiled encouragingly at him. Truth was that Manny was more dangerous and much better backup. But Manny was like me. He didn't look dangerous. Charles did. I needed a good bluff tonight, not firepower.

I glanced at my watch. It was almost midnight. Jean-Claude had kept me waiting an hour. I looked behind me and caught Willie's gaze. He came towards me immediately. I would try to use this power only for good.

He bent close, but not too close. He glanced at Charles, acknowledging him with a nod. Charles nodded back. Mr. Stoic.

"What ya want?" Willie said.

"Is Jean-Claude ready to see me or not?"

"Yeah, I was just coming to get ya. I didn't know you was expecting company tonight." He looked at Charles.

"He's a coworker."

"A zombie raiser?" Willie asked.

Charles said, "Yes." His dark face was impassive. His look was quietly menacing.

Willie seemed impressed. He nodded. "Sure, ya got zombie work after you see Jean-Claude?"

"Yeah," I said. I stood and spoke softly to Charles, though chances were that Willie would hear it. Even the newly dead hear better than most dogs.

"I'll be as quick as I can."

"Alright," he said, "but I need to get home soon."

I understood. He was on a short leash. His own fault, but it seemed to bother me more than it bothered Charles. Maybe it was one of the reasons I'm not married. I'm not big on compromise.

## 21

WILLIE LED ME through a door and a short hallway. As soon as the door closed behind us, the noise was muted, distant as a dream. The lights were bright after the dimness of the club. I blinked against it. Willie looked rosy-cheeked in the bright light, not quite alive, but healthy for a deadman. He'd fed tonight on something, or someone. Maybe a willing human, maybe animal. Maybe.

The first door on the left said "Manager's Office." Willie's office? Naw.

Willie opened the door and ushered me in. He didn't come in the office. His eyes flicked towards the desk, then he backed out, shutting the door behind him.

The carpeting was pale beige; the walls eggshell-white. A large black-lacquered desk sat against the far wall. A shiny black lamp seemed to grow out of the desk. There was a blotter perfectly placed in the center of the desk. There were no papers, no paper clips, just Jean-Claude sitting behind the desk.

His long pale hands were folded on the blotter. Soft curling black hair, midnight-blue eyes, white shirt with its strange button-down cuffs. He was perfect sitting there, perfectly still like a painting. Beautiful as a wet dream, but not real. He only looked perfect. I knew better.

There were two brown metal filing cabinets against the left wall. A black leather couch took up the rest of the wall. There was a large oil painting above the couch. It was a scene of St. Louis in the 1700s. Settlers coming downriver in flatboats. The sunlight was autumn thick. Children ran and played. It didn't match anything in the room.

"The picture yours?" I asked.

He gave a slight nod.

"Did you know the painter?"

He smiled then, no hint of fangs, just the beautiful spread of lips. If there had been a vampire GQ, Jean-Claude would have been their cover boy.

"The desk and couch don't match the rest of the decor," I said.

"I am in the midst of remodeling," he said.

He just sat there looking at me. "You asked for this meeting, Jean-Claude. Let's get on with it."

"Are you in a hurry?" His voice had dropped lower, the brush of fur on naked skin.

"Yes, I am. So cut to the chase. What do you want?"

The smile widened, slightly. He actually lowered his eyes for a moment. It was almost coy. "You are my human servant, Anita."

He used my name. Bad sign that. "No," I said, "I'm not."

"You bear two marks, only two more remain." His face still looked pleasant, lovely. The expression didn't match what he was saying.

"So what?"

He sighed. "Anita . . ." He stopped in midsentence and stood. He came around the desk. "Do you know what it means to be Master of the City?" He leaned on the desk, half sitting. His shirt gaped open showing an expanse of pale chest. One nipple showed small and pale and hard. The cross-shaped scar was an insult to such pale perfection.

I had been staring at his bare chest. How embarrassing. I met his gaze and managed not to blush. Bully for me.

"There are other benefits to being my human servant, *ma petite*." His eyes were all pupil, black and drowning deep.

I shook my head. "No."

"No lies, *ma petite*, I can feel your desire." His tongue flicked across his lips. "I can taste it."

Great, just great. How do you argue with someone who can feel what you're feeling? Answer: don't argue, agree. "Alright, I lust after you. Does that make you happy?"

He smiled. "Yes." One word, but it flowed through my mind, whispering things that he had not said. Whispers in the dark.

"I lust after a lot of men, but that doesn't mean I have to sleep with them."

His face was almost slack, eyes like drowning pools. "Casual lust is easily defeated," he said. He stood in one smooth motion. "What we have is not casual, *ma petite*. Not lust, but desire." He moved towards me, one pale hand outstretched.

My heart was thudding in my throat. It wasn't fear. I didn't think it was a mind trick. It felt real. Desire, he called it, maybe it was. "Don't," my voice was hoarse, a whisper.

He, of course, did not stop. His fingers traced the edge of my cheek, barely touching. The brush of skin on skin. I stepped away from him, forced to draw a deep shaking breath. I could be as uncool as I wanted, he could feel my discomfort. No sense pretending.

I could feel where he had touched me, a lingering sensation. I looked at the ground while I spoke. "I appreciate the possible fringe benefits, Jean-Claude, really. But I can't. I won't." I met his eyes. His face was a terrible blankness. Nothing. It was the same face of a moment ago, but some spark of humanity, of life, was gone.

My pulse started thudding again. It had nothing to do with sex. Fear. It had a lot to do with fear.

"As you like, my little animator. Whether we are lovers or not, it does not change what you are to me. You are my human servant."

"No," I said.

"You are mine, Anita. Willing or not, you are mine."

"See, Jean-Claude, here's where you lose me. First you try seducing me, which has its pleasant side. When that doesn't work, you resort to threats."

"It is not a threat, *ma petite*. It is the truth."

"No, it isn't. And stop calling me *ma* fucking *petite*."

He smiled at that.

I didn't want him amused by me. Anger replaced fear in a quick warm rush. I liked anger. It made me brave, and stupid. "Fuck you."

"I have already offered that." His voice made something low jerk in my stomach.

I felt the rush of heat as I blushed. "Damn you, Jean-Claude, damn you."

"We need to talk, *ma petite*. Lovers or not, servant or not, we need to talk."

"Then talk. I haven't got all night."

He sighed. "You don't make this easy."

"If it was easy you wanted, you should have picked on someone else."

He nodded. "Very true. Please, be seated." He went back to lean on the desk, arms crossed over his chest.

"I don't have that kind of time," I said.

He frowned slightly. "I thought we agreed to talk this out, *ma petite*."

"We agreed to meet at eleven. You're the one who wasted an hour, not me."

His smile was almost bitter. "Very well. I will give you a . . . condensed version."

I nodded. "Fine with me."

"I am the new Master of the City. But to survive with Nikolaos alive, I had to hide my powers. I did it too well. There are those who think I am not powerful enough to be the Master of all. They are challenging me. One of the things they are using against me is you."

"How?"

"Your disobedience. I cannot even control my own human servant. How can I possibly control all the vampires in the city and surrounding areas?"

"What do you want from me?"

He smiled then, wide and genuine, flashing fangs. "I want you to be my human servant."

"Not in this lifetime, Jean-Claude."

"I can force the third mark on you, Anita." There was no threat as he said it. It was just a fact.

"I would rather die than be your human servant." Master vampires can smell the truth. He would know I meant it.

"Why?"

I opened my mouth to try to explain, but didn't. He would not understand. We stood two feet apart but it might have been miles. Miles across some dark chasm. We could not bridge that gap. He was a walking corpse. Whatever he had been as a living man, it was gone. He was the Master of the City, and that was nothing even close to human.

"If you force this issue, I will kill you," I said.

"You mean that." There was surprise in his voice. It isn't often a girl gets to surprise a centuries-old vampire.

"Yes."

"I do not understand you, *ma petite*."

"I know," I said.

"Could you pretend to be my servant?"

It was an odd question. "What does pretending mean?"

"You come to a few meetings. You stand at my side with your guns and your reputation."

"You want the Executioner at your back." I stared at him for a space of heartbeats. The true horror of what he'd just said floated slowly through my mind. "I thought the two marks were accident. That you panicked. You meant all along to mark me, didn't you?"

He just smiled.

"Answer me, you son of a bitch."

"If the chance arose, I was not averse to it."

"Not averse to it!" I was almost yelling. "You cold-bloodedly chose me to be your human servant! Why?"

"You are the Executioner."

"Damn you, what does that mean?"

"It is impressive to be the vampire who finally caught you."

"You haven't caught me."

"If you would behave yourself, the others would think so. Only you and I need know that it is pretense."

I shook my head. "I won't play your game, Jean-Claude."

"You will not help me?"

"You got it."

"I offer you immortality. Without the compromise of vampirism. I offer you myself. There have been women over the years who would have done anything I asked just for that."

"Sex is sex, Jean-Claude. No one's that good."

He smiled slightly. "Vampires are different, *ma petite*. If you were not so stubborn, you might find out how different."

I had to look away from his eyes. The look was too intimate. Too full of possibilities.

"There's only one thing I want from you," I said.

"And what is that, *ma petite*?"

"All right, two things. First, stop calling me *ma petite*; second, let me go. Wipe these damn marks away."

"You may have the first request, Anita."

"And the second?"

"I cannot, even if I wanted to."

"Which you don't," I said.

"Which I don't."

"Stay away from me, Jean-Claude. Stay the fuck away from me, or I'll kill you."

"Many people have tried through the years."

"How many of them had eighteen kills?"

His eyes widened just a bit. "None. There was this man in Hungary who swore he killed five."

"What happened to him?"

"I tore his throat out."

"You understand this, Jean-Claude. I would rather have my throat torn out. I would rather die trying to kill you than submit to you." I stared at him, trying to see if he understood any of what I said. "Say something."

"I have heard your words. I know you mean them." He was suddenly standing in front of me. I hadn't seen him move, hadn't felt him in my head. He was just suddenly inches in front of me. I think I gasped.

"Could you truly kill me?" His voice was like silk on a wound, gentle with an edge of pain. Like sex. It was like velvet rubbing inside my skull. It felt good, even with fear tearing through my body. Shit. He could still have me. Still take me down. No way.

I looked up into his so-blue eyes and said, "Yes."

I meant it. He blinked once, gracefully, and stepped back. "You are the most stubborn woman I have ever met," he said. There was no play in his voice this time. It was a flat statement.

"That's the nicest compliment you've ever paid me."

He stood in front of me, hands at his sides. He stood very still. Snakes or birds can stand utterly still but even a snake has a sense of aliveness, of action waiting to resume. Jean-Claude stood there with no sense of anything, as if despite what my eyes told me, he had vanished. He was not there at all. The dead make no noise.

"What happened to your face?"

I touched the swollen cheek before I could stop myself. "Nothing," I lied.

"Who hit you?"

"Why, so you can go beat him up?"

"One of the fringe benefits of being my servant is my protection."

"I don't need your protection, Jean-Claude."

"He hurt you."

"And I shoved a gun into his groin and made him tell me everything he knew," I said.

Jean-Claude smiled. "You did what?"

"I shoved a gun into his balls, alright?"

His eyes started to sparkle. Laughter spread across his face and burst out between his lips. He laughed full-throated.

The laugh was like candy: sweet, and infectious. If you could bottle Jean-Claude's laugh, I know it would be fattening. Or orgasmic.

"*Ma petite, ma petite*, you are absolutely marvelous."

I stared at him, letting that wonderful, touchable laugh roll around me. It was time to go. It is very hard to be dignified when someone is laughing uproariously at you. But I managed.

My parting shot made him laugh harder. "Stop calling me *ma petite*."

## 22

I STEPPED BACK out into the noise of the club. Charles was standing beside the table, not sitting. He looked uncomfortable from a distance. What had gone wrong now?

His big hands were twisted together. Dark face scrunched up into near pain. A kind God had made Charles look big and bad, because inside he was all marshmallow. If I'd had Charles's natural size and strength, I'd have been a guaranteed bad ass. It was sort of sad and unfair.

"What's wrong?" I asked.

"I called Caroline," he said.

"And?"

"The baby-sitter's sick. And Caroline's been called in to the hospital. Someone has to stay with Sam while she goes to work."

"Mm-huh," I said.

He didn't look the least bit tough when he said, "Can going down to the Tenderloin wait until tomorrow?"

I shook my head.

"You're not going to go down there alone," Charles said. "Are you?"

I stared up at the great mountain of a man, and sighed. "I can't wait, Charles."

"But the Tenderloin." He lowered his voice as if just saying the word too loud would bring a cloud of pimps and prostitutes to descend upon us. "You can't go down there alone at night."

"I've gone worse places, Charles. I'll be all right."

"No, I won't let you go alone. Caroline can just get a new sitter or tell the hospital no." He smiled when he said it. Always happy to help a friend. Caroline would give him hell for it. Worst of all, now I didn't want to take Charles with me. You had to do more than look tough.

What if Gaynor got wind of me questioning Wanda? What if he found Charles and thought he was involved? No. It had been selfish to risk Charles. He had a four-year-old son. And a wife.

Harold Gaynor would eat Charles raw for dinner. I couldn't involve him. He was a big, friendly, eager-to-please bear. A lovable, cuddly bear. I didn't need a teddy bear for backup. I needed someone who would be able to take any heat that Gaynor might send our way.

I had an idea.

"Go home, Charles. I won't go alone. I promise."

He looked uncertain. Like maybe he didn't trust me. Fancy that. "Anita, are you sure? I won't leave you hanging like this."

"Go on, Charles. I'll take backup."

"Who can you get at this hour?"

"No questions. Go home to your son."

He looked uncertain, but relieved. He hadn't really wanted to go to the Tenderloin. Maybe Caroline's short leash was what Charles wanted, needed. An excuse for all the things he really didn't want to do. What a basis for a marriage.

But, hey, if it works, don't fix it.

Charles left with many apologies. But I knew he was glad to go. I would remember that he had been glad to go.

I knocked on the office door. There was a silence, then, "Come in, Anita."

How had he known it was me? I wouldn't ask. I didn't want to know.

Jean-Claude seemed to be checking figures in a large ledger. It looked antique with yellowed pages and fading ink. The ledger looked like something Bob Crachit should have been scribbling in on a cold Christmas Eve.

"What have I done to merit two visits in one night?" he said.

Looking at him now, I felt silly. I spent all this time avoiding him. Now I was going to invite him to accompany me on a bit of sleuthing? But it would kill two bats with one stone. It would please Jean-Claude, and I really didn't want him angry with me, if I could avoid it. And if Gaynor did try to go up against Jean-Claude, I was betting on Jean-Claude.

It was what Jean-Claude had done to me a few weeks ago. He had chosen me as the vampire's champion. Put me up against a monster that had slain three master vampires. And he had bet that I would come out on top against Nikolaos. I had, but just barely.

What was sauce for the goose was sauce for the gander. I smiled sweetly at him. Pleased to be able to return the favor so quickly.

"Would you care to accompany me to the Tenderloin?"

He blinked, surprise covering his face just like a real person. "To what purpose?"

"I need to question a prostitute about a case I'm working on. I need backup."

"Backup?" he asked.

"I need backup that looks more threatening than I do. You fit the bill."

He smiled beatifically. "I would be your bodyguard."

"You've given me enough grief, do something nice for a change."

The smile vanished. "Why this sudden change of heart, *ma petite*?"

"My backup had to go home and baby-sit his kid."

"And if I do not go?"

"I'll go alone," I said.

"Into the Tenderloin?"

"Yep."

He was suddenly standing by the desk, walking towards me. I hadn't seen him rise.

"I wish you'd stop doing that."

"Doing what?"

"Clouding my mind so I can't see you move."

"I do it as often as I can, *ma petite*, just to prove I still can."

"What's that supposed to mean?"

"I gave up much of my power over you when I gave you the marks.

I practice what little games are left me." He was standing almost in front of me. "Lest you forget who and what I am."

I stared up into his blue, blue eyes. "I never forget that you are the walking dead, Jean-Claude."

An expression I could not read passed over his face. It might have been pain. "No, I see the knowledge in your eyes of what I am." His voice dropped low, almost a whisper, but it wasn't seductive. It was human. "Your eyes are the clearest mirror I have ever seen, *ma petite*. Whenever I begin to pretend to myself. Whenever I have delusions of life. I have only to look into your face and see the truth."

What did he expect me to say? Sorry, I'll try to ignore the fact that you're a vampire. "So why keep me around?" I asked.

"Perhaps if Nikolaos had had such a mirror, she would not have been such a monster."

I stared at him. He might be right. It made his choice of me as human servant almost noble. Almost. Oh, hell. I would not start feeling sorry for the freaking Master of the City. Not now. Not ever.

We would go down to the Tenderloin. Pimps beware. I was bringing the Master as backup. It was like carrying a thermonuclear device to kill ants. Overkill has always been a specialty of mine.

## 23

THE TENDERLOIN WAS originally the red light district on the River-front in the 1800s. But the Tenderloin, like so much of St. Louis, moved uptown. Go down Washington past the Fox Theater, where you can see Broadway traveling companies sing bright musicals. Keep driving down Washington to the west edge of downtown St. Louis and you will come to the resurrected carcass of the Tenderloin.

The night streets are neon-coated, sparkling, flashing, pulsing—colors. It looks like some sort of pornographic carnival. All it needs is a Ferris wheel in one of the empty lots. They could sell cotton candy shaped like naked people. The kiddies could play while Daddy went to get his jollies. Mom would never have to know.

Jean-Claude sat beside me in the car. He had been utterly silent on the drive over. I had had to glance at him a time or two just to make sure he was still there. People make noise. I don't mean talking or belching or anything overt. But people, as a rule, can't just sit without making noise. They fidget, the sound of cloth rubbing against the seats; they breathe, the soft intake of air; they wet their lips, wet, quiet, but noise. Jean-Claude didn't do any of these things as we drove. I couldn't even swear he blinked. The living dead, yippee.

I can take silence as good as the next guy, better than most women and a lot of men. Now, I needed to fill the silence. Talk just for the noise. A waste of energy, but I needed it.

"Are you in there, Jean-Claude?"

His neck turned, bringing his head with it. His eyes glittered, reflecting the neon signs like dark glass. Shit.

"You can play human, Jean-Claude, better than almost any vampire I've ever met. What's all this supernatural crap?"

"Crap?" he said, voice soft.

"Yeah, why are you going all spooky on me?"

"Spooky?" he asked, and the sound filled the car. As if the word meant something else entirely.

"Stop that," I said.

"Stop what?"

"Answering every question with a question."

He blinked once. "So sorry, *ma petite*, but I can feel the street."

"Feel the street? What does that mean?"

He settled back against the upholstery, leaning his head and neck into the seat. His hand clasped over his stomach. "There is a great deal of life here."

"Life?" He had me doing it now.

"Yes," he said, "I can feel them running back and forth. Little creatures, desperately seeking love, pain, acceptance, greed. A lot of greed here, too, but mostly pain and love."

"You don't come to a prostitute for love. You come for sex."

He rolled his head so his dark eyes stared at me. "Many people confuse the two."

I stared at the road. The hairs at the back of my neck were standing at attention. "You haven't fed yet tonight, have you?"

"You are the vampire expert. Can you not tell?" His voice had dropped to almost a whisper. Hoarse and thick.

"You know I can never tell with you."

"A compliment to my powers, I'm sure."

"I did not bring you down here to hunt," I said. My voice sounded firm, a tad loud. My heart was loud inside my head.

"Would you forbid me to hunt tonight?" he asked.

I thought about that one for a minute or two. We were going to have to turn around and make another pass to find a parking space. Would I forbid him to hunt tonight? Yes. He knew the answer. This was a trick question. Trouble was I couldn't see the trick.

"I would ask that you not hunt here tonight," I said.

"Give me a reason, Anita."

He had called me Anita without me prompting him. He was definitely after something. "Because I brought you down here. You wouldn't have hunted here, if it hadn't been for me."

"You feel guilt for whomever I might feed on tonight?"

"It is illegal to take unwilling human victims," I said.

"So it is."

"The penalty for doing so is death," I said.

"By your hand."

"If you do it in this state, yes."

"They are just whores, pimps, cheating men. What do they matter to you, Anita?"

I don't think he had ever called me Anita twice in a row. It was a bad sign. A car pulled away not a block from The Grey Cat Club. What luck. I slid my Nova into the slot. Parallel parking is not my best thing, but luckily the car that pulled away was twice the size of my car. There was plenty of room to maneuver, back and forth from the curb.

When the car was lurched nearly onto the curb but safely out of traffic, I cut the engine. Jean-Claude lay back in his seat, staring at me. "I asked you a question, *ma petite*, what do these people mean to you?"

I undid my seat belt and turned to look at him. Some trick of light and shadow had put most of his body in darkness. A band of nearly gold light lay across his face. His high cheekbones were very prominent against his pale skin. The tips of his fangs showed between his lips. His eyes gleamed like blue neon. I looked away and stared at the steering wheel while I talked.

"I have no personal stake in these people, Jean-Claude, but they are people. Good, bad, or indifferent, they are alive, and no one has the right to just arbitrarily snuff them out."

"So it is the sanctity of life you cling to?"

I nodded. "That and the fact that every human being is special. Every death is a loss of something precious and irreplaceable." I looked at him as I finished the last.

"You have killed before, Anita. You have destroyed that which is irreplaceable."

"I'm irreplaceable, too," I said. "No one has the right to kill me, either."

He sat up in one liquid motion, and reality seemed to collect around him. I could almost feel the movement of time in the car, like a sonic boom for the inside of my head, instead of my ear.

Jean-Claude sat there looking entirely human. His pale skin had a certain flush to it. His curling black hair, carefully combed and styled, was rich and touchable. His eyes were just midnight-blue, nothing exceptional but the color. He was human again, in the blink of an eye.

"Jesus," I whispered.

"What is wrong, *ma petite?*"

I shook my head. If I asked how he did it, he'd just smile. "Why all the questions, Jean-Claude? Why the worry about my view of life?"

"You are my human servant." He raised a hand to stop the automatic objection. "I have begun the process of making you my human servant, and I would like to understand you better."

"Can't you just . . . scent my emotions like you can the people on the street?"

"No, *ma petite.* I can feel your desire but little else. I gave that up when I made you my marked servant."

"You can't read me?"

"No."

That was really nice to know. Jean-Claude didn't have to tell me. So why did he? He never gave anything away for free. There were strings attached that I couldn't even see. I shook my head. "You are just to back me up tonight. Don't do anything to anybody unless I say so, okay?"

"Do anything?"

"Don't hurt anyone unless they try to hurt us."

He nodded, face very solemn. Why did I suspect that he was laughing at me in some dark corner of his mind? Giving orders to the Master of the City. I guess it was funny.

The noise level on the sidewalk was intense. Music blared out of every other building. Never the same song, but always loud. The flashing signs proclaimed, "Girls, Girls, Girls. Topless." A pink-edged sign read, "Talk to the Naked Woman of Your Dreams." Eeek.

A tall, thin black woman came up to us. She was wearing purple shorts so short that they looked like a thong bikini. Black fishnet panty hose covered her legs and buttocks. Provocative.

She stopped somewhere between the two of us. Her eyes flicked from one to the other. "Which one of ya does it, and which one of ya watches?"

Jean-Claude and I exchanged glances. He was smiling ever so slightly. "Sorry, we were looking for Wanda," I said.

"A lot of names down here," she said. "I can do anything this Wanda can do and do it better." She stepped very close to Jean-Claude, almost touching. He took her hand in his and lifted it gently to his lips. His eyes watched me as he did it.

"You're the doer," she said. Her voice had gone throaty, sexy. Or maybe that was just the effect Jean-Claude had on women. Maybe.

The woman cuddled in against him. Her skin looked very dark against the white lace of his shirt. Her fingernails were painted a bright pink, like Easter basket grass.

"Sorry to interrupt," I said, "but we don't have all night."

"This is not the one you seek then," he said.

"No," I said.

He gripped her arms just above the elbows and pushed her away. She struggled just a bit to reach him again. Her hands grabbed at his arms, trying to pull herself closer to him. He held her straight-armed, effortlessly. He could have held a semitruck effortlessly.

"I'll do you for free," she said.

"What did you do to her?" I asked.

"Nothing."

I didn't believe him. "Nothing, and she offers to do you for free?" Sarcasm is one of my natural talents. I made sure that Jean-Claude heard it.

"Be still," he said.

"Don't tell me to shut up."

The woman was standing perfectly still. Her hands dropped to her sides, limp. He hadn't been talking to me at all.

Jean-Claude took his hands away from her. She never moved. He stepped around her like she was a crack in the pavement. He took my arm, and I let him. I watched the prostitute, waiting for her to move.

Her straight, nearly naked back shuddered. Her shoulders slumped. She threw back her head and drew a deep trembling breath.

Jean-Claude pulled me gently down the street, his hand on my elbow. The prostitute turned around, saw us. Her eyes never even hesitated. She didn't know us.

I swallowed hard enough for it to hurt. I pulled free of Jean-Claude's hand. He didn't fight me. Good for him.

I backed up against a storefront window. Jean-Claude stood in front of me, looking down. "What did you do to her?"

"I told you, *ma petite*, nothing."

"Don't call me that. I saw her, Jean-Claude. Don't lie to me."

A pair of men stopped beside us to look in the window. They were holding hands. I glanced in the window and felt color creep up my cheeks. There were whips, leather masks, padded handcuffs, and things I didn't even have a name for. One of the men leaned into the other and whispered. The other man laughed. One of them caught me looking. Our eyes met, and I looked away, fast. Eye contact down here was a dangerous thing.

I was blushing and hating it. The two men walked away, hand in hand.

Jean-Claude was staring in the window like he was out for a Saturday afternoon of window-shopping. Casual.

"What did you do to that woman?"

He stared in the storefront. I couldn't tell exactly what had caught his attention. "It was careless of me, *ma* . . . Anita. My fault entirely."

"What was your fault?"

"My . . . powers are greater when my human servant is with me." He stared at me then. His gaze solid on my face. "With you beside me, my powers are enhanced."

"Wait, you mean like a witch's familiar?"

He cocked his head to one side, a slight smile on his face. "Yes, very close to that. I did not know you knew anything about witchcraft."

"A deprived childhood," I said. I was not going to be diverted from the important topic. "So your ability to bespell people with your eyes is stronger when I'm with you. Strong enough that without trying, you bespelled that prostitute."

He nodded.

I shook my head. "No, I don't believe you."

He shrugged, a graceful gesture on him. "Believe what you like, *ma petite*. It is the truth."

I didn't want to believe it. Because if it were true, then I was in fact his human servant. Not in my actions but by my very presence. With sweat trickling down my spine from the heat, I was cold. "Shit," I said.

"You could say that," he said.

"No, I can't deal with this right now. I can't." I stared up at him. "You keep whatever powers we have between us in check, okay?"

"I will try," he said.

"Don't try, dammit, do it."

He smiled wide enough to flash the tips of his fangs. "Of course, *ma petite*."

Panic was starting in the pit of my stomach. I gripped my hands into fists at my sides. "If you call me that one more time, I'm going to hit you."

His eyes widened just a bit, his lips flexed. I realized he was trying not to laugh. I hate it when people find my threats amusing.

He was an invasive son of a bitch; and I wanted to hurt him. To hurt him because he scared me. I understand the urge, I've had it before with other people. It's an urge that can lead to violence. I stared up at his softly amused face. He was a condescending bastard, but if it ever came to real violence between us, one of us would die. Chances were good it would be me.

The humor leaked out of his face, leaving it smooth and lovely, and arrogant. "What is it, Anita?" His voice was soft and intimate. Even in the heat and movement of this place, his voice could roll me up and under. It was a gift.

"Don't push me into a corner, Jean-Claude. You don't want to take away all my options."

"I don't know what you mean," he said.

"If it comes down to you or me, I'm going to pick me. You remember that."

He looked at me for a space of heartbeats. Then he blinked and nodded. "I believe you would. But remember, *ma* ... Anita, if you hurt me, it hurts you. I could survive the strain of your death. The question, *amante de moi*, is could you survive mine?"

*Amante de moi?* What the hell did that mean? I decided not to ask. "Damn you, Jean-Claude, damn you."

"That, dear Anita, was done long before you met me."

"What does that mean?"

His eyes were as innocent as they ever were. "Why, Anita, your own Catholic Church has declared all vampires as suicides. We are automatically damned."

I shook my head. "I'm Episcopalian, now, but that isn't what you meant."

He laughed then. The sound was like silk brushed across the nape of the neck. It felt smooth and good, but it made you shudder.

I walked away from him. I just left him there in front of the obscene window display. I walked into the crowd of whores, hustlers, customers. There was nobody on this street as dangerous as Jean-Claude. I had brought him down here to protect me. That was laughable. Ridiculous. Obscene.

A young man who couldn't have been more than fifteen stopped me. He was wearing a vest with no shirt and a pair of torn jeans. "You interested?"

He was taller than me by a little. His eyes were blue. Two other boys just behind him were staring at us.

"We don't get many women down here," he said.

"I believe you." He looked incredibly young. "Where can I find Wheelchair Wanda?"

One of the boys behind him said, "A crip lover, Jesus."

I agreed with him. "Where?" I held up a twenty. It was too much to pay for the information, but maybe if I gave it to him, he could go home sooner. Maybe if he had twenty dollars, he could turn down one of the cars cruising the street. Twenty dollars, it would change his life. Like sticking your finger in a nuclear meltdown.

"She's just outside of The Grey Cat. At the end of the block."

"Thanks." I gave him the twenty. His fingernails had grime embedded in them.

"You sure you don't want some action?" His voice was small and uncertain, like his eyes.

Out of the corner of my eye I saw Jean-Claude moving through the crowd. He was coming for me. To protect me. I turned back to the boy. "I've got more action than I know what to do with," I said.

He frowned, looking puzzled. That was all right. I was puzzled, too. What do you do with a master vampire that won't leave you alone? Good question. Unfortunately, what I needed was a good answer.

## 24

WHEELCHAIR WANDA WAS a small woman sitting in one of those sport wheelchairs that are used for racing. She wore workout gloves, and the muscles in her arms moved under her tanned skin as she pushed herself along. Long brown hair fell in gentle waves around a very pretty face. The makeup was tasteful. She wore a shiny metallic blue shirt and no bra. An ankle-length skirt with at least two layers of multicolored crinoline and a pair of stylish black boots hid her legs.

She was moving towards us at a goodly pace. Most of the prostitutes, male and female, looked ordinary. They weren't dressed outrageously, shorts, middrifts. In this heat who could blame them? I guess if you wear fishnet jumpsuits, the police just naturally get suspicious.

Jean-Claude stood beside me. He glanced up at the sign that proclaimed "The Grey Cat" in a near blinding shade of fuchsia neon. Tasteful.

How does one approach a prostitute, even just to talk? I didn't know. Learn something new every day. I stood in her path and waited for her to come to me. She glanced up and caught me watching her. When I didn't look away, she got eye contact and smiled.

Jean-Claude moved up beside me. Wanda's smile broadened or deepened. It was a definite "come along smile" as my Grandmother Blake used to say.

Jean-Claude whispered, "Is that a prostitute?"

"Yes," I said.

"In a wheelchair?" he asked.

"Yep."

"My," was all he said. I think Jean-Claude was shocked. Nice to know he could be.

She stopped her chair with an expert movement of hands.

She smiled, craning to look up at us. The angle looked painful.

"Hi," she said.

"Hi," I said.

She continued to smile. I continued to stare. Why did I suddenly feel awkward? "A friend told me about you," I said.

Wanda nodded.

"You are the one they refer to as Wheelchair Wanda?"

She grinned suddenly, and her face looked real. Behind all those lovely but fake smiles was a real person. "Yeah, that's me."

"Could we talk?"

"Sure," she said. "You got a room?"

Did I have a room? Wasn't she supposed to do that? "No."

She waited.

Oh, hell. "We just want to talk to you for an hour, or two. We'll pay whatever the going rate is."

She told me the going rate.

"Jesus, that's a little steep," I said.

She smiled beatifically at me. "Supply and demand," she said. "You can't get a taste of what I have anywhere else." She smoothed her hands down her legs as she said it. My eyes followed her hands like they were supposed to. This was too weird.

I nodded. "Okay, you got a deal." It was a business expense. Computer paper, ink pens medium point, one prostitute, manila file folders. See, it fit right in.

Bert was going to love this one.

## 25

WE TOOK WANDA back to my apartment. There are no elevators in my building. Two flights of stairs are not exactly wheelchair accessible. Jean-Claude carried her. His stride was even and fluid as he walked ahead of me. Wanda didn't even slow him down. I followed with the wheelchair. It did slow me down.

The only consolation I had was I got to watch Jean-Claude climb the stairs. So sue me. He had a very nice backside for a vampire.

He was waiting for me in the upper hallway, standing with Wanda cuddled in his arms. They both looked at me with a pleasant sort of blankness.

I wheeled the collapsed wheelchair over the carpeting. Jean-Claude followed me. The crinoline in Wanda's skirts crinkled and whispered as he moved.

I leaned the wheelchair against my leg and unlocked the door. I pushed the door all the way back to the wall to give Jean-Claude room. The wheelchair folded inwards like a cloth baby stroller. I struggled to make the metal bars catch, so the chair would be solid again. As I suspected, it was easier to break it than to fix it.

I glanced up from my struggles and found Jean-Claude still standing outside my door. Wanda was staring at him, frowning.

"What's wrong?" I asked.

"I have never been to your apartment."

"So?"

"The great vampire expert . . . come, Anita."

Oh. "You have my permission to enter my home."

He gave a sort of bow from the neck. "I am honored," he said.

The wheelchair snapped into shape again. Jean-Claude set Wanda in her chair. I closed the door. Wanda smoothed her long skirts over her legs.

Jean-Claude stood in the middle of my living room and gazed about. He gazed at the penguin calendar on the wall by the kitchenette. He rifled the pages to see future months, gazing at pictures of chunky flightless birds until he'd seen every picture.

I wanted to tell him to stop, but it was harmless. I didn't write appointments on the calendar. Why did it bother me that he was so damned interested in it?

I turned back to the prostitute in my living room. The night was entirely too weird. "Would you like something to drink?" I asked. When in doubt, be polite.

"Red wine if you have it," Wanda said.

"Sorry, nothing alcoholic in the house. Coffee, soft drinks with real sugar in them, and water, that's about it."

"Soft drink," she said.

I got her a can of Coke out of the fridge. "You want a glass?"

She shook her head.

Jean-Claude was leaning against the wall, staring at me as I moved about the kitchen. "I don't need a glass either," he said softly.

"Don't get cute," I said.

"Too late," he said.

I had to smile.

The smile seemed to please him. Which made me frown. Life was hard around Jean-Claude. He sort of wandered off towards the fish tank. He was giving himself a tour of my apartment. Of course, he would. But at least it would give Wanda and I some privacy.

"Shit, he's a vampire," Wanda said. She sounded surprised. Which surprised me. I could always tell. Dead was dead to me, no matter how pretty the corpse.

"You didn't know?" I asked.

"No, I'm not coffin-bait," she said. There was a tightness to her face. The flick of her eyes as she followed Jean-Claude's casual movements around the room was new. She was scared.

"What's coffin-bait?" I handed her the soft drink.

"A whore that does vampires."

Coffin-bait, how quaint. "He won't touch you."

She turned brown eyes to me then. Her gaze was very thorough, as if she were trying to read the inside of my head. Was I telling the truth?

How terrifying to go away with strangers to rooms and not know if they will hurt you or not. Desperation, or a death wish.

"So you and I are going to do it?" she asked. Her gaze never left my face.

I blinked at her. It took me a moment to realize what she meant. "No." I shook my head. "No, I said I just wanted to talk. I meant it." I think I was blushing.

Maybe the blush did it. She popped the top on the soda can and took a drink. "You want me to talk about doing it with other people, while you do it with him?" She motioned her head towards the wandering vampire.

Jean-Claude was standing in front of the only picture I had in the room. It was modern and matched the decor. Grey, white, black, and palest pink. It was one of those designs that the longer you stared at it, the more shapes you could pick out.

"Look, Wanda, we are just going to talk. That's it. Nobody is going to do anything to anybody. Okay?"

She shrugged. "It's your money. We can do what you want."

That one statement made my stomach hurt. She meant it. I'd paid the money. She would do anything I wanted. Anything? It was too awful. That any human being would say "anything" and mean it. Of course, she drew the line at vampires. Even whores have standards.

Wanda was smiling up at me. The change was extraordinary. Her face glowed. She was instantly lovely. Even her eyes glowed. It reminded me of Cicely's soundless laughing face.

Back to business. "I heard you were Harold Gaynor's mistress a while back." No preliminaries, no sweet talk. Off with the clothes.

Wanda's smile faded. The glow of humor died in her eyes, replaced by wariness. "I don't know the name."

"Yeah, you do," I said. I was still standing, forcing her to look up at me in that near painful angle.

She sipped her drink and shook her head without looking up at me.

"Come on, Wanda, I know you were Gaynor's sweetie. Admit you know him, and we'll work from there."

She glanced up at me, then down. "No. I'll do you. I'll let the vamp watch. I'll talk dirty to you both. But I don't know anybody named Gaynor."

I leaned down, putting my hands on the arms of her chair. Our faces were very close. "I'm not a reporter. Gaynor will never know you talked to me unless you tell him."

Her eyes had gotten bigger. I glanced where she was staring. The Windbreaker had fallen forward. My gun was showing, which seemed to upset her. Good.

"Talk to me, Wanda." My voice was soft. Mild. The mildest of voices is often the worst threat.

"Who the hell are you? You're not cops. You're not a reporter. Social workers don't carry guns. Who are you?" That last question had the lilt of fear in it.

Jean-Claude strolled into the room. He'd been in my bedroom. Great, just great. "Trouble, *ma petite*?"

I didn't correct him on the nickname. Wanda didn't need to know there was dissent in the ranks. "She's being stubborn," I said.

I stepped back from her chair. I took off the Windbreaker and laid it over the kitchen counter. Wanda stared at the gun like I knew she would.

I may not be intimidating, but the Browning is.

Jean-Claude walked up behind her. His slender hands touched her shoulders. She jumped like it had hurt. I knew it hadn't hurt. Might be better if it did.

"He'll kill me," Wanda said.

A lot of people seemed to say that about Mr. Gaynor. "He'll never know," I said.

Jean-Claude rubbed his cheek against her hair. His fingers kneading her shoulders, gently. "And, my sweet coquette, he is not here with you tonight." He spoke with his lips against her ear. "We are." He said something else so soft I could not hear. Only his lips moved, soundlessly for me.

Wanda heard him. Her eyes widened, and she started to tremble. Her entire body seemed in the grip of some kind of fit. Tears glittered in her eyes and fell down her cheeks in one graceful curve.

Jesus.

"Please, don't. Please don't let him." Her voice was squeezed small and thin with fear.

I hated Jean-Claude in that moment. And I hated me. I was one of the good guys. It was one of my last illusions. I wasn't willing to give it up, not even if it worked. Wanda would talk or she wouldn't. No torture. "Back off, Jean-Claude," I said.

He gazed up at me. "I can taste her terror like strong wine." His eyes were solid, drowning blue. He looked blind. His face was still lovely as he opened his mouth wide and fangs glistened.

Wanda was still crying and staring at me. If she could have seen the look on Jean-Claude's face, she would have been screaming.

"I thought your control was better than this, Jean-Claude?"

"My control is excellent, but it is not endless." He stood away from her and began to pace the room on the other side of the couch. Like a leopard pacing its cage. Contained violence, waiting for release. I could not see his face. Had the spook act been for Wanda's benefit? Or real?

I shook my head. No way to ask in front of Wanda. Maybe later. Maybe.

I knelt in front of Wanda. She was gripping the soda can so hard, she was denting it. I didn't touch her, just knelt close by. "I won't let him hurt you. Honest. Harold Gaynor is threatening me. That's why I need information."

Wanda was looking at me, but her attention was on the vampire in back of her. There was a watchful tension in her shoulders. She would never relax while Jean-Claude was in the room. The lady had taste.

"Jean-Claude, Jean-Claude."

His face looked as ordinary as it ever did when he turned to face me.

A smile crooked his full lips. It was an act. Pretense. Damn him. Was there something in becoming a vampire that made you sadistic?

"Go into the bedroom for a while. Wanda and I need to talk in private."

"Your bedroom." His smile widened. "My pleasure, *ma petite*."

I scowled at him. He was undaunted. As always. But he left the room as I'd asked.

Wanda's shoulders slumped. She drew a shaky breath. "You really aren't going to let him hurt me, are you?"

"No, I'm not."

She started to cry then, soft, shaky tears. I didn't know what to do. I've never known what to do when someone cries. Did I hug her? Pat her hand comfortingly. What?

I finally sat back on the ground in front of her, leaning back on my heels, and did nothing. It took a few moments, but finally the crying stopped. She blinked up at me. The makeup around her eyes had faded, just vanished. It made her look vulnerable, more rather than less attractive. I had the urge to take her in my arms and rock her like a child. Whisper lies, about how everything would be alright.

When she left here tonight, she was still going to be a whore. A crippled whore. How could that be alright? I shook my head more at me than at her.

"You want some Kleenex?"

She nodded.

I got her the box from the kitchen counter. She wiped at her face and blew her nose softly, very ladylike.

"Can we talk now?"

She blinked at me and nodded. She took a shaky sip of pop.

"You know Harold Gaynor, right?"

She just stared at me, dully. Had we broken her? "If he finds out, he will kill me. Maybe I don't want to be coffin-bait, but I sure as hell don't want to die either."

"No one does. Talk to me, Wanda, please."

She let out a shaky sigh. "Okay, I know Harold."

Harold? "Tell me about him."

Wanda stared at me. Her eyes narrowed. There were fine lines around her eyes. It made her older than I had thought. "Has he sent Bruno or Tommy after you yet?"

"Tommy came for a personal meeting."

"What happened?"

"I drew a gun on him."

"That gun?" she asked in a small voice.

"Yes."

"What did you do to make Harold mad?"

Truth or lie? Neither. "I refused to do something for him."

"What?"

I shook my head. "It doesn't matter."

"It can't have been sex. You aren't crippled." She said the last word like it was hard. "He doesn't touch anyone who's whole." The bitterness in her voice was thick enough to taste.

"How did you meet him?" I asked.

"I was in college at Wash U. Gaynor was donating money for something."

"And he asked you out?"

"Yeah." Her voice was so soft, I had to lean forward to hear it.

"What happened?"

"We were both in wheelchairs. He was rich. It was great." She rolled her lips under, like she was smoothing lipstick, then out, and swallowed.

"When did it stop being great?" I asked.

"I moved in with him. Dropped out of college. It was . . . easier than college. Easier than anything. He couldn't get enough of me." She stared down at her lap again. "He started wanting variety in the bedroom. See, his legs are crippled, but he can feel. I can't feel." Wanda's voice had dropped almost to a whisper. I had to lean against her knees to hear. "He liked to do things to my legs, but I couldn't feel it. So at first I thought that was okay, but . . . but he got really sick." She looked at me suddenly, her face only inches from mine. Her eyes were huge, swimming with unshed tears. "He cut me up. I couldn't feel it, but that's not the point, is it?"

"No," I said.

The first tear trailed down her face. I touched her hand. Her fingers wrapped around mine and held on.

"It's alright," I said, "it's alright."

She cried. I held her hand and lied. "It's alright now, Wanda. He can't hurt you anymore."

"Everyone hurts you," she said. "You were going to hurt me." There was accusation in her eyes.

It was a little late to explain good cop, bad cop to her. She wouldn't have believed it anyway.

"Tell me about Gaynor."

"He replaced me with a deaf girl."

"Cicely," I said.

She looked up, surprised. "You've met her?"

"Briefly."

Wanda shook her head. "Cicely is one sick chickie. She likes torturing people. It gets her off." Wanda looked at me as if trying to gauge my reaction. Was I shocked? No.

"Harold slept with both of us at the same time, sometimes. At the end it was always a threesome. It got real rough." Her voice dropped lower and lower, a hoarse whisper. "Cicely likes knives. She's real good at skinning things." She rolled her lips under again in that lipstick-smoothing gesture. "Gaynor would kill me just for telling you his bed-room secrets."

"Do you know any business secrets?"

She shook her head. "No, I swear. He was always very careful to keep me out of that. I thought at first it was so if the police came, I wouldn't be arrested." She looked down at her lap. "Later, I realized it was be-cause he knew I would be replaced. He didn't want me to know anything that could hurt him when he threw me away."

There was no bitterness now, no anger, only a hollow sadness. I wanted her to rant and rave. This quiet despair was aching. A hurt that would never heal. Gaynor had done worse than kill her. He'd left her alive. Alive and as crippled inside as out.

"I can't tell you anything but bedroom talk. It won't help you hurt him."

"Is there any bedroom talk that isn't about sex?" I asked.

"What do you mean?"

"Personal secrets, but not sex. You were his sweetie for nearly two years. He must have talked about something other than sex."

She frowned, thinking. "I . . . I guess he talked about his family."

"What about his family?"

"He was illegitimate. He was obsessed with his real father's family."

"He knew who they were?"

Wanda nodded. "They were rich, old money. His mother was a hooker turned mistress. When she got pregnant, they threw her out."

Like Gaynor did to his women, I thought. Freud is so often at work in our lives. Out loud I said, "What family?"

"He never said. I think he thought I'd blackmail them or go to them with his dirty little secrets. He desperately wants them to regret not welcoming him into the family. I think he only made his money so he could be as rich as they were."

"If he never gave you a name, how do you know he wasn't lying?"

"You wouldn't ask if you could hear him. His voice was so intense. He hates them. And he wants his birthright. Their money is his birthright."

"How does he plan to get their money?" I asked.

"Just before I left him, Harold had found where some of his ancestors were buried. He talked about treasure. Buried treasure, can you believe it?"

"In the graves?"

"No, his father's people got their first fortune from being river pirates. They sailed the Mississippi and robbed people. Gaynor was proud of that and angry about it. He said that the whole bunch of them were descended from thieves and whores. Where did they get off being so high and mighty to him?" She was watching my face as she spoke the last. Maybe she saw the beginnings of an idea.

"How would knowing the graves of his ancestors help him get their treasure?"

"He said he'd find some voodoo priest to raise them. He'd force them to give him their treasure that had been lost for centuries."

"Ah," I said.

"What? Did that help?"

I nodded. My role in Gaynor's little scheme had become clear. Painfully clear. The only question left was why me? Why didn't he go to someone thoroughly disreputable like Dominga Salvador? Someone who would take his money and kill his hornless goat and not lose any sleep over it. Why me, with my reputation for morality?

"Did he ever mention any names of voodoo priests?"

Wanda shook her head. "No, no names. He was always careful about names. There's a look on your face. How could what I have told you just now help you?"

"I think the less you know about that, the better, don't you?"

She stared at me for a long time but finally nodded. "I guess so."

"Is there any place . . ." I let it trail off. I was going to offer her a plane ticket or a bus ticket to anywhere. Anywhere where she wouldn't have to sell herself. Anywhere where she could heal.

Maybe she read it in my face or my silence. She laughed, and it was a rich sound. Shouldn't whores have cynical cackles?

"You are a social worker type after all. You want to save me, don't you?"

"Is it terribly naive to offer you a ticket home or somewhere?"

She nodded. "Terribly. And why should you want to help me? You're not a man. You don't like women. Why should you offer to send me home?"

"Stupidity," I said and stood.

"It's not stupid." She took my hand and squeezed it. "But it wouldn't do any good. I'm a whore. Here at least I know the town, the people. I have regulars." She released my hand and shrugged. "I get by."

"With a little help from your friends," I said.

She smiled, and it wasn't happy. "Whores don't have friends."

"You don't have to be a whore. Gaynor made you a whore, but you don't have to stay one."

There were tears trembling in her eyes for the third time that night. Hell, she wasn't tough enough for the streets. No one was.

"Just call a taxi, okay. I don't want to talk anymore."

What could I do? I called a taxi. I told the driver the fare was in a wheelchair like Wanda told me to. She let Jean-Claude carry her back downstairs because I couldn't do it. But she was very tight and still in his arms. We left her in her chair on the curb.

I watched until the taxi came and took her away. Jean-Claude stood beside me in the golden circle of light just in front of my apartment building. The warm light seemed to leech color from his skin.

"I must leave you now, *ma petite*. It has been very educational, but time grows short."

"You're going to go feed, aren't you?"

"Does it show?"

"A little."

"I should call you *ma vérité*, Anita. You always tell me the truth about myself."

"Is that what *vérité* means? Truth?" I asked.

He nodded.

I felt bad. Itchy, grumpy, restless. I was mad at Harold Gaynor for victimizing Wanda. Mad at Wanda for allowing it. Angry with myself for not being able to do anything about it. I was pissed at the whole world tonight. I'd learned what Gaynor wanted me to do. And it didn't help a damn bit.

"There will always be victims, Anita. Predators and prey, it is the way of the world."

I glared up at him. "I thought you couldn't read me anymore."

"I cannot read your mind or your thoughts, only your face and what I know of you."

I didn't want to know that Jean-Claude knew me that well. That intimately. "Go away, Jean-Claude, just go away."

"As you like, *ma petite*." And just like that he was gone. A rush of wind, then nothing.

"Show-off," I murmured. I was left standing in the dark, tasting the first edge of tears. Why did I want to cry over a whore whom I'd just met? Over the unfairness of the world in general?

Jean-Claude was right. There would always be prey and predator. And I had worked very hard to be one of the predators. I was the Executioner. So why were my sympathies always with the victims? And why did the despair in Wanda's eyes make me hate Gaynor more than anything he'd ever done to me?

Why indeed?

## 26

THE PHONE RANG. I moved nothing but my eyes to glance at the bedside clock: 6:45 A.M. Shit. I lay there waiting, half drifted to sleep again when the answering machine picked up.

"It's Dolph. We found another one. Call my pager . . ."

I scrambled for the phone, dropping the receiver in the process. "H'lo, Dolph. I'm here."

"Late night?"

"Yeah, what's up?"

"Our friend has decided that single family homes are easy pickings." His voice sounded rough with lack of sleep.

"God, not another family."

" 'Fraid so. Can you come out?"

It was a stupid question, but I didn't point that out. My stomach had dropped into my knees. I didn't want a repeat of the Reynolds house. I didn't think my imagination could stand it.

"Give me the address. I'll be there."

He gave me the address.

"St. Peters," I said. "It's close to St. Charles, but still . . ."

"Still what?"

"It's a long way to walk for a single family home. There are lots of houses that fit the bill in St. Charles. Why did it travel so far to feed?"

"You're asking *me*?" he said. There was something almost like laughter in his voice. "Come on out, Ms. Voodoo Expert. See what there is to see."

"Dolph, is it as bad as the Reynolds house?"

"Bad, worse, worst of all," he said. The laughter was still there, but it held an edge of something hard and self-deprecating.

"This isn't your fault," I said.

"Tell that to the top brass. They're screaming for someone's ass."

"Did you get the warrant?"

"It'll come in this afternoon late."

"No one gets warrants on a weekend," I said.

"Special panic-mode dispensation," Dolph said. "Get your ass out here, Anita. Everyone needs to go home." He hung up.

I didn't bother saying bye.

Another murder. Shit, shit, shit. Double shit. It was not the way I wanted to spend Saturday morning. But we were getting our warrant. Yippee. The trouble was I didn't know what to look for. I wasn't really a voodoo expert. I was a preternatural crimes expert. It wasn't the same thing. Maybe I should ask Manny to come along. No, no, I didn't want him near Dominga Salvador in case she decided to cut a deal and give him to the police. There is no statute of limitations on human sacrifice. Manny could still go down for it. It'd be Dominga's style to trade my friend for her life. Making it, in a roundabout way, my fault. Yeah, she'd love that.

The message light on my answering machine was blinking. Why hadn't I noticed it last night? I shrugged. One of life's mysteries. I pressed the playback button.

"Anita Blake, this is John Burke. I got your message. Call me anytime here. I'm eager to hear what you have." He gave the phone number, and that was it.

Great, a murder scene, a trip to the morgue, and a visit to voodoo land, all in one day. It was going to be a busy and unpleasant day. It matched last night perfectly, and the night before. Shit, I was on a roll.

# 27

THERE WAS A patrol cop throwing up his guts into one of those giant, elephant-sized trash cans in front of the house. Bad sign. There was a television news van parked across the street. Worse sign. I didn't know how Dolph had kept zombie massacres out of the news so long. Current events must have been really hopping for the newshounds to ignore such easy headlines. ZOMBIES MASSACRE FAMILY. ZOMBIE SERIAL MURDERER ON LOOSE. Jesus, it was going to be a mess.

The camera crew, complete with microphone-bearing suit, watched me as I walked towards the yellow police tape. When I clipped the official plastic card on my collar, the news crew moved like one animal. The uniform at the police tape held it for me, his eyes on the descending press. I didn't look back. Never look back when the press are gaining on you. They catch you if you do.

The blond in the suit yelled out, "Ms. Blake, Ms. Blake, can you give us a statement?"

Always nice to be recognized, I guess. But I pretended not to hear. I kept walking, head determinedly down.

A crime scene is a crime scene is a crime scene. Except for the unique nightmarish qualities of each one. I was standing in a bedroom of a very nice one-story ranch. There was a white ceiling fan that turned slowly.

It made a faint whirring creak, as if it wasn't screwed in tight on one side.

Better to concentrate on the small things. The way the east light fell through the slanting blinds, painting the room in zebra-stripe shadows. Better not to look at what was left on the bed. Didn't want to look. Didn't want to see.

Had to see. Had to look. Might find a clue. Sure, and pigs could fucking fly. But still, maybe, maybe there would be a clue. Maybe. Hope is a lying bitch.

There are roughly two gallons of blood in the human body. As much blood as they put on television and the movies, it's never enough. Try dumping out two full gallons of milk on your bedroom floor. See what a mess it makes, now multiply that by . . . something. There was too much blood for just one person. The carpet squeeched underfoot, and blood came up in little splatters like mud after a rain. My white Nikes were spotted with scarlet before I was halfway to the bed.

Lesson learned: wear black Nikes to murder scenes.

The smell was thick in the room. I was glad for the ceiling fan. The room smelled like a mixture of slaughterhouse and outhouse. Shit and blood. The smell of fresh death, more often than not.

Sheets covered not just the bed, but a lot of the floor around the bed. It looked like giant paper towels thrown over the world's biggest Kool-Aid spill. There had to be pieces all over, under the sheets. The lumps were so small, too small to be a body. There wasn't a single scarlet-soaked bump that was big enough for a human body.

"Please don't make me look," I whispered to the empty room.

"Did you say something?"

I jumped and found Dolph standing just behind me. "Jesus, Dolph, you scared me."

"Wait until you see what's under the sheets. Then you can be scared."

I didn't want to see what was under the army of blood-soaked sheets. Surely, I'd seen enough for one week. My quota of gore had to have been exceeded, night before last. Yeah, I was over my quota.

Dolph stood in the doorway waiting. There were tiny pinched lines by his eyes that I had never noticed. He was pale and needed a shave.

We all needed something. But first I had to look under the sheets. If Dolph could do it, I could do it. Ri-ight.

Dolph stuck his head out in the hallway. "We need some help in here lifting the sheets. After Blake sees the remains we can go home." I think he added that last because no one had moved to help. He wasn't going to get any volunteers. "Zerbrowski, Perry, Merlioni, get your butts in here."

The bags under Zerbrowski's eyes looked like bruises. "Hiya, Blake."

"Hi, Zerbrowski, you look like shit."

He laughed. "And you still look fresh and lovely as a spring morning." He grinned at me.

"Yeah, right," I said.

Detective Perry said, "Ms. Blake, good to see you again."

I had to smile. Perry was the only cop I knew who would be gracious even over the bloody remains. "Nice to see you, too, Detective Perry."

"Can we get on with this," Merlioni said, "or are the two of you planning to elope?" Merlioni was tall, though not as tall as Dolph. But then who was? He had grey curling hair cut short and buzzed on the sides and over his ears. He wore a white dress shirt with the sleeves rolled up to his elbows and a tie at half-mast. His gun stuck out on his left hip like a lumpy wallet.

"You take the first sheet then, Merlioni, if you're in such a damn hurry," Dolph said.

Merlioni sighed. "Yeah, yeah." He stepped to the sheet on the floor. He knelt. "You ready for this, girlie?"

"Better girlie than dago," I said.

He smiled.

"Do it."

"Showtime," Merlioni said. He raised the sheet and it stuck in a wet swatch that pulled up one wet inch at a time.

"Zerbrowski, help him raise the damn thing," Dolph said.

Zerbrowski didn't argue. He must have been tired. The two men lifted the sheet in one wet motion. The morning sunlight streamed through the red sheet and painted the rug even redder than it was, or maybe it didn't make any difference. Blood dripped from the edges of the sheet where the men held it. Wet, heavy drops, like a sink that needed fixing. I'd never seen a sheet saturated with blood before. A morning of firsts.

I stared at the rug and couldn't make sense of it. It was just a pile of lumps, small lumps. I knelt beside them. Blood soaked through the knee of my jeans, it was cold. Better than warm, I guess.

The biggest lump was wet and smooth, about five inches long. It was pink and healthy-looking. It was a scrap of upper intestine. A smaller lump lay just beside it. I stared at the lump but the longer I stared the less it looked like anything. It could have been a hunk of meat from any animal. Hell, the intestine didn't have to be human. But it was, or I wouldn't be here.

I poked the smaller glob with one gloved finger. I had remembered my surgical gloves this time. Goody for me. The glob was wet and heavy and solid. I swallowed hard, but I was no closer to knowing what it was. The two scraps were like morsels dropped from a cat's mouth. Crumbs from the table. Jesus.

I stood. "Next." My voice sounded steady, ordinary. Amazing.

It took all four men lifting from different corners to peel the sheet back from the bed. Merlioni cursed and dropped his corner, "Dammit!"

Blood had run down his arm onto the white shirt. "Did um's get his shirt messy?" Zerbrowski asked.

"Fuck yes. This place is a mess."

"I guess the lady of the house didn't have time to clean up before you came, Merlioni," I said. My eyes flicked down to the bed and the remains of the lady of the house. But I looked back up at Merlioni instead. "Or can't the dago cop take it?"

"I can take anything you can dish out, little lady," he said. I frowned and shook my head. "Betcha can't."

"I'll take some of that action," Zerbrowski said.

Dolph didn't stop us, tell us this was a crime scene, not a betting parlor. He knew we needed it to stay sane. I could not stare down at the remains and not make jokes. I couldn't. I'd go crazy. Cops have the weirdest sense of humor, because they have to.

"How much you bet?" Merlioni said.

"A dinner for two at Tony's," I said.

Zerbrowski whistled. "Steep, very steep."

"I can afford to foot the bill. Is it a deal?"

Merlioni nodded. "My wife and I haven't been out in ages." He offered his blood-soaked hand. I took it. The cool blood clung to the
outside of my surgical gloves. It felt wet, like it had soaked through to
the skin, but it hadn't. It was a sensory illusion. I knew that when I took
off the gloves my hands would be powder dry. It was still unnerving.

"How we prove who's toughest?" Merlioni asked.

"This scene, here and now," I said.

"Deal."

I turned my attention back to the carnage with renewed determination. I would win the bet. I wouldn't let Merlioni have the satisfaction.
It gave me something to concentrate on rather than the mess on the
bed.

The left half of a rib cage lay on the bed. A naked breast was still
attached to it. The lady of the house? Everything was brilliant scarlet
red, like someone had poured buckets of red paint on the bed. It was
hard to pick out the pieces. There a left arm, small, female.

I picked up the fingers and they were limp, no rigor mortis. There
was a wedding band set on the third finger. I moved the fingers back
and forth. "No rigor mortis. What do you think, Merlioni?"

He squinted down at the arm. He couldn't let me out-do him so he
fiddled with the hand, turning it at the wrist. "Could be rigor came and
went. You know the first rigor doesn't last."

"You really think nearly two days have passed?" I shook my head.
"The blood's too fresh for that. Rigor hasn't set in. The crime isn't
eight hours old yet."

He nodded. "Not bad, Blake. But what do you make of this?" He
poked the rib cage enough to make the breast jiggle.

I swallowed hard. I would win this bet. "I don't know. Let's see. Help
me roll it over." I stared into his face while I asked. Did he pale just a
bit? Maybe.

"Sure."

The three others were standing at the side of the room, watching the
show. Let them. It was a lot more diverting than thinking of this as
work.

Merlioni and I moved the rib cage over on its side. I made sure to give him the fleshy parts, so he ended up groping the dead body. Was breast tissue breast tissue? Did it matter that it was bloody and cold? Merlioni looked just a little green. I guess it mattered.

The insides of the rib cage were snatched clean like Mr. Reynolds's rib cage. Clean and bloody smooth. We let the rib cage fall back on the bed. It splattered blood in a faint spray onto us. His white shirt showed it worse than my blue polo shirt did. Point for me.

He grimaced and brushed at the blood specks. He smeared blood from his gloves down the shirt. Merlioni closed his eyes and took a deep breath.

"Are you alright, Merlioni?" I asked. "I wouldn't want you to continue if it's upsetting you."

He glared at me, then smiled. A most unpleasant smile. "You ain't seen it all, girlie. I have."

"But have you touched it all?"

A trickle of sweat slid down his face. "You won't want to touch it all."

I shrugged. "We'll see." There was a leg on the bed, from the hair and the one remaining tennis shoe it looked male. The round, wet mound of the ball socket gleamed out at us. The zombie had just torn the leg off, tearing flesh without tearing bone.

"That must have hurt like a son of a bitch," I said.

"You think he was alive when the leg was pulled off?"

I nodded. "Yeah." I wasn't a hundred percent sure. There was too much blood to tell who had died when, but Merlioni looked a little paler.

The rest of the pieces were just bloody entrails, globs of flesh, bits of bone. Merlioni picked up a handful of entrails. "Catch."

"Jesus, Merlioni, that isn't funny." My stomach was one tight knot.

"No, but the look on your face is," he said.

I glared at him and said, "Throw it or don't, Merlioni, no teasing."

He blinked at me for a minute, then nodded. He tossed the string of entrails. They were awkward to throw but I managed to catch them. They were wet, heavy, flaccid, squeeshy, and altogether disgusting, like touching raw calf's liver but more so.

Dolph made an exasperated sound. "While you two are playing gross out, can you tell me something useful?"

I dropped the flesh back on the bed. "Sure. The zombie came in through the sliding glass door like last time. It chased the man or woman back in here and got them both." I stopped talking. I just froze.

Merlioni was holding up a baby blanket. Some trick had left a corner of it clean. It was edged in satiny pink with tiny balloons and clowns all over it. Blood dripped heavily from the other end of it.

I stared at the tiny balloons and clowns while they danced in useless circles. "You bastard," I whispered.

"Are you referring to me?" Merlioni asked.

I shook my head. I didn't want to touch the blanket. But I reached out for it. Merlioni made sure that the bloody edge slapped my bare arm. "Dago bastard," I said.

"You referring to me, bitch?"

I nodded and tried to smile but didn't really manage it. We had to keep pretending that this was alright. That this was doable. It was obscene. If the bet hadn't held me I'd have run screaming from the room.

I stared at the blanket. "How old?"

"Family portrait out front, I'd guess three, four months."

I was finally on the other side of the bed. There was another sheet-draped spot. It was just as bloody, just as small. There was nothing whole under the sheet. I wanted to call the bet off. If they wouldn't make me look I'd take them all to Tony's. Just don't make me lift that last sheet. Please, please.

But I had to look, bet or no bet, I had to see what there was to see. Might as well see it and win, as run and lose.

I handed the blanket back to Merlioni. He took it and laid it back on the bed, up high so the clean corner would stay clean.

I knelt on one side of the sheet. He knelt on the other. Our eyes met. It was a challenge then, to the gruesome end. We peeled back the sheet.

There were only two things under the sheet. Only two. My stomach contracted so hard I had to swallow vomit. I coughed and almost lost it there, but I held on. I held on.

I'd thought the blood-soaked form was the baby, but it wasn't. It was a doll. So blood-soaked I couldn't tell what color its hair had been, but it was just a doll. A doll too old for a four-month-old baby.

A tiny hand lay on the carpet, covered in gore like everything else, but it was a hand. A tiny hand. The hand of a child, not a baby. I spread my hand just above it to size it. Three, maybe four. About the same age as Benjamin Reynolds. Was that coincidence? Had to be. Zombies weren't that choosy.

"I'm breast-feeding the baby, maybe, when I hear a loud noise. Husband goes to check. Noise wakes the little girl, she comes out of her room to see what's the matter. Husband sees the monster, grabs the child, runs for the bedroom. The zombie takes them here. Kills them all, here." My voice sounded distant, clinical. Bully for me.

I tried to wipe some of the blood off the tiny hand. She was wearing a ring like Mommy. One of those plastic rings you get out of bubble gum machines.

"Did you see the ring, Merlioni?" I asked. I lifted the hand from the carpet and said, "Catch."

"Jesus!" He was on his feet and moving before I could do anything else. Merlioni walked very fast out the door. I wouldn't really have thrown the hand. I wouldn't.

I cradled the tiny hand in my hands. It felt heavy, as if the fingers should curl round my hand. Should ask me to take it for a walk. I dropped the hand on the carpet. It landed with a wet splat.

The room was very hot and spinning ever so slightly. I blinked and stared at Zerbrowski. "Did I win the bet?"

He nodded. "Anita Blake, tough chick. One night of delectable feasting at Tony's on Merlioni's tab. I hear they make great spaghetti."

The mention of food was too much. "Bathroom, where?"

"Down the hall, third door on the left," Dolph said.

I ran for the bathroom. Merlioni was just coming out. I didn't have time to savor my victory. I was too busy tossing my cookies.

# 28

I KNELT WITH my forehead against the cool porcelain of the bathtub. I was feeling better. Lucky I hadn't taken time to eat breakfast.

There was a tap on the door.

"What?" I said.

"It's Dolph. Can I come in?"

I thought about that for a minute. "Sure."

Dolph came in with a washcloth in his hand. Linen closet, I guessed. He stared at me for a minute or two and shook his head. He rinsed the washrag in the sink and handed it to me. "You know what to do with it."

I did. The rag was cold and felt wonderful on my face and neck. "Did you give Merlioni one, too?" I asked.

"Yeah, he's in the kitchen. You're both assholes, but it was entertaining."

I managed a weak smile.

"Now that you're through grandstanding, any useful observations?" He sat on the closed lid of the stool.

I stayed on the floor. "Did anybody hear anything, this time?"

"Neighbor heard something around dawn, but he went on to work. Said, he didn't want to get involved in a domestic dispute."

I stared up at Dolph. "Had he heard fighting from this house before?"

Dolph shook his head.

"God, if he had just called the police," I said.

"You think it would have made a difference?" Dolph asked.

I thought about that for a minute. "Maybe not to this family, but we might have trapped the zombie."

"Spilled milk," Dolph said.

"Maybe not. The scene is still very fresh. The zombie killed them, then took the time to eat four people. That isn't quick. At dawn the thing was still killing them."

"Your point."

"Seal the area."

"Explain."

"The zombie has to be nearby, within walking distance. It's hiding, waiting for nightfall."

"I thought zombies could go out in daylight," Dolph said.

"They can, but they don't like it. A zombie won't go out in the day unless ordered to."

"So the nearest cemetery," he said.

"Not necessarily. Zombies aren't like vamps or ghouls. It doesn't need to be coffins or even graves. The zombie will just want to get out of the light."

"So where do we look?"

"Sheds, garages, any place that will shield it."

"So he could be in some kid's tree house," Dolph said.

I smiled. Nice to know I still could. "I doubt the zombie would climb if given a choice. Notice that all the houses are one-stories."

"Basements," he said.

"But no one runs down to the basement," I said.

"Would it have helped?"

I shrugged. "Zombies aren't great at climbing, as a rule. This one is faster and more alert but . . . At best the basement might have delayed it. If there were windows, they might have gotten the children out." I rubbed the cloth on the back of my neck. "The zombie picks one-story houses with sliding glass doors. It might rest near one."

"The medical examiner says the corpse is tall, six feet, six-two. Male, white. Immensely strong."

"We knew the last, and the rest doesn't really help."

"You got a better idea?"

"As a matter of fact," I said, "have all the officers about the right height walk the neighborhood for an hour. Then block off that much of the area."

"And search all the sheds and garages," Dolph said.

"And basements, crawl spaces, old refrigerators," I said.

"If we find it?"

"Fry it. Get an exterminator team out here."

"Will the zombie attack during the day?" Dolph asked.

"If disturbed enough, yes. This one's awfully aggressive."

"No joke," he said. "We'd need a dozen exterminator teams or more. The city'll never go for that. Besides, we could walk a pretty damn wide circle. We might search and miss it completely."

"It'll move at dark. If you're ready, you'll find it then."

"Okay. You sound like you're not going to help search."

"I'll be back to help, but John Burke returned my call."

"You taking him to the morgue?"

"Yeah, in time to try to use him against Dominga Salvador. What timing," I said.

"Good. You need anything from me?"

"Just access to the morgue for both of us," I said.

"Sure thing. You think you'll really learn anything from Burke?"

"Don't know till I try," I said.

He smiled. "Give it the old college try, eh?"

"Win one for the Gipper," I said.

"You go visit the morgue and deal with voodoo John. We'll turn this fucking neighborhood upside down."

"Nice to know we've both got our days planned," I said.

"Don't forget this afternoon we check out Salvador's house."

I nodded. "Yeah, and tonight we hunt zombies."

"We're going to end this shit tonight," he said.

"I hope so."

He looked at me, eyes narrowed. "You got a problem with our plans?"

"Just that no plan is perfect."

He was quiet a moment, then stood. "Wish this one was."

"Me, too."

## 29

The St. Louis county morgue was a large building. It needs to be. Every death not attended by a physician comes to the morgue. Not to mention every murder. In St. Louis that made for some very heavy traffic.

I use to come to the morgue fairly regularly. To stake suspected vampire victims so they wouldn't rise and feast on the morgue attendants. With the new vamp laws, that's murder. You have to wait for the puppies to rise, unless they've left a will strictly forbidding coming back as a vampire. My will says to put me out of my misery if they think I'm coming back with fangs. Hell, my will asks for cremation. I don't want to come back as a zombie either, thank you very much.

John Burke was as I remembered him. Tall, dark, handsome, vaguely villainous. It was the little goatee that did it. No one wears goatees outside of horror movies. You know, the ones with strange cults that worship horned images.

He looked a little faded around the eyes and mouth. Grief will do that to you even if your skin tone is dark. His lips were set in a thin line as we walked into the morgue. He held his shoulders as if something hurt.

"How's it going at your sister-in-law's?" I asked.

"Bleak, very bleak."

I waited for him to elaborate, but he didn't. So I let it go. If he didn't want to talk about it, that was his privilege.

We were walking down a wide empty corridor. Wide enough for three gurneys to wheel abreast. The guard station looked like a WWII bunker, complete with machine guns. In case the dead should rise all at once and make for freedom. It had never happened here in St. Louis, but it had happened as close as Kansas City.

A machine gun will take the starch out of any walking dead. You're only in trouble if there are a lot of them. If there is a crowd, you're pretty much cooked.

I flashed my ID at the guard. "Hi, Fred, long time no see."

"I wish they let you come down here like before. We've had three get up this week and go home. Can you believe that?"

"Vampires?"

"What else? There's going to be more of them than of us someday."

I didn't know what to say, so I said nothing. He was probably right. "We're here to see the personal effects of Peter Burke. Sergeant Rudolph Storr was supposed to clear it."

Fred checked his little book. "Yeah, you're authorized. Take the right corridor, third door on the left. Dr. Saville is waiting for you."

I raised an eyebrow at that. It wasn't often that the chief medical examiner did errands for the police or anybody else. I just nodded as if I had expected royal treatment.

"Thanks, Fred, see you on the way out."

"More and more people do," he said. He didn't sound happy about it.

My Nikes made no sound in the perpetual quiet. John Burke wasn't making any noise either. I hadn't pegged him as a tennis shoe man. I glanced down, and I was right. Soft-soled brown tie-ups, not tennis shoes. But he still moved beside me like a quiet shadow.

The rest of his outfit sort of matched the shoes. A dressy brown sport jacket so dark brown it was almost black, over a pale yellow shirt, brown dress slacks. He only needed a tie, and he could have gone to corporate America. Did he always dress up, or was this just what he had brought for his brother's funeral? No, the suit at the funeral had been perfectly black.

The morgue was always quiet, but on a Saturday morning it was deathly still. Did the ambulances circle like planes until a decent hour on the weekend? I knew the murder count went up on the weekend, yet Saturday and Sunday morning were always quiet. Go figure.

I counted doors on the left-hand side. Knocked on the third door. A faint "Come in," and I opened the door.

Dr. Marian Saville is a small woman with short dark hair bobbed just below her ears, an olive complexion, deeply brown eyes, and fine high cheekbones. She is French and Greek and looks it. Exotic without being intimidating. It always surprised me that Dr. Saville wasn't married. It wasn't for lack of being pretty.

Her only fault was that she smoked, and the smell clung to her like nasty perfume.

She came forward with a smile and an offered hand. "Anita, good to see you again."

I shook her hand, and smiled. "You, too, Dr. Saville."

"Marian, please."

I shrugged. "Marian, are those the personal effects?"

We were in a small examining room. On a lovely stainless-steel table were several plastic bags.

"Yes."

I stared at her, wondering what she wanted. The chief medical examiner didn't do errands. Something else was up, but what? I didn't know her well enough to be blunt, and I didn't want to be barred from the morgue, so I couldn't be rude. Problems, problems.

"This is John Burke, the deceased's brother," I said.

Dr. Saville's eyebrows raised at that. "My condolences, Mr. Burke."

"Thank you." John shook the hand she offered him, but his eyes were all for the plastic bags. There was no room today for attractive doctors or pleasantries. He was going to see his brother's last effects. He was looking for clues to help the police catch his brother's killer. He had taken the notion very seriously.

If he wasn't involved with Dominga Salvador, I would owe him a big apology. But how was I to get him to talk with Dr. Marian hovering around? How was I supposed to ask for privacy? It was her morgue, sort of.

"I have to be here to make sure no evidence is tampered with," she said. "We've had a few very determined reporters lately."

"But I'm not a reporter."

She shrugged. "You're not an official person, Anita. New rules from on high that no nonofficial person is to be allowed to look at murder evidence without someone to watch over them."

"I appreciate it being you, Marian."

She smiled. "I was here anyway. I figured you'd resent my looking over your shoulder less than anyone else."

She was right. What did they think I was going to do, steal a body? If I wanted to, I could empty the damn place and get every corpse to play follow the leader.

Perhaps that was why I needed watching. Perhaps.

"I don't mean to be rude," John said, "but could we get on with this?"

I glanced up at his handsome face. The skin was tight around the mouth and eyes as if it had thinned. Guilt speared me in the side. "Sure, John, we're being thoughtless."

"Your forgiveness, Mr. Burke," Marian said. She handed us both little plastic gloves. She and I slipped into them like pros, but John wasn't used to putting on examining gloves. There is a trick to it—practice. By the time I finished helping him on with his gloves, he was grinning. His whole face changed when he smiled. Brilliant and handsome and not the least villainous.

Dr. Saville popped the seal on the first bag. It was clothing.

"No," John said, "I don't know his clothing. It maybe his, and I wouldn't know. Peter and I had . . . hadn't seen each other in two years." The guilt in those last words made me wince.

"Fine, we'll go on to the smaller items," Marian said, and smiled as she said it. Nice and cheery, practicing her bedside manner. She so seldom got to practice.

She opened a much smaller bag and spilled the contents gently on the shiny silver surface. A comb, a dime, two pennies, a movie ticket stub, and a voodoo charm. A gris-gris.

It was woven of black and red thread with human teeth worked into the beading. More bones dangled all the way around it. "Are those human finger bones?" I asked.

"Yes," John said, his voice very still. He looked strange as he stood there, as if some new horror were dawning behind his eyes.

It was an evil piece of work, but I didn't understand the strength of his reaction to it.

I leaned over it, poking it with one finger. There was some dried skin woven in the center of it all. And it wasn't just black thread, it was black hair.

"Human hair, teeth, bones, skin," I said softly.

"Yes," John repeated.

"You're more into voodoo than I am," I said. "What does it mean?"

"Someone died to make this charm."

"Are you sure?"

He glared down at me with withering contempt. "Don't you think if it could be anything else I wouldn't say it? Do you think I enjoy learning my brother took part in human sacrifice?"

"Did Peter have to be there? He couldn't have just bought it afterwards?"

"NO!" It was almost a yell. He turned away from us, pacing to the wall. His breathing was loud and ragged.

I gave him a few moments to collect himself, then asked what had to be asked. "What does the gris-gris do?"

He turned a calm enough face to us, but the strain showed around his eyes. "It enables a less powerful necromancer to raise older dead, to borrow the power of some much greater necromancer."

"How borrow?"

He shrugged. "That charm holds some of the power of the most powerful among us. Peter paid dearly for it, so he could raise more and older dead. Peter, God, how could you?"

"How powerful would you need to be to share your power like this?"

"Very powerful," he said.

"Is there any way to trace it back to the person who made it?"

"You don't understand, Anita. That thing is a piece of someone's power. It is one substance to what soul they have left. It must have been a great need or great greed to do it. Peter could never have afforded it. Never."

"Can it be traced back?"

"Yes, just get it in the room with the person who truly owns it. The thing will crawl back to him. It's a piece of his soul gone missing."

"Would that be proof in court?"

"If you could make the jury understand it, yes, I guess so." He stepped towards me. "You know who did this?"

"Maybe."

"Who, tell me who?"

"I'll do better than that. I'll arrange for you to come on a search of their house."

A grim smile touched his lips. "I'm beginning to like you a great deal, Anita Blake."

"Compliments later."

"What's this mean?" Marian asked. She had turned the charm completely over. There, shining among the hair and bone, was a small charm, like from a charm bracelet. It was in the shape of a musical symbol—a treble clef.

What had Evans said when he touched the grave fragments; they slit her throat, she had a charm bracelet with a musical note on it and little hearts. I stared at the charm and felt the world shift. Everything fell together in one motion. Dominga Salvador hadn't raised the killer zombie. She had helped Peter Burke raise it. But I had to be sure. We only had a few hours until we'd be back at Dominga's door trying to prove a case.

"Are there any women that came in around the same time as Peter Burke?"

"I'm sure there are," Marian said with a smile.

"Women with their throats slit," I said.

She stared at me for a heartbeat. "I'll check the computer."

"Can we take the charm with us?"

"Why?"

"Because if I'm right, she had a charm bracelet with a bow and arrow and little hearts on it, and this came from the bracelet." I held the gold charm up to the light. It sparkled merrily as if it didn't know its owner was dead.

## 30

DEATH TURNS YOU grey before any other color. Oh, a body that loses a lot of blood will look white or bluish. But once a body starts to decay, not rot, not yet, it looks greyish.

The woman looked grey. Her neck wound had been cleaned and searched. The wound looked puckered like a second giant mouth below her chin.

Dr. Saville pulled her head back casually. "The cut was very deep. It severed the muscles in the neck and the carotid artery. Death was fairly quick."

"Professionally done," I said.

"Well, yes, whoever cut her throat knew what they were doing. There are a dozen different ways to injure the neck that won't kill or won't kill quickly."

John Burke said, "Are you saying that my brother had practice?"

"I don't know," I said. "Do you have her personal effects?"

"Right here." Marian unfastened a much smaller bag and spilled it out on an empty table. The golden charm bracelet sparkled under the fluorescent lights.

I picked the bracelet up in my still gloved hand. A tiny strung bow complete with arrow, a different musical note, two entwined hearts. Everything Evans had said.

"How did you know about the charm and the dead woman?" John Burke asked.

"I took some evidence to a clairvoyant. He saw the woman's death and the bracelet."

"What's that got to do with Peter?"

"I believe a voodoo priestess had Peter raise a zombie. It got away from him. It's been killing people. To hide what she's done, she killed Peter."

"Who did it?"

"I have no proof unless the gris-gris will be proof enough."

"A vision and a gris-gris." John shook his head. "Hard sell to a jury."

"I know. That's why we need more proof."

Dr. Saville just watched us talk, like an eager spectator.

"A name, Anita, give me a name."

"Only if you swear not to go after her until the law has its chance. Only if the law fails, promise me."

"I give you my word."

I studied his face for a minute. The dark eyes stared back, clear and certain. Bet he could lie with a clear conscience. "I don't trust just anybody's word." I stared at him a moment longer. He never flinched. I guess my hard-as-nails look has faded a little. Or maybe he meant to keep his word. It happens sometimes.

"Alright, I'll take your word. Don't make me regret it."

"I won't," he said. "Now give me the name."

I turned to Dr. Saville. "Excuse us, Marian. The less you know about all this, the greater your chances of never waking to a zombie crawling through your window." An exaggeration, sort of, but it made my point.

She looked like she wanted to protest but finally nodded. "Very well, but I would dearly love to hear the complete story someday, if it's safe."

"If I can tell it, it's yours," I said.

She nodded again, shut the drawer the Jane Doe lay on, and left. "Yell when you're finished. I've got work to do," she said and the door closed behind her.

She left us with the evidence still clutched in our hands. Guess she trusted me. Or us?

"Dominga Salvador," I said.

He drew a sharp breath. "I know that name. She is a frightening force if all the stories are true."

"They're true," I said.

"You've met her?"

"I've had the misfortune."

There was a look on his face that I didn't much like. "You swore no revenge."

"The police will not get her. She is too crafty for that," he said.

"We can get her legally. I believe that."

"You aren't sure," he said.

What could I say? He was right. "I'm almost sure."

"Almost is not good enough for killing my brother."

"That zombie has killed a lot more people than just your brother. I want her, too. But we're going to get her legally, through the court system."

"There are other ways to get her," he said.

"If the law fails us, feel free to use voodoo. Just don't tell me about it."

He looked amused, puzzled. "No outrage about me using black magic?"

"The woman tried to kill me once. I don't think she'll give up."

"You survived an attack by the Señora?" he asked. He looked amazed.

I didn't like him looking amazed. "I can take care of myself, Mr. Burke."

"I don't doubt that, Ms. Blake." He smiled. "I've bruised your ego. You don't like me being so surprised, do you?"

"Keep your observations to yourself, okay?"

"If you have survived a head-on confrontation with what Dominga Salvador would send to you, then I should have believed some of the stories I heard of you. The Executioner, the animator who can raise anything no matter how old."

"I don't know about that last, but I'm just trying to stay alive, that's all."

"If Dominga Salvador wants you dead that won't be easy."

"Damn near impossible," I said.

"So let us get her first," he said.

"Legally," I said.

"Anita, you are being naive."

"The offer to come on a raid of her house still stands."

"You're sure you can arrange that?"

"I think so."

His eyes had a sort of dark light to them, a sparkling blackness. He smiled, tight-lipped, and very unpleasant, as if he were contemplating tortures for one Dominga Salvador. The private vision seemed to fill him with pleasure.

The skin between my shoulders crept with that look. I hoped John never turned those dark eyes on me. Something told me he would make a bad enemy. Almost as bad as Dominga Salvador. Almost as bad, but not quite.

## 31

DOMINGA SALVADOR SAT in her living room smiling. The little girl who had been riding her tricycle on my last trip here was sitting in her grandma's lap. The child was as relaxed and languorous as a kitten. Two older boys sat at Dominga's feet. She was the picture of maternal bliss. I wanted to throw up.

Of course, just because she was the most dangerous voodoo priestess I'd ever met didn't mean she wasn't a grandma, too. People are seldom just one thing. Hitler liked dogs.

"You are more than welcome to search, Sergeant. My house is your house," she said in a candy-coated voice that had already offered us lemonade, or perhaps iced tea.

John Burke and I were standing to one side, letting the police do their job. Dominga was making them feel silly for their suspicions. Just a nice old lady. Right.

Antonio and Enzo were also standing to one side. They didn't quite fit this picture of grandmotherly bliss, but evidently she wanted witnesses. Or maybe a shootout wasn't out of the question.

"Mrs. Salvador, do you understand the possible implications of this search?" Dolph said.

"There are no implications because I have nothing to hide." She smiled sweetly. Damn her.

"Anita, Mr. Burke," Dolph said.

We came forward like props in a magic show. Which wasn't far off. A tall police officer had the video camera ready to go.

"I believe you know Ms. Blake," Dolph said.

"I have had the pleasure," Dominga said.

Butter wouldn't have melted in her lying mouth.

"This is John Burke."

Her eyes widened just a little. The first slip in her perfect camouflage. Had she heard of John Burke? Did the name worry her? I hoped so.

"So glad to meet you at last, Mr. John Burke," she said finally.

"Always good to meet another practitioner of the art," he said.

She bowed her head slightly in acknowledgment. At least she wasn't trying to pretend complete innocence. She admitted to being a voodoo priestess. Progress.

It was obscene for the godmother of voodoo to be playing the innocent.

"Do it, Anita," Dolph said. No preliminaries, no sense of theater, just do it. That was Dolph for you.

I took a plastic bag out of my pocket. Dominga looked puzzled. I pulled out the gris-gris. Her face became very still, like a mask. A funny little smile curled her lips. "What is that?"

"Come now, Señora," John said, "do not play the fool. You know very well what it is."

"I know that it is a charm of some kind, of course. But do the police now threaten old women with voodoo?"

"Whatever works," I said.

"Anita," Dolph said.

"Sorry." I glanced at John, and he nodded. I sat the gris-gris on the carpet about six feet from Dominga Salvador. I had had to take John's word on a lot of this. I had checked some of it over the phone with Manny. If this worked and if we could get it admitted into court, and if we could explain it to the jury, then we might have a case. How many ifs was that?

The gris-gris just sat there for a moment, then the finger bones rippled as if an invisible finger had ruffled them.

Dominga lifted her granddaughter from her lap and shooed the boys over to Enzo. She sat alone on the couch and waited. The strange little smile was still on her face, but it looked sickly now.

The charm began to ooze towards her like a slug, pushing and struggling with muscles it did not have. The hairs on my arms stood to attention.

"You recording this, Bobby?" Dolph asked.

The cop with the video camera said, "I'm getting it. I don't fucking believe it, but I'm getting it."

"Please, do not use such words in front of the children," Dominga said.

The cop said, "Sorry, ma'am."

"You are forgiven." She was still trying to play the perfect hostess while that thing crawled towards her feet. She had nerve. I'd give her that.

Antonio didn't. He broke. He strode forward as if he meant to pluck the thing from the rug.

"Don't touch it," Dolph said.

"You are frightening my grandmother with your tricks," he said.

"Don't touch it," Dolph said again. This time he stood. His bulk seemed to fill the room. Antonio looked suddenly small and frail beside him.

"Please, you are frightening her." But it was his face that was pale and covered with a sheen of sweat. What was ol' Tony in such a fret about? It wasn't his ass going to jail.

"Stand over there," Dolph said, "now, or do we have to cuff you?"

Antonio shook his head. "No, I . . . I will go back." He did, but he glanced at Dominga as he moved. A quick, fearful glance. When she met his eyes, there was nothing but rage in them. Her black eyes glittered with rage. Her face was suddenly contorted with it. What had happened to strip the act away? What was going on?

The gris-gris made its painful way to her. It fawned at her feet like a dog, rolling on the toes of her shoes in abandon like a cat who wants its belly rubbed.

She tried to ignore it, to pretend.

"Would you refuse your returned power?" John asked.

"I don't know what you mean." Her face was under control again.

She looked puzzled. Gosh, she was good. "You are a powerful voodoo priest. You are doing this to trap me."

"If you don't want the charm, I will take it," he said. "I will add your magic to mine. I will be the most powerful practitioner in the States." For the first time, John's power flowed across my skin. It was a breath of magic that was frightening. I had begun to think of John as ordinary, or as ordinary as any of us get. My mistake.

She just shook her head.

John strode forward and knelt, reaching for the writhing gris-gris. His power moved with him like an invisible hand.

"No!" She grabbed it, cradling it in her hands.

John smiled up at her. "Do you acknowledge that you made this charm? If not, I can take it and use it as I see fit. It was found in my brother's effects. It's legally mine, correct, Sergeant Storr?"

"Correct," Dolph said.

"No, you cannot."

"I can and I will, unless you look into that camera and admit making it."

She snarled at him. "You will regret this."

"You will regret having killed my brother."

She stared at the video camera. "Very well, I made this charm, but I admit nothing else. I made the charm for your brother, but that is all."

"You performed human sacrifice to make this charm," John said.

She shook her head. "The charm is mine. I made it for your brother, that is all. You have the charm but nothing else."

"Señora, forgive me," Antonio said. He looked pale and shaken and very, very scared.

"Calenta," she said, "shut up!"

"Zerbrowski, take our friend here into the kitchen and take his statement," Dolph said.

Dominga stood at that. "You fool, you miserable fool. Tell them anything more, and I will rot the tongue out of your mouth."

"Get him out of here, Zerbrowski."

Zerbrowski led a nearly weeping Antonio from the room. I had a feeling that ol' Tony had been responsible for getting the charm back. He failed, and he was going to pay the consequences. The police were the least of his problems. If I were him, I'd make damn sure grandma was locked up tonight. I wouldn't want her near her voodoo paraphernalia. Ever.

"We're going to search now, Mrs. Salvador."

"Help yourself, Sergeant. You will find nothing else to help you."

She was very calm when she said it. "Even the stuff behind the doors?" I asked.

"They are gone, Anita. You will find nothing that is not legal and . . . wholesome." She made that last sound like a bad word.

Dolph glanced my way. I shrugged. She seemed awfully sure.

"Okay, boys, take the place apart." Uniforms and detectives moved like they had a purpose. I started to follow Dolph out. He stopped me.

"No, Anita, you and Burke stay up here."

"Why?"

"You're civilians."

A civilian, me? "Was I a civilian when I walked the cemetery for you?"

"If one of my people could have done it, I wouldn't have let you do that either."

"Let me?"

He frowned. "You know what I mean."

"No, I don't think I do."

"You may be a bad ass, you may even be as good as you think you are, but you aren't police. This is a job for cops. You stay in the living room with the civies just this once. When it's all clear, you can come down and identify the bogeymen for us."

"Don't do me any favors, Dolph."

"I didn't peg you for a pouter, Blake."

"I am not pouting," I said.

"Whining?" he said.

"Cut it out. You've made your point. I'll stay behind, but I don't have to like it."

"Most of the time you're ass deep in alligators. Enjoy being out of the line of fire for once, Anita." With that he led the way towards the basement.

I hadn't really wanted to go down into the darkness again. I certainly didn't want to see the creature that had chased Manny and I up the stairs. And yet . . . I felt left out. Dolph was right. I was pouting. Great.

John Burke and I sat on the couch. Dominga sat in the recliner where she had been since we hit the door. The children had been shooed out to play, with Enzo to watch them. He looked relieved. I almost volunteered to go with them. Anything was better than just sitting here straining to hear the first screams.

If the monster, and that was the only word that matched the noises, was down there, there would be screaming. The police were great with bad guys, but monsters were new to them. It had been simpler, in a way, when all this shit was taken care of by a few experts. A few lone people fighting the good fight. Staking vampires. Turning zombies. Burning witches. Though there is some debate whether I might have ended up on the receiving end of some fire a few years back. Say, the 1950s.

What I did was undeniably magic. Before we got all the bogeymen out in the open, supernatural was supernatural. Destroy it before it destroys you. Simpler times. But now the police were expected to deal with zombies, vampires, the occasional demon. Police were really bad with demons. But then who isn't?

Dominga sat in her chair and stared at me. The two uniforms left in the living room stood like all police stand, blank-faced, bored, but let anyone move and the cops saw it. The boredom was just a mask. Cops always saw everything. Occupational hazard.

Dominga wasn't looking at the police. She wasn't even paying attention to John Burke, who was much closer to her equal. She was staring at little old me.

I met her black gaze and said, "You got a problem?"

The cop's eyes flicked to us. John shifted on the couch. "What's wrong?" he asked.

"She's staring at me."

"I will do a great deal more than stare at you, *chica*." Her voice crawled low. The hairs at the nape of my neck tried to crawl down my shirt.

"A threat." I smiled. "I don't think you're going to be hurting anybody anymore."

"You mean this." She held out the charm. It writhed in her hand as if thrilled that she had noticed it. She crushed it in her hand. It made futile movements as if pushing against her. Her hand covered it completely. She stared straight at me, as she brought her hand slowly to her chest.

The air was suddenly heavy, hard to breathe. Every hair on my body was creeping down my skin.

"Stop her!" John said. He stood.

The policeman nearest her hesitated for only an instant, but it was enough. When he pried her fingers open, they were empty.

"Sleight of hand, Dominga. I thought better of you than that."

John was pale. "It isn't a trick." His voice was shaky. He sat down heavily on the couch beside me. His dark face looked pale. His power seemed to have shriveled up. He looked tired.

"What is it? What did she do?" I asked.

"You have to bring back the charm, ma'am," the uniform said.

"I cannot," she said.

"John, what the hell did she do?"

"Something she shouldn't have been able to do."

I was beginning to know how Dolph must feel having to depend on me for information. It was like pulling fucking teeth. "What did she do?"

"She absorbed her power back into herself," he said.

"What does that mean?"

"She absorbed the gris-gris into her body. Didn't you feel it?"

I had felt something. The air was clearer now, but it was still heavy. My skin was tingling with the nearness of something. "I felt something, but I still don't understand."

"Without ceremony, without help from the loa, she absorbed it back into her soul. We won't find a trace of it. No evidence."

"So all we have is the tape?"

He nodded.

"If you knew she could do this, why didn't you speak up earlier? We wouldn't have let her hold the thing."

"I didn't know. It's impossible without ceremonial magic."

"But she did it."

"I know, Anita, I know." He sounded scared for the first time. Fear didn't sit well on his darkly handsome face. After the power I'd felt from him, the fear seemed even more out of place. But it was real nonetheless.

I shivered, like someone had walked on my grave. Dominga was staring at me. "What are you staring at?"

"A dead woman," she said softly.

I shook my head. "Talk is cheap, Señora. Threats don't mean squat."

John touched my arm. "Do not taunt her, Anita. If she can do that instantly, there's no telling what else she can do."

The cop had had enough. "She's not doing anything. If you so much as twitch wrong, lady, I'm going to shoot you."

"But I am just an old woman. Would you threaten me?"

"Don't talk either."

The other uniform said, "I knew a witch once who could bespell you with her voice."

Both uniforms had their hands near their guns. Funny how magic changes how people perceive you. They were fine when they thought she needed human sacrifice and ceremony. Let her do one instant trick, and she was suddenly very dangerous. I'd always known she was dangerous.

Dominga sat silently under the watchful eyes of the cops. I had been distracted by her little performance. There were still no screams from downstairs. Nothing. Silence.

Had it gotten them all? That quickly, without a shot fired. Naw. But still, my stomach was tight, sweat trickled down my spine. Are you alright, Dolph? I thought.

"Did you say something?" John asked.

I shook my head. "Just thinking really hard."

He nodded as if that made sense to him.

Dolph came into the living room. I couldn't tell anything by his face. Mr. Stoic.

"Well, what was it?" I asked.

"Nothing," he said.

"What do you mean, nothing?"

"She's cleaned the place out completely. We found the rooms you told me about. One door had been busted from inside, but the room's been scrubbed down and painted." He held up one big hand. It was stained white. "Hell, the paint's still wet."

"It can't all be gone. What about the cement-covered doors?"

"Looks like someone took a jackhammer to them. They're just freshly painted rooms, Anita. The place stinks of pine-scented bleach and wet paint. No corpses, no zombies. Nothing."

I just stared at him. "You've got to be kidding."

He shook his head. "I'm not laughing."

I stood in front of Dominga. "Who warned you?"

She just stared up at me, smiling. I had a great urge to slap that smile off her face. Just to hit her once would feel good. I knew it would.

"Anita," Dolph said, "back off."

Maybe the anger showed on my face, or maybe it was the fact that my hands were balled into fists and I seemed to be shaking. Shaking with anger and the beginnings of something else. If she didn't go to jail, that meant she was free to try to kill me again tonight. And every night after that.

She smiled as if she could read my mind. "You have nothing, *chica*. You have gambled all on a hand with nothing in it."

She was right. "Stay away from me, Dominga."

"I will not come near you, *chica*, I will not need to."

"Your last little surprise didn't work out so well. I'm still here."

"I have done nothing. But I am sure there are worse things that could come to your door, *chica*."

I turned to Dolph. "Dammit, isn't there anything we can do?"

"We got the charm, but that's it."

Something must have showed on my face because he touched my arm. "What is it?"

"She did something to the charm. It's gone."

He took a deep breath and stalked away, then back. "Dammit to hell, how?"

I shrugged. "Let John explain. I still don't understand it." I hate admitting that I don't know something. It's always bothered me to admit ignorance. But hey, a girl can't be an expert on everything. I had worked hard to stay away from voodoo. Work hard and where does it get you?

Staring into the black eyes of a voodoo priestess who's plotting your death. A most unpleasant death by the looks of it.

Well, in for a penny, in for a pound. I went back to her. I stood and stared into her dark face and smiled. Her own smile faltered, which made my smile bigger.

"Someone tipped you off and you've been cleaning up this cesspit for two days." I leaned over her, putting my hands on the arms of the chair. It brought our faces close together.

"You had to break down your walls. You had to let out or destroy all your creations. Your inner sanctum, your hougun, is cleaned and white-washed. All the verve gone. All the animal sacrifices gone. All that slow building of power, line by line, drop by bloody drop, you're going to have to start over, you bitch. You're going to have to rebuild it all."

The look in those black eyes made me shiver, and I didn't care. "You're getting old to rebuild that much. Did you have to destroy many of your toys? Dig up any graves?"

"Have your joke now, *chica*, but I will send what I have saved to you some dark night."

"Why wait? Do it now, in daylight. Face me or are you afraid?"

She laughed then, and it was a warm, friendly sound. It startled me so much I stood up straight, almost jumped back.

"Do you think I am foolish enough to attack you with the police all around? You must think me a fool."

"It was worth a try," I said.

"You should have joined with me in my zombie enterprises. We could have been rich together."

"The only thing we're likely to do together is kill each other," I said.

"So be it. Let it be war between us."

"It always was," I said.

She nodded and smiled some more.

Zerbrowski came out of the kitchen. He was grinning from ear to ear. Something good was up.

"The grandson just spilled the beans."

Everyone in the room stared at him. Dolph said, "Spilled what?"

"Human sacrifice. How he was supposed to get the gris-gris back from Peter Burke after he killed him, on his grandmother's orders, but some joggers came by and he panicked. He's so afraid of her"—he motioned to Dominga—"he wants her behind bars. He's terrified of what she'll do to him for forgetting the charm."

The charm that we didn't have anymore. But we had the video and now we had Antonio's confession. The day was looking up.

I turned back to Dominga Salvador. She looked tall and proud and terrifying. Her black eyes blazed with some inner light. Standing this close to her, the power crawled over my skin, but a good bonfire would take care of that. They'd fry her in the electric chair, then burn the body and scatter the ashes at a crossroad.

I said softly, "Gotcha."

She spit at me. It landed on my hand and burned like acid. "Shit!"

"Do that again and we'll shoot you, and save the taxpayers some money," Dolph said. He had his gun out.

I went in search of the bathroom to wash her spit off my hand. A blister had formed where it had hit. Second fucking degree burns from her spit. Dear God.

I was glad Antonio had broken. I was glad she was going to be locked away. I was glad she was going to die. Better her than me.

## 32

RIVERRIDGE WAS A modern housing development. Which meant that there were three models to choose from. You could end up with four identical houses in a row, like cookies on a baking sheet. There was also no river within sight. No ridge either.

The house that was the center of the police search area was identical to its neighbor, except for color. The murder house, which is what the news was calling it, was grey with white shutters. The house that had been passed safely by was blue with white shutters. Neither's shutters worked. They were just for show. Modern architecture is full of perks that are just for show; balcony railings without a balcony, peaked roofs that make it look like you have an extra room that you don't have, porches so narrow that only Santa's elves could sit on them. It makes me nostalgic for Victorian architecture. It might have been overdone, but everything worked.

The entire housing project had been evacuated. Dolph had been forced to give a statement to the press. More's the pity. But you can't evacuate a housing development the size of a small town and keep it quiet. The cat was out of the bag. They were calling them the zombie massacres. Geez.

The sun was going down in a sea of scarlet and orange. It looked like someone had melted two giant crayons and smeared them across the sky. There wasn't a shed, garage, basement, tree house, playhouse, or anything else we could think of that had been left unsearched. Still, we had found nothing.

The newshounds were prowling restlessly at the edge of the search area. If we had evacuated hundreds of people and searched their premises without a warrant and found no zombie . . . we were going to be in deep fucking shit.

But it was here. I knew it was here. Alright, I was almost sure it was here.

John Burke was standing next to one of those giant trash cans. Dolph had surprised me by allowing John to come on the zombie hunt. As Dolph said, we needed all the help we could get.

"Where is it, Anita?" Dolph asked.

I wanted to say something brilliant. My God, Holmes, how did you know the zombie was hiding in the flower pot? But I couldn't lie. "I don't know, Dolph. I just don't know."

"If we don't find this thing . . ." He let the thought trail off, but I knew what he meant.

My job was secure if this fell apart. Dolph's was not. Shit. How could I help him? What were we missing? What?

I stared at the quiet street. It was eerily quiet. The windows were all dark. Only the streetlights pushed back the coming dark. Soft halos of light.

Every house had a mailbox on a post near the sidewalk that edged the curb. Some of the mailboxes were unbelievably cute. One had been shaped like a sitting cat. Its paw went up if there was mail in its tummy. The family name was Catt. It was too precious.

Every house had at least one large super duper trash can in front of it. Some of them were bigger than I was. Surely, Sunday couldn't be trash day. Or had today been trash day, and the police line had stopped it?

"Trash cans," I said aloud.

"What?" Dolph asked.

"Trash cans." I grabbed his arm, feeling almost lightheaded. "We've stared at those fucking trash cans all day. That's it."

John Burke stood quietly beside me, frowning.

"Are you feeling okay, Blake?" Zerbrowski came up behind us, smoking. The end of his cigarette looked like a bloated firefly.

"The cans are big enough for a large person to hide in."

"Wouldn't your arms and legs fall asleep?" Zerbrowski asked.

"Zombies don't have circulation, not like we do."

Dolph yelled, "Everybody check the trash cans. The zombie is in one of them. Move it!"

Everyone scattered like an anthill stirred with a stick, but we had a purpose now. I ended up with two uniformed officers. Their nameplates said "Ki" and "Roberts." Ki was Asian and male. Roberts was blond and female. A nicely mixed team.

We fell into a rhythm without discussing it. Officer Ki would move up and dump the trash can. Roberts and I would cover him with guns. We were all set to yell like hell if a zombie came tumbling out. It would probably be the right zombie. Life is seldom that cruel.

We'd yell and an exterminator team would come running. At least, they'd better come running. This zombie was entirely too fast, too destructive. It might be more resistant to gunfire. Better not to find out. Just french-fry the sucker and be done with it.

We were the only team working on the street. There was no sound but our footsteps, the rubber crunch of trash cans overturning, the rattle of cans and bottles as the trash spilled. Didn't anybody tie their bags up anymore?

Darkness had fallen in a solid blackness. I knew there were stars and a moon up there somewhere, but you couldn't prove it from where we stood. Clouds as thick and dark as velvet had come in from the west. Only the streetlights made it bearable.

I didn't know how Roberts was doing, but the muscles in my shoulders and neck were screaming. Every time Ki put his hands to the can and pushed, I was ready. Ready to fire, ready to save him before the zombie leapt up and ripped his throat out. A trickle of sweat dripped down his high-cheekboned face. Even in the dim light it glimmered.

Glad to know I wasn't the only one feeling the effort. Of course, I wasn't the one putting my face over the possible hiding place of a berserk zombie. Trouble was, I didn't know how good a shot Ki was, or Roberts either for that matter. I knew I was a good shot. I knew I could slow the thing down until help arrived. I had to stay on shooting detail. It was the best division of labor. Honest.

Screams. To the left. The three of us froze. I whirled towards the screaming. There was nothing to see, nothing but dark houses and pools of streetlight. Nothing moved. But the screams continued high and horrified.

I started running towards the screams. Ki and Roberts were at my back. I ran with the Browning in a two-handed grip pointed up. Easier to run that way. Didn't dare holster the gun. Visions of blood-coated teddy bears, and the screams. The screams sort of faded. Someone was dying up ahead.

There was a sense of movement everywhere in the darkness. Cops running. All of us running but it was too late. We were all too late. The screaming had stopped. No gunshots. Why not? Why hadn't someone gotten off a shot?

We ran down the side yards of four houses when we hit a metal fence. Had to holster the guns. Couldn't climb it with one hand. Dammit. I did my best to vault the fence using my hands for leverage.

I stumbled to my knees in the soft dirt of a flower bed. I was trampling some tall summer flowers. On my knees I was considerably shorter than the flowers. Ki landed beside me. Only Roberts landed on her feet.

Ki stood up without drawing his gun. I drew the Browning while I crouched in the flowers. I could stand up after I was armed.

I had a sense of rushing movement but not clear sight. The flowers obscured my vision. Roberts was suddenly tumbling backwards, screaming.

Ki was drawing his gun, but something hit him, knocked him on top of me. I rolled but was still half under him. He lay still on top of me.

"Ki, move it, dammit!"

He sat up and crawled towards his partner, his gun silhouetted against the streetlight. He was staring down at Roberts. She wasn't moving.

I searched the darkness trying to see something, anything. It had moved more than human fast. Fast as a ghoul. No zombie moved like that. Had I been wrong all along? Was it something else? Something worse? How many lives would my mistake cost tonight? Was Roberts dead?

"Ki, is she alive?" I searched the darkness, fighting the urge to look only at the lighted areas. There was shouting, but it was confusion, "Where is it? Where did it go?" The sounds were getting farther away.

I screamed, "Here, here!" The voices hesitated, then started our way. They were making so much noise, like a herd of arthritic elephants.

"How bad is she hurt?"

"Bad." He'd put his gun down. He was pressing his hands over her neck. Something black and liquid was spreading over his hands. God.

I knelt on the other side of Roberts, gun ready, searching the darkness. Everything was taking forever, yet it was only seconds.

I checked her pulse, one-handed. It was thready, but there. My hand came away covered in blood. I wiped it on my pants. The thing had damn near slit her throat.

Where was it?

Ki's eyes were huge, all pupil. His skin looked leprous in the streetlight. His partner's blood was dripping out between his fingers.

Something moved, too low to the ground to be a man, but about that size. It was just a shape creeping along the back of the house in front of us. Whatever it was had found the deepest shadow and was trying to creep away.

That showed more intelligence than a zombie had. I was wrong. I was wrong. I was fucking wrong. And Roberts was dying because of it.

"Stay with her. Keep her alive."

"Where are you going?" he asked.

"After it." I climbed the fence one-handed. The adrenaline must have been pumping because I made it.

I gained the yard and it was gone. A streaking shape fast as a mouse caught in the kitchen light. A blur of speed, but big, big as a man.

It rounded the corner of the house and I lost sight of it. Dammit. I ran as far from the wall as I could, my stomach tight with anticipation of fingers ripping my throat out. I came round the house gun pointed, two-handed, ready. Nothing. I scanned the darkness, the pools of light. Nothing.

Shouts behind me. The cops had arrived. God, let Roberts live.

There, movement, creeping across the streetlight around the edge of another house. Someone shouted, "Anita!"

I was already running towards the movement. I shouted as I ran, "Bring an exterminator team!" But I didn't stop. I didn't dare stop. I was the only one in sight of it. If I lost it, it was gone.

I ran into the darkness, alone, after something that might not be a zombie at all. Not the brightest thing I've ever done, but it wasn't going to get away. It wasn't.

It was never going to hurt another family. Not if I could stop it. Now. Tonight.

I ran through a pool of light and it made the darkness heavier, blinding me temporarily. I froze in the dark, willing my eyes to adjust faster.

"Perssisstent woman," a voice hissed. It was to my right, so close the hair on my arms stood up.

I froze, straining my peripheral vision. There, a darker shape rising out of the evergreen shrubs that hugged the edge of the house. It rose to its full height, but didn't attack. If it wanted me, it could have me before I could turn and fire. I'd seen it move. I knew I was dead.

"You arrre not like the resst." The voice was sibilant, as if parts of the mouth were missing, so it put great effort into forming each word. A gentleman's voice decayed by the grave.

I turned towards it, slowly, slowly.

"Put me back."

I had turned my head enough to be able to see some of it. My night vision is better than most. And the streetlights made it lighter than it should have been.

The skin was pale, yellowish-white. The skin clung to the bones of his face like wax that had half-melted. But the eyes, they weren't decayed. They burned out at me with a glitter that was more than just eyes.

"Put you back where?" I asked.

"My grave," he said. His lips didn't work quite right, there wasn't enough flesh left on them.

Light blazed into my eyes. The zombie screamed, covering his face. I couldn't see shit. It crashed into me. I pulled the trigger blind. I thought I heard a grunt as the bullet hit home. I fired the gun again one-handed, throwing an arm across my neck. Trying to protect myself as I fell half-blind.

When I blinked up into the electric-shot darkness, I was alone. I was unhurt. Why? Put me back, it had said. In my grave. How had it known what I was? Most humans couldn't tell. Witches could tell sometimes, and other animators always spotted me. Other animators. Shit.

Dolph was suddenly there, pulling me to my feet. "God, Blake, are you hurt?"

I shook my head. "What the hell was that light?"

"A halogen flashlight."

"You damn near blinded me."

"We couldn't see to shoot," he said.

Police had run past us in the darkness. There were shouts of, "There it is!" Dolph and I and the offending flashlight, bright as day, were left behind as the chase ran merrily on.

"It spoke to me, Dolph," I said.

"What do you mean, it spoke to you?"

"It asked me to put it back in its grave." I stared up at him as I said it. I wondered if my face looked like Ki's had, pale, eyes wide and black. Why wasn't I scared?

"It's old, a century at least. It was a voodoo something in life. That's what went wrong. That's why Peter Burke couldn't control it."

"How do you know all this? Did it tell you?"

I shook my head. "The way it looked, I could judge the age. It recognized me as someone who could lay it to rest. Only a witch or another animator could have recognized me for what I am. My money's on an animator."

"Does that change our plan?" he asked.

I stared up at him. "It's killed how many people?" I didn't wait for him to answer. "We kill it. Period."

"You think like a cop, Anita." It was a great compliment from Dolph, and I took it as one.

It didn't matter what it had been in life. So it had been an animator, or rather a voodoo practioner. So what? It was a killing machine. It hadn't killed me. Hadn't hurt me. I couldn't afford to return the favor.

Shots echoed far way. Some trick of the summer air made them echo. Dolph and I looked at each other.

I still had the Browning in my hand. "Let's do it."

He nodded.

We started running, but he outdistanced me quickly. His legs were as tall as I was. I couldn't match his pace. I might be able to run him into the ground, but I'd never match his speed.

He hesitated, glancing at me.

"Go on, run," I said.

He put on an extra burst of speed and was gone into the darkness. He didn't even look back. If you said you were fine in the dark with a killer zombie on the loose, Dolph would believe you. Or at least he believed me.

It was a compliment but it left me running alone in the dark for the second time tonight. Shouts were coming from two opposite directions. They had lost it. Damn.

I slowed. I had no desire to run into the thing blind. It hadn't hurt me the first time, but I'd put at least one bullet into it. Even a zombie gets pissed about things like that.

I was under the cool darkness of a tree shadow. I was on the edge of the development. A barbed-wire fence cut across the entire back of the subdivision. Farmland stretched as far as I could see. At least the field was planted in beans. The zombie'd have to be lying flat to hide in there. I caught glimpses of policemen with flashlights, searching the darkness, but they were all about fifty yards to either side of me.

They were searching the ground, the shadows, because I'd told them zombies didn't like to climb. But this wasn't any ordinary zombie. The tree rustled over my head. The hair on my neck crawled down my spine. I whirled, looking upwards, gun pointing.

It snarled at me and leapt.

I fired twice before its weight hit me and knocked us both to the ground. Two bullets in the chest, and it wasn't even hurt.

I fired a third time, but I might as well have been hitting a wall.

It snarled in my face, broken teeth with dark stains, breath foul as a new opened grave. I screamed back, wordless, and pulled the trigger again. The bullet hit it in the throat. It paused, trying to swallow. To swallow the bullet?

Those glittering eyes stared down at me. There was someone home, like Dominga's soul-locked zombies. There was someone looking out of those eyes. We froze in one of those illusionary seconds that last years. He was straddling my waist, hands at my throat, but not pressing, not hurting, not yet. I had the gun under his chin. None of the other bullets had hurt him; why would this one?

"Didn't mean to kill," it said softly, "didn't undersstand at firsst. Didn't remember what I wass."

The police were there on either side, hesitating. Dolph screamed, "Hold your fire, hold your fire, dammit!"

"I needed meat, needed it to remember who I wass. Tried not to kill. Tried to walk past all the houssess, but I could not. Too many houssess," he whispered. His hands tensed, stained nails digging in. I fired into his chin. His body jerked backwards, but the hands squeezed my neck.

Pressure, pressure, tighter, tighter. I was beginning to see white star bursts on my vision. The night was fading from black to grey. I pressed the gun just above the bridge of his nose and pulled the trigger again, and again.

My vision faded, but I could still feel my hands, pulling the trigger. Darkness flowed over my eyes and swallowed the world. I couldn't feel my hands anymore.

I woke to screams, horrible screams. The stink of burning flesh and hair was thick and choking on my tongue.

I took a deep shaking breath and it hurt. I coughed and tried to sit up. Dolph was there supporting me. He had my gun in his hand. I drew one ragged breath after another and coughed hard enough to make my throat raw. Or maybe the zombie had done that.

Something the size of a man was rolling over the summer grass. It burned. It flamed with a clean orange light that sent the darkness shattering in fire shadows like the sun on water.

Two exterminators in their fire suits stood by it, covering it in napalm, as if it were a ghoul. The thing screamed high in its throat, over and over, one loud ragged shriek after another.

"Jesus, why won't it die?" Zerbrowski was standing nearby. His face was orange in the firelight.

I didn't say anything. I didn't want to say it out loud. The zombie wouldn't die because it had been an animator when alive. That much I knew about animator zombies. What I hadn't known was that they came out of the grave craving flesh. That they remembered only when they ate flesh.

That I hadn't known. Didn't want to know.

John Burke stumbled into the firelight. He was cradling one arm to his chest. Blood stained his clothing. Had the zombie whispered to John? Did he know why the thing wouldn't die?

The zombie whirled, the fire roaring around it. The body was like the wick of a candle. It took one shaking step towards us. Its flaming hand reached out to me. To me.

Then it fell forward, slowly, into the grass. It fell like a tree in slow motion, fighting for life. If that was the word. The exterminators stayed ready, taking no chances. I didn't blame them.

It had been a necromancer once upon a time. That burning hulk, slowly catching the grass on fire, had been what I was. Would I be a monster if raised from the grave? Would I? Better not to find out. My will said cremation because I didn't want someone raising me just for kicks. Now I had another reason to do it. One had been enough.

I watched the flesh blacken, curl, peel away. Muscles and bone popped in miniature explosions, tiny pops of sparks.

I watched the zombie die and made a promise to myself. I'd see Dominga Salvador burned in hell for what she'd done. There are fires that last for all eternity. Fires that make napalm look like a temporary inconvenience. She'd burn for all eternity, and it wouldn't be half long enough.

# 33

I WAS LYING on my back in the emergency room. A white curtain hid me from view. The noises on the other side of the curtain were loud and unfriendly. I liked my curtain. The pillow was flat, the examining table was hard. It felt white and clean and wonderful. It hurt to swallow. It even hurt a little bit just to breathe. But breathing was important. It was nice to be able to do it.

I lay there very quietly. Doing what I was told for once. I listened to my breathing, the beating of my own heart. After nearly dying, I am always very interested in my body. I notice all sorts of things that go unnoticed during most of life. I could feel blood coursing through the veins in my arms. I could taste my calm, orderly pulse in my mouth like a piece of candy.

I was alive. The zombie was dead. Dominga Salvador was in jail. Life was good.

Dolph pushed the curtain back. He closed the curtain like you'd close a door to a room. We both pretended we had privacy even though we could see people's feet passing under the hem of the curtain.

I smiled up at him. He smiled back. "Nice to see you up and around."

"I don't know about the up part," I said. My voice had a husky edge to it. I coughed, tried to clear it, but it didn't really help.

"What'd the doc say about your voice?" Dolph asked.

"I'm a temporary tenor." At the look on his face, I added, "It'll pass."

"Good."

"How's Burke?" I asked.

"Stitches, no permanent damage."

I had figured as much after seeing him last night, but it was good to know.

"And Roberts?"

"She'll live."

"But will she be alright?" I had to swallow hard. It hurt to talk.

"She'll be alright. Ki was cut up, too, on the arm. Did you know?"

I shook my head and stopped in mid-motion. That hurt, too. "Didn't see it."

"Just a few stitches. He'll be fine." Dolph plunged his hands in his pants pockets. "We lost three officers. One hurt worse than Roberts, but he'll make it."

I stared up at him. "My fault."

He frowned. "How do you figure that?"

"I should have guessed," I had to swallow, "it wasn't an ordinary zombie."

"It was a zombie, Anita. You were right. You were the one who figured out it was hiding in one of those damn trash cans." He grinned down at me. "And you nearly died killing it. I think you've done your part."

"Didn't kill it. Exterminators killed it." Big words seemed to hurt more than little words.

"Do you remember what happened as you were passing out?"

"No."

"You emptied your clip into its face. Blew its damn brains out the back of its head. You went limp. I thought you were dead. God"—he shook his head—"don't ever do that to me again."

I smiled. "I'll try not to."

"When its brains started leaking out the back of its head, it stood up. You took all the fight out of it."

Zerbrowski pushed into the small space, leaving the curtain gaping behind him. I could see a small boy with a bloody hand crying into a woman's shoulder. Dolph swept the curtain closed. I bet Zerbrowski was one of those people who never shut a drawer.

"They're still digging bullets out of the corpse. And every bullet's yours, Blake."

I just looked at him.

"You are such a bad ass, Blake."

"Somebody has to be with you around, Zerbrow . . ." I couldn't finish his name. It hurt. It figures.

"Are you in pain?" Dolph asked.

I nodded, carefully. "The doc's getting me painkiller. Already got tetanus booster."

"You've got a necklace of bruises blossoming on that pale neck of yours," Zerbrowski said.

"Poetic," I said.

He shrugged.

"I'll check in on the rest of the injured one more time, then I'll have a uniform drive you back to your place," Dolph said.

"Thanks."

"I don't think you're in any condition to drive."

Maybe he was right. I felt like shit, but it was happy shit. We'd done it. We'd solved the crime, and people were going to jail for it. Yippee.

The doctor came back in with the painkillers. He glanced at the two policemen. "Right." He handed me a bottle with three pills in it. "This should see you through the night and into the next day. I'd call in sick if I were you." He glanced at Dolph as he said it. "You hear that, boss?"

Dolph sort of frowned. "I'm not her boss."

"You're the man in charge, right?" the doctor asked.

Dolph nodded.

"Then . . ."

"I'm on loan," I said.

"Loan?"

"You might say we borrowed her from another department," Zerbrowski said.

The doctor nodded. "Then tell her superior to let her off tomorrow. She may not look as hurt as the others, but she's had a nasty shock. She's very lucky there was no permanent damage."

"She doesn't have a superior," Zerbrowski said, "but we'll tell her boss." He grinned at the doctor.

I frowned at Zerbrowski.

"Well, then, you're free to go. Watch those scratches for infection. And that bite on your shoulder." He shook his head. "You cops earn your money." With that parting wisdom, he left.

Zerbrowski laughed. "Wouldn't do for the doc to know we'd let a civie get messed up."

"She's had a nasty shock," Dolph said.

"Very nasty," Zerbrowski said.

They started laughing.

I sat up carefully, swinging my legs over the edge of the bed. "If you two are through yukking it up, I need a ride home."

They were both laughing so hard that tears were creeping out of their eyes. It hadn't been that funny, but I understood. For tension release laughter beats the hell out of tears. I didn't join them because I suspected strongly that laughing would hurt.

"I'll drive you home," Zerbrowski gasped between giggles.

I had to smile. Seeing Dolph and Zerbrowski giggling was enough to make anyone smile.

"No, no," Dolph said. "You two in a car alone. Only one of you would come out alive."

"And it'd be me," I said.

Zerbrowski nodded. "Ain't it the truth."

Nice to know there was one subject we agreed on.

# 34

I WAS HALF asleep in the back of the squad car when they pulled up in front of my apartment building. The throbbing pain in my throat had slid away on a smooth tide of pain medication. I felt nearly boneless. What had the doctor given me? It felt great, but it was like the world was some sort of movie that had little to do with me. Distant and harmless as a dream.

I'd given Dolph my car keys. He promised to have someone park the car in front of my apartment building before morning. He also said he'd call Bert and tell him I wouldn't be in to work today. I wondered how Bert would take the news. I wondered if I cared. Nope.

One of the uniformed police officers leaned back over the seat and said, "You going to be alright, Miss Blake?"

"Ms.," I corrected automatically.

He gave me a half smile as he held the door for me. No door handles on the inside of a squad car. He had to hold the door for me, but he did it with relish, and said, "You going to be alright, Ms. Blake?"

"Yes, Officer"—I had to blink to read his name tag—"Osborn. Thank you for bringing me home. To your partner, too."

His partner was standing on the other side of the car, leaning his arms on the roof of the car. "It's a kick to finally meet the spook squad's Executioner." He grinned as he said it.

I blinked at him and tried to pull all the pieces together enough to talk and think at the same time. "I was the Executioner long before the spook squad came along."

He spread his hands, still grinning. "No offense."

I was too tired and too drugged to worry about it. I just shook my head. "Thanks again."

I was a touch unsteady going up the stairs. I clutched the railing like it was a lifeline. I'd sleep tonight. I might wake up in the middle of the hallway, but I'd sleep.

It took me two tries to put the key in the door lock. I staggered into my apartment, leaning my forehead against the door to close it. I turned the lock and was safe. I was home. I was alive. The killer zombie was destroyed. I had the urge to giggle, but that was the pain medication. I never giggle on my own.

I stood there leaning the top of my head against the door. I was staring at the toes of my Nikes. They seemed very far away, as if distances had grown since last I looked at my feet. The doc had given me some weird shit. I would not take it tomorrow. It was too reality-altering for my taste.

The toes of black boots stepped up beside my Nikes. Why were there boots in my apartment? I started to turn around. I started to go for my gun. Too late, too slow, too fucking bad.

Strong brown arms laced across my chest, pinning my arms. Pinning me against the door. I tried to struggle now that it was too late. But he had me. I craned my neck backwards trying to fight off the damn medication. I should have been terrified. Adrenaline pumping, but some drugs don't give a shit if you need your body. You belong to the drug until it wears off, period. I was going to hurt the doctor. If I lived through this.

It was Bruno pinning me to the door.

Tommy came up on the right. He had a needle in his hands.

"NO!"

Bruno cupped his hand over my mouth. I tried to bite him, and he slapped me. The slap helped a little but the world was still cotton-coated, distant. Bruno's hand smelled like after-shave. A choking sweetness.

"This is almost too easy," Tommy said.

"Just do it," Bruno said.

I stared at the needle as it came closer to my arm. I would have told them that I was drugged already, if Bruno's hand hadn't been clasped over my mouth. I would have asked what was in the syringe, and whether it would react badly with what I had already taken. I never got the chance.

The needle plunged in. My body stiffened, struggling, but Bruno held me tight. Couldn't move. Couldn't get away. Dammit! Dammit! The adrenaline was finally chasing the cobwebs away, but it was too late. Tommy took the needle out of my arm and said, "Sorry, we don't have any alcohol to swab it off with." He grinned at me.

I hated him. I hated them both. And if the shot didn't kill me, I was going to kill them both. For scaring me. For making me feel helpless. For catching me unaware, drugged, and stupid. If I lived through this mistake, I wouldn't make it again. Please, dear God, let me live through this mistake.

Bruno held me motionless and mute until I could feel the injection taking hold. I was sleepy. With a bad guy holding me against my will, I was sleepy. I tried to fight it, but it didn't work. My eyelids fluttered. I struggled to keep them open. I stopped trying to get away from Bruno and put everything I had into not closing my eyes.

I stared at my door and tried to stay awake. The door swam in dizzying ripples as if I were seeing it through water. My eyelids went down, jerked up, down. I couldn't open my eyes. A small part of me fell screaming into the dark, but the rest of me felt loose and sleepy and strangely safe.

# 35

I WAS IN that faint edge of wakefulness. Where you know you're not quite asleep, but don't really want to wake up either. My body felt heavy. My head throbbed. And my throat was sore.

The last thought made me open my eyes. I was staring at a white ceiling. Brown water marks traced the paint like spilled coffee. I wasn't home. Where was I?

I remembered Bruno holding me down. The needle. I sat up then. The world swam in clear waves of color. I fell back onto the bed, covering my eyes with my hands. That helped a little. What had they given me?

I had an image in my mind that I wasn't alone. Somewhere in that dizzying swirl of color had been a person. Hadn't there? I opened my eyes slower this time. I was content to stare up at the water-ruined ceiling. I was on a large bed. Two pillows, sheets, a blanket. I turned my head carefully and found myself staring into Harold Gaynor's face. He was sitting beside the bed. It wasn't what I wanted to wake up to.

Behind him, leaning against a battered chest of drawers was Bruno. His shoulder holster cut black lines across his blue short-sleeved dress shirt. There was a matching and equally scarred vanity table near the foot of the bed. The vanity sat between two high windows. They were boarded with new, sweet-smelling lumber. The scent of pine rode the hot, still air.

I started to sweat as soon as I realized that there was no air-conditioning.

"How are you feeling, Ms. Blake?" Gaynor asked. His voice was still that jolly Santa voice with an edge of sibilance. As if he were a very happy snake.

"I've felt better," I said.

"I'm sure you have. You have been asleep for over twenty-four hours. Did you know that?"

Was he lying? Why would he lie about how long I'd been asleep? What would it gain him? Nothing. Truth then, probably.

"What the hell did you give me?"

Bruno eased himself away from the wall. He looked almost embarrassed. "We didn't realize you'd already taken a sedative."

"Painkiller," I said.

He shrugged. "Same difference when you mix it with Thorazine."

"You shot me up with animal tranquilizers?"

"Now, now, Ms. Blake, they use it in mental institutions, as well. Not just animals," Gaynor said.

"Gee," I said, "that makes me feel a lot better."

He smiled broadly. "If you feel good enough to trade witty repartee, then you're well enough to get up."

Witty repartee? But he was probably right. Truthfully, I was surprised I wasn't tied up. Glad of it, but surprised.

I sat up much slower than last time. The room only tilted the tiniest bit, before settling into an upright position. I took a deep breath, and it hurt. I put a hand to my throat. It hurt to touch the skin.

"Who gave you those awful bruises?" Gaynor asked.

Lie or truth? Partial lie. "I was helping the police catch a bad guy. He got a little out of hand."

"What happened to this bad guy?" Bruno asked.

"He's dead now," I said.

Something flickered across Bruno's face. Too quick to read. Respect maybe. Naw.

"You know why I've had you brought here, don't you?"

"To raise a zombie for you," I said.

"To raise a very old zombie for me, yes."

"I've refused your offer twice. What makes you think I'll change my mind?"

He smiled, such a jolly old elf. "Why, Ms. Blake, I'll have Bruno and Tommy persuade you of the error of your ways. I still plan on giving you a million dollars to raise this zombie. The price hasn't changed."

"Tommy offered me a million five last time," I said.

"That was if you came voluntarily. We can't pay full price when you force us to take such chances."

"Like a federal prison term for kidnapping," I said.

"Exactly. Your stubbornness has cost you five hundred thousand dollars. Was it really worth that?"

"I won't kill another human being just so you can go looking for lost treasure."

"Little Wanda has been bearing tales."

"I was just guessing, Gaynor. I read a file on you and it mentioned your obsession with your father's family." It was an outright lie. Only Wanda had known that.

"I'm afraid it's too late. I know Wanda talked to you. She's confessed everything."

Confessed? I stared at him, trying to read his blankly good-humored face. "What do you mean, confessed?"

"I mean I gave her to Tommy for questioning. He's not the artist that Cicely is, but he does leave more behind. I didn't want to kill my little Wanda."

"Where is she now?"

"Do you care what happens to a whore?" His eyes were bright and birdlike as he stared at me. He was judging me, my reactions.

"She doesn't mean anything to me," I said. I hoped my face was as bland as my words. Right now they weren't going to kill her. If they thought they could use her to hurt me, they might.

"Are you sure?"

"Listen, I haven't been sleeping with her. She's just a chippie with a very bent angle."

He smiled at that. "What can we do to convince you to raise this zombie for me?"

"I will not commit murder for you, Gaynor. I don't like you that much," I said.

He sighed. His apple-cheeked face looked like a sad Kewpie doll. "You are going to make this difficult, aren't you, Ms. Blake?"

"I don't know how to make it easy," I said. I put my back to the cracked wooden headboard of the bed. I was comfortable enough, but I still felt a little fuzzy around the edges. But it was as good as it was going to get for a while. It beat the hell out of being unconscious.

"We have not really hurt you yet," Gaynor said. "The reaction of the Thorazine with whatever other medication you had in you was accidental. We did not harm you on purpose."

I could argue with that, but I decided not to. "So where do we go from here?"

"We have both your guns," Gaynor said. "Without a weapon you are a small woman in the care of big, strong men."

I smiled then. "I'm used to being the smallest kid on the block, Harry."

He looked pained. "Harold or Gaynor, never Harry."

I shrugged. "Fine."

"You are not in the least intimidated that we have you completely at our mercy?"

"I could argue that point."

He glanced up at Bruno. "Such confidence, where does she get it?"

Bruno didn't say anything. He just stared at me with those empty doll eyes. Bodyguard eyes, watchful, suspicious, and blank all at the same time.

"Show her we mean business, Bruno."

Bruno smiled, a slow spreading of lips that left his eyes dead as a shark's. He loosened his shoulders, and did a few stretching exercises against the wall. His eyes never left me.

"I take it, I'm going to be the punching bag?" I asked.

"How well you put it," Gaynor said.

Bruno stood away from the wall, limber and eager. Oh, well. I slid off the bed on the opposite side. I had no desire for Gaynor to grab me. Bruno's reach was over twice mine. His legs went on forever. He had to outweigh me by nearly a hundred pounds, and it was all muscle. I was about to get badly hurt. But as long as they didn't tie me up, I'd go down swinging. If I could cause him any serious damage, I'd be satisfied.

I came out from behind the bed, hands loose at my side. I was already in that partial crouch that I used on the judo mat. I doubted seriously if Bruno's fighting skill of choice was judo. I was betting karate or tae kwon do.

Bruno stood in an awkward-looking stance, halfway between an x and a t. It looked like someone had taken his long legs and crumbled them at the knees. But as I moved forward he scooted backwards like a crab, fast and out of reach.

"Jujitsu?" I made it half question.

He raised an eyebrow. "Most people don't recognize it."

"I've seen it," I said.

"You practice?"

"No."

He smiled. "Then I am going to hurt you."

"Even if I knew jujitsu, you'd hurt me," I said.

"It'd be a fair fight."

"If two people are equal in skill, size matters. A good big person will always beat a good small person." I shrugged. "I don't have to like it, but it's the truth."

"You're being awful calm about this," Bruno said.

"Would being hysterical help?"

He shook his head. "Nope."

"Then I'd just as soon take my medicine like, if you'll excuse the expression, a man."

He frowned at that. Bruno was accustomed to people being scared of him. I wasn't scared of him. I'd decided to take the beating. With the decision came a certain amount of calm. I was going to get beat up, not pleasant, but I had made my mind up to take the beating. I could do it. I'd done it before. If my choices were a) getting beat up or b) performing human sacrifice, I'd take the beating.

"Ready or not," Bruno said.

"Here you come," I finished for him. I was getting tired of the bravado. "Either hit me or stand up straight. You look silly crouched down like that."

His fist was a dark blur. I blocked it with my arm. The impact made the arm go numb. His long leg kicked out and connected solidly with my stomach. I doubled over like I was supposed to, all the air gone in one movement. His other foot came up and caught me on the side of the face. It was the same cheek ol' Seymour had smashed. I fell to the floor not sure what part of my body to comfort first.

His foot came for me again. I caught it with both hands. I came up in a rush, hoping to trap his knee between my arms and pop the joint. But he twisted away from me, totally airborne for a moment.

I dropped to the ground and felt the air pass overhead as his legs kicked out where my head had been. I was on the ground again, but by choice. He stood over me, impossibly tall from this angle. I lay on my side, knees drawn up.

He came for me, evidently planning to drag me to my feet. I kicked out with both feet at an angle to his kneecap. Hit it just right above or below and you dislocate it.

The leg buckled, and he screamed. It had worked. Hot damn. I didn't try to wrestle him. I didn't try to grab his gun. I ran for the door.

Gaynor grabbed for me, but I flung open the door and was out in a long hallway before he could maneuver his fancy chair. The hallway was smooth with a handful of doors and two blind corners. And Tommy.

Tommy looked surprised to see me. His hand went for his shoulder holster. I pushed on his shoulder and foot-swept his leg. He fell backwards and grabbed me as he fell. I rode him down, making sure my knee ground into his groin. His grip loosened enough for me to slip out of reach. There were sounds behind me from the room. I didn't look back. If they were going to shoot me, I didn't want to see it.

The hallway took a sharp turn. I was almost to it when the smell slowed me from a run to a walk. The smell of corpses was just around the corner. What had they been doing while I slept?

I glanced back at the men. Tommy was still lying on the floor, cradling himself. Bruno leaned against the wall, gun in hand, but he wasn't pointing it at me. Gaynor was sitting in his chair, smiling.

Something was very wrong.

Around the blind corner came that something that was wrong, very, very wrong. It was no taller than a tall man, maybe six feet. But it was nearly four feet wide. It had two legs, or maybe three, it was hard to tell. The thing was leprously pale like all zombies, but this one had a dozen eyes. A man's face was centered where the neck would have been. Its eyes dark and seeing, and empty of everything sane. A dog's head was growing out of the shoulder. The dog's decaying mouth snapped at me. A woman's leg grew out of the center of the mess, complete with black high-heeled shoe.

The thing shambled towards me. Pulling with three of a dozen arms, dragging itself forward. It left a trail behind it like a snail.

Dominga Salvador stepped around the corner. "*Buenas noches, chica.*"

The monster scared me, but the sight of Dominga grinning at me scared me just a little bit more.

The thing had stopped moving forward. It squatted in the hallway, kneeling on its inadequate legs. Its dozens of mouths panted as if it couldn't get enough air.

Or maybe the thing didn't like the way it smelled. I certainly didn't. Covering my mouth and nose with my arm didn't block out much of the smell. The hallway suddenly smelled like bad meat.

Gaynor and his wounded bodyguards had stayed at the end of the hall. Maybe they didn't like being near Dominga's little pet. I know it didn't do much for me. Whatever the reason we were isolated. It was just her and me and the monster.

"How did you get out of jail?" Better to deal with more mundane problems first. The mind-melting ones could wait for later.

"I made my bail," she said.

"This quickly on a murder involving witchcraft?"

"Voodoo is not witchcraft," she said.

"The law sees it as the same thing when it comes to murder."

She shrugged, then smiled beatifically. She was the Mexican grandmother of my nightmares.

"You've got a judge in your pocket," I said.

"Many people fear me, *chica*. You should be one of them."

"You helped Peter Burke raise the zombie for Gaynor."

She just smiled.

"Why didn't you just raise it yourself?" I asked.

"I didn't want someone as unscrupulous as Gaynor to witness me murdering someone. He might use it for blackmail."

"And he didn't realize that you had to kill someone for Peter's gris-gris?"

"Correct," she said.

"You hid all your horrors here?"

"Not all. You forced me to destroy much of my work, but this I saved. You can see why." She caressed a hand down the slimy hide.

I shuddered. Just the thought of touching that monstrosity was enough to make my skin cold. And yet . . .

"How did you make it?" I had to know. It was so obviously a creation of our shared art that I had to know.

"Surely, you can animate bits and pieces of the dead," Dominga said.

I could, but no one else I had ever met could do it. "Yes," I said.

"I found I could take these odds and ends and meld them together."

I stared at the shambling thing. "Meld them?" The thought was too horrible.

"I can create new creatures that have never existed before."

"You make monsters," I said.

"Believe what you will, *chica*, but I am here to persuade you to raise the dead for Gaynor."

"Why don't you do it?"

Gaynor's voice came from just behind us. I whirled, putting the wall at my back so I could watch everybody. What good that would do me, I wasn't sure. "Dominga's power went wrong once. This is my last chance. The last known grave. I won't risk it on her."

Dominga's eyes narrowed, her age-thinned hands forming fists. She didn't like being dismissed out of hand. Couldn't say I blamed her.

"She could do it, Gaynor, easier than I could."

"If I truly believed that, I would kill you because I wouldn't need you anymore."

Hmm, good point. "You've had Bruno rough me up. Now what?"

Gaynor shook his head. "Such a little girl to have taken both my bodyguards down."

"I told you ordinary methods of persuasion will not work on her," Dominga said.

I stared past her at the slathering monster. She called this ordinary?

"What do you propose?" Gaynor asked.

"A spell of compulsion. She will do as I bid, but it takes time to do such a spell for one as powerful as she. If she knew any voodoo to speak of, it would not work at all. But for all her art, she is but a baby in voodoo."

"How long will you need?"

"Two hours, no more."

"This had better work," Gaynor said.

"Do not threaten me," Dominga said.

Oh, goody, maybe the bad guys would fight and kill each other.

"I am paying you enough money to set up your own small country. I should get results for that."

Dominga nodded her head. "You pay well, that is true. I will not fail you. If I can compel Anita to kill another person, then I can compel her to help me in my zombie business. She will help me rebuild what she forced me to destroy. It has a certain irony, no?"

Gaynor smiled like a demented elf. "I like it."

"Well, I don't," I said.

He frowned at me. "You will do as you are told. You have been very naughty."

Naughty? Me?

Bruno had worked himself close to us. He was leaning heavily on the wall, but his gun was very steadily pointed at the center of my chest. "I'd like to kill you now," he said. His voice sounded raw with pain.

"A dislocated knee hurts like hell, doesn't it?" I smiled when I said it. Better dead than a willing servant of the voodoo queen.

I think he ground his teeth. The gun wavered just a little, but I think that was rage, not pain. "I will enjoy killing you."

"You didn't do so good last time. I think the judges would have given the match to me."

"There are no fucking judges here. I am going to kill you."

"Bruno," Gaynor said, "we need her alive and whole."

"After she raises the zombie?" Bruno asked.

"If she is a willing servant of the Señora, then you are not to hurt her. If the compulsion doesn't work, then you may kill her."

Bruno gave a fierce flash of teeth. It was more snarl than smile. "I hope the spell fails."

Gaynor glanced at his bodyguard. "Don't let personal feelings interfere with business, Bruno."

Bruno swallowed hard. "Yes, sir." It didn't sound like a title that came easily to him.

Enzo came around the corner behind Dominga. He stayed near the wall as far from her "creation" as he could get.

Antonio had finally lost his job as bodyguard. It was just as well. He was much better suited to stool pigeon.

Tommy came limping down the hall, still sort of scrunched over himself. The big Magnum was in his hands. His face was nearly purple with rage, or maybe pain. "I'm gonna kill you," he hissed.

"Take a number," I said.

"Enzo, you help Bruno and Tommy tie this little girl to a chair in the room. She's a lot more dangerous than she seems," Gaynor said.

Enzo grabbed my arm. I didn't fight him. I figured I was safer in his hands than either of the other two. Tommy and Bruno both looked as if they were looking forward to me trying something. I think they wanted to hurt me.

As Enzo led me past them, I said, "Is it because I'm a woman or are you always this bad at losing?"

"I'm gonna shoot her," Tommy grunted.

"Later," Gaynor said, "later."

I wondered if he really meant that. If Dominga's spell worked, I'd be like a living zombie, obeying her will. If the spell didn't work, then Tommy and Bruno would kill me, a piece at a time. I hoped there was a third choice.

## 36

THE THIRD CHOICE was being tied to a chair in the room where I woke up. It was the best of the three choices, but that wasn't saying much. I don't like being tied up. It means your options have gone from few to none. Dominga had clipped some of my hair and the tips of my fingernails. Hair and nails for her compulsion spell. Shit.

The chair was old and straight-backed. My wrists were tied to the slats that made up the back of the chair. Ankles tied separately to a leg of the chair. The ropes were tight. I tugged at the ropes, hoping for some slack. There wasn't any.

I had been tied up before, and I always have this Houdini fantasy that this time I'll have enough slack to wiggle free. It never works that way. Once you're tied up, you stay tied up until someone lets you go.

The trouble was when they let me go, they were going to try a nasty little spell on me. I had to get away before then. Somehow, I had to get away. Dear God, please let me get away.

The door opened as if on cue, but it wasn't help.

Bruno entered, carrying Wanda in his arms. Blood had dried down the right side of her face from a cut above the eye. Her left cheek was ripe with a huge bruise. The lower lip had burst in a still bleeding cut. Her eyes were shut. I wasn't even sure she was conscious.

I had an aching line on the left side of my face where Bruno had kicked me, but it was nothing to Wanda's injuries.

"Now what?" I asked Bruno.

"Some company for you. When she wakes up, ask her what else Tommy did to her. See if that will persuade you to raise the zombie."

"I thought Dominga was going to bespell me into helping you."

He shrugged. "Gaynor doesn't put much faith in her since she screwed up so badly."

"He doesn't give second chances, I guess," I said.

"No, he doesn't." He laid Wanda on the floor near me. "You best take his offer, girl. One dead whore and you get a million dollars. Take it."

"You're going to use Wanda for the sacrifice," I said. My voice sounded tired even to me.

"Gaynor don't give second chances."

I nodded. "How's your knee?"

He grimaced. "I put it back in place."

"That must have hurt like hell," I said.

"It did. If you don't help Gaynor, you're going to find out exactly how much it hurt."

"An eye for an eye," I said.

He nodded and stood. He favored his right leg. He caught me looking at the leg.

"Talk to Wanda. Decide what you want to end up as. Gaynor's talking about making you a cripple, then keeping you around as his toy. You don't want that."

"How can you work for him?"

He shrugged. "Pays real well."

"Money isn't everything."

"Spoken by somebody who's never gone hungry."

He had me there. I just looked at him. We stared at each other for a few minutes. There was something human in his eyes at last. I couldn't read it though. Whatever emotion it was, it was nothing I understood.

He turned and left the room.

I stared down at Wanda. She lay on her side without moving. She was wearing another long multicolored skirt. A white blouse with a wide lace collar was half-ripped from one shoulder. The bra she wore was the color of plums. I bet there had been panties to match before Tommy got hold of her.

"Wanda," I said it softly. "Wanda, can you hear me?"

Her head moved slowly, painfully. One eye opened wide and panic-stricken. The other eye was glued shut with dried blood. Wanda pawed at the eye, frantic for a moment. When she could open both eyes, she blinked at me. Her eyes took a moment to focus and really see who it was. What had she expected to see in those first few panicked moments? I didn't want to know.

"Wanda, can you speak?"

"Yes." The voice was soft, but clear.

I wanted to ask if she was alright, but I knew the answer to that. "If you can get over here and free me, I'll get us out of here."

She looked at me like I'd lost my mind. "We can't get out. Harold's gonna kill us." She made that last sound like a statement of pure fact.

"I don't believe in giving up, Wanda. Untie me and I'll think of something."

"He'll hurt me if I help you," she said.

"He's planning on you being the human sacrifice to raise his ancestor. How much more hurt can you get?"

She blinked at me, but her eyes were clearing. It was almost as if panic were a drug, and Wanda was fighting off the influence. Or maybe it was Harold Gaynor who was the drug. Yeah, that made sense. She was a junkie. A Harold Gaynor junkie. Every junkie is willing to die for one more fix. But I wasn't.

"Untie me, Wanda, please. I can get us out of this."

"And if you can't?"

"Then we're no worse off," I said.

She seemed to think about that for a minute. I strained for sounds from the hallway. If Bruno came back while we were in the middle of escaping, it would be very bad.

Wanda propped herself up on her arms. Her legs trailed out behind her under the skirt, dead, no movement at all. She began dragging herself towards me. I thought it would be slow work, but she moved quickly. The muscles in her arms bunched and pushed, working well. She was by the chair in a matter of minutes.

I smiled. "You're very strong."

"My arms are all I have. They have to be strong," Wanda said.

She started picking at the ropes that bound my right wrist. "It's too tight."

"You can do it, Wanda."

She picked at the knot with her fingers, until after what seemed hours, but was probably about five minutes, I felt the rope give. Slack, I had slack. Yea!

"You've almost got it, Wanda." I felt like a cheerleader.

The sound of footsteps clattered down the hall towards us. Wanda's battered face stared up at me, terror in her eyes. "There's not time," she whispered.

"Go back where you were. Do it. We'll finish later," I said.

Wanda hand-walked back to where Bruno had laid her. She had just arranged herself into nearly the same position when the door opened. Wanda was pretending to be unconscious, not a bad idea.

Tommy stood in the doorway. He'd taken off his jacket and the black webbing of the shoulder rig stood out on his white polo shirt. Black jeans emphasized his pinched-in waist. He looked top-heavy from lifting so many weights.

He'd added one new thing to the outfit. A knife. He twirled it in his hand like a baton. It was almost a perfect sheen of light. Manual dexterity. Wowee.

"I didn't know you used a knife, Tommy." My voice sounded calm, normal, amazing.

He grinned. "I have a lot of talents. Gaynor wants to know if you've changed your mind about the zombie raising."

It wasn't exactly a question, but I answered it. "I won't do it."

His grin widened. "I was hoping you'd say that."

"Why?" I was afraid I knew the answer.

"Because he sent me in here to persuade you."

I stared at the glittering knife, I couldn't help myself. "With a knife?"

"With something else long and hard, but not so cold," he said.

"Rape?" I asked. The word sort of hung there in the hot, still air.

He nodded, grinning like a damn Cheshire cat. I wished I could make him disappear except for his smile. I wasn't afraid of his smile. It was the other end I was worried about.

I jerked at the ropes helplessly. The right wrist gave a little more. Had Wanda loosened the rope enough? Had she? Please God, let it be.

Tommy stood over me. I stared up the length of his body and what I saw in his eyes was nothing human. There were all sorts of ways to become a monster. Tommy had found one. There was nothing but an animal hunger in his gaze. Nothing human left.

He put a leg on either side of the chair, straddling me without sitting down. His flat stomach was pressed against my face. His shirt smelled of expensive after-shave. I jerked my head back, trying not to touch him.

He laughed and ran fingers through the tight waves of my hair. I tried to jerk my head out of his reach, but he grabbed a handful of hair and forced my head back.

"I'm going to enjoy this," he said.

I didn't dare jerk at the ropes. If my wrist came free he'd see it. I had to wait, wait until he was distracted enough not to notice. The thought of what I might have to do to distract him, allow him to do to me, made my stomach hurt. But staying alive was the goal. Everything else was gravy. I didn't really believe that, but I tried.

He sat down on me, his weight settling on my legs. His chest was pressed against my face, and there was nothing I could do about it.

He rubbed the flat of the knife across my cheek. "You can stop this anytime. Just say yes, and I'll tell Gaynor." His voice was already growing thick. I could feel him growing hard where he was pressed against my belly.

The thought of Tommy using me like that was almost enough to make me say yes. Almost. I jerked on the ropes and the right one gave a little more. One more hard tug and I could get free. But I'd have just one hand to Tommy's two, and he had a gun and a knife. Not good odds, but it was the best I was going to get tonight.

He kissed me, forcing his tongue in my mouth. I didn't respond, because he wouldn't have believed that. I didn't bite his tongue either because I wanted him close. With only one hand free, I needed him close. I needed to do major damage with one hand. What? What could I do?

He nuzzled my neck, face buried in my hair on the left side. Now or never. I pulled with everything I had and the right wrist popped free. I froze. Surely he'd felt it, but he was too busy sucking on my neck to notice. His free hand massaged my breast.

He had his eyes closed as he kissed to the right side of my neck. His eyes were closed. The knife was loose in his other hand. Nothing I could do about the knife. Had to take the chance. Had to do it.

I caressed the side of his face, and he nuzzled my hand. Then his eyes opened. It had occurred to him that I was supposed to be tied. I plunged my thumb into his open eye. I dug it in, feeling the wet pop as his eye exploded.

He shrieked, rearing back, hand to his eye. I grabbed the wrist with the knife and held on. The screams were going to bring reinforcements. Dammit.

Strong arms wrapped around Tommy's waist and pulled him backwards. I grabbed the knife as he slid to the floor. Wanda was struggling to hold him. The pain was so severe, it hadn't occurred to him to go for his gun. Putting out an eye hurts and panics a lot more than a kick to the groin.

I cut my other hand free and knicked my arm doing it. If I hurried too much, I'd end up slitting my own wrist. I forced myself to be more careful slicing my ankles free.

Tommy had managed to get free of Wanda. He staggered to his feet, one hand still over the eye. Blood and clear liquid trailed down his face. "I'll kill you!" He reached for his gun.

I reversed my grip on the knife and threw it. It thunked into his arm. I'd been aiming for his chest. He screamed again. I picked up the chair and smashed it into his face. Wanda grabbed his ankles, and Tommy went down.

I pounded at his face with the chair until the chair broke apart in my hands. Then I beat him with a chair leg until his face was nothing but a bloody mess.

"He's dead," Wanda said. She was tugging at my pants leg. "He's dead. Let's get out of here."

I dropped the blood-coated chair leg and collapsed to my knees. I couldn't swallow. I couldn't breathe. I was splattered with blood. I'd never beaten someone to death before. It had felt good. I shook my head. Later, I'd worry about it later.

Wanda put an arm over my shoulders. I grabbed her around the waist, and we stood. She weighed a lot less than she should have. I didn't want to see what was under the pretty skirt. It wasn't a full set of legs, but for once that was good. She was easier to move.

I had Tommy's gun in my right hand. "I need this hand free, so hold on tight."

Wanda nodded. Her face was very pale. I could feel her heart pounding against her ribs. "We're going to get out of this," I said.

"Sure," but her voice was shaky. I don't think she believed me. I wasn't sure I believed me.

Wanda opened the door, and out we went.

# 37

THE HALLWAY WAS just like I remembered it. A long stretch with no cover, then a blind corner at each end.

"Right or left?" I whispered to Wanda.

"I don't know. This house is like a maze. Right I think."

We went right, because at least it was a decision. The worst thing we could do was just stand there waiting for Gaynor to come back.

I heard footsteps behind us. I started to turn, but with Wanda in my arms, I was slow. The gunshot echoed in the hallway. Something hit my left arm, around Wanda's waist. The impact spun me around and sent us both crashing to the floor.

I ended up on my back with my left arm trapped under Wanda's weight. The left arm was totally numb.

Cicely stood at the end of the hallway. She held a small caliber handgun two-handed. Her long, long legs were far apart. She looked like she knew what she was doing.

I raised the .357 and aimed at her, still lying flat on my back on the floor. It was an explosion of sound that left my ears ringing. The recoil thrust my hand skyward, backwards. It was everything I could do not to drop the gun. If I'd needed a second shot I'd have never gotten it off in time. But I didn't need a second shot.

Cicely lay crumpled in the middle of the hallway. Blood was spreading on the front of her blouse. She didn't move, but that didn't mean anything. Her gun was still gripped in one hand. She could be pretending, then when I walked up, she'd shoot me. But I had to know.

"Can you get off my arm, please?" I asked.

Wanda didn't say anything, but she lifted herself to a sitting position, and I could finally see my arm. It was still attached. Goody. Blood was seeping down my arm in a crimson line. A point of icy burning had started to chase away the numbness. I liked the numbness better.

I did my best to ignore the arm as I stood up and walked towards Cicely. I had the Magnum pointed at her. If she so much as twitched, I'd hit her again. Her miniskirt had hiked up her thighs, displaying black garters and matching underwear. How undignified.

I stood over her, staring down. Cicely wasn't going to twitch, not voluntarily. Her silk blouse was soaked with blood. A hole big enough for me to put my fist through took up most of her chest. Dead, very dead.

I kicked the .22 out of her hand, just in case. You can never tell with someone who plays voodoo. I've had people get up before with worse injuries. Cicely just lay there, bleeding.

I was lucky she'd had a ladylike caliber pistol. Anything bigger and I might have lost the arm. I stuck her pistol in the front of my pants, because I couldn't figure out where else to put it. I did click the safety on first.

I'd never been shot before. Bitten, stabbed, beaten, burned, but never shot. It scared me because I wasn't sure how badly I was hurt. I walked back to Wanda. Her face was pale, her brown eyes like islands in her face. "Is she dead?"

I nodded.

"You're bleeding," she said. She tore a strip from her long skirt. "Here, let me wrap it."

I knelt and let her tie the multicolored strip just above the wound. She wiped the blood away with another piece of skirt. It didn't look that bad. It looked almost like a raw, bloody scrap.

"I think the bullet just grazed me," I said. A flesh wound, nothing but a flesh wound. It burned and was almost cold at the same time.

Maybe the cold was shock. One little bullet graze and I was going into shock? Surely not.

"Come on, we've got to get out of here. The shots will bring Bruno." It was good that I had pain in the arm. It meant I could feel and I could move the arm. The arm did not want to be wrapped around Wanda's waist again, but it was the only way to move her and keep my right hand free.

"Let's go left. Maybe Cicely came in this way," Wanda said. There was a certain logic to that. We turned and walked past Cicely's body.

She lay there, blue eyes staring impossibly wide. There is never a look of horror on the face of the newly dead, more surprise than anything. As if death had caught them while they weren't looking.

Wanda stared down at the body as we passed it. She whispered, "I never thought she'd die first."

We rounded the corner and came face-to-face with Dominga's monster.

# 38

THE MONSTER STOOD in the middle of a narrow little hall that seemed to take up most of the back of the house. Many-paned windows lined the wall. And in the middle of those windows was a door. Through the windows I could see black night sky. The door led outside. The only thing standing between us and freedom was the monster.

The only thing, sheesh.

The shambling mound of body parts struggled towards us. Wanda screamed, and I didn't blame her. I raised the Magnum and sighted on the human face in the middle. The shot echoed like captive thunder.

The face exploded in a welter of blood and flesh and bone. The smell was worse. Like rotten fur on the back of my throat. The mouths screamed, an animal howling at its wound. The thing kept coming, but it was hurt. It seemed confused as to what to do now. Had I taken out the dominant brain? Was there a dominant brain? No way to be sure.

I fired three more times, exploding three more heads. The hallway was full of brains and blood and worse. The monster kept coming.

The gun clicked on empty. I threw the gun at it. One clawed hand batted it away. I didn't bother trying the .22. If the Magnum couldn't stop it, the .22 sure as hell couldn't.

We started backing down the hallway. What else could we do? The monster pulled its twisted bulk after us. It was that same sliding sound that had chased Manny and I out of Dominga's basement. I was looking at her caged horror.

The flesh between the different textures of skin, fur, and bone was seamless. No Frankenstein stitches. It was like the different pieces had melted together like wax.

I tripped over Cicely's body, too busy watching the monster to see where my feet were. We sprawled across her body. Wanda screamed.

The monster scrambled forward. Misshapen hands grabbed at my ankles. I kicked at it, struggling to climb over Cicely's body, away from it. A claw snagged in my jeans and pulled me towards it. It was my turn to scream. What had once been a man's hand and arm wrapped around my ankle.

I grabbed onto Cicely's body. Her flesh was still warm. The monster pulled us both easily. The extra weight didn't slow it down. My hands scrambled at the bare wood floor. Nothing to hold on to.

I stared back at the thing. Eager rotting mouths yawned at me. Broken, discolored teeth, tongues working like putrid snakes in the openings. God!

Wanda grabbed my arm, trying to hold me, but without legs to brace she just succeeded in being pulled closer to the thing. "Let go!" I screamed it at her.

She did, screaming, "Anita!"

I was screaming myself, "No! Stop it! Stop it!" I put everything I had into that yell, not volume, but power. It was just another zombie, that was all. If it wasn't under specific orders, it would listen to me. It was just another zombie. I had to believe that, or die.

"Stop, right now!" My voice broke with the edge of hysteria. I wanted nothing more than just to start screaming and never stop.

The monster froze with my foot halfway to one of its lower mouths. The mismatched eyes stared at me, expectantly.

I swallowed and tried to sound calm, though the zombie wouldn't care. "Release me."

It did.

My heart was threatening to come out my mouth. I lay back on the floor for a second, relearning how to breathe. When I looked up, the monster was still sitting there, waiting. Waiting for orders like a good little zombie.

"Stay here, do not move from this spot," I said.

The eyes just stared at me, obedient as only the dead can be. It would sit there in the hallway until it got specific orders contradicting mine. Thank you, dear God, that a zombie is a zombie is a zombie.

"What's happening?" Wanda asked. Her voice was broken into sobs. She was near hysterics.

I crawled to her. "It's alright. I'll explain later. We have a little time, but we can't waste it. We've got to get out of here."

She nodded, tears sliding down her bruised face.

I helped her up one last time. We limped towards the monster. Wanda shied away from it, pulling on my sore arm.

"It's alright. It won't hurt us, if we hurry." I had no idea how close Dominga was. I didn't want her changing the orders while we were right next to it. We stayed near the wall and squeezed past the thing. Eyes on the back of the body, if it had a back and a front, followed our progress. The smell from the running wounds was nearly overwhelming. But what was a little gagging between friends?

Wanda opened the door to the outside world. Hot summer wind blew our hair into spider silk strands across our faces. It felt wonderful.

Why hadn't Gaynor and the rest come to the rescue? They had to have heard the gunshots and the screaming. The gunshots at least would have brought somebody.

We stumbled down three stone steps to the gravel of a turn around. I stared off into the darkness at hills covered in tall, waving grass and decaying tombstones. The house was the caretaker's house at Burrell Cemetery. I wondered what Gaynor had done to the caretaker.

I started to lead Wanda away from the cemetery towards the distant highway, then stopped. I knew why no one had come now.

The sky was thick and black and so heavy with stars if I'd had a net I could have caught some. There was a high, hot wind blowing against the stars. I couldn't see the moon. Too much starlight. On the hot seeking fingers of the wind I felt it. The pull. Dominga Salvador had completed her spell. I stared off into the rows of headstones and knew I had to go to her. Just as the zombie had had to obey me, I had to obey her. There was no saving throw, no salvaging it. As easy as that I was caught.

## 39

I STOOD VERY still on the gravel. Wanda moved in my arms, turning to look at me. Her face by starlight was incredibly pale. Was mine as pale? Was the shock spread over my face like moonlight? I tried to take a step forward. To carry Wanda to safety. I could not take a step forward. I struggled until my legs were shaking with the effort. I couldn't leave.

"What's the matter? We have to get out of here before Gaynor comes back," Wanda said.

"I know," I said.

"Then what are you doing?"

I swallowed something cold and hard in my throat. My pulse was thudding in my chest. "I can't leave."

"What are you talking about?" There was an edge of hysteria to Wanda's voice.

Hysterics sounded perfect. I promised myself a complete nervous breakdown if we got out of here alive. If I could ever leave. I fought against something that I couldn't see, or touch, but it held me solid. I had to stop or my legs were going to collapse. We had enough problems in that direction already. If I couldn't go forward, maybe, backwards.

I backed up a step, two steps. Yeah, that worked.

"Where are you going?" Wanda asked.

"Into the cemetery," I said.

"Why!"

Good question, but I wasn't sure I could explain it so that Wanda would understand. I didn't understand it myself. How could I explain it to anyone else? I couldn't leave, but did I have to take Wanda back with me? Would the spell allow me to leave her here?

I decided to try. I laid her down on the gravel. Easy, some of my choices were still open.

"Why are you leaving me?" She clutched at me, terrified.

Me, too.

"Make it to the road if you can," I said.

"On my hands?" she asked.

She had a point, but what could I do? "Do you know how to use a gun?"

"No."

Should I leave her the gun, or should I take it with me, and maybe get a chance to kill Dominga? If this worked like ordering a zombie, then I could kill her if she didn't specifically forbid me to do it. Because I still had free will, of a sort. They'd bring me, then send someone back for Wanda. She was to be the sacrifice.

I handed her the .22. I clicked off the safety. "It's loaded and it's ready to fire," I said. "Since you don't know anything about guns, keep it hidden until Enzo or Bruno is right on top of you, then fire point-blank. You can't miss at point-blank range."

"Why are you leaving me?"

"A spell, I think," I said.

Her eyes widened. "What kind of spell?"

"One that allows them to order me to come to them. One that forbids me to leave."

"Oh, God," she said.

"Yeah," I said. I smiled down at her. A reassuring smile that was all lie. "I'll try to come back for you."

She just stared at me, like a kid whose parents left her in the dark before all the monsters were gone.

She clutched the gun in her hands and watched me walk off into the darkness.

The long dry grass hissed against my jeans. The wind blew the grass in pale waves. Tombstones loomed out of the weeds like the backs of small walls, or the humps of sea monsters. I didn't have to think where I was going, my feet seemed to know the way.

Was this how a zombie felt when ordered to come? No, you had to be within hearing distance of a zombie. You couldn't do it from this far away.

Dominga Salvador stood at the crown of a hill. She was highlighted against the moon. It was sinking towards dawn. It was still night, but the end of night. Everything was still velvet, silver, deep pockets of night shadows, but there was the faintest hint of dawn on the hot wind.

If I could delay until dawn, I couldn't raise the zombie. Maybe the compulsion would fade, too. If I was luckier than I deserved.

Dominga was standing inside a dark circle. There was a dead chicken at her feet. She had already made a circle of power. All I had to do was step into it and slaughter a human being. Over my dead body, if necessary.

Harold Gaynor sat in his electric wheelchair on the opposite side of the circle. He was outside of it, safe. Enzo and Bruno stood by him, safe. Only Dominga had risked the circle.

She said, "Where is Wanda?"

I tried to lie, to say she was safe, but truth spilled out of my mouth, "She's down by the house on the gravel."

"Why didn't you bring her?"

"You can only give me one order at a time. You ordered me to come. I came."

"Stubborn, even now, how curious," she said. "Enzo, go fetch the girl. We need her."

Enzo walked away over the dry, rustling grass without a word. I hoped Wanda killed him. I hoped she emptied the gun into him. No, save a few bullets for Bruno.

Dominga had a machete in her right hand. Its edge was black with blood. "Enter the circle, Anita," she said.

I tried to fight it, tried not to do it. I stood there on the verge of the circle, almost swaying. I stepped across. The circle tingled up my spine, but it wasn't closed. I don't know what she'd done to it, but it wasn't closed. The circle looked solid enough but it was still open. Still waiting for the sacrifice.

Shots echoed in the darkness. Dominga jumped. I smiled.

"What was that?"

"I think it was your bodyguard biting the big one," I said.

"What did you do?"

"I gave Wanda a gun."

She slapped me with her empty hand. It wouldn't really have hurt, but she slapped the same cheek Bruno and what's-his-name had hit. I'd been smacked three times in the same place. The bruise was going to be a beaut.

Dominga looked at something behind me and smiled. I knew what it would be before I turned and saw it.

Enzo was carrying Wanda up the hill. Dammit. I'd heard more than one shot. Had she panicked and shot too soon, wasted her ammunition? Damn.

Wanda was screaming and beating her small fists against Enzo's broad back. If we were alive come morning, I would teach Wanda better things to do with her fists. She was crippled, not helpless.

Enzo carried her over the circle. Until it closed everyone could pass over it without breaking the magic. He dropped Wanda to the ground, holding her arms out behind her at a painful angle. She still struggled and screamed. I didn't blame her.

"Get Bruno to hold her still. The death needs to be one blow," I said.

Dominga nodded. "Yes, it does." She motioned for Bruno to enter the circle. He hesitated, but Gaynor told him, "Do what she says."

Bruno didn't hesitate after that. Gaynor was his greenback god. Bruno grabbed one of Wanda's arms. With a man on each arm, and her legs useless, she was still moving too much.

"Kneel and hold her head still," I said.

Enzo dropped first, putting a big hand on the back of Wanda's head. He held her steady. She started to cry. Bruno knelt, putting his free hand on her shoulders to help steady her. It was important for the death to be a single blow.

Dominga was smiling now. She handed me a small brown jar of ointment. It was white and smelled heavily of cloves. I used more rosemary in mine, but cloves were fine.

"How did you know what I needed?"

"I asked Manny to tell me what you used."

"He wouldn't tell you shit."

"He would if I threatened his family." Dominga laughed. "Oh, don't look so sad. He didn't betray you, *chica*. Manuel thought I was merely curious about your powers. I am, you know."

"You'll see soon enough, won't you," I said.

She gave a sort of bow from the neck. "Place the ointment on yourself in the appointed places."

I rubbed ointment on my face. It was cool and waxy. The cloves made it smell like candy. I smeared it on over my heart, under my shirt, both hands. Last the tombstone.

Now all we needed was the sacrifice.

Dominga told me, "Do not move."

I stayed where I was, frozen as if by magic. Was her monster still frozen in the hallway, like I was now?

Dominga laid the machete on the grass near the edge of the circle, then she stepped out of the circle. "Raise the dead, Anita," she said.

"Ask Gaynor one question first, please." That please hurt, but it worked.

She looked at me curiously. "What question?"

"Is this ancestor also a voodoo priest?" I asked.

"What difference does it make?" Gaynor asked.

"You fool," Dominga said. She whirled on him, hands in fists. "That is what went wrong the first time. You made me think it was my powers!"

"What are you babbling about?" he asked.

"When you raise a voodoo priest or an animator, sometimes the magic goes wrong," I said.

"Why?" he asked.

"Your ancestor's magic interfered with my magic," Dominga said. "Are you sure this ancestor had no voodoo?"

"Not to my knowledge," he said.

"Did you know about the first one?" I asked.

"Yes."

"Why didn't you tell me?" Dominga said. Her power blazed around her like a dark nimbus. Would she kill him, or did she want the money more?

"I didn't think it was important."

I think Dominga was grinding her teeth. I didn't blame her. He'd cost her her reputation and a dozen lives. He saw nothing wrong with it. But Dominga didn't strike him dead. Greed wins out.

"Get on with it," Gaynor said. "Or don't you want your money?"

"Do not threaten me!" Dominga said.

Peachy keen, the bad guys were going to fight among themselves.

"I am not threatening you, Señora. I merely will not pay unless this zombie is raised."

Dominga took a deep breath. She literally squared her shoulders and turned back to me. "Do as I ordered, raise the dead."

I opened my mouth to think of some other excuse to delay. Dawn was coming. It had to come.

"No more delays. Raise the dead, Anita, now!" That last word had the tone of a command.

I swallowed hard and walked towards the edge of the circle. I wanted to get out, to leave, but I couldn't. I stood there, leaning against that invisible barrier. It was like beating against a wall that I couldn't feel. I stayed there straining until my entire body trembled. I took a deep shaking breath.

I picked up the machete.

Wanda said, "No, Anita, please, please don't!" She struggled, but she couldn't move. She would be an easy kill. Easier than beheading a chicken with one hand. And I did that almost every night.

I knelt in front of Wanda. Enzo's hand on the back of her head kept her from moving. But she whimpered, a desperate sound low in her throat.

God, help me.

I placed the machete under her neck and told Enzo, "Raise her head up so I can make sure of the kill."

He grabbed a handful of hair and bowed her neck at a painful angle. Her eyes were showing a lot of white. Even by moonlight I could see the pulse in her throat.

I placed the machete back against her neck. Her skin was solid and real under the blade. I raised it just above her flesh, not touching for an instant. I drove the machete straight up into Enzo's throat. The point speared his throat. Blood gushed out in a black wave.

Everyone froze for an instant, but me. I jerked the machete out of Enzo and plunged it into Bruno's gut. His hand with the gun half-drawn fell away. I leaned on the machete and drew it up towards his throat. His insides spilled out in a warm rush.

The smell of fresh death filled the circle. Blood sprayed all over my face, chest, hands, coating me. It was the last step, and the circle closed.

I'd felt a thousand circles close, but nothing like this. The shock of it left me gasping. I couldn't breathe over the rush of power. It was like an electric current was running over my body. My skin ached with it.

Wanda was covered in other people's blood. She was having hysterics in the grass. "Please, please, don't kill me. Don't kill me! Please!"

I didn't have to kill Wanda. Dominga had told me to raise the dead, and I would do just that.

Killing animals never gave me this kind of rush. It felt like my skin was going to crawl off on its own. I shoved the power flowing through me into the ground. But not just into the grave in the circle. I had too much power for just one grave. Too much power for just a handful of graves. I felt the power spreading outward like ripples in a pool. Out and out, until the power was spread thick and clean over the ground. Every grave that I had walked for Dolph. Every grave but the ones with ghosts. Because that was a type of soul magic, and necromancy didn't work around souls.

I felt each grave, each corpse. I felt them coalesce from dust and bone fragments to things that were barely dead at all.

"Arise from your graves all dead within sound of my call. Arise and serve me!" Without naming them all I shouldn't have been able to call a single one from the grave, but the power of two human deaths was too much for the dead to resist.

They rose upward like swimmers through water. The ground rippled underfoot like a horse's skin.

"What are you doing?" Dominga asked.

"Raising the dead," I said. Maybe it showed in my voice. Maybe she felt it. Whatever, she started running towards the circle, but it was too late.

Hands tore through the earth at Dominga's feet. Dead hands grabbed her ankles and sent her sprawling into the long grass. I lost sight of her but I didn't lose control of the zombies. I told them, "Kill her, kill her."

The grass shuddered and surged like water. The sound of muscles pulling away from bone in wet thick pieces filled the night. Bones broke with sharp cracks. Over the sounds of tearing flesh, Dominga shrieked.

There was one last wet sound, thick and full. Dominga's screams broke off abruptly. I felt the dead hands tearing out her throat. Her blood splattered the grass like a black sprinkler.

Her spell shredded on the wind, but I didn't need her urging now. The power had me. I was riding it like a bird on a current of air. It held me, lifted me. It felt solid and insubstantial as air.

The dry sunken earth cracked open over Gaynor's ancestor's grave. A pale hand shot skyward. A second hand came through the crack. The zombie tore the dry earth. I heard other old graves breaking in the still, summer night. It broke its way out of his grave, just like Gaynor had wanted.

Gaynor sat in his wheelchair on the crest of the hill. He was surrounded by the dead. Dozens of zombies in various stages of decay crowded close to him. But I hadn't given the order yet. They wouldn't hurt him unless I told them to.

"Ask him where the treasure is," Gaynor shouted.

I stared at him and every zombie turned with my eyes and stared at him, too. He didn't understand. Gaynor was like a lot of people with money. They mistake money for power. It isn't the same thing at all.

"Kill the man Harold Gaynor." I said it loud enough to carry on the still air.

"I'll give you a million dollars for having raised him. Whether I find the treasure or not," Gaynor said.

"I don't want your money, Gaynor," I said.

The zombies were moving in on every side, slow, hands extended, like every horror movie you've ever seen. Sometimes Hollywood is accurate, whatta ya know.

"Two million, three million!" His voice was breaking with fear. He'd had a better seat for Dominga's death than I had. He knew what was coming. "Four million!"

"Not enough," I said.

"How much?" he shouted. "Name your price!" I couldn't see him now. The zombies hid him from view.

"No money, Gaynor, just you dead, that's enough."

He started screaming, wordlessly. I felt the hands begin to rip at him. Teeth to tear.

Wanda grabbed my legs. "Don't, don't hurt him. Please!"

I just stared at her. I was remembering Benjamin Reynolds's blood-coated teddy bear, the tiny hand with that stupid plastic ring on it, the blood-soaked bedroom, the baby blanket. "He deserves to die," I said. My voice sounded separate from me, distant and echoing. It didn't sound like me at all.

"You can't just murder him," Wanda said.

"Watch me," I said.

She tried to climb my body, but her legs betrayed her and she fell in a heap at my feet, sobbing.

I didn't understand how Wanda could beg for his life after what he had done to her. Love, I suppose. In the end she really did love him. And that, perhaps, was the saddest thing of all.

When Gaynor died, I knew it. When pieces of him stained almost every hand and mouth of the dead, they stopped. They turned to me, waiting for new orders. The power was still buoying me up. I wasn't tired. Was there enough to lay them all to rest? I hoped so.

"Go back, all of you, go back to your graves. Rest in the quiet earth. Go back, go back."

They stirred like a wind had blown through them, then one by one they went back to their graves. They lay down on the hard dry earth and the graves just swallowed them whole. It was like magic quicksand. The earth shuddered underfoot like a sleeper moving to a more comfortable position.

Some of the corpses had been as old as Gaynor's ancestor, which meant that I didn't need a human death to raise one three-hundred-year-old corpse. Bert was going to be pleased. Human deaths seemed to be cumulative. Two human deaths and I had emptied a cemetery. It wasn't possible. But I'd done it anyway. Whatta ya know?

False dawn passed like milk on the eastern sky. The wind died with the light. Wanda knelt in the bloody grass, crying. I knelt beside her.

She jerked back at my touch. I guess I couldn't blame her, but it bothered me anyway.

"We have to get out of here. You need a doctor," I said.

She stared up at me. "What are you?"

Today for the first time I didn't know how to answer that question. Human didn't seem to cover it. "I'm an animator," I said finally.

She just kept staring at me. I wouldn't have believed me either. But she let me help her up. I guess that was something.

But she kept looking at me out of the edge of her eyes. Wanda considered me one of the monsters. She may have been right.

Wanda gasped, eyes wide.

I turned, too slowly. Was it the monster?

Jean-Claude stepped out of the shadows.

I didn't breathe for a moment. It was so unexpected.

"What are you doing here?" I asked.

"Your power called to me, *ma petite*. No dead in the city could fail to feel your power tonight. And I am the city, so I came to investigate."

"How long have you been here?"

"I saw you kill the men. I saw you raise the graveyard."

"Did it ever occur to you to help me?"

"You did not need any help." He smiled, barely visible in the moonlight. "Besides, would it not have been tempting to rend me to pieces, as well?"

"You can't possibly be afraid of me," I said.

He spread his hands wide.

"You're afraid of your human servant? Little ol' *moi*?"

"Not afraid, *ma petite*, but cautious."

He was afraid of me. It almost made some of this shit worthwhile.

I carried Wanda down the hill. She wouldn't let Jean-Claude touch her. A choice of monsters.

# 40

DOMINGA SALVADOR MISSED her court date. Fancy that. Dolph had searched for me that night, after he discovered that Dominga had made bail. He had found my apartment empty. My answers about where I had gone didn't satisfy him, but he let it go. What else could he do?

They found Gaynor's wheelchair, but no trace of him. It's one of those mysteries to tell around campfires. The empty, blood-coated wheelchair in the middle of the cemetery. They did find body parts in the caretaker's house: animal and human. Only Dominga's power had held the thing together. When she died, it died. Thank goodness. Theory was that the monster got Gaynor. Where the monster came from no one seemed to know. I was called in to explain the body parts, that's how the police knew they'd once been attached.

Irving wanted to know what I really knew about Gaynor's vanishing act. I just smiled and played inscrutable. Irving didn't believe me, but all he had were suspicions. Suspicions aren't a news story.

Wanda is waiting tables downtown. Jean-Claude offered her a job at The Laughing Corpse. She declined, not politely. She'd saved quite a bit of money from her "business." I don't know if she'll make it or not, but with Gaynor gone, she seems free to try. She was a junkie whose drug of choice was dead. It was better than rehab.

By Catherine's wedding the bullet wound was just a bandage on my arm. The bruises on my face and neck had turned that sickly shade of greenish-yellow. It clashed with the pink dress. I gave Catherine the option of me not being in the wedding. The wedding coordinator was all for that, but Catherine wouldn't hear of it. The wedding coordinator applied makeup to the bruises and saved the day.

I have a picture of me standing in that awful dress with Catherine's arm around me. We're both smiling. Friendship is strange stuff.

Jean-Claude sent me a dozen white roses in the hospital. The card read, "Come to the ballet with me. Not as my servant, but as my guest."

I didn't go to the ballet. I had enough problems without dating the Master of the City.

I had performed human sacrifice, and it had felt good. The rush of power was like the memory of painful sex. Part of you wanted to do it again. Maybe Dominga Salvador was right. Maybe power talks to everyone, even me.

I am an animator. I am the Executioner. But now I know I'm something else. The one thing my Grandmother Flores feared most. I am a necromancer. The dead are my specialty.

# AFTERWORD
## by Laurell K. Hamilton

IT WAS THE second summer in a row that St. Louis had suffered weeks of one hundred-plus temperatures, with a hundred percent humidity. As the heat closed around us like some gigantic sweaty fist, I began thinking of murder. It was my second summer of plotting murder. Maybe it was the heat, or maybe I'm just not right. The family who raised me would probably agree with the latter, but that means nothing; most of us are strangers to our birth families. The real telling point is that my friends would agree, but they like me anyway, or sometimes even *because* I'm not quite right. Because they aren't quite right either. To the handful of normal, well-adjusted friends that I have, my apologies. To the rest of you, argue if you can.

Once upon a time, it bothered me that I don't think like the majority of people. That I walk through a world where the worst can happen, and often does. That I see danger where most people see nothing. I am told that I think like a cop. I'd ignore that, except that it's policemen who told me. I'm told by people in the military that I think like a soldier. Though both the police and the military add that I'd make a good detective but a lousy uniform; a good officer, but a bad enlisted. I'm just not good at taking other people's orders. Sorry, but I'm not.

The book you're holding in your hands was a paperback original almost ten years ago. The fact that it is coming out in hardback is a testament to how devoted the fans of this series have become, and how two stubborn petite women managed to change the publishing industry, almost by accident.

This particular petite woman found hard-boiled detective fiction the summer after college. The male detectives got to cuss, have sex, and kill people. The women, even the most liberated of them, didn't cuss much, if there was sex it was sanitized or off stage, and if they killed someone they had to feel very, very bad about it. This seemed unfair to me, so I decided to write a character who would even the playing field. Enter Anita Blake, the other stubborn petite woman. I might have gotten a little carried away with the whole idea that Anita needed to be tougher, rougher, and just *more*, than the men. To my knowledge, she has the highest kill count in literature outside of war novels. She cusses like a sailor, and the sex is hot enough that many fans claim as couples they read my books to each other as foreplay.

My original plan was actually to never have to do sex on paper. I wanted every touch, every caress, to be so amazing that I didn't have to resort to writing actual intercourse. But six books into the series, we did the dirty deed on paper, and because I'd spent five books building up to it, I couldn't skimp on the scene. Or felt I couldn't. Besides, I'd written books where every crime, every bit of necessary violence was kept on full camera, no flinching. So that when it came to sex, and I wanted the camera to do that 1940s pan to the sky; I couldn't do it. What did it say about me as a person that I hadn't paled at showing murder and mayhem in every book, but the first real sex scene had me panicked. Actually, it just proved that I think like an American. Violence is dandy, but God forbid you show sex on stage. Let alone enjoyable sex between two people that know and like, and maybe love, each other.

I didn't plan to be the spokesperson for women's sexuality. Really, I didn't. But I had too many people in the publishing industry tell me that my books were disturbing, not because of the violence and sex, but because a woman wrote the sex and violence. And even worse my main character, a first person point of view, was female. I had one well-known mystery editor tell me that the Anita books would never have sold as straight mystery. This was when, I think, only three books were out, so we hadn't even crossed the sexual divide. No, her objection was to the level of violence. A straight mystery heroine was not allowed to be that violent. If I'd been a man, and, or, my main character had been male, then it would have been okay. I really thought that we'd come further than that in this country. Guess I was wrong.

Anita and I are very different people, but one trait we do share. If you tell us we can't, then we are more determined than ever. Stubborn. Contrary, my grandmother would say. So be it. What everyone kept telling us was that the sex had gone far enough. Had my editor told me to slow down, tone it down? No, she hadn't. It was other people, at other publishing houses, and it was other writers, mostly male, who told me I'd gone too far. Then I started hearing from other countries. Americans think that we're backwards when it comes to sex, and the Europeans are having lots more sex, and kinkier sex. It's true that the European fans are more bothered by the violence and hardly at all by the sex, but if they were bothered, it was again about the fact that I was a woman and so was Anita. I began to hear from women in this country and in others, that they had been raised to believe that women didn't enjoy sex. That womens' appetites were less than mens'.

Who starts these stories?

The truth is that some women do not enjoy sex. Some women do not have the sexual appetite of a man. The truth is that some men don't enjoy sex. That some men don't have as large a sexual appetite as some women.

I think this idea that men are sexually predatory and we women are just victims, gets both men and women in trouble. If a man isn't that interested in sex, he's considered less of a man. If a woman is more interested in sex, she's a slut. Both of these are false assumptions.

People say I'm a feminist, but in truth, I am an equalist. I believe that everyone, male and female, should be free to be whom and what they are. Not to fit into some tight cultural box. The best quick example I have in this country is the double-standard for strippers. A male stripper has a female customer tear off his G-string, and the police arrest him, not her. A female stripper has a male customer tear off her G-string, and the customer is thrown out of the club and arrested. The idea is that men should be okay with sexual contact, because they like it, and women don't like it, so they should be protected from it. That is unfair, and untrue. Assault is assault, no matter who's stripping whose dignity.

By the way, who decided that men don't want doors in the bathrooms? I know a lot of men who'd like a little privacy, if they could get it.

Now all this talk about sex may be misleading, since there is no sex in *The Laughing Corpse*. But there is something in this book that also was new and different when I started out. Mixing genres.

It took more than two and a half years to sell the first Anita Blake novel, *Guilty Pleasures*, because nobody knew what to do with it. The mystery houses thought it was horror. The horror houses thought it wasn't scary enough, and called it fantasy or science fiction. The science fiction houses called it fantasy. The fantasy houses called it horror. Etc. . . .

I was literally told that mixed genre fiction does not sell. Period, end of story. Since the last five books I wrote have all been *New York Times* bestsellers, and all of them have mixed genres, I'm glad I didn't listen to the doomsayers.

I combine mystery, fantasy, horror, romance, and science fiction, usually all in one book. Why pick one genre when you can play in all of them?

Thanks to my success the publishing industry has actually begun to solicit mixed genre books, especially urban fantasy mixed genre. I have heard back from editors and agents that people are actually asking writers to send them something "Hamiltonesque." I feel a little young to be an "esque", but once I got over the weirdness factor, it was sort of flattering.

None of the imitators, so far, have done nearly as well. Why? I'm writing exactly what I want to write. I think a lot of the imitators are writing this because they think it will sell. I think if your heart isn't in a book, especially a series, it shows. Most people who are just reading me to try to figure out what I do that has captured so much attention, see the sex and violence and monsters. They think, oh, I'll put in some vampires, some sex, some violence, and it'll sell. Not exactly.

If you asked me what I wrote I wouldn't say I write vampire novels. I certainly wouldn't say that I write erotica or horror. If pushed, I'd say fantasy because it has the broadest definition. I don't sit down to a book and think this one will be more of a mystery, or more of a romance. I sit down to a book, and let my characters come talk to me.

I don't write books about vampires. I write books about people who happen to be vampires. Everybody must be a person first and whatever else second. Anita raises zombies for a living and is a legal vampire executioner, but first she is Anita Blake who lost her mother when she was eight and has never forgiven her father for remarrying. The fact that some of my characters are vampires shapes their character, profoundly, but I think of them first as characters, not first as vampires. Anyone who reads this, and doesn't understand the distinction, I'm not sure I can explain it to you. Anita has been shaped by her job, by her preternatural abilities with the dead. Shaped and broken and changed by what she has seen and experienced. But first, she was a little girl, and somewhere under all the violence and sex, she is still that little girl, crying for her mother. Jean-Claude is an immortal vampire, the Master Vampire of the City. He is the demon-lover, the dark prince that you both want and fear, but he is also still the peasant boy that was taken from his family, at a very tender age, because the wife of the nobleman who owned their land thought he was beautiful and would be a fit companion for the noble's son. Somewhere under all that suave charm is still the confusion he must have felt from being taken out of a world of poverty to a world of opulence.

Having written that last sentence, I realize, that I didn't know Jean-Claude's back-story when I wrote *The Laughing Corpse*. He was just a cute dead guy to me back then. I was still yelling loud and long that I would never use him as a romantic lead. I'd kill him first. In fact, he was supposed to die at the end of the third book, *Circus of the Damned*. But when the time came, I couldn't do it. Because, by then, Anita would have missed him, and so would I. I began the series believing, as Anita did, that the monsters are monstrous, and people are somehow better just because they aren't vampires. It would take us several books to realize that the world was not black and white, but oh, so gray. Anita's journey as a character was part of my own journey as I struggled to understand what I was writing and why. I write first so I can read it. So I can enjoy the books. I write what I want to read. Lucky for me, lots of other people want to read it, too.

But I am also writing to make sense of my world. So different from Anita's, but her world helps me think about ours more clearly. It may take me years after I've written something to understand why I wrote a particular book. Then one day it will dawn on me, and I'll think, oh, that was why. It's like having therapy in public, and getting paid for it.

It's May, almost summer, and I'm sitting down to the computer, and thinking of murder. And sex. And love. And what exactly loyalty means, and who do you owe it to? And the age old question, what is love, and how do you know when you've got the real thing? Oh, and one other question: whodunit? Truthfully, even I don't know yet. But I can hardly wait to find out.